HETR

LAVANAI

PIRIDET

NITHLE

VELOTH

N

W E

S

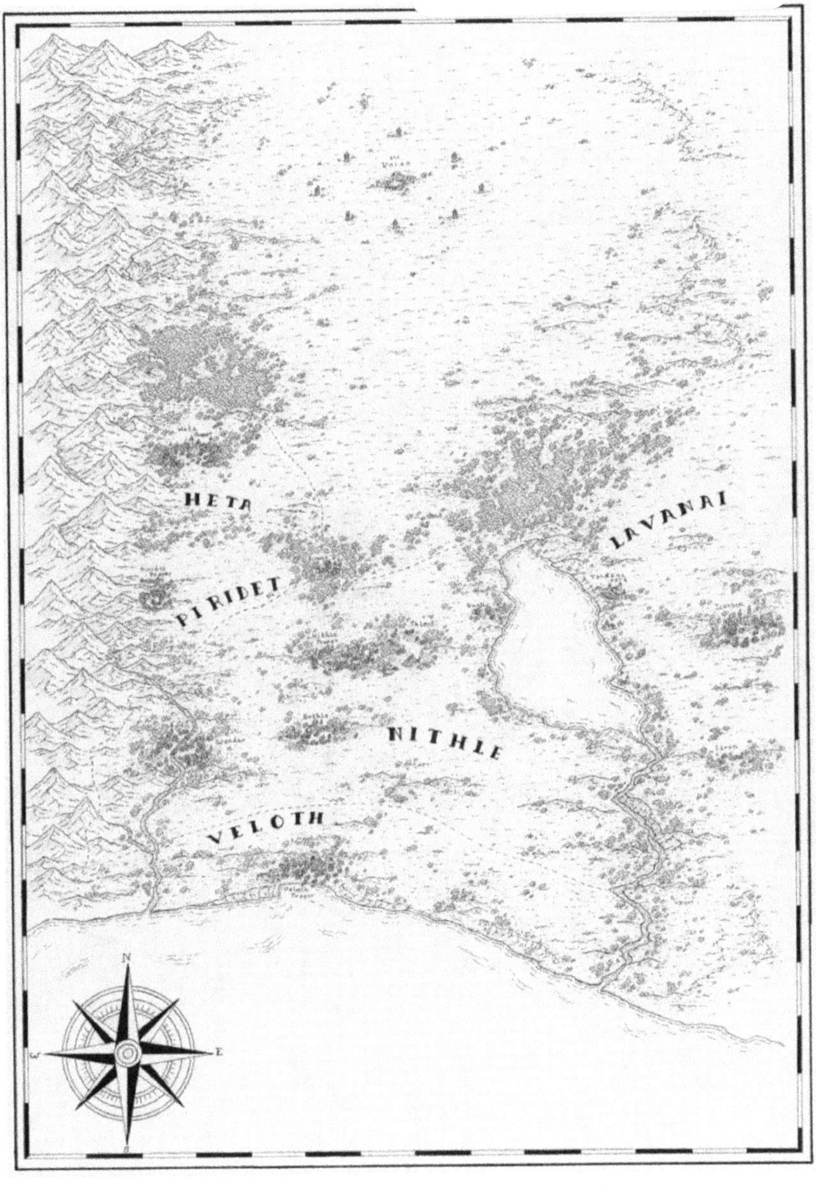

KILLING SECRETS

SECRET MINDERS
BOOK ONE

LAURA A. BARTON

For those who've felt powerless to change their realities.

CHAPTER
ONE

S parks scattered across Prince Arran's vision, cracks and sizzles an accompanying note. People crowding around the spectacle gasped but drew in closer.

In dramatic style, players cast themselves across the low stage set up in the middle of Nithle Proper's square, as though they'd been hit by real magic instead of the magic manufactured for the theatrical performance. They fell to the platform floor with unceremonious thumps as other players skulked with methodical footsteps toward them, bearing wooden weapons and "magical" abilities. Magicless, the humans cowered under the threat.

While the players prostrate on the stage wore the same kind of tunics and slacks, though exaggerated, as the crowd around them, the skulking players looked much more monstrous.

Arran scoffed quietly over the display from where he was content to stand at the back of the crowd. Dahems didn't actually look like the fanged, clawed monstrosities with double-pointed ears before him. Even the clothing the dahem players wore—tattered rags at best—didn't match what he'd seen in the books he'd studied over his seventeen years. Dahems wore battle leathers and armour, just as a human army might.

The only correct parts of the costume were the amber-hued eyes, narrowed for the menacing effect, painted on the flesh-coloured masks. Amber eyes that signified an affinity for magic and an ability to use it safely. Otherwise, dahems barely looked any different from humans.

Like many in the United, the prince had been only a toddler when he'd learned of the dangers of magic. It caused corruption of the soul, seen through the gold stain of magic in the eyes, and eventual death either from the magic fully consuming a person or someone mercifully ending their life. Sometimes the damage could be reversed before it came to that, but not always.

As for the "magic" in the play, it was no more threatening than sparks from a fire. But Arran had seen true magic—or at least the effects of it on a human. One of his earliest memories was of a teenaged boy brought before the king because he'd endeavoured to harness magic, only to have it begin to devour his soul and corrupt his mind as it turned his eyes the colour of pure gold.

That the dahems could wield such a dangerous force of nature was cause enough to be leery of them. Their multitude of attacks against the United over the centuries solidified it.

Cheers from those gathered interrupted Arran's silent critique. Another player wearing a silver crown and an extravagant, flowing overcoat and swinging a sword jumped into the fray to save those who'd been knocked down. They thrust the wooden blade to force the dahems back.

Nithle's only heir adjusted his own navy overcoat against the cool evening breeze that swept through the large city square. Behind and around him, he knew other Harvest Festival attendees would be milling about Nithle Proper and stopping at vendor stands while waiting for the feast and the dance area to be set up in the square later into the evening.

The last lingering rays of light cast a blend of cool and warm tones along the sides of the neutral-coloured buildings branching off from the square in a variety of different directions. Long shadows had festival attendees preemptively hanging and lighting lanterns from the twisting, cast-iron hooks set high above the crowds.

As the biggest of the five remaining cities and villages in Nithle Kingdom, it wasn't unlikely that the crowds would have dispersed beyond the Nithle Proper's main square, even if only to catch a glimpse of the castle, illuminated by torch light where it stood on a hill. The large, dark-stone building with its high outer walls, defense towers, and tall inner structure overlooked its people from along the western-most edge of the city's main populace.

The Harvest Festival was one of four staple occasions where all four kingdoms of the United—Nithle, Heta, Piridet, and Veloth—gathered. While everyone came to Nithle for the Harvest Festival, the United would gather in Veloth for the Midwinter Festival, in Heta for Reawakening Festival, and Piridet for the Midsummer Festival.

There had once been a fifth kingdom, Wendur, farther southwest, nearer to the mountains. But after Wendur and its royal family had fallen to a dahem attack, Nithle had taken over protection and rule of its people and noble houses.

Another breeze ruffled through Arran's dark, curly hair and rattled the decorations strung up between the shops and homes crowded around the square in equal measure. Navy, burgundy, and silver pennants waved to the festival goers. Silver stitching depicting Nithle's proud stag encircled by a thick ring glimmered along the rippling navy fabrics.

The same crest adorned the collar of Arran's overcoat and shirt underneath, as well as the shoulder of the dress attire worn by Royal Knight Ley, the prince's personal guardsman, who was never too far out of reach. Glancing over his shoulder now,

Arran saw him only a few paces away in his navy and silver-stitched overcoat and dark trousers, with his sword sheathed at his left hip. The knight's questioning glance made its way through the throngs of people that passed between them. Arran waved him off and returned his attention to the play.

The gallant royal player who'd jumped in to save the non-magic players, now noticeably absent from the stage, was backed to a corner. A blast of fire shot into the air, casting a wave of heat out into the crowd before the chill air returned. Just when it looked like all might be lost, new figures made a grand entrance onto the stage from somewhere on the other side. One was hooded, features obscured, and the other wore some sort of armour; the hooded one took up position beside the royal while the armoured warrior attacked the dahems.

"This is quite the spectacle, My Prince."

Arran glanced toward the voice at his right. His blue gaze came to rest upon the young Lord Davi of Wendur. The increasing shadows made him look simultaneously his proper age and older than he was with the way they cast across his dishevelled hair and defined jaw. A deep navy, almost black, brocade also added to the older appearance, the silver crest of the stag stitched on the collar.

The prince thought he'd detected a whisper of sarcasm in Davi's statement, but it was hard to tell over the din. "Are you not enjoying it, Lord Davi?"

Davi tilted his head just enough to address Arran before countering with his own question. "It's a bit overstated, don't you think?"

"Naturally. It is a play after all," Arran replied. He wouldn't tell Davi that he shared similar criticisms only moments ago. "If you're looking for historical accuracy on how the Union came to protect the United kingdoms, I suggest petitioning the royal archives. I can put a word in for you."

Arran was intimately familiar with the royal archives. Nithlean heirs were trained in the arts of strategy, and how better to learn than by studying the past? He had grown up immersed in historical accounts and even eye-witness journals of how the dahems of Lavanai, the enemy kingdom, had one day broken through Nithle's borders with an expansive army in an attempt to overthrow human kingdoms with their magic. Though the five smaller human kingdoms banded together against the large dahem kingdom, the dahems' use of magic left them at a disadvantage. Wendur had fallen, five kingdoms became four—but in the midst of panic, the Union had arrived.

According to the archives, a hooded figure, much like the one on the stage, was said to have arrived with a young warrior in tow. The warrior, the hooded one had promised, was trained for the sole purpose of defeating the magic-using fiends. Sure enough, even the magic-users fled from the warrior, and that, alongside the Union's tactical guidance, allowed the human kingdoms to push Lavanai back east, across Lake Pol and within its borders. From then on, the hooded figure, called a Keeper, gave a promise—the Oath—that the Union would protect all the kingdoms. In exchange for the Keepers' and their warriors' protection, the Union would have leave to take newborns from the four kingdoms and train them to become their warriors. Warriors known as Killers.

Fifteen and a half years had passed since Lavanai last attacked. The Union had sent a warrior and guidance then, too, but Arran had been too young to remember anything. Not that the dahems had gotten close enough for him to see, anyway.

It was only through studying texts like those in the royal archives and the books given to him by his tutors that Arran knew the play and its depiction of dahems were farcical. All the same, he understood the purpose of reminding his people not only of the Union's protection, but the dangers the Union protected them from. Without the Union, Nithle and the other kingdoms would probably have been overrun by the dahems decades ago.

Arran's gaze, which had ventured back to the stage, now came to rest on Lord Davi again as silence lulled between them. "Shall I put in the request?"

"That won't be necessary, Your Highness." The young man shook his head. "I do wonder, though, if what the Union provides truly is protection."

"None of that, Lord Davi." Arran's tone was edged with warning. "I can't allow such treasonous talk."

"Who said anything about treason, Your Highness?" he asked innocently, though a slight quirk of his lips gave him away. "I'm only asking questions."

Arran ignored the stage now to fully face the young man. He stood nearly eye-to-eye with the young lord, but the prince was just slightly shorter. Out of his peripheral, Arran noticed Ley had drawn nearer, but he focused his attention on Davi. "Questions you know cross a line."

"I just—" Davi started.

"Davi!" a booming voice called above the noise of the performance and crowds.

The attentions of both young men and the royal knight fell to the person who'd called. Standing at a vendor stand several yards away was a man who looked like an older version of Davi and wore similar garb. He waved a hand for Davi to come to him.

Lord Robyr, Arran placed the man. The lord stood beside the stand's vendor, who seemed to be holding something between them to look at, perhaps to work out some sort of sale.

"Coming, Father!" Davi called to Lord Robyr before facing Arran again. "Excuse me, Your Highness."

Arran took hold of Davi's arm as he turned to leave, the brocade rough under his fingers. It stopped the young man in his tracks. "Remember what I said, Davi."

Releasing a sigh, Davi replied, "Of course, Your Highness."

He contemplated holding him further and lecturing him more, but ultimately Arran let the lord make his way to his father and the vendor. Arran watched after them a moment as the three fell into conversation. *I'll have to report this conversation to Father.*

Ley's tenor voice echoed his thoughts, "Your father will want to hear about this, Your Highness. I have no idea what the young lord was thinking with that line of conversation."

Arran only nodded and looked away from the lords and their conversation. "I feel there's more to his 'innocent' questioning."

"Your instinct is usually good on these matters," Ley remarked. He stood, feet shoulder width apart and his hands behind his back as he spoke. While his dark eyes did meet Arran's, from time to time, they drifted in their ever watchful way to the throngs of people.

Arran let his own attention drift. The crowd had dispersed from the stage, and the players were removing the meager props. Later, the musicians would take place of the players to entertain during the evening meal and refreshments.

"Excuse me, Your Highness."

A young woman planted herself in front of Arran, head held high as she stared up at him with sharp green eyes, while her cream-coloured gloved hands clasped before her. Red hair stood out like fire against her pale, freckled skin, a few ringlets framing her face while the rest was pulled back. It somehow blended almost seamlessly with the bodice of her burgundy dress.

"Ashla."

Arran hoped the easy grin he gave his friend hid the little leap his heart did in his chest. His attention wandered from the young woman before him. *If Ashla's here...*

"You shouldn't keep a lady waiting," Ashla insisted, her voice stern.

That's when he caught sight of her: Adel, Heta's princess and his best friend. More importantly, the young woman he was courting.

Ashla, Ley, the festival...it all faded away as his world shrunk to only him and Adel.

A smile tugged at his lips as his heart did a flip this time. Adel waited a short distance away, wearing an outfit practically identical to Ashla's. Her burgundy gown, slightly more detailed in its stitching, hugged her slender form as she wrung her gloved fingers before its flowing skirts. She didn't break eye contact, and he could see the delicate blush creeping onto her fair skin and the sparkle in her hazel eyes.

"Well, don't just stare!" Ashla's voice shattered the moment as a firm shove between his shoulder blades sent the prince stumbling into full reality.

"Ashla!" Adel protested, rushing forward.

Arran's shoes scuffed against the stone of the city square, but he avoided a fall. With a sweep of his hand through his hair and a brief tug at his overcoat, he righted himself. Seeing the two stand side-by-side, he could more clearly see the intentional similarities in appearance from their attire to their hair style. Adel's dirty-blonde hair, cut shorter since he'd last seen her months before, was also in ringlets and otherwise pinned back out of her face.

The princess turned from her lady-in-waiting to look Arran over, hands outstretched, but not quite touching him. Concern pinched her features. "Are you okay?" Her soft voice invited a warmth that he'd missed.

"It was nothing. I'm fine," he said quickly.

"*See*, he's *fine*." Ashla rolled her eyes and crossed her arms.

Adel's hands dropped, and she rounded on Ashla again. "You can't go around shoving people!"

"No harm came of it. People know we're friends." Another eye roll.

"It's still not a smart thing to do," Adel fired back.

"You are always a worrier," Ashla insisted but eventually gave in under the princess's withering gaze. "All right, all right. I'll behave," she huffed.

"Good," Adel said, her attention falling back to Arran. "You look great."

"As do you." Great seemed too small a word, be he couldn't find a sufficient one to describe the delicate edges to her features and the way the smile graced her pink lips. "I'm glad you're here. Are your parents and brother around somewhere?"

"My parents are." She looked absently into the masses for them. "Rynn wasn't feeling well, though, so he didn't come."

"He made quite a scene of it," Ashla interjected excitedly. "He kept on about how it's not fair that because he was a 'little woozy' he had to miss the whole festival…and then he keeled right on over. It was pretty funny."

"Ashlaaaa," Adel groaned, tilting her head back and sighing.

"What? He was fine. Your father caught him before he fell." Ashla shrugged.

Arran shook his head with a mirthful grin. Adel and Ashla had grown up together, and it was pretty much *the* reason the lady-in-waiting could get away with saying and doing what she did. To an extent. Missing titles here or there, bantering so openly with her princess… Those were fairly minor infractions, depending on the setting. But Arran had seen more than a few times where she'd pushed the boundaries too far and ended up with extra, unpleasant duties as punishment.

It wasn't so much that Ashla *didn't* know decorum and properness. She was just choosy with when she used it, occasionally to her detriment.

The Harvest Festival might be a bit more lenient of a setting, but Arran had other plans than standing in the square as Adel and Ashla bantered. "Shall we walk? We can get refreshments, perhaps dance later…?"

Adel's smile returned. "That'd be great."

He held out his arm, which she easily hooked hers into. The weight of her arm and hand on his forearm had him smiling despite himself. As they walked and she leaned into him, he caught a glimpse of a bracelet under the cuff of her glove: a silver band inlaid with blue gemstones. It was the one he'd given her when he'd taken the chance to evolve their friendship into a courtship.

The way he'd agonized for weeks over the decision was still fresh in his mind. The thought of asking his best friend to be his romantic partner had made him practically ill with worry about how it might negatively impact their friendship. The relief and joy he'd felt when she'd agreed had been the perfect antidote.

The several days' journey that separated their kingdoms kept them from seeing each other more, but their letters had become frequent. However, nothing was the same as her calming presence or spending an afternoon doing he didn't care what with her, so he relished in every moment.

"When did you get here?" Arran asked.

"Not too long ago. We're disappointed to have missed the first day, but Mother wanted to see if Rynn would get better. We wouldn't miss the festival, though," Adel replied.

Eyes trailed them as they walked, as did footsteps. It wasn't just their guard, but Ashla also hung back, probably talking Ley's ear off. Arran was grateful for the way she gave them space without question once the dynamic of their relationship had changed.

"Remember when we were little, and we'd run down the streets to find the best pastry stands?" Adel said wistfully.

Arran chuckled softly. "Ashla always found the best ones."

Their glances over their shoulders to the redhead were practically in sync. Sure enough, as Arran had suspected, she was going on animatedly with Ley. A good-natured smile poked through Ley's short facial hair and crinkled his eyes as he nodded along to what she was saying.

Adel's voice was small as she spoke next. "I can't help but feel everyone is gossiping about us."

Arran caught her eyes scanning the crowd, where people lingered in place and did indeed seem to be watching them closely. The courtship hadn't officially been announced. By some miracle, they'd staved off any sort of public declaration as they navigated the changing waters of their relationship. But given their increased closeness over the past year, Arran knew people had their assumptions.

"Does it bother you?" Arran ventured.

The sounds of chatter congested the silence that followed his question as a string of distant music grated against his sudden nerves.

"No. I wouldn't say it does, but I still wish they wouldn't. If that makes any sense." She peered up at him, her hazel eyes sparkling as they caught the lights.

The tightness in his chest released. "It does," he replied with a soft smile, reminding himself over his anxieties that Adel was more reserved with other people. "It's only going to get worse once it's officially announced."

"You're right," she agreed, biting her lip ever so slightly as she concentrated on the path before them. "But at least we'll have each other."

"Of course." He dropped his free hand over hers where it still rested on his arm.

She squeezed his arm gently, a smile replacing the concentration as she gazed up at him. "Let's enjoy these moments while we can. We can start by getting Ashla to find us some good pastries and then go dance."

Adel slipped her arm from Arran's, and he watched as the princess picked up her skirts to rush back to her lady-in-waiting. That smile tugged at his lips again as Adel relayed the plan, the lights seeming to find her in just the right ways to highlight the shine of her hair and the curve of her cheek as she beamed at her friend.

The word he'd been searching for earlier suddenly came to him. *Stunning.*

CHAPTER
TWO

"These look and smell *amazing*!" Ashla exclaimed. She leaned over the wide countertop of the vendor stand, her hand extended as if she were about to select a pastry but couldn't decide which.

The sweet smell wafted around them as Arran simply watched Adel and Ashla peruse the pastries lined up before them. About half the size of an adult's palm, they had golden brown crusts and some were sprinkled with icing sugar while others were plain. The saccharine aroma of fruit hinted at what lay within their fluffy centres.

"They're called tora, My Lady," commented the vendor, a woman with dark hair held back in a loose braid that draped down the front of her plain, brown dress.

"Tora," Adel repeated, the word rolling off her tongue as if trying to taste it from the sound alone. She leaned in beside Ashla, taking stock of the selection. Her shoulders rose as she inhaled again before she straightened and turned to Arran. "Have I ever had one of these before?"

He shrugged. "I'm not sure. They're a seasonal dessert. It could be your visits haven't lined up with when they're in season."

She rose a brow. "What do you mean? We attend the Harvest Festival each year."

Arran glanced at the vendor. "This batch is a bit early this year, is that right?"

"Yes, Your Highness. The grains we use for tora were ready for harvest a little earlier than normal thanks to the all the rains we got," she replied with a nod. "Please, Princess, My Lady, try some. You, too, Your Highness."

While Adel and Ashla paused another moment to debate their choices, Arran stepped up to the stand and picked one without hesitation. The crust flaked and crumbled as he bit into it, the thick, sweet yet tart filling rich on his taste buds and threatening to spill out the sides where he'd bitten.

"You said this one is plain?" Ashla asked, pointing at one of the tora sitting on the tray on the countertop.

The woman nodded with a smile. "Yes, that's right, My Lady."

Ashla removed her glove, then plucked it up and stepped back to take a bite as Adel continued to decide.

"Delicious!" Ashla declared. "Adel, pick one. You must try it."

Adel's mouth twisted, and she again looked to Arran. "Which do you recommend?"

He swallowed the final bite of his own, watching with faint amusement and brushing crumbs from his hands and overcoat. Her indecision over something so small was endearing. "Any of them, but you'd probably like one with icing best."

"If I may, Princess?" the vendor spoke up again. Her eyes shifted ever so slightly as she gauged the princess's reaction. When Adel nodded, she picked up a pastry with icing on top, gently pinching it at the sides as her other hand hovered underneath. "This is one of my favourites. There isn't any filling, but the icing is sweet enough to still provide that dessert satisfaction."

Adel removed her own gloves now, handing them to Ashla.

"Thank you," she said as she took the treat from the woman, who curtsied slightly after the pastry was out of her hands.

A smile crept onto Arran's face when Adel bit into the tora and her eyes lit up.

"See, see? I told you!" Ashla prodded her shoulder just slightly.

"This *is* very good," Adel agreed.

"When I was young, I'd sneak down to the kitchens when I knew the baker was making them," Arran shared as she chewed. He met the vendor's gaze. "Pack up one of each, would you?"

"Of course, Your Highness." The woman crouched behind the stand to retrieve what he assumed was something to carry the pastries in.

Arran fished into a jacket pocket and pulled out a small coin pouch. He tugged at the leather strings to open the top, then fished out a few coins to place them on the countertop, where they gave the sure *thunk* of metal against wood.

The vendor straightened, spotted the coins, and connected with Arran's gaze. "I couldn't, Your Highness."

"I insist," he said, returning the pouch to his jacket.

"Thank you." She curtsied low this time before putting one pastry of each flavour into a small basket with burlap-like cloth lining.

Soon the trio continued making their way through the crowds, which parted for them. Ashla carried the basket, promising not to eat any more of the pastries. As they stopped at various stands, the basket filled with more treats both familiar and new.

Darkness blanketed Nithle Proper by the time they returned to the city square where crowds had gathered to dine and dance. The space was bright with lanterns and seemed to glint whenever the light caught any metal, adding warm tones to the banners and other décor.

Most had gathered into this area, with royal families seated at a group of tables to one side. The kings and queens of Nithle and Heta sat near each other, and whatever King Alden of Nithle and King Criph of Heta were talking about had the boyhood friends in stitches of laughter. Alden leaned back with his hands resting on his stomach as Criph hammered his fist against the table.

Their wives, Queen Shron and Queen Mela respectively, seemed to be having a less eventful conversation. Mela looked to be describing or explaining something with the way she moved her hands about as if to demonstrate the size of an object while Shron nodded along as if she understood completely.

As for the Piridet royal family, they occupied several seats at a different table. From what Arran could see, King Timith and Queen Diah of Piridet had brought their daughter, Princess Mihel, and three of their four sons, who were all in conversation about something.

I wonder if there's still tension between them, Arran thought as his gaze trailed from Mihel to Adel.

A couple years before, Mihel had pursued a courtship with Arran. He could still pretty clearly remember how she'd approached him at the Midsummer Festival, asking to speak with him alone. She'd taken him to the palace gardens where she'd sprung it on him. He'd had little idea before then that she was even interested in him at all, but from the earnestness in her expression, he'd doubted it was her parents' idea.

For the first little while after he'd turned her down and begun courting Adel, it had created some awkwardness at the events that followed, as Mihel seemed to constantly find reason to stare at them. It used to make Adel uncomfortable, but judging by how Mihel's gaze passed over them now, it seemed like she had moved on.

Adel's voice broke through Arran's reverie. "Look who's here." Her tone rung with astonishment.

Arran followed her gaze and was shocked to see none other than the three royal children of Veloth: Jase, Nea, and Rold. It had been several years since they'd last attended any event outside their own borders, kept within their kingdom by their protective father. King Hadden himself tended to stay within the castle walls ever since his wife, Queen Lelleth, had been killed by dahems seven years before in a random, one-off attack. The ambitious woman had departed from Veloth in search of a way to stop Lavanai from ever attacking again and never returned home.

It had taken weeks to find her body, but she'd eventually been discovered on the outskirts of Veloth where it skirted along the southern border of Lavanai. It was a tragedy that had rocked the kingdoms, and one that King Hadden still hadn't recovered from.

While the royal children enjoyed a meal at their table with a swath of their Royal Knights standing nearby, their father was still noticeably absent. Arran suspected it wasn't just because he was preoccupied elsewhere.

"I wonder how they managed to convince their father to let them come," Ashla commented quietly from Adel's opposite side.

A shrug was all either of her friends could offer.

The crowd erupted into applause as the band's performance came to an end. Some abandoned dancing while others closed in to take up the space and wait for the next song to begin from the stage in the centre of the square. A single musician drew a slow note from his stringed instrument; the other six musicians joined in as the tempo increased. There were hoots and hollers from those familiar with the boisterous tune.

Arran, Adel, and Ashla stood watching as people from across the United skipped across the dancing area or twirled in place. A whirling rainbow of fabric flashed under the lantern light as shadows kept pace along the ground.

Arran leaned toward Adel. "What do you think?"

"They're very good," she replied instantly, her tone betraying her hesitation.

Arran smirked. "I know you know that's not what I mean."

"There's no way," she replied with a shake of her head. Her brows pinched together as her eyes traced the dancing bodies moving about the square.

A small chuckle escaped him before he pressed his lips to her temple, onlookers be damned. "Okay."

"Let's find somewhere to sit and get refreshments instead," Ashla suggested from where she stood watching the dancers beside Adel. She then looked at her best friend and said, "My feet hurt anyway, and since we're wearing the same kind of shoes, I bet yours do, too."

"I'm okay," Adel insisted with a shake of her head. "But we can still sit."

"There's a table near our parents reserved for us." Arran pointed across the crowd. Among the moving bodies, he could see the smooth, navy table cloth with silver trim, the goblets set in a line, and the smaller table lanterns lighting the area in a soft glow.

As they made their way around the dance area to the table, attendants slipped into motion, first wiping the goblets clean and checking for tampering, and then pouring tart ciders for them. Their guard moved into position nearby, and by the time the trio got seated, there were trays of food spread out before them and someone had taken the basket of desserts.

Various steaming plates of meat and vegetables, as well as a warm loaf of bread, accompanied hearty smells that made Arran's mouth water and his stomach grumble.

In this more conspicuous position, Ashla was on better behaviour. She waited dutifully for Arran and Adel to fill their plates and for Adel to give her leave before taking anything for herself.

Soon the three fell into easy conversation about the food, the dance, and just about anything they could think of. This continued until Adel and Ashla excused themselves to use the privy. Their departure seemed a cue to the attendants, who swept in to remove things from the table, first checking with Arran that they were no longer needed.

Nithle's prince stood and stretched, thinking as he did about how it'd be nice to dance once Adel got back. He guessed there'd still be a little while until the musicians paused for a break. If she didn't take too long, they should be able to get at least one dance in.

While waiting, he did a sweep over the crowd, which was when he noticed a small faction of field fighters led by a field knight quickly, but discreetly, making their way around the crowd. Almost as soon as he saw them, Ley was at his side.

Arran glanced at his royal knight, almost eye level with his darker gaze. Ley looked just as bemused as he did, but still Arran asked, "What do you suppose this is about?"

"I'd hope for just a general report that the festival remains secure, but their pace…" Ley trailed off, keeping his voice low enough that only Arran could hear him.

Arran nodded, his mind already flipping from the festival to his militaristic side. As strategist for Nithle's army, it was his job to provide direction. He considered converging on the group, a tingle of worry creeping through his limbs, but he didn't want to draw any more attention. The group already stood out, wearing less formal and more battle-ready garb, mainly armour. Arran could see the stag carved into the field knight's shoulder plate as he turned to say something to one of the fielders.

Rather than approaching them, Arran schooled his expression, trying to keep it as neutral and light as possible. "What's going on?" Arran asked as soon as the group reached him. His eyes locked in on the field knight, a man named Feon.

"There's been an attack," the knight replied quickly; the purple scar along his left cheek twitched just slightly from the tension.

"Where? By whom?" He hoped against hope that it wasn't who he thought it'd be. *But there's no one else it would be...*

"Bunthle," Feon responded. "Word by pigeon says it's forces from Lavanai."

The trickle of worry solidified to ice. Only hours earlier, he'd been watching a play about Lavanai attacking his kingdom, and now, they were actually doing so.

Bunthle was Nithle's farthest remaining village and one of its smallest, located along Lake Pol and across from Lavanai. Knights and fighters protected the residents, given its proximity to the enemy kingdom.

Arran swallowed the fear lodging in his throat, trying to force it down so he could focus on figuring out how to handle the situation. *They're depending on me,* he reminded himself. "How many?"

"Several hundred. Maybe close to a thousand. They weren't sure," Feon said gravely.

Ley swore beside him. Arran felt like the air had been sucked out of Nithle Proper.

He moved on to his next question. "How many were sent

to aid them?" Bunthle was at least a half day's journey from the edge of Thlent, the rural village on the outskirts of Nithle Proper, but Arran had confidence in his forces holding them off. Hopefully it would be long enough for reinforcements to get there.

Feon shook his head. "Your Highness, the message came from Knight Harben. Most of the village has been captured. Some of Lavanai's people are holding them, but a good portion of Lavanai's forces are on the way to Nithle Proper."

It was Arran's turn to swear. "Ley, get Royal Commander Calar. We need to act now."

"Yes, Sire." Ley's tone was clipped and his movements sharp as he turned to find the royal commander. He wouldn't be far as he usually lingered near King Alden.

"We're pulling forces as we speak to form a line in Thlent to make sure they don't get through to Nithle Proper. We aren't sure how much time we have though," Feon continued.

Arran nodded again, outwardly calm while his heart hammered painfully in his chest. He'd been training as Nithle's war strategist since before he was a teenager, but with no active attacks, everything had been drills and hypotheticals. Figures on maps in the safety of the study. Now the reality of it was unfolding around him. He couldn't hesitate. Had to make the right call to protect his people.

Ley, Calar, his father, and King Criph joined them a few moments later. Their tense expressions told Arran they'd been filled in on the situation.

"We need to act now," Alden stated without preamble.

Arran nodded in agreement. "Stop the festival and bring everyone to the castle. It's the safest place. We'll have the protection of the outer walls and the advantage of elevation to see Lavanai's forces coming. We don't know how much time we have. Commander, have your captains organize and get people to safety as quickly and calmly as possible."

"Yes, Your Highness," Calar, a taller man with dark hair, said and turned away from the group.

"Father, you and Mother should fall back to the castle as well. Lead the other royal families to the safe holds," Arran continued, his mind moving quickly.

Ley gave Arran a stern look. "You should fall back to the safehold as well, Your Highness."

Arran stopped his protest short. He didn't need the concern etched into the set of Ley's mouth and jaw and the pinch of his brows to know his knight was right. Strategy, Arran was good at. Physical combat was something he'd never mastered. He didn't even carry a sword. Putting himself in the thick of battle would make him a liability.

"Where's Adel?" King Criph interrupted, drawing Arran from his thoughts.

Another spike of ice through his veins. Arran looked over his shoulder in the direction Adel and Ashla had gone, hoping they were somehow on their way back. All he saw were Calar's captains dispersing into the crowd to start corralling people.

"She and Ashla left to go to the privy. They have their guard with them," Arran said when he faced Criph again.

The king, just shorter than Arran, nodded before ducking out of the circle to speak with his own guard. Arran resisted following him. He was needed here, and Adel's father could protect her as well as, if not better than, he could.

"Don't worry, Arran." It was Ley that spoke, his voice low and reassuring. "The king will find them and get them to the castle."

Arran put a hand on the knight's shoulder and gave it an appreciative squeeze. He then turned back to Feon. "Return to Thlent. Whatever forces I can send will be on your heels and join you there. Send word to me if anything happens."

"Of course, Your Highness," Feon said, his voice hard. He and his fielders didn't hesitate to weave their way through the crowd.

Unsurprised to see him still standing there, Arran addressed King Alden. "Father, go to the castle now," he pleaded with him. "I'm more than capable of ensuring our forces are in place before I retreat myself. You and Mother need to get to safety." Alden opened his mouth to speak, but Arran cut in, "Ley will make sure of it."

The king paused and regarded Ley a long moment. The knight said nothing, but some understanding passed between them because Alden said, "Very well. Protect him, Knight Ley."

Ley didn't hesitate. "Of course, Your Majesty."

The king retreated next, leaving Arran and Ley standing in place near the table he'd shared with Adel and Ashla. The village square was still in motion, but the music had died, the excitement dampened, and laughs extinguished. What had once been the warm glow of lanterns now felt frenetic as they swayed in the breeze and cast fast-moving shadows about the square.

Arran watched as knights in the crowd ushered people from the square down the road toward the castle. Their faces and movements betrayed their unease, even fear, but no one fought the knights.

Still, the feeling of chaos closed in around him. It seemed Ley could sense it, too.

"The Union will protect us, Your Highness."

Davi's earlier words rang in Arran's mind. *Is it protection though?*

Of course it was, and Ley was right. The Union wouldn't let them fall.

CHAPTER

THREE

"What a fantastic night," Ashla commented as the
princess and lady-in-waiting duo strolled through
a quieter part of the streets.

There were some lights in the windows of homes and shops,
but the decorations were fewer and farther between this far
out from the festivities. The princess's guards followed close
behind, boot steps crunching along the dirt and gravel of the
roadway. The sounds of the crowd continued ricocheting off
the buildings, but the music had stopped. Adel guessed the
performers were taking a short reprieve.

After finishing up in the privy, Adel had asked for a
much needed reprieve of her own. The Harvest Festival's loud
music, throngs of people, and watchful eyes—it was getting
to be a bit too much. In many ways, the princess was used to
people watching her every move. After all, her mother had
always impressed upon her how even when she didn't think
anyone was, someone was watching. But this was different.
Her relationship with Arran was something she held dearly.
She didn't want the pressures of royal intrigue and politics to
taint the beautiful thing they had.

"So how are you feeling about tomorrow?" Ashla asked
when Adel didn't reply to her comment.

Adel wrung her fingers. "The same as before. Like I'm
going to throw up in front of the entirety of the United."

Ashla nudged her shoulder gently. "The entirety of the United won't be there, Adel."

Tomorrow, on the last day of the Harvest Festival, the little bubble Adel had been clinging to would burst. A joint royal announcement would set the courtship officially in motion in the public eye. She sighed and the heaviness of the thought settled on her shoulders.

"I told you you should talk to your father about having a less public announcement. Surely they could send a royal decree by parchment," Ashla continued.

Adel glanced at her with a half-hearted glare. "And I told you I already did talk to him."

"Once."

"And? I still did."

"But if you ask him about it again, he might understand it better and see how important it is to you."

"Once my father's decided something, I just have to go with it. You know this."

Ashla sighed but didn't say anything else at first. Comfortable silence fell between them, the footsteps and a flurry of wings as night birds took off somewhere nearby being the only sounds accompanying them in the dark streets.

Finally, Ashla spoke again. "It'll be fine. You two will still be you two. You can still be just as you are."

"I know," Adel replied.

"Do you though?" Ashla challenged playfully.

"I do. But while we might be the same, our worlds will shift." She felt silly saying it, but still couldn't shake the way it clutched at her chest.

"Just think though: Public courtship means people will be expecting to see the two of you together more. It could mean more visits," Ashla said brightly.

Adel wasn't lured by the silver lining. "Things will change for you as well, you know. More eyes on me means more eyes on you."

Ashla shrugged and tossed her curls over her shoulder. "I can handle it."

Adel wasn't so sure and worried what toll suppressing her lively spirit would take on her best friend. As she caught glimpses of her though the meager light, she admired the determination she saw there. Nothing seemed to faze her, even when she did get in trouble for overstepping. She learned the boundary, yes, but never let it fully restrain her.

Ashla caught her staring and smiled. "We should head back soon. They'll be wondering where we are."

"You're right," Adel ceded.

They changed course, picking a side street that would lead them back to the city square. As they made their way, a cat darted out across the intersection ahead of them. They thought nothing of it until they saw two figures stop in the middle of the junction. Weapons glinted in the lantern-light, before they suddenly took off at inhuman speeds.

Before Adel could even think, Ashla had grabbed her and pulled her into the shadows of one of the nearby buildings, pressing them both against the wall. The building felt cold even through the thick fabric of her dress. Without command, two of the guards dashed ahead while the others joined the girls in the shadows.

Adel focused on controlling her breathing as her heart hammered against her ribcage. They'd practiced for this kind of situation in which danger was upon them and getting Adel to safety became top priority. She knew she should remain perfectly still, but she needed to see Ashla's reaction. She needed to see this was actually happening.

Please, let it be nothing, Adel prayed, trying to conjure up some reasonable scenario where weapon-wielding individuals would be rushing off at breakneck speeds.

She turned her head ever so slowly, and although they were in the shadows, she was close enough to Ashla that she could make out her features. Her friend's eyes were wide and watchful, somehow seeming to take up her round face. Her breathing was laboured but quiet. Adel felt blindly and found Ashla's hand; Ashla gripped hers in return.

That grip tightened when they heard a scuffle and then shouting in the direction that the two guards had gone. Most of the shouts were indiscernible, but Adel could have sworn she heard one word above all the others.

No. Not dahems. It can't be.

"Princess, we need to get you to safety," one of her remaining guards said, his voice fast and low. "We'll take you to the castle and have your lady along with the rest of the guard meet us there."

"No!" Adel hissed instantly. "I know that's protocol, but no!"

To her horror, Ashla let go of her hand and fished two dark-coloured scarves from the folds of her dress that hinted at some hidden pocket. She draped one of them over Adel's head and worked on tying the thin fabric under her chin.

"We have to, Adel," Ashla said before Adel could protest again. Her words, like the guard's, were quick and low. There was a firmness to them and a steadiness to her hands that Adel couldn't comprehend. Once Adel's scarf was secure, Ashla draped the second scarf over her own head and knotted it.

"We can go together! They haven't seen us," Adel tried.

"They'll know we're out here because of the guard," Ashla continued. She placed her hands on either side of Adel's face. They were warm, and now she felt a slight tremble in them. "It's better if we go to the castle separately. We'll meet you there."

Pain in her jaw told Adel she was clenching her teeth anxiously, and she forced herself to relax it. She placed her hands over Ashla's and then gave a firm nod. She was right.

"We'll see each other at the castle," Ashla said reassuringly. "Be brave."

"You, too."

Ashla's hands slipped out from under Adel's, and then she and a few guards stepped out of the shadows to start their escape to the castle. Adel lingered in the shadows with her remaining guards with a sick feeling in her stomach. How was this actually happening? She and Ashla splitting up, their matching attire… They were just drills before. She never expected to need them in reality. Her eyes remained fixated on the direction they'd gone even after they disappeared into the night.

Her heart continued to pound in her chest, but while her heart raced, her feet felt leaden.

You have to move, she ordered herself. *You have to make it to the castle to meet up with Ashla and Arran.*

She took a deep breath that did nothing to calm her nerves, looked to her protectors, and gave another nod to signal she was ready. In truth, she didn't feel ready at all.

CHAPTER

FOUR

With the calmest tones Arran could muster, he urged a family of three to follow the crowds to the castle as they crossed the nearly evacuated city square. He was about to say something more to them, but a sudden roar and glow of flames cut his words short and snared his attention.

The inferno towered high enough into the air that it seemed to lick the tops of the tallest buildings in the distance. He and Ley both froze in place, eyes wide as the fire disappeared just as quickly as it had appeared, bringing darkness down more thickly than just moments ago. There was only a fraction of a moment of silence before screams and tramping of feet retreating down the pathway. Anyone remaining in the city square now fled at full speed toward safety, save for Arran and Ley, who remained frozen.

"Magic." Arran's voice was barely a whisper, as if speaking any louder would invite the death magic promised. *They brought magic users!*

"And close," Ley continued, drawing his sword. "They'll be upon us in moments. You need to hide."

The prince's mind wasn't on what Ley had said though. His eyes trailed the square, where a few remaining lanterns flickered away in the darkness.

"We have to douse the lanterns," Arran said instead. "We can't risk them fueling the magic."

Ley stepped in front of him, his expression hard. "The lanterns are the least of our worries."

Arran stared him down but knew he couldn't argue. The city could be rebuilt. Nithle's only heir couldn't be brought back to life.

He glanced over his shoulder to where the crowd had disappeared down the street, worrying over them, too. *There are guards and knights with them. They'll be safe.*

As Ley lead Arran down Nithle Proper's side streets, the knight's attention seemed to flit here and there among the swaying lantern light, looking for somewhere to stow him away. Finally, they came upon a building that had a cellar entrance in the small space between it and its neighbour. They pulled open the worn wooden doors, and Arran sunk into the darkness.

"Someone with the password will come get you. Don't leave, don't make a sound," Ley commanded. His usual friendliness had been stripped away. "I'll lead them away from this area."

Another nod was Arran's response, backing into the corner nearest to the stairs of the small cellar room. Once the doors were closed, it was pitch dark, and he could see nothing. The hum of silence welcomed him in the chill dampness. Even as he suppressed a shiver, he was grateful for the cold. He could only imagine the cellar's smell in the summer months.

The blackness and hush brought on a scramble of worried thoughts. Had his parents made it to safety? Were Adel and Ashla safe? What about Ley?

One of the loudest worries: *How are we going to fight a force of magic-using dahems?*

His stomach clenched. Physical combat was hard enough, what with the dahems' extra speed and strength. Although they looked remarkably human, they were somehow born with heightened physical skills despite no noticeable difference in physique.

Still, it was the thought of their amber eyes that chilled him the most. He remembered the childhood stories where amber-eyed demons took children from their parents and parents from their children. Stories where they tortured innocent people by sucking the air out of their lungs with their magical powers.

The stories also warned against humans trying to harness magic for themselves. One came to mind in particular of a royal knight who was desperate to save his king from an attack. In his desperation, the knight invited the magic to himself, only to be overtaken by madness as his eyes turned brilliant gold and it devoured his soul. While the knight managed to slay the dahem, he also tragically killed his king.

While most children only had these cautionary tales, Arran also had historical accounts of dahems slaughtering villages and humans losing their souls to magic. There was one logbook in particular he remembered in which a field knight had written about the screams of his fellows falling to dahem attacks, magical and otherwise, in battle.

Arran shivered. *That could be my people right now.*

Time passed excruciatingly slowly, each moment testing his trust in his knights and guards to keep everyone safe while he waited for someone to come with the right series of knocks to free him.

He worried whether or not someone *would* come. His feet and legs began to ache from standing so long in the damp cellar. Still, he dared not move, not even to try to sit or crouch, lest he accidentally knock something over and give himself away.

He wasn't sure what was worse: waiting in the silence or

the sounds of a group that eventually drew closer. At first, a flicker of hope fluttered through him, but that quickly died as he heard the distinct sounds of destruction. It sounded like smashing wood, the wrenching of metal, and shattering glass.

The prince's breathing laboured with panic. There was no way to escape from the cellar except through the door he'd come in.

He tried to determine how close those forces were. The particular muffle of chaos made it seem as though they weren't on top of him just yet... Maybe he could slip out and run.

His own thoughts chided him. *Run where? They're probably crawling through all of Nithle Proper.*

Still, if he were to stay put, he'd be found for sure. They were leaving no door unopened or hiding place unchecked. As soon as they opened the door and climbed into the cellar, they'd see him, and that'd be it. He'd be dead.

He cursed, willing his limbs to loosen and move. Splinters from the narrows steps poked at Arran's hands as he climbed them in a crouched position and then slowly pushed open one of the doors a crack. The glow of flames from somewhere else in the village caught his eye, but he focused on his escape. Looking one way down the space between the buildings, there was no one. He peered around the door in the other direction and didn't see anyone there either.

Ley's order to stay rang in his head one last time before he inched out the door, trying to keep to the shadows. He pressed himself against the wall, using one hand to guide the door closed as quietly as possible while also listening to the village around him. Another smash came from his right; to his left, it was quieter. That'd have to be the way he'd go. He took a moment to look up, half-expecting to see someone perched on the edge of a roof like bird of prey, but there were only twinkling stars, partially hidden by smoke.

It took a lot to keep his shaking legs from collapsing under him as he moved, but Arran started his way between the buildings as quickly as he dared. He couldn't help the occasional glance over his shoulder, fearing he'd see glowing, amber eyes staring back at him, but when he wasn't looking over his shoulder, he was focused on his surroundings.

Unfamiliar with this part of Nithle Proper, he wasn't quite sure which way he was going but hoped it was toward the castle. Toward safety. Whichever direction it was, he successfully made it a few streets, creeping along in the shadows, before he found himself stuck again.

The sounds of dahems scouring the city surrounded him. They were close enough that he could hear them talking pretty distinctly, although he didn't understand the words of their sharp-sounding language at all.

Arran wedged himself into a small alcove he found in one of the buildings, leaning his head back and closing his eyes a moment to try to calm his racing heart and thoughts. He needed to focus on hiding long enough for the dahems to move on or he needed to figure out how to slip by them.

Both felt like an impossibility.

He opened his eyes and his heart stopped. A pair of mirthful amber eyes stared back at him.

CHAPTER

FIVE

E ven as Arran dipped his shoulder to try to barrel past, the dahem slammed him back into the alcove with both hands. The wind left the prince, and he felt his head connect with the wall behind him. Star-filled darkness danced before his eyes as the dahem pulled at his collar to give it a closer look, called something out to its fellows, then wrenched him forward.

Amidst the sudden wooziness, Arran wondered that he wasn't instantly meeting death. Instead, the dahem dragged him stumbling over his own two feet into the main street where the torches made the space glow. The dahems exchanged more sharp words amongst themselves. As they did, the prince tried to assess how many there were. Through the dizziness, it wasn't easy.

Maybe twenty, he thought, trying to squint away his distorted vision.

Before he could think about what that might mean or what he could do, the dahems collectively moved. With the dahem holding his arms behind his back, he was swept up in their surprisingly human-paced procession. They wove through the streets, other groups of dahems joining them along the way and seeming to share a moment of celebration.

The more his mind cleared, the more he was able to take Lavanai's forces in. As much as he'd known the players' renditions of dahems had been a huge farce in the stage drama earlier that evening, seeing just how human they looked was surreal. Dahems of all statures and builds chatted away, their words cutting through the air with each syllable. They carried all variety of weapons, and their battle leathers creaked and also smelled of sweat as they walked.

By the time they reached an area Arran was familiar with, he'd regained most of his wits. Approaching the village square, he could see the stonework stained with blood as bodies littered the ground. His stomach turned, then clenched as his eyes found groups of humans held captive under the threat of weapons and, he was sure, magic. A shorter dahem with cropped, dark hair and a blade sheathed at each hip paced around them. Every once in a while, she barked something at one of her fellows, who reacted instantly to follow whatever command had been given.

In almost the centre of the square stood a taller, youthful-looking dahem, also with dark hair. He stood with his shoulders back and jaw set as he listened to another dahem that spoke to him. Whatever that dahem said caused the taller dahem to turn to look their way and grin at the sight of them.

"So this is Prince Arran of Nithle."

Arran was shocked the dahem even knew his language. His heavy accent meant Nithle was pronounced as Neet-lay instead of Nith-lay, but his words were otherwise clear, and the accented pronunciation took nothing away from the wave of fear rolling over Arran.

They know who I am. He thought of how the dahem tugged at his collar and swore silently. *Nithle's crest.* He'd never been ashamed to wear it, but all of a sudden, he wished it wasn't there.

The smaller dahem that had been barking orders also

looked in his direction as the group around him dispersed, leaving only him and the one holding his arms to step forward to meet the tall dahem in the middle. The dahem assessed him, his amber eyes looking him up and down a few times before coming to settle on his face. He said something in his own language, which prompted the dahem holding Arran's arms to release him.

He glanced over his shoulder just slightly to see if the dahem was still there, and his eyes caught sight of none other than Ley among one of the groups of captured humans.

He's alive! Arran rejoiced silently. From his brief glimpse, it looked like his knight was sporting a bloody, swelling lip and maybe a black eye—but he was alive.

Arran brought his gaze back to the dahem, whose mere presence felt imposing even without his height and stronger build. Was this Lavanai's Lord Jasim he'd heard so much of?

Too young, he thought as he swallowed back fear and tried to keep his expression firm.

"Where are your parents, Prince?" the dahem asked finally, his tone even and cold.

Arran inhaled. There was no chance he'd answer that question.

"This could be over much more quickly," the dahem continued, taking a step forward.

Arran involuntarily took a step back, catching the quirk of the dahem's mouth as he did. He cursed at himself silently. *Get it together. How can we fight back?*

"Your hesitation does your people no good," the dahem continued. "You'd best tell me where the king and queen are."

Arran swallowed, knowing a threat when he heard one. His eyes darted to the human captives, then to Ley, trying to silently converse with him and find a solution. The knight shook his head almost imperceptibly.

I can't give up my parents, Arran told himself. *But I also can't allow them to harm my people.*

A crack of lightning crashed through the prince's thoughts, followed quickly by a chorus of shrieks and a thump as a body fell.

"No!" he shouted, eyes finding the victim among a part in the crowd. He could smell the scorch of the stonework and something he didn't even want to think about. *Flesh*, his mind supplied anyway. It took everything not to wretch.

"I told you, Prince," the dahem spoke again, his voice somehow more menacing as it pitched lower.

Arran ripped his eyes from the victim to the dahem, who lowered the mace he held in his right hand. The spike-laden ball on the end of a dark, wooden handle looked just as menacing as its wielder.

"Hesitation does not serve your people. Now tell me."

Panic and a need to keep calm warred within him. He tried to rein in his scattering thoughts that screamed to come up with some way to save everyone.

Before he could think of anything else, the dahem struck him hard across the face, sending him crashing sideways, where his right shoulder smarted against the hard stone ground. He tried to push himself up, but the shoulder gave way under his weight, and he crashed back down on his stomach.

He flipped onto his back as he heard a new wave of screams and boot steps approach, looking up from where he was on the ground to see the dahem had his mace at the ready again.

The dahem raised his arm, the weapon rising and prepared to strike, while sparks of lightning began jumping from spike to spike. Arran's breath quickened with his hammering heart. He heard a scuffle somewhere beyond him and more shouting.

He swore he heard Ley, but he also heard that sharp dahem language as well.

"Naxela! Yastalai!"

Arran had no idea what those words meant, but the female dahem's tone sounded urgent. Anxious even. He had no time to think about it. He tried to scramble away but his shoulder gave out again. The dahem's arm swung.

CHAPTER

SIX

Ryla's right shoulder connected firmly into the side of the dahem swinging the mace. A collection of gasps chorused as she stopped in her tracks while the dahem flew through the air to land hard on the ground several feet away. The sound of the mace's wooden handle clunking across the stones pierced sharply through the air as the electric charge died.

Her brown-eyed gaze trailed to the young man on the ground. He gawped back at her. In only a moment, she took in as much of him as she could: blue eyes, defined features, short, curly brown hair, clean-shaven. No weapon at all, and the crest on his garment gave him away as the Nithlean prince. With the subtle shift of his eyes, she could read he was studying her, too.

Her arrival was incendiary. Dahems left their positions, running to their fallen commander and at her. She was ready for it: feet shoulder-width apart and her sword gripped firmly in her left, gloved hand while her right was extended for balance. Her eyes shifted calmly from side to side, and she checked over her shoulders, too. They were coming in from all sides.

She stooped a fraction of a second. "Stay down," she instructed Nithle's prince, her voice deadpan even among the eruption of chaos.

Her sword flashed, meeting a dahem's. The metals cried

out as reverberations shook through her hand and up her arm. Amber eyes pierced her, searching her features for something, perhaps trying to read her next moves or figure out who she was. Rather than give them an answer, she pushed them back and, in another quick motion, sliced through with a spray of blood.

Another check over her shoulder, and sure enough, dahems were about to close in on the young man on the ground. Other human fighters had managed to break free from their captors in the chaos and had begun hacking their way through the dahems. Still, Ryla moved closer to the prince, who was doing what he could to heed her command. At most, he scrambled to get out of the way of tramping feet, noticeably avoiding the blood that painted the stones and the fallen dahem body.

Another dahem, getting too close, met its end with a graceful pivot of Ryla's boot steps and a swing of her blade. A surge of energy rushed through her as she did, pushing her body to keep up its efforts. Regular humans couldn't match dahems for their speed or strength—but she wasn't a regular human.

She was trained for this.

As her assault continued, she left her senses open. The hum of nature's magic surrounded them, but it was the distinct sense of magic users among the dahems she sought out. There were two. One had been the dahem she'd collided with originally, and the other was somewhere beyond her sightline but still in the fray. Why they weren't using their magic, she wasn't sure.

It wasn't long before she heard a call in the dahem tongue. "Fall back!"

There was little doubt one among them had recognized what she was.

Despite the command, the attacking dahems hesitated. The dahem directly in front of Ryla made a face, almost like a snarl, before lurching forward; Ryla struck first with her sword before running it through when it leapt backward. She stared down the next wave of attackers without so much as flinching.

"*Fall back!*" the voice called again, much sharper.

This time, the group made quick work to heed the order by pushing their way through the humans and disappearing down the myriad of city streets. Armour clanked as knights followed through the darkness, but Ryla stayed still, watching and making sure the prince went without further assault.

As it was, a knight crouched at his side, looking a little roughed up himself, but showing only concern for the prince.

"Are you okay?" she heard the knight ask quickly, although his words sounded slightly strained, probably from the swelling lip.

"My shoulder and hip hurt," the prince replied, his voice shaking.

Ryla saw the prince had indeed shifted his weight to his left side. That he wasn't crying out in pain was either indicative of the injury's low severity or a testament to his ability to hold a façade. It was perhaps slightly too early to give him a complete judge of character, but she was very certain it was the former and not the latter.

It was only when she felt the whispers of magic fade beyond the fairly wide radius of her senses that Ryla crouched and tore fabric from a fallen body to wipe the blood and gore from her sword. She felt eyes on her as the fabric whispered up the blade, but she continued through the motions before discarding the cloth, standing, and sheathing the weapon at her right hip.

The prince had climbed to his feet, though leaning heavily against the roughed up knight. Her earlier intake of his features recommenced: the prince was roughly average height for a man, standing about eye-to-eye with her. He had the build of a non-fighter, which his scuffed royal garb only seemed to accentuate. His expression, shaken as it was, was sharp in his observation of her.

She pulled at the fingers of the glove on her left hand, feeling it tug at the fabric of her sleeve where it stopped near her elbow. When it came free and slid from her fingers, she held the hand up for them to see.

"I am Killer Ryla," she supplied for the unasked question.

Eyes widened around her, a combined reaction, she knew, to her expressionless voice and the symbol tattooed to the back of her hand. The black ink marked into her skin looked like a stylized, slanted *S* with an inward-pointing line hovering at each of the "letter's" tips. They couldn't see it, but the same mark was tattooed over her heart and on her scalp.

"High Protector! We're honoured," the scuffed up knight said. Others around him bowed, which seemed to prompt him to say, "If you'll please forgive myself and my prince for this improper greeting."

Ryla only nodded in response, unperturbed either way. She lowered her hand and pulled the glove back on with practiced ease.

"I am Prince Arran of Nithle," the young man spoke now from where he stood, supported by his knight. The tension in his voice and slight tremble of his hands told her he was forcing evenness as he spoke. "This is Royal Knight Ley. We're grateful for the Union's assistance." His jaw tightened as he shifted. "How should we prepare for the next dahem attack?"

"It'll be some time before they attack again," Ryla replied without hesitation.

His brows furrowed just slightly. "You're certain?"

"I am." She left no room for further rebuttal. "We must

meet with the Keepers."

This was met with more wide eyes. Considering how long it had been since the last Killer had been sent to defend Nithle, it wasn't surprising to her they weren't accustomed to the protocol.

The last time Lavanai had made any attempt on Nithle was when the young prince that now stood before her had been a toddler, and the Union had protected the kingdom then just as it would now. Ryla hadn't been sent as the protector last time—she'd been only a child herself, in the early years of her training. But she knew of Nithle's history with the Union.

Arran spoke again. "Someone fetch the royal healer and tell him to wait for me in my chambers. I'll meet with him after the Keepers."

Ryla detected a slight shift in his tone as he gave his orders, and although he didn't give them to anyone specifically, more than one knight jumped into action to find the healer he spoke of.

He addressed a group of knights and fighters next. "See to it that everyone here is cared for. Gather the dead." He stumbled subtly over that command and cleared his throat before continuing. "Check the damages to the city and report back to me as quickly as possible."

Ryla waited as he continued to delegate tasks. She allowed this effort for the prince to regain a sense of control and reclaim safety. If it came to it, she could order them to move this along, but she wouldn't need to impose her rank here. The Keepers would understand the delay.

It wasn't long before they began to pick their way through the disheveled city toward Nithle Castle. Someone had been sent ahead to inform the castle of their approach, but their group of the prince, his Royal Knight, an entourage of other guard, and the Killer made slow progress due to the prince's limping steps. Ryla remained in step with Prince Arran, her attention focused on him alongside their surroundings in the cool air of the night.

The streets were quiet, devoid of anyone except for a few frightened folks coming out of hiding. No one approached; many looked on with concern and curiosity. All let them pass. When one older woman spotted the group, it was Ryla that caught and held her attention. The woman held up a hand with her palm facing outward and fingers splayed before moving her arm in a clockwise circle in the air.

Arran seemed to consider the motion a moment. "Killer Ryla, if I may, that was the old hand signal of respect for the Union, was it not?"

"Correct," Ryla replied, the emotionlessness of her tone snaring the prince's attention a moment longer. She didn't look at him but could see the lingering gaze out of the corner of her eye.

The motion the woman had made was meant to symbolize the Union crest—a stylized sun. It was a simple design of a circle with eight alternating longer and shorter spokes.

"If any kingdom were to have people keeping that practice, I suppose it would be Nithle," Ley said conversationally without any reaction to her voice. "Other kingdoms don't have the relationship we do with the Union, after all."

While the Union protected all kingdoms in the United, Nithle had been the kingdom who'd benefited from the Union's aid the most. Many speculated that it was Nithle's proximity to Lavanai that drew the dahems to them. After all, they shared a long border on either side of Lake Pol. Veloth's border with Lavanai was much smaller. Nithle was also the largest of the four kingdoms after its acquisition of Wendur, so perhaps

Lavanai thought starting their conquest by eliminating the biggest kingdom would be best.

None of that truly mattered to Ryla. Her duty was to protect whom she was ordered to and kill the dahems, not guess as to their overarching thought processes.

Conversation died, everyone on the lookout for any danger that might pop out of the shadows. First, they'd meet with the Keepers to get their directives, then Ryla could gather whatever information she needed from them to perform her duty.

A winding, lantern-lit pathway led them to the large, stone castle once they'd made it past the outer walls. Lights illuminated the entryway and lower levels of the castle, but the towers, parapets, merlons, windows, and otherwise were cloaked in darkness.

By the time they reached the castle, attendants waited for them on the entrance stairs. Armed guards stood at the ready, an effort and step in precaution that Ryla understood despite it being unnecessary. An array of drawn swords and nocked arrows lined their trek up the castle's grey, stone steps and through the large, dark, wooden doors.

The doors closed them in, leaving them to a castle alive with anticipation. Even more attendants filled the large, high-ceilinged entryway, each waiting with calm expressions but nervous energy. A variety of tense forms and shifting gazes met her, as did reverence with low bows and bright expressions.

A servant approached, looking remarkably put together for the commotion that had taken place that night. His light-coloured hair was combed back out of his face and his tan trousers with a dark-coloured tunic were neatly pressed.

"High Protector." The servant bowed low, then turned to the prince, who was now standing on his own though still favouring his left side. "Your Highness, Healer Dalam has been called to meet you in your chambers. The king and queen have already made their way to the High Chambers to await your party to meet with the Keepers."

"Excellent," Arran replied. His voice had steadied.

"High Protector, is there anything I might get or prepare for you?" the servant continued, facing Ryla once again.

"Not at this time. Be on standby," she replied.

The man nodded briskly. "Of course. My name is Huth. Call on me whenever you may need. In the meantime, I shall prepare a room for you. Do you have any special requirements?"

"No," Ryla replied.

"Very well. If you'll excuse me." The man bowed again before scurrying off.

"Killer Ryla," Arran said, bringing her attention to him. "The High Chambers are this way, in the north wing." He gestured generally to the wide staircase that spilled down into the entrance directly in front of them. Unlike the exterior, the stairs were made of a lighter stonework, flanked by banisters carved into thick spirals and railings that appeared as smooth as glass.

As she glanced up the stairs, Ryla saw two guards positioned on either side near the banisters at the top as well as servants. The wall behind them was lined with portraits and paintings and other décor nearly all the way up to the high ceilings. Everything appeared exactly as she'd have expected it.

She looked back to the prince, who was watching her with quiet expectation. Her eyes flicked to how he held his arm, and she noted again that he was still favouring the injured hip.

Registering her gaze, he said, "Don't worry about me. I can make it to the High Chambers." Another limping step forward led to another grimace.

Her eyes flickered to Knight Ley. "Help him up the stairs."

The man jumped into action without a second thought, reaching for the prince's arm.

Arran pulled his arm away. "I said I can make it. There isn't much pain." His tone was slightly indignant, maybe even offended.

Ryla pressed on calmly. "Unnecessarily aggravating the injury for the sake of your pride is pointless. Accept the aid and reduce the longevity of the wound."

The prince's jaw tightened as if he were going to retort, but he said nothing as Ley again took his arm and draped it around his shoulders.

Going up the flight of stairs was slow work, but when they did make it to the top and went to the right, Arran shrugged out of Ley's support and led the way to the High Chambers with his slow limp. Ley was in step with him, speaking quietly with the prince as Ryla followed a pace or two behind. Despite their hushed tones, she still heard them.

"You know the High Protector is right, Arran," Ley implored.

"They're not that bad, and I'm not a fighter. My injuries don't matter as much. We should be tending to yours more immediately," Arran replied, glancing at the knight.

"I'm fine. Bruising and swelling. Dried blood and nothing broken," Ley said dismissively. "Fighter or not, your injuries matter just as much as anyone's."

Ryla paid little mind to their exchange, instead taking in the surroundings of the halls and mentally mapping the route they took to the High Chambers. It lined up perfectly with the map the Keepers had of the castle, and while she had no doubt of the map's accuracy, she continued with the exercise.

They finally came to the guarded double-doors at the entrance of the High Chambers. Like the castle entrance, they were a heavy, dark-coloured wood, although these were both engraved with the stag crest of Nithle and the solar crest of the Union. The silver leafing originally used to highlight the carvings was flaked and faded, but the crests still stood out strong.

The doors opened soundlessly as the guards pushed them inward to give the group entrance. Ryla stepped around the prince and knight to cross the threshold first, walking in to a scene of the queen wringing her skirts where they met the bodice of her dress and the king pacing the room. Both stopped to stare.

"High Protector!" the king declared, stepping forward as if to approach her.

Ryla ignored him. Her footfalls were silent as she traversed the carpeted floor which led to a raised platform that ran the width of the room. On it were three high-backed chairs, ornately carved and cushioned for exalted guests. She bypassed the seats entirely to examine the stone wall behind them.

It took only a moment for her to find what she was looking for. *Here*, she thought as she again removed her left glove, then removed the thin piece of stone along the wall.

Behind it was a small compartment, home to a scuffed Cherrywood box, which she extracted. She undid the small, golden clasp, then lifted the lid to reveal an amulet inside. It was a simple thing sitting on a small plush cushion of dark fabric. It could have just as easily been worn on a chain, but generally, kingdoms kept the amulet just as she'd found this one—secreted in a wall in a box.

The unblemished silver surface of the round amulet had the Union crest etched into it. Each kingdom had one of these magic-infused charms as a way to quickly contact the Keepers. It was considered too dangerous for Killers to carry an amulet themselves. Balancing the box in her right hand, she brushed the amulet's cool surface with her left index and middle fingertips. The slightest of touches elicited a pulse of magic, after which she withdrew her hand.

It was only when everything was returned to its place that she gave her attention to the royal family and their knights, who were watching her intently. Their expressions shifted as three cloaked figures silently appeared before the chairs while Ryla came to stand to the left of the left-most chair. She stood with her feet apart and her right hand resting easily on the hilt of her sword. The cloaked figures took their seats.

Everyone else in the room bowed.

CHAPTER

SEVEN

The room was barely above chilly, but the Keepers invited a completely different kind of chill to Arran's bones. Any sort of mental preparation he'd once thought he might have for the day he met the kingdoms' protectors for the first time was swept away.

Their obscured appearances matched every depiction he'd seen or read: charcoal-coloured cloaks with each kingdom's crest in silver stitching along the hems. Even without seeing their faces, their presences were commanding as they sat perfectly still, seemingly staring down from the platform. It was a surreal feeling, as though they'd stepped out of the pages of his texts.

Next to them, Killer Ryla looked almost normal.

No, she doesn't, he decided as his gaze trailed back to where she stood silently and stoically beside the chair farthest to his right.

Varying shades of black, charcoal, and grey made up her attire, all of it form fitted to her lean frame. Those things were fairly normal—female warriors were not uncommon among his people and many had similar body types.

The oddity started with the style of the outfit. It didn't appear to be made of metal or even leathers, but rather some sort of fabric that he could hardly fathom would be protective enough. Yet, not a stitch was out of place nor a single scrap of it torn despite her earlier combat. Her heavy-looking boots ended just below her knees, coming to a rounded point at the kneecap and looking like they sloped off behind the bend of the knee. The strange part, however, was the thick straps at the ankles with a silver buckle each along the outside—it struck him as a fashion choice instead of necessity.

The jacket she wore came up under her chin and tapered down only her left hip since her sword belt was fastened on her right. The sleeves of the jacket disappeared into the elbow-length gloves she wore.

The clothing, while odd, he could get past. It was the perfect stillness with which she held herself, the complete lack of exertion he'd seen as she'd fended off attackers, and the absence of emotions that was more perplexing to him. The even, calm of her voice was almost unnerving as she spoke, yet there was no doubt it held authority. Then there were her eyes: a deep brown with the ability to bore into a person. Even now, he felt pinned by her blank stare and unable to read her.

She didn't look much older than him. Her face still held youth, framed by strands of hair that had escaped the long ponytail tied at the base of her neck. He half-wondered that the Union had sent someone seemingly so young.

The thought brought his attention back to the three hooded figures. Although they looked no different from one another, he got the impression the one in the middle led this group. That Keeper sat forward just slightly.

King Alden's voice cut through the silence from where he stood to Arran's immediate left. "Esteemed Keepers, thank you for coming again to Nithle's aid. As always, you've arrived at exactly the right moment to save us from being overrun by Lavanai's forces."

"As per the Oath," one of the Keepers replied. The voice

was a rich, male baritone that Arran was certain came from the forward-leaning middle figure.

While newborns were a price of the Oath, being perched atop the hierarchy wasn't something the Keepers had ever asked. Yet, they'd ended up there all the same, even with their known use of magic.

They've never weaponized magic though, Arran mused, thinking about how they'd suddenly appeared in the room. *They use it to get to us quickly. To protect us.*

And it didn't seem to have the same negative effects on them that it did other humans. They behaved nothing like the erratic people that those tainted by or lost to magic became. If the Keepers could safely use magic to protect his people, he'd accept it. *Besides, we owe so much to the Union.* Arran was alive because of the young woman standing before him, as well as the Keepers who'd sent her.

The same Keeper that spoke before continued. "Killer Ryla will remain with Nithle until Lavanai's efforts have again subsided. Until then she will guard Prince Arran directly."

The statement hit Arran unexpectedly. *What?* It took a lot for him to not ask the question aloud, but his efforts to hold his tongue left his face to do what it pleased.

"We understand your confusion, Prince Arran," the Keeper continued. "This decision was made based on a number of factors, primarily that you are Nithle's only heir and you are largely unprotected. You don't even carry a sword."

Humiliation prickled along Arran's neck, leaving him feeling too warm, but he continued to say nothing.

"While we understand that you are Nithle's strategist, Lavanai will likely return to their pattern of targeting the royal family directly. You will need higher protection, and Killer Ryla will provide it for you," the Keeper explained.

"We're grateful for this, Esteemed Keepers," Queen Shron said, and although Arran wasn't looking at her, he could hear the relief in her voice and rustle of her skirts as she bowed again.

The idea didn't sit so easily with him.

Arran took a grounding breath, ignoring the way his shoulder pinched just slightly. "If I may, Esteemed Keepers?"

The hood of the centre figure bobbed with a nod. "Proceed."

"Would it not be more sensible to have Killer Ryla join the forces along our borders? There, she could confront any attacking dahems, which would see the entire kingdom—and by association, me—protected and hopefully speed up Lavanai's retreat. I witnessed the almost visceral reaction the dahems had to her in Nithle Proper, and her skills are like none I've ever seen. I have full confidence she would be a great asset in that way." He forced his tone to stay even as he pled his case.

"No," the Keeper replied almost instantly. "She will guard you."

There was a finality to the Keeper's tone that stayed any further protests Arran had. From the corner of his eye, he caught the way his mother shifted on the other side of his father; an inhale and the way she changed her weight from one foot to the other told him she was nervous for him. She probably wanted to remind him to not challenge the Keepers. He knew just as well that he shouldn't.

But he'd read the historical writings himself. He knew that Killers had been used exactly as he wanted to use Ryla—they'd been intermingled with various fighting forces, where they could fight against the dahems head on. Although Killers had also acted as personal guards, including for his family, the insistence this time around didn't make sense to him. Even with what the Keeper had said about the dahems targeting the royal family, he felt strongly about using her skills in the army.

His thoughts took a dark turn. *Is it really because I can't protect myself in battle? Am I putting the kingdom at risk because I can't wield a sword?*

A flash of the lightning from earlier in the night lit up his mind. The body falling to the ground because he didn't act quickly enough. The screams and the blood of those he couldn't protect because of his own ineptitude.

Guilt joined the humiliation.

"Have we made ourselves clear?" the Keeper broke the silence that had formed.

"Yes, of course, Esteemed Keepers," Alden replied quickly, his voice even and strong.

"Prince Arran."

He looked up, not realizing that his gaze had shifted to the floor. Only the dark shadow of the hood greeted him when he looked to where he assumed the Keeper's face was under the cloak. He had a distinct sense that all eyes were on him in that moment, but he didn't dare remove his gaze from the figure beneath the charcoal cloak.

"Yes. I understand, Esteemed One," he finally replied. In truth, he didn't. Not really, but there was nothing he could do about it.

"Very good." The fabric of the hood shifted as the Keeper nodded and moved on. "To ensure Nithle's forces have ample strength, you'll also have the Union's decree that each Nithle city and village should prepare to send new recruits and provide whatever resources are necessary."

Arran spoke again, "Thank you, Esteemed One." Nithle could have done that alone, but with the Union's decree, it'd be much simpler.

The Keeper in the middle stood then, joined a moment

later by the other two.

"Killer Ryla will summon us if there is need," the Keeper said, then he and the other two Keepers vanished.

Silence hummed in the room for only a second before the Killer's boot steps brought her to the centre of the platform. Arran wondered if she'd make some speech, but she only stood there.

When she didn't say anything, Alden spoke again. "High Protector, we'll have a room prepared for you near our son's and have a servant ready for you whenever you need."

"A man named Huth has already seen to it and promised to be at my ready," Killer Ryla supplied, her eyes coming to rest on the king.

Alden paused, as if mentally pulling up Huth's credentials. "Very well then. If there's anything you require, you only need ask for it."

Ryla gave a small nod before changing the course of the conversation. "It's time Prince Arran saw the healer."

His parents' eyes flew to him, but his mother rounded to face him and spoke first. "What's happened? Are you injured?"

"I'm fine, Mother." Arran waved it off, careful to use his left arm. He watched her brows pinch together as she extended her hands to touch him but hesitated before doing so.

"His injuries are likely minor."

Arran jumped and then winced as the movement sent a spasm of pain through his shoulder. An involuntary step back put distance between him and Killer Ryla, whom he hadn't even heard approach. She wasn't looking at him, though; her eyes were on his mother.

"A relief," Queen Shron sighed. She used her extended hands to push her dark, wavy locks behind her ears instead and looked between Arran and Killer Ryla. "What happened?

Didn't you get out of the city?"

Arran clenched his jaw, not wanting to recount the tale but knowing she wouldn't let it rest. "No," he replied before providing a summary of events, skimming as quickly as he could over the horrific details. His father, Ley, and Calar had gathered around as if it were some fire story.

When he finished, Shron took his left hand and gave it a gentle squeeze. Her blue eyes, the same colour as his, shone up at him. "Thank the Union Killer Ryla arrived."

"I see now what they meant by Lavanai targeting our family," Alden said next. "But we can discuss it at length later. For now, let's get you to your chambers to see Healer Dalam."

"I'd like to have someone send for Adel and Ashla while I'm being tended to," Arran requested. "I'd like to see for myself that they're safe."

There was a pause, and the looks that crossed his parents' faces renewed the chill in his bones.

"What is it?"

Alden and Shron exchanged a glance before Shron ultimately answered the question. "They haven't arrived at the castle. At least, not last we'd left Mela and Criph. Perhaps that's changed."

Alden added, "And if it hasn't, a search will commence immediately."

Arran wanted to believe the confident look on his father's face, but the sudden roiling in his gut warred against it. His mother's hand came to rest on his good arm.

"They'll be found, Arran." She gave a reassuring squeeze.

It did little to allay the worry.

T here was some comfort to being back in his own room, but Arran still felt a sense of unease. Probably because Healer Dalam, a middle-aged man with greying hair and bespectacled eyes, was tending to injuries that reminded him of all the terrible things that had happened that night.

Then there was Killer Ryla standing in his room's entryway near the door. She seemed more interested in watching the door than watching the healer gently inspect and prod at his injuries, but subtle shifts of her body told him that she was very much paying attention to everything.

Healer Dalam broke through his thoughts. "It doesn't appear that anything is broken. Neither your shoulder nor your hip, which is a good sign. Likely bruising, and you'll want to rest for a few days to not aggravate the injuries further. Try not to be on your feet too often for the next day or two especially. If I may, Your Highness?"

When Arran brought his focus back to the man, he saw he was holding up a strip of light brown cloth. It took a moment, but it registered that the healer meant to tie it around his neck to support his arm.

"Of course," Arran replied and leaned forward in his chair to accommodate the man. The fire crackled away behind him, casting shadows as the healer worked.

Healer Dalam secured the cloth at the back of Arran's

neck, then adjusted the fabric so it covered from his elbow to his wrist. When he stepped back, he said, "Give that a go."

Arran let the weight of his arm into the sling, which did take some pressure off his shoulder, although it felt strange to have the weight on the back of his neck.

"Seems it'll be fine," the prince replied.

Dalam nodded approvingly. "If it's not or something doesn't feel right, call for me. There's another way we can try binding your shoulder. We can also use topical or oral remedies."

"Thank you, Healer Dalam," Arran dismissed him.

"Not at all," he replied, turning to pack up his things. He made quick work of it. "Good night, Your Highness. High Protector," he added as he slipped past where she stood and out the door.

With impeccable timing, Ley stepped into the room only moments later. The blood had been cleaned from his face, but the cuts and scrapes stood out against his pale skin. Then there were the deep red marks and swelling of his lip and around his eye. All the same, his expression was even, not showing any of the pain that Arran was sure he must be in, even with medicines he would have received from Healer Dalam's apprentices.

Dressed in a more casual tunic and trousers now, the royal knight stopped and bowed to Killer Ryla. He was only a little taller than she was. "Thank you, High Protector, for coming to us and saving His Highness."

She nodded, which Ley seemed to understand was all the response he'd get. Ley's expression shifted from quiet respect to something warmer with a smile as he approached Arran. Arran returned the gesture.

"Looks like you're taken care of, Ley," Arran commented.

"Yes. The dahems only roughed me up a bit. What did

Healer Dalam say of your injuries?" Ley asked.

"Nothing broken it seems, but I need to be mindful of my injuries to be sure things heal properly," Arran replied conversationally. "Is there any word of Adel and Ashla?"

The knight shook his head. "King Criph has personally ridden out with his guard to search for them."

A lump lodged itself in Arran's throat. "I should go look for them, too."

"Between King Criph and his guard alongside those your parents sent, there's no need," Ley said gently.

Arran chewed at his lip, but nodded. He couldn't help his eyes trailing to where the Killer stood by the door, however, as if wondering if she really were still there. She was.

Could she find them more quickly? he wondered. *Could I even ask that of her given that she's* my *guard?*

Ley followed Arran's sightline before turning back to him with a lift of a brow. Ley's curiosity brought back his earlier anxieties, and he felt a gnawing sense of needing to talk them out.

"Killer Ryla," Arran called from where he still sat, and she looked to him immediately. "Would it be all right if I had a private conversation with Knight Ley?" The gesture he made toward the knight felt awkward under her impassive gaze, which shifted between the two of them.

It was just a moment before she said, "Very well," then left the room without another word.

When the door snicked shut, Ley asked, "What is it, Arran?"

"Have a seat, Ley," Arran started, motioning toward the empty chair across from him.

The knight removed his sword belt, set it aside, and sank into the plush chair without hesitation. The sword was still in reach of course, just in case. Up until now, every just in case had felt hypothetical, like a strong maybe instead of a very likely.

A shiver wracked him as his mind brought him back to the city square, a pair of amber eyes bearing down on him and a mace crackling with lightning descending to crush his bones. His eyes squeezed shut.

"Arran?"

The prince opened his eyes to see the lines of concern traced into his knight's features. It made him look older than the mid-thirties he was.

Arran took a steadying breath. "I have something I want to talk with you about, but I need you to keep it in confidence."

Ley's expression didn't change, but he nodded. "Of course."

The prince opened his mouth to speak, then closed it again, gritting his teeth. Even the thought of what he was about to say felt wrong. "The Keepers...their instruction. It leaves me feeling uneasy, and I don't understand why. They stepped in to protect me. They've protected us all, but I don't understand their decision in this case."

Ley's features softened, tension leaving his shoulders. "You were also almost killed tonight."

"Someone died because of me tonight," Arran couldn't help but interrupt.

Ley swallowed, as if remembering the scene himself. "You can't take the blame for that, Your Highness. Dahems kill as they please. You know this." When Arran didn't respond, Ley continued on. "I'm sure this experience is colouring your thoughts and how the Keepers' decision will impact the people of Nithle. Trust in their experience with Lavanai. Trust this is the best course."

Arran released a breath, trying to ease his shoulders as

the injury pinched again. Even though it still lingered in his recent memory, somehow it hadn't occurred to him that it might be influencing his reactions to the Union's decision.

Ley's right. I need to trust their judgement.

There was a pause, filled only by the crackle of fire, before Ley continued conversationally. "Have I ever told you about when my sibling was chosen by the Union?"

Arran's eyebrows rose in wonder. "Never. I had no idea."

The knight nodded. "I was four or five at the time. My mother and father were in the birthing room. They closed the door to keep me out, of course, but I wanted to see what was going on.

"I opened the door just a crack to peek in and saw the Keepers standing around the bed. The baby was already gone, and the Keepers were telling my parents about how they couldn't seek out the child, how the child would become a warrior, and so on. I felt frozen in place. I had so many questions."

Arran nodded. "No doubt."

"My parents always raised me to respect and honour the Union, as any parent would, but things shifted for me after that experience. Even at that young age, I went headlong into my studies to learn about the Union and how I could properly honour the Keepers and Killers alike," Ley said.

"Have you ever wondered about them? Your sibling?" Arran heard himself ask in a soft voice, barely above a whisper.

"I did at first, but I know that whatever their fate, they were or are under the care of the Keepers. That they've contributed to protecting not only me, but all of us from dahems."

Silence fell between them again. There was something surreal about the story and the way Ley was so calm telling it. It was one thing to know about the Union's practices and another to encounter someone directly impacted by them.

"Ley, I—"

A knock at the door interrupted him, and both looked across the room to it. Ley took hold of his sword, his expression serious and focused now.

Killer Ryla should be just outside the door. She wouldn't have allowed a knock if it were danger, Arran talked himself through the shot of anxiety that pierced him. "Enter."

The door swung open to reveal a page, who stepped into the room and bowed.

"Forgive my intrusion, Your Highness, but we've located Princess Adel and her lady-in-waiting," he said quickly.

"You have?" Arran's heart leapt to his throat, and his hip protested as he rose to his feet. He didn't like the way this man stood, his shoulders drawn inward just so, his hands wringing slightly.

"Yes, Your Highness. Princess Adel is alive and uninjured," the page began.

Relief washed over him like a wave and happy tears stung at his eyes. *She's safe!* He resisted the urge to run across the room and demand to immediately be taken to her. *Why does the page look so distressed?*

"What of Ashla?"

The page inhaled. "She's dead, Your Highness."

CHAPTER

NINE

T he waking nightmare gouged Adel's soul. She felt hollow.
The princess clutched her coat at her throat, feeling the
biting autumn air despite her woolen clothes and hat. She didn't
know whether to blame it on how the castle's vast courtyard
seemed to conjure wind vortexes or just the weather in general.
She'd decided she wouldn't complain. At least she was alive.

A knot formed in her stomach, and her throat closed in.
Tears pricked her eyes, which she squeezed shut, only to feel
them collect along the lashes.

Deep breath in. Deep breath out.

She felt too exposed. Too many people could see her
wounds. People's pitying gazes bore into her as she stood
near the castle wall with her parents. She felt silly now for
having worried about the announcement of her courtship.
This was worse.

She'd overheard her mother telling her father that most
non-Nithleans had left almost immediately the night before,
not wanting to risk the danger. The only ones who came to
speak with them, besides King Alden and Queen Shron,
were the young royals from Piridet and Veloth. She'd briefly
spoken with each of them but couldn't recall the details of
the conversation.

Adel focused on the groundskeepers feeding wood into
the flames for the ceremony. The large rock structure at the

head of the courtyard had a high, blackened back wall. The two charred sides sloped down to meet with a waist-high wall at the front, where groundskeepers leaned while they worked.

"Adel."

She turned at the sound of the voice, familiar and present yet foreign and faraway. Even as her gaze came into focus on Arran, she felt detached from the world. It took a good moment before her mind registered him properly. When she did, she ran to him and wrapped her arms around his neck.

The warmth of his cloak enveloped her while she pressed her face into the crook of his shoulder and fought back the tears. She tried to speak but couldn't muster anything more than garbled sounds. The pair stayed like that for a while—silent, with his arm holding her closely as if she might fall to pieces. She wasn't sure she wouldn't.

It was only when she heard a large crack from the fire that she pulled back. As she composed herself, she took note of Arran's bandaged arm for the first time.

"I'm so sorry," she managed to say and looked up worriedly into his blue eyes. "Did I hurt you?"

"I'm fine," he said reassuringly. His voice was quiet and strained. Tears, like hers, threatened to spill over.

Seeing his injury reminded her of the other horrors of the evening. "Mother and Father told me about what happened. That must have been terrifying."

"I admit it was," he replied softly. "Never in my life… Then she came out of nowhere."

Adel followed his gaze to where a woman watched them from several feet away. Her blank expression grated against Adel's high emotions. Her parents had told her about the arrival of the Union's warrior the night before and again that morning, so her presence didn't come as a complete surprise.

But it was surprising—and annoying—how emotionless she seemed to be.

Don't judge her at first glance, Adel scolded herself.

The Killer looked away, surveying the rest of the crowd with that same blank stare.

"What's she like?" Adel heard herself ask, still staring at the other woman.

"I can't read her," Arran replied with what she thought was supposed to be a dismissive shrug. She knew him better than that.

She offered him a weak smile. "That's the point, isn't it? Being unreadable makes it harder for her enemies to know how to attack."

"You're right..." A breath of quiet passed between them. "I'm beyond glad that you're safe, but to think that Ashla..."

Adel bit her lip, and her eyes cast downward, the tightness flooding back to her chest.

"I'm sorry." Arran's voice sounded barely above a whisper, his hand trailing up and down her back.

A nod was about all she could manage.

Deep breath in. Deep breath out.

Her tongue felt leaden as she spoke. "We were walking when the dahems invaded Nithle Proper. We split up and...I guess they found her instead of me."

A loud bell echoed across the courtyard, interrupting anything else they might say. The signal of the beginning of the ceremony reverberated through her bones.

Wordlessly, swaths of people converged around the contained fire, although they left room for the royal families to approach. Adel reached into her deep coat pocket, pulling out a purple sash.

It had been Ashla's. One of her favourites, actually, and

she'd often worn it tied around her waist, even when it clashed with the rest of her ensemble. She'd said it gave her luck and protected her.

She should have been wearing it, Adel thought with bitter sadness. Other times, Ashla might have worn the sash underneath her matching ensemble, but it wouldn't fit under the festival's outfit. *I should have chosen a different dress.*

Guilt lanced her. She clenched her fist, but when she realized it creased the fabric, she opened her hand and tried to smooth out the satiny purple material again.

The Passing Ceremony called for mourners to throw the passed loved one's item into the flames to free the soul of the deceased so it could pass into the next realm. Whether there was any truth to the practice, Adel had no idea, but she wasn't going to chance it. Not with her best friend.

Her gaze drifted to Arran, and he nodded silently. With his arm still around her, Adel walked toward the flames. Reality warped and made the fire appear to draw farther away rather than closer, but suddenly, they were standing right in front of the flaming hearth.

The heat caressed her skin. Her fists closed around the sash again, feeling like throwing it in meant losing her best friend forever. It felt too final.

Arran squeezed her arm as they stood there. She closed her eyes as he leaned in and kissed her temple. Before she could rethink it again, she tossed the sash in the flames. The thin fabric alighted and burned through quickly.

Her heart hammered, and she concentrated on keeping herself composed.

Goodbye... Just thinking the word was enough to set her off, the pain both clawing through her and clenching tightly around her chest. The tears fell freely with her sobs and threatened to drag her to the ground.

She felt warmer and warmer the longer they stood by the hearth, but she couldn't bring herself to move. Others coming to throw items into the fire were nothing more than figures in her peripheral. She watched as clothing, toys, boxes, and all kinds of things burned away to nothing.

It wasn't until a figure approached to Arran's immediate right that Adel broke her gaze from the flames. The Killer. Tall and stoic, the fire cast a warm glow on her complexion.

At first, Adel wasn't sure what the other woman was going to do, but as the princess wiped her eyes, she saw the Killer, too, threw something into the eager flames. Through her blurred vision, it looked like nothing more than earth and leaves.

"Fanahray ehntehs oahcl."

The lilting words and halting syllables were foreign to Adel's ears but rolled off the Killer's tongue as if they were her native language. It was almost enough to distract from the deadpan tone.

"What does it mean?" Adel asked and cleared her throat as her voice cracked. She was about to repeat the question, but there wasn't any need.

"Be free of life's burdens," the Killer translated.

The words echoed in Adel's mind as she looked back to the fire. Somehow, they became a salve.

"Thank you, High Protector," Adel said.

"Killer Ryla," the woman replied.

Adel nodded. *Killer Ryla,* she thought, trying to commit the name to memory. She wasn't sure she'd be able to hold onto new information given the circumstances, but she'd try.

"When are you returning to Heta?" Arran asked suddenly.

Adel's brow furrowed as she leaned back to get a better look at him. She couldn't read where his thoughts were, but his features were strained and his jaw tight. "Father said we're leaving after the Passing. We'll postpone announcing our courtship. I'd like to stay longer—"

"No," he cut in.

Her heart twisted. He didn't want her there? Her emotion must have been evident on her face.

Arran quickly continued, "It's not safe here. I feel like we've been living in some sort of naïve bliss, but seeing how close the dahems got and considering how many died—*who* died—you need to get away from here. I don't want you to be in danger."

She didn't feel any more at ease. If anything, it intensified the sinking feeling in her gut, and she chose her next words carefully. "I don't want you to be in danger, either. But the reality is danger is around us."

"Your kingdom is safer."

"Even if they're not marching on Heta, the fear of dahems still lives there. And for all we know, Lavanai could decide to march on us next," she continued softly. "Let me stand by you through this."

He shook his head. "Not now."

"*Especially* now!" she snapped, jerking away from him and feeling her eyes well up again. Had they ever actually dried? "We've just been through this awful thing, and you're pushing me away! We need each other right now more than ever."

His jaw was set, eyes almost severe. "I'm doing this to protect you!"

Gone was his tenderness from the night before and even moments ago. In its place was the strong headed resolve of a strategist—a wall she knew she had no chance of getting through. Her fists clenched at her sides.

Adel sensed eyes lingering on them, as though they were a

spectacle. Her parents must have stepped away, or surely they would have intervened. It felt like everything was burning up around her. Or maybe she was burning up, having been tossed in the Passing's flame.

Her voice was small, plaintive. "We can protect each other."

She knew she couldn't ask him to come to Heta to ensure their safety, but she wanted to at least stay with him. They were stronger together. That was how it'd always been.

"Adel—"

All it took was his tone for her to know he wouldn't relent. Before he could even finish, she turned away from him and ran.

CHAPTER
TEN

T he very last thing Arran wanted to do was stand on display while his father made a speech to the people of Nithle. Between nearly dying and Ashla's death the previous night, and Adel literally running from him earlier that morning, he wanted nothing more than to lock himself in his room. The look on Adel's face haunted him: hazel eyes wide and glassy, a mix of brokenness and betrayal etched into her features.

Why couldn't she understand there was too much danger in Nithle right now?

Will it ever be safe again? he wondered.

Only the day before, things had felt safe and, well, normal. Lavanai had shattered that picturesque reality.

Then there were his conflicted feelings toward the Union and its Killers. To speak against the Union was treason that even a royal couldn't escape. Yet, during the Passing Ceremony, he couldn't help his wandering thoughts that teased ideas of how things may have been different if the Union had shown up sooner, sent more Killers, or even unleashed a direct attack on Lavanai. At the very least let him put Ryla among the Nithle army.

The fur lining of his thick cloak tickled his jaw and ears as it ruffled in the cool wind. It was chillier up where he stood to his father's right, overlooking a gathering area on the east side of the castle grounds just outside the outer wall where the Nithlean people could congregate to hear royal decrees. Arran could see them assembling below.

To Arran's right, Ryla stood impassively. He wondered at the fact that she wasn't shivering as the wind sent strands of her bound hair waving around her body. She hadn't donned a cloak like he and the others had and, in fact, looked practically bare compared to the queen, bundled to the brim on the other side of the king. It was as though even the elements couldn't touch her.

He followed her line of vision out to the crowd, where he was certain she was surveying for signs of trouble. She wasn't the only one.

Apart from the swords-people, some of the royal knights and guards had bows and arrows at the ready. He was grateful since, admittedly, he felt like an easy target standing where he was. His attention drifted to where Ley stood off to the side, and the man looked back at him as if he had sensed the prince's gaze. The knight's bow had an arrow nocked in place, even though he held it with both hands at his waist.

Arran returned a nod from Ley, then settled his gaze on his father. The king squinted against the overcast, yet somehow still bright, sky, looking out at his people and waiting for more to gather before he started to speak. Arran only had a vague idea of what his father was going to say since he hadn't given him any sort of brief until moments ago.

If anything, Arran wished this could have waited until after they'd had the chance to speak with the other cities and villages to get a sense of what had happened and the damage done. Unfortunately, he suspected it'd be another day or so before any word arrived, and after what had happened right here in Nithle Proper, they'd need to say something.

A missive would have been much safer.

The sound of a bell, much the same as the one before the Passing, settled the crowd for the king.

"My people," Alden began, his voice loud and carrying in the wind. "I know you must all be feeling fearful, but I urge you to take heart. We are not taking last night's tragedy lightly, and we *will not* allow Lavanai to accost us so. For too long, they have targeted us for nothing more than senseless killing. To assert their power over us through magic. They have brought destruction and invaded our lands for no other reason than bloodshed. We have lived under their terror for too long."

The king paused, and even from where they stood above their people, Arran could hear the murmurs of agreement and the stifled cries of anger. It didn't take much to stir people up when it came to dahems. All the same, there was something about it that sent chills through him. He felt simultaneously strong and afraid.

"In these times, we must stand together against Lavanai and ensure each other's safety. And in these times, the Union has sent a Killer to stand with us!" He made a grand, sweeping gesture in Ryla's direction, the crowd roaring in response.

Fists pumped into the air among the masses, and Arran thought he may have seen even a few more folks make the hand signal the woman they'd passed the night before had. Their confidence and hope made him feel lighter, if only marginally.

"With Killer Ryla, we will remind the dahems that our humanness does not make us weak," Alden continued.

Arran's gaze again fell to Ryla, wondering how she was reacting to this fanfare. Not even a muscle in her face twitched as she observed the crowd.

The king persisted. "We will remind them that Nithle will *not* stand idly by. We will *not* tolerate their evil ways!"

The cheers rose even louder than before. Arran's heart thumped at an accelerating pace as the clamour continued to grow. His hip pinched suddenly, and he shifted his weight to try to ease it, but it persisted.

Ryla's brown eyes connected with his, and suddenly he felt himself transported back to the first time he'd seen them staring down at him in the city square with that impassive gaze. A gaze that didn't belong on the face of someone who'd just killed, even if the victim was a dahem. The cheers of the crowd around him phased in and out, mixed with memories of screams and slaughter and death.

The longer he stared, the more his thoughts dove into darkness. The more reality faded.

The thumping in his heart became the panic he'd felt as the mace arced above the dahem's head.

It startled him when Ryla stepped closer. The world dissolved around Arran then, everything apart from him and Ryla a blur. He was certain his heartbeat was loud enough for all to hear. Her presence was overwhelming.

"Listen to me," Ryla said, her voice loud enough for only the two of them. "Ground yourself in this moment."

What? Arran thought, only half realizing he hadn't said it aloud.

Something on his face must have conveyed his confusion because she continued. "Tell me something you feel in this moment," she instructed in her emotionless way.

He swallowed, and when he spoke, his voice was barely a whisper. "Fear." He didn't know if he would normally admit that, but sharing it with a Killer felt okay. Like she would understand, somehow.

"Outside of emotions," she clarified.

He searched his mind. "The cold."

"Specific to *this* moment." She hadn't emphasized the word. Not really.

A tickle brushed against his skin again. "The fur of my cloak."

Saying it aloud sent a fissure through the bedlam in his mind, allowing reality to peek through. His breath caught in wonder. Almost as if possessed, his fingers rubbed together of their own accord, feeling the fabric of the soft gloves he wore. He looked down at them, seeing the worn, dark brown fabric.

"My gloves," he murmured without prompt, sending another fissure through the previous night's horror. It was enough to cause it to fully fall away, and daylight seeped into his vision. He brought his gaze up to meet Ryla's again. This time, it didn't sweep him into the night prior.

"What just happened?"

"The memory was overtaking you. Focusing on what's here, now, separates you from it," Ryla explained easily, not breaking his gaze.

Arran's brows pinched together. "You saw that just from looking at me?"

"Yes. I've seen it before, many times."

He felt a pang of shame. Another weakness to add to his roster. "Is it over?"

"For the time being. This is a tool. One that can be built upon and strengthened over time," she clarified.

He swallowed. "Can you train me, Killer Ryla?"

She nodded. "But not now."

The stares suddenly slammed into him. As he glanced around at the crowd and those in his more immediate presence, Arran noticed Ley in particular was watching them with concern. His mother looked like she was a breath away from rushing to him. His father, too, shot glances his way, but mostly continued to address the crowd. Arran wondered suddenly how much time had passed.

"Thank you, High Protector," the prince said finally, straightening up in an effort to regain composure. The effort pinched his shoulder this time.

She nodded again, then stepped back and resumed her former position. The weight of her presence eased as well.

As Arran returned to watching the crowd, he tried to ignore those watching him and whispering to each other. The thought that they might be talking about *him* made him feel sick. How much had they noticed?

He couldn't have his people questioning Nithle's rule, especially not after what had happened with the dahem attack.

The air felt sharp in his lungs as he inhaled deeply. He hoped the Killer could truly help him master whatever techniques she knew because this couldn't happen again.

CHAPTER

ELEVEN

L ord Jasim of Lavanai's clipped steps came to an abrupt
halt as he entered the infirmary at Yandana Fort. The
midday sun poured through high set windows over rows of
beds and stools filled with members of the Lavanai army. The
cacophony of conversation and movement were practically an
assault on his senses. That wasn't even considering the smell of
ointments and herbs of all sorts being administered by healers
and apprentices throughout the wide room.

Barely an hour had passed since the group had returned
to the fort from the prior day's attack on Nithle, but Jasim
looked around the room for his seconds in command. He
needed to know what had happened. It only took a moment
for him to spot them, seated close to one another on stools
near the centre of the room with healers tending to their
wounds. Others moved out of his way as he advanced through
the crowd. Reaching them, he gave them each a quick once-
over and was grateful to see neither of the injuries looked
particularly dire.

"The Union sent a Killer," he stated more than asked,
trying to ignore the tightness in his chest.

"Yes, My Lord," the female of the pair, Mithos, replied.
She flinched as a healer applied something to clean a minor
wound on her upper arm.

Jasim glanced to his other commander, Naxela, who

didn't say anything as the healer's assistant tightly wrapped a stitched-up wound on his torso.

"Who is it?" the lord persisted.

The room's descending hush and more attention on their conversation felt like a weight. Even the warmth from the amount of people in the room seemed to increase with the silence.

The fact that the Union might get involved was something Jasim and his commanders had discussed when planning the attack on Nithle. If history showed them anything, it was the organization's proclivity for protecting the kingdom when even the most minor attacks arose, let alone one which outright targeted the royal family. The plan had been for the initial attack on Bunthle to draw the Union's attention while Mithos and Naxela killed the entire royal family, or as many of them as they could, in Nithle Proper. From there, he and his commanders would have prepared for the fallout.

From the initial reports he'd heard, the ruse hadn't worked. The Union had sent no one to Bunthle and a Killer to Nithle Proper.

Lord Jasim's records, those of his brother, Lord Lamis, before him, and so on down their family line documented not only the Killers sent to Nithle, but any they'd encountered in other skirmishes as well. If it was a Killer they were familiar with, they might have a modicum of an advantage.

Mithos shook her head. "No one I'm familiar with, My Lord."

"Nor I," Naxela added, his voice gruff.

"It's Ryla, Lord Jasim."

The dahem lord's eyebrows shot up as ice rushed through his body, and he whirled on the voice. Captain Anxer rose from a nearby bed, his broad form tense and expression serious as he stood in his scuffed and torn combat leathers.

Anyone but her. The name alone winded Jasim, and he had to make an effort to keep his voice even. "You're certain?"

Anxer nodded. "It's been fifteen or sixteen years, but I recognized her in an instant."

"*That* was Ryla?" It was Naxela who spoke now, his tone a mix of disbelief tinged with dismay.

Of all the Killers, Ryla's name was perhaps the most well-known throughout Yandana Fort, even among those who hadn't fought her like Jasim and Anxer had. After that encounter, Jasim had done everything he could to learn who she was and to keep track of her. It had been no easy task, from consorting with spies to finding dahem sympathizers among human villages. It was a miracle he'd even gotten her name; apart from that, all they knew was that she'd only been out in the field a few other times.

It didn't matter. She was deadly, and that was something he could never forget.

How did I not consider this? Jasim turned back to Mithos and Naxela. "Did you use your magic against her?"

"Not me. I was coordinating the rest of the ranks with the hostages when she arrived. Naxela felt the brunt of her attack," Mithos explained, tilting her head toward her co-commander as she did.

"I didn't either. She knocked me aside, and I lost hold of my mace," Naxela admitted.

Jasim cursed, irritation narrowing his amber eyes. He only partially noted the abashed look on his commander's face. Without a doubt, Ryla had known what she was doing. She would know to disarm them so that they couldn't use their weapons to hone their magical attacks. He fell silent.

"My Lord?" Anxer interjected and continued when Jasim

looked at him. "Perhaps we should take this discussion to more private quarters."

It was as if Anxer's words stripped away whatever had been shielding him from noticing all the eyes on him. He took a deep breath, forcing himself into a composed state.

Be calm. Don't cause more panic, he chided himself. "Anxer, Mithos, Naxela, meet me in the war room as soon as you're done here."

"Yes, sir," they each replied, almost in sync.

Jasim turned on his heel and strode away, still focusing on his composure as he did. Inwardly, he was reeling, their next steps suddenly unclear. Preparing for a Killer was one thing.

Preparing for the Killer who'd slain his brother was another.

About half an hour passed before Anxer, Mithos, and Naxela strode into the war room, the larger space complete with various tables, chairs, maps, and books. Jasim heard their steps as he stared out the window, watching the horizon for a figure he knew wouldn't come. As this room was elevated within the fort, he had a partial view of the top of Lake Pol and the hills around it. Even this almost northernmost part of the lake was wide enough that Bunthle was a mere smudge on the opposite side, and only on the clearest days.

The Union wouldn't dare approach Lavanai, let alone Yandana Fort, where he and the army resided. Yet, he couldn't shake the sudden feeling that he had to keep watch, at least until they devised some way to deal with this new development.

Without him having to ask, one of his commanders or the captain closed the door. When he turned from the window, they were waiting there attentively, freshly dressed with almost all signs of the battle they'd just come from buried underneath their earth-toned apparel. Normally, his advisors would have joined them as well, but he'd sent them away, wanting to hear from his commanders and captain first without their interference.

But for their tired eyes, Jasim might not know that anything had happened. Mithos and Naxela's faces held similar expressions of wonder and determination despite the tiredness. Anxer's aged features alone matched the intensity Jasim felt roiling in his gut.

"Ryla as Nithle's protector changes everything," Jasim said without preamble. "The first time we encountered her, she couldn't have been more than seven years old. We knew no Killer should be underestimated, and yet somehow we still underestimated her then. We lost many that day, my brother included."

They knew this story of Lord Lamis and Killer Ryla. Saying it aloud now would remind them of the gravity of the situation. Indeed, Naxela's jaw tightened, and Mithos took a deep breath, as if digesting his words.

"All we'd done in that instance was seek aid from a village to the north. Considering the damage Ryla did to us then, it is a miracle she hasn't been Nithle's protector every time since. But even that was one day, a few hours. This time, the Union won't recall Ryla until the job is done and she's brought our army to its knees like others have before her." His tone grew darker and darker. He hadn't seen Ryla run his brother through with her blade, but he'd seen the aftermath. Lamis's blood, warm on his hands as he held him dying, was suddenly vivid in his mind.

"We won't be able to continue with our plans as they were," Mithos supplied when a silence fell over them.

"No," Jasim agreed.

"What would you have us do, My Lord?" Naxela asked. "We can double the training schedules, ensure our warriors are in top condition—"

"No—well, yes, but we can't rely on that alone. It's fortunate magic is in practice again after all this time."

Magic use in the army had died out for a period after an

assault on Nithle when Prince Arran was barely two years old. The Union had sent a Killer then, too, and their magic users had gotten so caught up in doing anything they could to destroy the Killer, they'd lost control of their powers. The result had been the deaths of a large portion of Lavanai's army. New to his role at that time, Lord Jasim had made the decision to reduce emphasis on magic use in war. It had only been over the last few years that he'd revived the search for magic users for his army.

Will the same thing happen again? Jasim wondered. As he looked over Mithos and Naxela, he felt confident. *These two are different. They'll be fine.* Aloud, he said, "We need more to ensure complete success." His eyes swept the wide space, as if its very nature as a war room would inspire him.

Anxer spoke for the first time since entering the room. "If I may, My Lord?"

Jasim focused on a tilted book on a far shelf instead of looking at Anxer. "Please."

"I think it's time we refocus on the Union," Anxer said.

Naxela's protest came sharp. "But what about the Nithle line?"

"The Nithle line won't matter a lick if Ryla destroys us," Anxer retorted sternly. Although Naxela outranked him, the young commander didn't have Anxer's years of experience. "We've been outdone by Killers time and time again. It takes *years* to recover. If we keep allowing that to happen, the cycle continues."

"We'll have to revisit everything we know. Scour the records, see what information we can find that might help us," Mithos chimed in next with a tone that hinted her mind was already working out how to uncover said information.

Jasim finally drew his eyes from the random book. Anxer, Mithos, and Naxela faced each other but then quickly turned their attention back to him. The dahem lord stayed silent for a long moment, the weight of his gaze keeping them silent as well.

"The Union is just as calculated as any other moving piece in this war, and they've sent Ryla for a reason. A warning, perhaps," Jasim voiced his thoughts. "We won't abandon the assault on Nithle, but we *need* to re-strategize for Ryla's involvement. If we can eliminate Ryla, we can eliminate the rest of their lot."

"We'll do everything in our power, Lord Jasim," Mithos vowed.

Jasim's instruction continued. "Anxer, ensure *everyone* gets an increased training schedule. Even if they can't handle double the schedule, it should be more than what they're currently receiving. I want you on lead for the physical training. Work with Gath. You know Killers—and Ryla—as well as I do. We'll need your expertise."

"Consider it done, My Lord," the captain nodded firmly, his longer, light-coloured hair shifting with the movement.

"Mithos and Naxela, continue to work with Woxla on your magic training and see to it that other magic users are working with him as well," Jasim said.

"Yes, My Lord," they said in unison.

"Mithos, since it seems you're interested in revisiting our records, do so and report back with any findings about Killers," he added and saw her nod affirmatively. "Although, if *anyone* finds anything that may help, I want to know about it."

"Yes, My Lord," they all said again.

He paused and thought a moment longer, but eventually

said, "Dismissed." His gaze lingered on them as they left the room, wishing they could take the tension he felt with them. It remained all the same.

He couldn't let Lavanai's people fall. He wouldn't let Ryla take anything else from him.

THIRTEEN

Adel adjusted the blanket around her shoulders and across her lap as she and her parents rode in the carriage taking them home. The sun shone through the window, and it wasn't that cold really, but the increasing wind seemed to steal any semblance of warmth with each gust. As they passed under a canopy of trees, its long-fallen leaves danced and fluttered across the dirt path.

Blanket adjusted, Adel fidgeted solemnly with the bracelet Arran had given her, staring at the blue gems inlaid in the silver band as they twinkled in the light. The closer to home the three-day trip brought them, the heavier she felt.

She couldn't understand why Arran was letting strategy overshadow emotion. She hated that it blinded him from seeing how much they needed each other—how much she needed him—right now.

She ached for his support.

Uncertainty over their relationship plagued her thoughts. The urge to write him was strong, but she wanted *him* to be the first to reach out. That would show he'd taken time to reflect, maybe even to understand her reaction.

The carriage was hollow, absent of the giggles that would have once filled it. Rather than conversations about whatever she and Ashla had found gossip-worthy at the event, there was only the wisp of page-turning and soft snores as her mother read and her father dozed. All she wanted to say was pent up in her chest, ready to burst, but no one to share it with. Some things could only be shared with best friends, and right how she had neither of hers.

Her thoughts skirted back to Arran. *What if that argument is the last I ever speak to him? What if that was the last time I see him?*

To distract herself, she watched the knights and guards that rode protectively around them. Their armour clinked with the horses' movements, and her eyes caught on the burgundy fabric underneath the animals' barding. The Heta kestrel with outstretched wings rippled in silver along the fabric when the wind picked up again, as if the bird were about to take flight. The knights braced themselves against the sudden gust.

Past the riders, the copses of trees thinned from the thicker forests along the edge of the Piridetian border to the sparser trees that would eventually end and give them full view of the mountain range in the distance. Already, Adel saw signs of the farmers' fields that wended throughout the outskirts of Heta. Most farmers lived closer to Heta Proper, but some still tended to fields in small villages this far out as well.

By nightfall, the carriage had wheeled through many familiar villages and towns. The outskirt towns they passed through without recieving much attention, but the people of Heta Proper were waiting for the procession along the roadways and among the dense collection of homes and shops. Lanterns hung aloft cast the crowds in a warm glow, while guards held flags with Heta's crest gleaming as the light caught the silver thread.

Once the castle was in sight, Adel stretched and stifled a yawn that didn't even begin to touch the exhaustion she felt.

Queen Mela glanced up from her book, then out the

curtained window before marking her place and closing the text with a gentle *thup*. She nudged her husband. "Darling."

He yawned and ran a hand through his receding hair before sitting up properly and rolling his neck and shoulders.

When the royal family pulled up to the steps at the entrance, servants emerged from the light-coloured stone castle to help the royal family out of the carriage and collect their belongings. Sconces with metal kestrels fastened to the front held flaming torches that illuminated the entryway with enough light for everyone to see what they were doing and where they were going. Adel had barely stepped down after her parents before she heard crunching footsteps coming towards them.

"Mama! Papa!"

Looking up, she saw her brother wrapping his arms around their father's torso, and then their mother giving him a kiss on the top of his head. Adel knew he was on that cusp of boyhood where he might soon reject this kind of affection in the name of being strong and independent, but for now, he welcomed it.

Seems he's feeling better, she mused.

She smiled wearily, suddenly very glad he'd missed the festival. There was no doubt in her mind he would have been killed. She could practically see it happening before her eyes; she had to blink it away and shake her head to make sure the image her mind had just conjured of his broken body didn't stick.

King Criph stifled his fatigue with a grin for his son. "How's the little prince?"

"I'm not little," Rynn insisted, "but I'm fine. And hungry. Cook was waiting for you to arrive before preparing anything and wouldn't give me a snack."

"Is that so? Well, I guess we'll have to get the cook to whip us up a meal, right?" Mela chuckled lightly, smoothing out her youngest's hair as he nodded firmly. "How about you greet your sister while your father and I go do that?"

"'Kay, Mama." The boy nodded again and made his way to Adel.

She wasn't sure how, but Adel found it in her to joke. "Cook wouldn't give you a snack? I can tell. It's completely stunted your growth."

He made to swat at her arm, but she dodged him. His attack seemed a ploy to get her to step out of the way anyway since he moved past her to the horses at the carriage. She watched as he first hovered his hand in front of the closest horse's muzzle; the animal's nostrils flared as it inhaled the boy's scent then pressed its nose into Rynn's palm.

"I guess he missed you." Adel grinned slightly.

When he looked at her, his brows pulled together. "What's wrong?"

"It was a long trip," she replied evasively.

"Where's Ashla?"

She shouldn't have been surprised he'd ask about her so quickly.

Adel used the coachman returning to pull the carriage away as an excuse to delay her answer. She stared after the vehicle as it disappeared beyond the torch-lit path, longing for her best friend to burst out of the door. Tears pricked her eyes as she turned her attention back to her brother who'd come to stand in front of her.

Adel took a deep breath, steeling herself to look him in the eye and be honest. He hadn't hit his growth spurt yet, so she still had to look down to meet his greenish-blue gaze. She could see the concern painted there.

She didn't take time to think about it. "Ashla…was killed protecting me. Lavanai attacked Nithle during the festival."

"What?" His voice was barely a whisper, his complexion paling. "How?"

"I don't know the details… Ashla and I were walking when we saw the dahems, so we separated. And then I… They told me…" Adel's throat closed in.

Rynn stepped closer and reached for her. "Did they hurt you?"

"Rynn."

Adel inhaled sharply at the voice, then looked up to see her mother standing at the top of the steps. The queen had a knowing look on her face. From her peripheral, Adel saw Rynn turn his attention to their mother.

"Let's go eat. We can talk about the festival and Ashla later," she said gently, but with enough command for him to leave inquisition behind for now.

Rynn's eyes fell back to Adel uncertainly. He let his hands fall away, though Adel got the distinct sense he didn't want to. He faced their mother again. "Okay, Mama."

Adel tried to control her breathing and quell the empty feeling in her chest as Rynn climbed the steps into the castle. She could tell the queen was holding her composure, shoulders rigid and hands clasped before her. Even the way her chin tilted ever-so-slightly upward told Adel this was her mother standing with careful consideration for what she was conveying to others.

The attack on Nithle Proper hadn't only meant Ashla's death and a strain on her relationship with Arran; it also meant a shift in the relationship between Nithle and Heta. How might the kingdoms' long-standing friendship endanger them all now that Lavanai had attacked again?

As Mela and Rynn disappeared into the castle, Adel thought about how all she wanted was for her brother to grow up in a safe, dahem-free world, where the only thing he'd have to worry about would be finding a companion and keeping the kingdom stable. She'd always done her best to use the little moments she had with him to give him that, but she feared she'd just effectively shattered that bright future for him.

She hugged herself as the wind swept around her anew and walked up the steps under the stars alone.

CHAPTER

FOURTEEN

Anxious energy teemed off Prince Arran. Even if Ryla hadn't been able to sense it, his squared shoulders and set jaw told her he was masking inner turmoil. She didn't acknowledge it; still, as she stood in the entryway to his expansive suite, door closed behind her, his gaze read wariness.

Brown eyes moving around the room, Ryla could see no one else was there, at least in the well-furnished and decorated sitting room. She doubted anyone lingered in his bedchambers behind the closed door. Meaning that she was the one making him wary.

He'll grow accustomed to me. They all did.

"Should we sit?" he asked. To his credit, his voice remained level as he gestured to the seating beside the mantle.

"Your prerogative," Ryla responded.

He hesitated only a moment before moving to the chairs, and she followed. Ryla removed her sword belt before settling into the plush seating but kept the weapon across her lap. The action and weight of the blade across her thighs felt no different than if she'd set her hands in her lap instead.

"I appreciate your guidance, Killer Ryla. I've never dealt with the likes of this and am quite caught off guard by it," Arran started, fidgeting slightly with the fabric on the arm of the chair as he did.

"It's a response to traumatic circumstances. For some,

experiences like what you went through become locked in your memory in a way that unleashes itself upon you and overtakes your mind." She continued to watch the young man, weighing his reaction. Not everyone responded well to this revelation. Some responded with rage, denial, accusations she was putting some disease on them. Others...

Arran's brows pinched together as he considered her words. Silence surrounded them, save for the sounds of the fire in the hearth, which cast shadows across his face even with the light coming through the unshaded windows.

"What's wrong with me?"

The words were quiet, probably only intended for his own musings. Ryla responded anyway. "Nothing."

His wide eyes flashed to her. Their blues betrayed his lack of understanding. Even among armies, few spoke of this consequence of surviving horrific experiences. Instead, most kept it to themselves as it broke their minds and spirits. In the past, she'd been called to bring an end to someone who'd tainted themselves with magic to try to alleviate the pain of it.

Arran found his voice again. "I have no doubt you've seen far more horrors than I ever have, High Protector, and yet, you seem to be unaffected by it."

"Do not measure yourself against me," Ryla countered. "I've been trained to be unaffected by everything."

"How does that work, exactly?" Arran asked, then seemed to realize what he said. "Forgive my curiosity."

Her reply came easily. "You're not the first to ask it. I cannot answer you."

The prince inhaled, then dragged his good hand through his curly hair and down his face, the scratch of light facial hair meeting her ears. He let out the breath like it was a weight in his chest. "Right," he said more firmly. "Whatever you can teach me to handle these…memories, I'll take."

"The strategies I have are all variations of similar tools to use the present moment to bring you out of the memory. There are also preventative measures you can take, but, given your current circumstances, mastery of the former will be more useful to begin with."

He nodded along without question, eyes trained expectantly on her.

If it could be called such, Ryla began her lesson. "Physical sensations are a powerful tool to draw yourself from a memory, but the key is to focus on something that exists uniquely in the present and not in the memory. This is why I pushed you to acknowledge more than the cold the other day. If we were in warmer months, perhaps it's something you could use, but not now."

Arran nodded again. "When I focused on the fur of my cloak and the fabric of my gloves, it sent cracks through the memory."

Ryla continued in her even-toned way. "If the memory is only beginning to take hold, you can also use techniques such as seeking out items and focusing on them and how they exist in the space around you. This gives your mind something else to focus on. Engage your mind and your senses."

"Engage my mind how?" Arran asked. He leaned forward, as though to absorb the information more fully. One arm rested on his thigh while he seemed mindful not to put pressure on the other, still in its sling.

"There are many strategies others have used. It could be describing some mundane task, reciting a passage from a book or a song, or even narrating your current situation." Reading the confusion on his face, she elaborated. "For instance, in this moment, you might say, 'I am Prince Arran of Nithle. I am seventeen years old. It is midmorning, and I am sitting in my quarters with Killer Ryla of the Union.'"

The confusion spread across his features and shifted to skepticism. "That really helps?"

"For many it has. You will need to seek out and determine which strategy is most effective for you."

The word strategy unsurprisingly resonated with him; his features relaxed into understanding. The conversation drifted away between them as he took in what she said. Ryla could hear the footsteps in the hall of servants going about their duties and of guards shifting their positions at the prince's door.

"I worry I am overstepping," Arran finally spoke again, "but I wonder if you would help me in these moments as I learn. Your guidance is invaluable."

Much like the anxiousness before it, the prince's vulnerability seeped into the space around her and seemed to brush against her skin.

Ryla's tone never changed as she replied. "My duty is to protect you, and that includes your mind."

The prince stared at her, as if expecting something more. She was familiar with eyes seeking compassion or empathy—at the very least sympathy—and that was how he looked at her now. Someone from whom he could draw comfort and understanding as he brought his turmoil to heel.

These were things she could not give.

Eventually, he swallowed, seeming to come to that conclusion himself. "Thank you, Killer Ryla. Please, continue with your instruction."

CHAPTER

FIFTEEN

As Arran listened to the official report that'd finally come in from Bunthle, he felt a sinking sense of guilt and shame over whatever he was struggling with. The small village near Lake Pol had been burned to the ground by Lavanai's forces. Thankfully, there were some survivors who'd escaped to Thlent, but Bunthle as a village was no more. It joined Jenthle, Thlake, and Harthlen, other villages Nithle had lost in the early days of the war.

These people lost everything…many of them their lives, he chided himself as he listened to the field knight's report.

It'd been days since the attack, and the field knight, Knight Harben, said he'd left a number of his company behind to continue to search the village wreckage in case there were survivors hidden away. Otherwise, he had reports of how a large segment of Lavanai's army had entered the village, immediately taken everyone hostage, and then sent the rest of their numbers to Nithle Proper.

"Our forces did what they could tuh rescue the captives and were able tuh help many escape," Harben described with a grave tone that mostly offset his rural accent. "But unfortunately, right now, our count stands at less than a hundred survivors. T'was an absolute slaughter."

Arran flinched at the word but hoped it wasn't too noticeable. His mental guards were up as he listened to Knight

Harben and staved off worries that anything he might say could trigger the memories he was feeling guilty over. From the moment he'd sat down, he'd put some of what Ryla had mentioned to him to work. It had started with paying attention to the room. Any other time, he would've simply taken stock of where the guards were, which doors were secured, and the atmosphere when walking into the large room to sit down in the chair to his father's right. This time, the smell of burned wood wafted into his nose, the large tapestry of his family's crest snared his attention behind the chairs, and the polished wood of the chair's arms felt smooth under his hands. The room had three tall windows along the far wall, letting the afternoon light pour in and illuminate the patterned carpet underfoot.

Whether he was doing this right or not, he wasn't entirely sure. But he took comfort that Ryla stood to his right, watching over him.

"This is terrible news," Shron uttered from where she sat to the left on the other side of Alden. Her pinched brow accompanied her pained voice and hands pressed together on her dark-coloured skirts.

"Is Thlent able to handle the intake? Does the village need anything?" Alden chimed in next. His tone was calmer, firm in how to proceed in this sort of situation, no matter how tragic. Even his posture was the picture of calm in his high-backed chair.

"We can always divert people to Sothle or Wendur if needed," Arran suggested. Sothle was another Nithlean city just south-west of Nithle Proper and on the way to Wendur.

Knight Feon, who stood beside Harben, answered. "We're managing, even with Thlent being half the size of Bunthle. If more survivors are found, that's when we'll need to consider diverting them elsewhere."

Alden nodded understandingly. "Very well. We'll make sure before sending you both back to your stations that you have enough supplies and whatever else you may need."

"Thank you, Your Highness." Feon bowed alongside Harben.

Arran spoke up now, trying to channel his father's calm tone. "While you're here, I'd like for you to join me, Knight Calar, and Killer Ryla. I want to make sure our people are protected in case Lavanai initiates another attack."

Despite what the Keepers had said about Lavanai's next moves, a strategic step for the dahems would be to wipe out Thlent, which was all that stood between them and Nithle Proper. It'd reduce their army, cause fear, and cast aspersions on the royal family's ability to protect them. It was another way to get at him and his parents, even if Lavanai's forces weren't directly at the castle doors.

The thought chilled him.

Luckily, Harben broke him from his thoughts. "Absolutely, My Prince. Whatever you need o' me."

"An excellent idea, Son," Alden agreed with a nod. "We can also use this as an opportunity to discuss taking action against Lavanai."

Arran started at the words, turning sharply to the king. "Action against Lavanai?"

"I promised our people we wouldn't sit idly by any longer, and I plan to do something about it. It's high time we take the reins, call on our allies, and march on Lavanai," Alden said firmly, his aged features hardened. "The Union has already sent their missive to all of Nithle to recruit for our protection. Now it's time we extend our reach and recruit for an offensive strike."

"Father, we have little chance if we meet them on their own land," Arran countered gently, trying to catch up with his father's thought trail. What good could come of this when every other attack on Lavanai had failed? *No one's marched on Lavanai in decades.*

He knew the story from the early days of the war when Nithle and the other kingdoms still dared set foot in Lavanai and had even succeeded in destroying the capital where their fort now stood. That had been at a great cost, however, with the majority of the humans meeting their death.

Alden's voice drew Arran from his thoughts. "I was hopeful, High Protector, that you might advise us in this matter."

Ryla's reply was simple. "Marching on Lavanai is an unwise strategy."

The king's jaw clenched subtly in response.

You shouldn't be surprised, Father, Arran wanted to say. *Even the Union won't march on Lavanai. They're protectors, not assassins. They won't advise we do something that will directly endanger us.*

Alden licked his lips before speaking again. "If I may, High Protector."

"Proceed," Ryla said.

"Defending ourselves has only prolonged the war. We know more now about the dahems than we ever have, and it makes sense to bring this to an end," the king continued with an attempt to persuade her.

Arran's eyes flicked to the Killer now and found her gaze fixed on his father.

"Do not forget that dahems use magic. Even if you find a way to last against their speed and strength, you cannot contend with that power." Her words held the gravity that her tone didn't.

Alden shook his head. "I haven't forgotten."

"Then you know the foolhardiness of your plan."

The silence that followed was palpable. Arran admired his father's desire to protect Nithle and its people, but agreed with Ryla that this wasn't the way to go about it.

"Don't worry, Father. We'll figure out how to stop Lavanai," Arran tried to reassure him. "Even if it means using all of our defensive forces to conquer them here on our own grounds."

Alden's gaze rested on Arran for a beat, his expression full of something that Arran couldn't read. Shron reached and grabbed her husband's hand, giving it a gentle squeeze that drew Alden's attention to her. Whatever the unreadable thing was, Arran let it go in favour of focusing on how to sort out the threat from Lavanai.

Figure it out, Arran.

CHAPTER

SIXTEEN

The hustle and bustle of the travelling market brought life to Yandana Fort like nothing else could. Every few weeks, vendors rolled in with wagons and carts from Lavanai's capital, Icarsen, with goods and wares that not only refilled the fort's pantries, but also brought a sense of normalcy Mithos loved.

Yandana had once been a part of Lavanai Capital, before it had fallen to human attacks closer to the beginning of the war. Being nearly a century ago, Mithos of course wasn't old enough to have seen it, but she was told it'd been bustling with the densest of Lavanai's population and was even home to the royal family itself, rich with splendor, balls, festivals, and all the finery one could want.

Now the fort was home to high walls, sparring grounds, war rooms, and blacksmith forges.

Stepping out of the barracks, Mithos made her way around the outdoor training areas, where a group was already at work with morning routines, and toward the outer wall where the stands would be set up. The bright sun guided Mithos's enthusiastic steps through the fort's simple roadway.

She couldn't help the smile that crossed her face when she saw the vendors with their brightly-coloured booths and garments. In comparison, her tan-coloured trousers, boots, and snugly-fitting tunic looked drab and boring, but she wouldn't allow her yearning for a more colourful ensemble dampen her spirits today. Other ranks were already making their way from stand to stand and chattering about, and Mithos happily slipped in to weave through the throngs of people.

While she intended to visit each of the dozen or so stands, she made a beeline for her favourite: a vegetable stand. The vendor, who wore a colourful scarf draped over her head and shoulders, smiled brightly as Mithos approached.

"Right on time, Commander. I've got your favourite," she said, her high voice just as bright as her smile. She reached behind the stand's counter and pulled up a small sack to hand to Mithos.

"Finally!" Mithos cheered as she accepted the rough sack and spied the inatin piled into a wooden crate atop the counter.

"I know. I was starting to think the late summer rains had drowned them out, but a few days ago, I saw these all over the stalks."

The commander plucked a few of the small orange vegetables, giving each of their dimpled surfaces a slight squeeze before placing them in the bag.

"How fare things in Icarsen?" Mithos asked conversationally as she made her selections.

"Well, as usual. Preparations are already underway for the end of season festivities. King Ottel is opening up the royal gardens for the occasion this year," the vendor replied.

Mithos's gaze flicked up from the vegetables. "The royal gardens?" When she saw the vendor nod, she continued. "That'll be a treat. I've never seen them, but I heard they're quite beautiful." She finished her selection of half a dozen inatin, trying to ignore a pang of jealousy in her chest.

The royal gardens were said to be expansive, filled with hundreds of different kinds of flora and fauna. In her mind, Mithos pictured giant flower bushes and willowing trees that gave home to all sorts of birds, rodents, and maybe even deer. There was an entire staff dedicated to tending to the flora alone, and the thought encouraged her imagination to stretch endlessly on the prospects of the royal gardens.

The vendor's cheerful voice brought her out of her day-dream. "Yes. Everyone is incredibly excited."

The commander fished some coins from a pocket in her fatigues, counting them in her palm before handing them to the vendor. "Thank you."

The vendor went about rearranging the display just slightly so that others would come their way as well. "It's my pleasure, Commander. Since you told me last time they were your favourite, I hoped to see you today."

"Well, I'm glad you did. Be well."

"You also, Commander."

With her favourite vegetable in tow, there was a little extra pep in Mithos's step as she went about visiting the other stalls. She didn't make it very far, however, before she heard a voice call to her through the crowd.

"Mithos!"

Looking up from the bolts of fabric lined across a rack in a stall, Mithos spotted Lord Jasim standing just outside the market area. His height gave him the advantage to see over some of the crowd and gave her the chance to spot him. Excusing herself, Mithos held her sack of inatin close to her as she wove her way toward him.

"Good morning, My Lord," Mithos greeted with a small inclination of her head.

"Walk with me," Jasim said and motioned in a direction away from the market.

Mithos fell into step beside him, if it could be called that. Him being several inches taller than her left her feet moving faster to keep up. The sack of vegetables swung back and forth with the movements of her hip beside one of her twin blades. "Is there something I can do for you, My Lord?"

"How are the ranks faring?"

"They're healing. Some are shaken after encountering Killer Ryla, but everyone so far is on schedule with the increased training with Gath. Captain Anxer was able to coordinate it all fairly quickly, and I even saw a group out early this morning on the training field."

"Good. I know a lot of our folks haven't had to deal with a Killer yet, let alone Ryla," he replied. "Of all the Killers they could have sent…" A shadow crossed his face.

Mithos nodded, pushed strands of her dark hair out of her face, and looked up at him. "Honestly, My Lord, I agree with what you said before about this being a warning. The Union didn't send her by chance. She wasn't just someone available they could slough off."

"We'll just have to keep an eye on how this unfolds. It seems you've bounced back from it all without too much trouble."

"Yes, My Lord," she said with a nod, a small swell of pride in her chest. "However, I've unfortunately not made progress with my research on the Union just yet."

"That's not unexpected. It's only been a few days since you've been fully back on your feet. How is training with Woxla? Is controlling the magic coming any easier?"

"It's a challenge I'm prepared to conquer. Fire is a volatile element, but I'm starting to master it," she answered with a determined nod of her head. Its volatility made her a bit uneasy, but knowing that she was doing this for her people and her kingdom encouraged her.

"I'd like to see a demonstration…" His tone trailed off.

Mithos saw a faraway look in his eyes. She had a feeling where his mind was, so she didn't pry.

Instead, Jasim divulged it himself. "I remember when Lamis began to learn to control the fire. He burned himself a few times, which I taunted him for, of course." He laughed, a hearty sound that made it impossible not to smile with him. "Did you ever have any such troubles, Commander?"

"Not quite. I first learned magic had accepted me by accidentally setting a small grass fire," Mithos said with a lopsided grin.

She remembered it well, that day when she and her two older brothers were playing in the yard in their home village. One of her brothers started raving about how mother and father had said he was old enough to invite nature's magic to him to see if he'd gain any powers. Young as she was, perhaps five, Mithos wondered what that'd be like. Like all dahems, she felt magic all around her, as intrinsically a part of nature as the air they breathed, but it was said children should wait to call to it in case a particularly powerful magic accepted them and they weren't ready for it. Being older also meant they'd be able to use a weapon as a conduit to better control the magic.

Somehow, in her wonderment of the experience, nature had responded. It was like a little surge of heat washed through her body, and she even remembered saying to her brothers that she felt too hot. Next thing she knew, the grass burst to flames around her, but didn't burn her. Mother came rushing out of their small home to see what had happened, Mithos had started crying, worried that she'd be in trouble, and it had kickstarted the whole journey of learning to control her powers.

For many years, she focused on dampening it so she didn't cause more trouble. Until she was accepted into the army for the very powers she bore.

"I imagine that was quite the spectacle," Jasim chuckled again. "I always was jealous I wasn't accepted by magic as Lamis was, which is why I poked fun. But I imagine fire would be a difficult element to master. Speaking of difficult elements, how is Naxela faring?"

"He's trying. I think he feels a lot of pressure to perfect his skill, especially after being tossed about by the Killer the way he was." She felt for him. Had their positions been reversed, she imagined she would be in the training centre every day, just as he was. "He should be with Woxla now if you want to check in on him, My Lord," she suggested, gesturing in the general direction of the facilities.

"Let's do that."

In a short time, the training building came within view. Fanciful designs adorned the large stone archway around the door and a flag with Lavanai's crest flew just above it. Both filigree and ancient runes that Mithos recognized but couldn't read made up much of the design work around the door. Given the building's purpose, she'd always imagined they were runes for strength, endurance, protection, and the like. She'd once tried to research them, but had found nothing in any lore or archives that matched their sharp points and multi-lined characters.

Despite not knowing what they meant, each time she passed under the runes, she felt a sense of protection and even comfort.

Cracks of electricity greeted the lord and commander as they entered the building, followed by the familiar smell of char. The stone interior was enough to contain not only her fire and Naxela's lightning, but also the way other magic-users' abilities manifested.

The wide space with buttressed ceilings provided lots of

area to work with, and as Mithos and Jasim strolled into the training space, they saw Woxla standing to the side with one arm crossed over his bare chest and tucked under his other arm where a battle axe hung loosely in his opposite hand. His longer hair was tied back and separated into three braids, then braided into each other; his dark skin showed the wear and tear of battle.

Naxela stood near the middle of the room, his dark hair matted to his head as he pushed himself up from the dirt floor where his mace stuck out of the ground. His loose training clothes were dirtied and wet with sweat; part of one pant leg appeared singed along the hem and up to the knee.

"Lord Jasim, Commander Mithos," Woxla greeted with a wide grin that reached his eyes. "Are you here for a demonstration?"

"If you could," Jasim said with a simple nod from where he and Mithos stood along the sidelines.

Mithos spied how Naxela steeled himself when his gaze locked on their lord. She knew magic didn't come as easily to others as it did to her, and she worried Naxela in particular was pushing himself too hard. He used his sleeve to swipe the sweat from his face, leaving a dirty smudge across his brow, and readied himself again.

Without warning, Woxla charged forward with the battle axe now securely gripped in both hands. He was one of the fastest dahems Mithos had ever faced or even seen, but Naxela was nearly as fast. The two danced around each other's swings and defenses, leaving her wondering who would strike first with magic. The spark of Naxela's mace answered her silent speculation.

Woxla responded quickly, electricity crackling around his own weapon—the perfect trainer for Naxela, although the trainer's magical signature toned lower than the co-commander's. Focusing on the essence of the magic allowed Mithos to track their attacks more easily than by sight alone.

A surge of magic accompanied a counter attack from Naxela, and the upward swing of the mace met the battle axe's blade. The two came together with a blinding flash and a resounding crack like thunder. As the world came into focus again, flashes of lightning that continued around Naxela's mace caused Mithos to tense involuntarily. It reminded her of a chaotic lightning storm, like one she'd seen as a child that had destroyed many crops and some homes in her native village.

A brief twitch in Naxela's expression gave away how tenuous his control was, but a small adjustment of his grip seemed to help him focus enough to reel it in, concentrating the electric storm to the ball of the mace.

Woxla's nod signaled the end of the demonstration. The magic extinguished almost as quickly as it had come alive, and both dahems took a step back, chests heaving. They exchanged a few words between them before facing their audience. Naxela made his way off the training floor.

"You two are working well together," Jasim praised once Naxela reached them.

"Thank you, My Lord," Naxela responded with a grin. His eyes practically sparkled as Jasim clapped him on the shoulder.

"Your abilities will be a great asset." He gave another pat before stepping out onto the training floor to meet with Woxla.

Naxela turned his wide grin on Mithos. Something about the look in his amber eyes gave her the distinct sense that he was looking for her approval, too.

Before she could dole out her assessment, he asked, "Care to spar?" He hoisted his mace up, resting it across his shoulders with his arms holding it in place.

"I'll pass," she replied with a shake of her head and wry grin. "You ought to be careful. You keep at it too hard, and you'll fry yourself. Besides, we both know I'm not as fast as you are."

"Someday you'll catch up." He ignored her warning and continued to grin, dimples showing in his cheeks. "Realistically, you only need to be fast enough to get by the Killer."

Mithos made a face, flashing back to the night of the festival. She'd never seen a human move so fast, nor with such precision and strength.

Is she even human? Mithos wondered, not for the first time.

She hadn't seen any amber in the woman's eyes, so it didn't seem she was a dahem. Even the crazy thought that she might be using magic was quickly dashed by the lack of gold tainting. It didn't make sense how she was as skilled as she was. Ryla simply *was*.

Woxla pulled her from her thoughts. "Come show off your skills, Little Flame."

Her gaze broke from Naxela to Woxla and acknowledged his call with a nod.

"Hold this for me?" Mithos asked Naxela, hoisting her sack of inatin for him to see.

"Sure," he said, taking the bag and then peeking inside. "Oh, excellent. Inatin!"

Mithos's eyes narrowed, and she stuck a finger in his face. "Don't you dare eat any of them."

He put his hands up in surrender. "I won't, I won't."

Only when she was sure he wouldn't touch her precious vegetables, she stepped out onto the training floor.

"Don't show off too much!" Naxela called after her.

The falchions sang as they left their sheaths, the blue-tinted blades gleaming before rippling to life with flames at her sides. The heat from the fire warmed her legs and waist, but she had enough control of it that it never touched nor burned her. Although magic had come pretty easily to her, the training was honing the skills she'd dampened for so long. Woxla didn't even step in to spar with her. Rather, he backed away and gently encouraged Jasim to do the same.

Once certain everyone was out of the way, Mithos dragged her arms forward from where they hung at her sides. Paths burned along the floor with the roar of a fire catching a particularly dry brush even though it was only dirt in her path. Released from the swords, the fire was harder to control, but she knew how to mentally call to the magic and manipulate it, preventing the blaze from getting wildly out of hand.

The control was important to her. Although they were at war, she had no intention of being barbaric, which was one of her qualms about how her powers manifested, and even Naxela's. It was hard to use them for anything but destruction.

With a nudge from her mind, the flames spider-webbed off in various directions, rushing toward the edges of the room. When she glanced around, she saw Woxla smiling with the quiet pride of a teacher. Jasim's gaze showed he was impressed. Naxela's features showed admiration. Just before the flames reached them all, she gave another mental nudge, leaving smoke and char where the flames had been a moment before.

Naxela gave a whoop, and Jasim and Woxla continued to look on approvingly.

That they could use magic was fine and well, and she knew it was one of the key reasons she and Naxela had been made co-commanders as young as they were. Still, magic alone wouldn't defeat a Killer. She'd need to find something that would.

CHAPTER

SEVENTEEN

Eagerness vibrated in Arran's chest that morning as he pulled on the loose tunic and looped the sling over his head to rest around his neck. Adjusting the fabric bunched underneath, he had high hopes this would be the last day of awkward, one-armed dressing, one-side-only sleeping, and essentially all one-handed functioning. The sun had barely reached out across the horizon, but the prince was already awake and ready for Healer Dalam's visit.

The weeks that had passed since he and his father came to an agreement on how to reorganize their forces to best protect the Nithlean people and prepare for any further attack had also mended his shoulder. Although, he admittedly felt more certain about his shoulder mending than he did about the state of the war. It'd been eerily quiet, which Killer Ryla assured him was because of her presence and the Lavanian army needing to regroup. In the meantime, she continued to guide him through staving off intrusive memories.

As he stepped out of his chambers, the door to the left, the room Ryla had been given, opened. A servant carrying a breakfast tray turned abruptly and almost collided with him.

She stopped short with a gasp and the dishes clattering on the metal tray. "My deepest apologies, Your Highness," she said, her voice small and eyes cast downward.

He gave it a quick glance, spying food left behind, but

none of it had even left the dishes let alone slopped on him. "No harm done. Be on your way."

The servant nodded her head, side-stepped and scurried away down the hall.

A mere moment later, Ryla herself exited the room, pulling her gloves taut as she crossed the threshold.

"Good morning, High Protector," Arran greeted. "I hope there was nothing wrong with your meal."

"It was satisfactory," Ryla replied.

"So even Killers have preferences, then?" he mused more to himself than anyone. The food left behind wasn't as if someone picked at a little bit of everything and may have been full. Rather, it looked as though her portion of breakfast vegetables had gone untouched.

She was human after all, he supposed, and having preferences would explain things like why she kept her hair long even though it no doubt could cause trouble in battle. His gaze landed on her boots, again resting on the seemingly useless belts around the ankles.

It's the only *explanation.*

As if she could read his mind, she said, "Being observant is a valuable skill."

He met her gaze, taking stock in the same moment of the details of his surroundings—sling on his arm, servants walking down the hall and waiting to tidy the rooms, the sound of someone coughing somewhere nearby. As much as he was grateful to her, Ryla's vacant eyes were one of the strongest triggers for his memories of the night of the festival.

Finally, he said, "I can only hope my observations will guide me in this war against Lavanai."

"The more you face them, the more you'll come to understand," Ryla replied.

Unbidden, his defenses flew up. "I've been studying them since I was a child. I've read everything we have about dahems, and Lavanai in particular. I've heard all the stories."

"Words on a page and stories from a tutor are much different than an actual experience." She gave no indication that she'd heard his tone. "You're seeing them through eyes other than your own, and that doesn't tell you everything."

"They tell me Lavanai and the dahems have always been our enemies," Arran rattled off from memory. They tell me the dahems attacked my kingdom when my great-grandfather ruled, for no reason other than they're tyrants. Had he not captured and killed the dahem king, they probably would have overtaken us from the beginning."

It was one of the earliest stories from his childhood, trumping even fairy tales and happy endings. Lavanai's king at the time, Irkis, sought to assert his power and force the humans to bow to their magic. He and his kingdom had arrived without warning, breaking through Nithle's defences and coming after its people. But Irkis had been an arrogant king, leading the battle with reckless abandon, which led to his capture and death at Nithle King Gerge's command. After that, the war had truly begun.

"What I've seen of the dahems is enough to show me the stories are true," Arran continued. A small pang of what he might call betrayal hit him. *You* know *this. You* know *what I've been fighting in my memories.*

She didn't miss a beat. "Even tyranny is backed by a motive. Knowing an opponent's motive is a part of strategy."

"And what's your motive, Killer Ryla?" Arran surprised himself with his words. He'd fully intended to ask what helpful observations had led her to understand dahems. Instead, those words came tumbling out. Humiliation crawled across his skin. "I apologize, High Protector. Forget I said anything."

"A Killer's motive is their duty," she replied, which also surprised him.

Ley's voice cut through the conversation. "Your Highness."

Arran turned quickly, sobered by his knight's voice. His eyes darted around the hallway to see how many had witnessed the exchange, but apart from his guard, there was maybe a servant or two that lingered. They each politely averted their gazes, but he knew the servants at least might gossip among themselves.

He cursed silently, then said to Ley, "Let's get going. Healer Dalam will be waiting."

A stifling feeling trailed Arran as he and his retinue began their trek to the castle infirmary, where they'd meet the healer. Although Ryla said nothing as she walked a few paces to his side, Arran couldn't help the anxiety bubbling in his gut over the words that had spilled out of his mouth.

Ley kept pace on his right, hovering close enough to speak but saying nothing until they came to a hall devoid of servants or other guards.

The royal knight kept his voice low. "What was that about?"

Arran didn't need him to specify. He both knew he'd ask about it and had hoped he wouldn't. "What she said…it just got under my skin."

"That's not like you," Ley prodded gently.

He cursed the man's instinct—how he always seemed to know when things should be hashed out. Arran ground his teeth together.

The prince pitched his voice low. "Ever since Killer Ryla and the Keepers arrived, all I see are my failures." Ley was probably one of the only people Arran would admit that to. "I can't protect myself well enough, so the Killer is assigned to me specifically. What happened the night of the festival has me reliving memories at the drop of a pin. Then her comments about dahems and observations…it's just something else I'm failing at. And it's not her fault. I know it's not."

Arran used being mindful of where he walked as an excuse to not look at Ley. The words felt just as uncomfortable out in the world as they had in his mind.

"I can understand why you'd have those feelings. For what it's worth, I don't think you're failing. And the aftermath of an assault of any kind is challenging for most," Ley replied gently.

"Have you…?" Arran's voice felt small. *He* felt small. "Have you faced what I'm going through? With memories trapping you in a moment?"

"I haven't, no," Ley answered.

As much as he wanted someone to relate to, Arran also felt relieved. "I'm grateful for that. No one should have to deal with this. It's got me on edge, wondering when the next time it happens will be. Wondering what it means for my rule."

"These are all learning opportunities. The chance to get better is available to you at each step," Ley offered. "I know you've had a few private meetings with Killer Ryla. Is it about this?"

Arran nodded. "Given that, her suggestion that I needed to observe the dahems more felt like a stab. Although now I feel I'm being ungrateful of her help."

"I'm sure she understands," Ley reassured him. "While she seems young still, even young Killers have seen many things. They have perspective most of us couldn't fathom."

The words rattled around in Arran's mind.

Ley continued when he didn't say anything else. "You're not in this alone, Arran. I am with you. The Union is with us all."

Arran felt another ache in his chest. *Is Adel with me?*

There'd been no word from her since the Passing Ceremony—another memory that continued to replay in his mind, though not in the same way. This one was more haunting, laced with guilt and anxiety that this would put a permanent fissure between them.

I'm just trying to keep you safe... he thought and willed his words to reach her. If she could only understand.

Of all the turmoil roiling in his gut, this was one he'd kept to himself. While he was sure Ley would listen if he confided in him about it, this didn't feel like a conversation to have with the knight.

If only he could simply talk with Adel. Maybe if he shared what he was going through with her, it'd show why she was better off in the safety of her own kingdom right now. He'd thought about going to her, but he couldn't leave Nithle so soon after an attack. And each time he put ink to parchment, the words wouldn't come out right. So far, his attempts at connecting with her were no more than ash in his hearth.

The infirmary was surprisingly warm when they arrived, with tables of instruments Arran couldn't name and jars of herbs and solutions for who knew what. Beds lined the plain walls, and the morning light began to filter in through a large, lone window at the far end of the room.

The space had an odd smell: a mix of woodiness from the fire crackling away in the far corner with the freshly cut wood sitting neatly beside it and what he assumed was the mix of things around him. Every once in a while, a single smell would become distinct, but most of the time it was a muddle of everything together that tickled his nose.

"Good morning, My Prince," Healer Dalam said with a smile, then looked to Ryla. "High Protector, it's an honour to see you again, as well."

Arran smiled in turn. "Thank you, Healer Dalam. I'm hoping there's good news, and I can finally take this off," he said, lifting his arm slightly. He thought it a good sign that his shoulder didn't pinch when he did.

"This should have been more than ample time to get you back to normal, but it's always best to be sure. Here, please have a seat."

The older man pulled out a stool from under one of the tables and, though it already looked spotless, wiped it off with a rag. Arran sat down and waited for his next instructions.

"I'm going to undo the knot," Dalam said, his movements precise and gentle. Arran barely felt him do anything, yet the healer spoke again after only a moment. "There we go. All right, let's take a look. Let me know if any of this hurts." He flung the cloth over his shoulder before leaning forward again to work.

Dalam's long fingers began poking at and massaging the shoulder, feeling for any missed internal damage. His focus was nowhere in particular, as if he were seeing with his fingertips while he worked instead of seeing anything of the world before his eyes. While some of his prodding was uncomfortable, nothing hurt Arran too badly.

Dalam grinned broadly. "I'd say you're healed up. And how's the hip?"

"Still tender sometimes, but nothing too bad. I think my shoulder took the brunt of it."

Dalam nodded knowingly. "I'm sure it'll be fine, but I'd be happy to take a look if you'd like."

"If it starts giving me trouble, I'll call for you again," Arran said as he stood, waving away the offer.

"In that case, I'll let you be on your way, Prince Arran. I'm sure you have plenty to do," Dalam said.

"I appreciate your care." It felt both nice and odd to Arran to be using both arms freely again. "Call on me if there's anything I can do for you."

"That's very generous of you, Your Highness," Dalam said with a grateful bow, sweeping his hair to the side when he was once again upright. "High Protector, are you still completing the Repelling today?"

"Yes," she replied.

The Repelling. He had forgotten. Arran felt cold all of a sudden despite the warmth of the infirmary.

Driven by the dahem attack, a couple of the Nithlean people had tried to harness magic for themselves. Despite the fears, despite how magic ultimately destroyed humans, sometimes the fear of falling to the dahems was more powerful. It wasn't unheard of for people to still *try* to use it to protect themselves and those they loved.

From what he'd been told, one of the two had been turned in by a family member. The other sounded worse off, and they'd been apprehended by knights after causing a bit of a ruckus and shouting through the streets of Nithle Proper. Both were being held in the dungeons for everyone's safety.

The thought of it all made Arran's stomach turn.

"I'll be along as quickly as I can with a couple of my apprentices. They should be arriving any moment," Healer Dalam said.

Ryla only nodded in response.

As they left the infirmary, Arran wished he'd worn a warmer tunic. The difference between the warmth of the healer's quarters and the hallway sent a shiver down his spine, and he also saw Ley rubbing his arms while he came up beside him.

"Your healing is certainly good news, Your Highness," Ley noted.

"It's at least one small shining moment for the day," Arran

agreed with a nod. "I'd like to find Mother and Father. I'm sure they'll want to hear about it."

"Absolutely," Ley said as the group began walking. He looked around Arran briefly. "Killer Ryla, are you venturing to the dungeons right away?"

She nodded. "Yes."

"Did you need an escort?" Ley offered.

"It's taken care of. Huth will be meeting me," she explained.

Ley nodded. "Very well."

Arran spoke next, his tone graver than a moment ago. "I'm hopeful you can help my people, Killer Ryla." He looked to her, mentally preparing all the while in case she looked back at him, too. *The light is streaming through that window. Someone's boots are scuffing on the carpet.*

Ryla replied without looking his way. "I will do everything I can."

EIGHTEEN

S parsely lit spiral stairs led Ryla and Huth in intervals of darkness down to a bright hallway in the belly of the castle. Torches chased away any shadows that might have lurked in the curved ceiling of the hall, and their echoing footsteps emphasized the hollowness of the space.

Huth was silent beside her, only speaking to give direction. The way he held his chin high and walked with his back straight hinted at pride in this simple task of leading her way. The farther they walked, the less she needed his direction. The hum of magic grew stronger, feeling chaotic and untamed, like an animal trapped by a snare.

Soon, they encountered a largely built guard at the end of the hall standing in front of a hefty-looking door. The dark wood and lack of window left no hint of what was beyond it.

"High Protector," the guard greeted without addressing Huth. "I've been expecting you. You're here for the Tainted?"

"Correct," Ryla replied.

"Would you like an escort?" the guard continued.

"Unnecessary." Her attention turned to Huth. "Healer Dalam will arrive shortly."

The servant swept a slight bow. "I shall make sure he finds his way to you, High Protector," he said, then turned to go back the way they'd come.

The guard pulled a single key from where it was stowed

between a dagger and some sort of pack on his belt. "Through here, High Protector." The door barely whispered across the stone floor once he'd unlocked and pushed it open. "If there is anything you need at all, just ask."

Wordlessly, she passed through the door to the next series of halls. The torches here burned lower, as though it had been some hours since anyone had travelled this route and attended to them. After rounding a slight corner, she came upon the dungeon's prison cells.

About a dozen fair-sized cells lined the edges of the room with a large, dirt space in the centre. The torches along the walls chased the shadows to the corners of the space, as if to ensure anyone and any movement could be accounted for. The air was dank and the lack of circulation made the smells more pungent.

Her ability to sense the magic continued to lead Ryla beyond the cells and down another hall. Judging by how far the hallway extended, she could tell she wasn't under the castle any longer. On castle grounds still, yes, but not directly under the building. It was customary that those tainted by magic would be kept separate to minimize any damage to themselves and others with their uncontrolled powers.

The space opened up into an antechamber of sorts. Four windowless, metal doors lined the walls, and the smell of scorched metal and rock competed against the dampness.

"Esteemed Killer," a new guard greeted. The man's stocky build looked good for tackling someone to the ground if he had to. He also wore heavy leathers that covered most of his body; a number of ropes and other binding materials hung at his waist alongside various close-combat weapons.

Ryla only motioned for the guard to open the first door to her right. The guard seemed hesitant at first, but a single flick of her gaze back to him spurred the man into action. He removed the metal beam barring the door with a little effort and then fished a key from around his neck to unlock it. The hinges creaked as he swung the door open, and Ryla stepped inside to meet its lone occupant.

The woman sat on the floor with her knees to her chest, eyes wide and staring blankly. Matted hair cascaded down her back and stuck to her mostly-clean face. All things considered, the smell could have been worse. The only light in the room came from the torches along the wall outside the open door, crawling toward the girl and casting Ryla's silhouette across the floor.

Ryla took a moment to feel out the magical energy, mentally throwing up walls to block out the other magical signature coming from across the hall. A low, but still strong, vibration hummed around her, and her mind's eye conjured a visual manifestation of the powers—a golden haze of sorts that hovered and shifted about the girl.

Invited, but not totally absorbed, Ryla determined. *More docile.*

Magic behaved as beasts and humans did—sometimes aggressively and sometimes gently—but all of it harmful to humans who dared invite it into their beings. Once they did, it seeped into every crevice until they no longer knew themselves or anyone else.

The magic this woman had invited into herself wasn't aggressive enough for a rapid descent into madness. This was slower working, leaving her in her current state, but still sure to eventually bring her mind to complete chaos as it devoured her soul.

Ryla crouched before her to look for physical signs of the magic. The woman startled, inhaling sharply as if seeing for the first time. The pair locked eyes. A corona of gold around the pupils with streaks into the rest of the young woman's grey irises seemed to glitter in the sparse light. This was all the indication Ryla needed.

The woman's gold-turning eyes seemed to be searching Ryla's brown ones. "You've been touched, too…" It was barely a whisper.

Despite the nonsense of her words, Ryla sensed that the woman wasn't completely lost to madness. *It's not too late for this one.*

This close, the unstable magic reacted to Ryla. The hum grew louder, the haze shifting more quickly. Goosebumps raised across her skin under her attire, but her mental barriers continued to protect her. Repelling, the Keepers called it, and Killers like herself could be called to take care of it as needed.

Come, Ryla invited the magic to herself.

The magic's energy shifted, became a bit more aggressive although it wasn't the aggressive sort. It pushed against her senses to knead at her defenses and attempt to bore its way in. Despite its efforts, it couldn't touch her. In the process, it drew away from the woman, the haze leaving her behind.

The gold slowly receded from the woman's eyes, but Ryla didn't look away or move even as they returned to being wholly grey. A snap followed, like a lead on a horse breaking. It was a physically jarring sensation, but neither of them actually flinched. Rather, the woman's eyes rolled to the back of her head, and her body went limp as she lost consciousness. Ryla caught her before her head hit the ground, and she set her gently on the dirt floor before rising to her feet.

The space felt hollow as the magic's resonance dissipated into nature—nondescript and unthreatening.

Looks of amazement greeted her where the guard stood,

mouth agape, in the doorway. A younger girl, presumably Healer Dalam's apprentice, wore a similar expression but regained her composure more quickly when her master nudged her. The pair pushed past the guard to examine the woman.

Ryla stepped around the healers and then the guard as she passed through the doorway. With that magic gone, the chaos of the other magical essence was much more evident. She crossed to the door with just a few long strides, and the guard followed. Two metal bars barricaded this door, and the guard first touched them in brief taps with his gloved hands as if to see if they were hot before completely taking hold to lift them out of the way.

As he set down the second beam, Ryla instructed, "Stay out of the cell."

Anxiety crossed his features. "Of course, Esteemed Killer."

When the door opened and she stepped into the small room, Ryla wasn't the least bit surprised to see a pair of completely golden, wide eyes turn her direction. A thick haze of smoke lingered in the air. The antechamber's torch flames gave a hearty roar, and she heard the guard make a sound like a strangled gasp.

The shorter, gold-eyed man blinked a few times as his sight adjusted to the light from the open door, then stared her down with a wild expression and backed away. His hands pressed against the wall with his fingers splayed. His eyes darted repeatedly toward the open door. The torch fire flared again.

Ryla's silent beckoning to the magic met with burning resistance. Her eyes traced the man's body, and it was as though she could see gold flowing through his veins rather than as a haze hanging in the air. She drew her sword.

He is lost.

The gold-eyed man lunged forward with more speed than

a mere human should have. Ryla's reaction was mostly instinct as her elbow connected sharply with the side of his head. He hit the ground hard enough that the blackened dirt, which seemed more like ash, puffed up around his body. She flicked a glance at the guard, but the man didn't dare intervene; he'd taken several steps back, mouth agape once again.

A fiery glow and flash of heat within the cell drew Ryla's attention. The man hadn't moved, but a thin layer of flames covered his body as a shield. Strike now, and flames would chase up her sword and her arm; her uniform would protect her, but she wouldn't unnecessarily try to fight fire. The volatility of this common manifestation of magic was well known to her.

Its essence goaded her to attack. Even though it'd claimed a human and had refused her initial invite, she felt as it now reached to manipulate her, pushing hard against her mental barriers. Unlike with the woman, it wasn't breaking away from the man.

Another rush of flames roared from the antechamber. Ryla watched the man with unwavering patience, unaffected by the magic's attempt to break her. But, just because she was fine, it didn't mean the others would be.

Without shifting her gaze, she said, "Go to safety."

"How far should we go?" the guard asked from where he was planted.

"To the castle."

"Yes, Esteemed Killer."

Among the flicker of the torchlight, the guard collected the healer, his apprentice, and the woman she'd relieved of magic. Their retreat afforded them safety while Ryla's resolve kept her in danger's wake. Indeed, the roar of fiery magic grew more frequent and aggressive as she stood by the unconscious man.

It was the heat that pressed against Ryla's nape where

there was bare skin between the collar of her uniform and her hairline that told her the flames had spread from the torches to the rest of the antechamber.

A decision needed to be made: tangle with the fire protecting the man's body or test fate to see if he awoke before the flames burned her alive.

As the thought crossed her mind, the glow of the flame shield began to fade. Ryla adjusted the grip on her sword just slightly. Although the fire raged on in the antechamber, the flames disappeared fully from around his body when the Lost man shifted. His movements were slow, and he shook his head slightly.

"*Fanahray ehntehs oahcl.*" The words had barely left her lips as her blade arced.

CHAPTER

NINETEEN

L ate afternoon light diffused through the sheer white curtains strewn from the four poster frame of Adel's bed. Dust motes danced lazily through the air, never seeming to land no matter how much her tired eyes trailed their movements. She couldn't fathom why there were so many of them.

Where do they come from? her mind wandered.

It didn't truly matter. Just another day where she laid alone on her plush bed and missed her studies and other duties. She couldn't help it. She'd held herself together for the journey home from Nithle and even into the castle, but when she'd entered her room for the first time, her world collapsed and her body gave out.

Her mind conjured up images of Ashla everywhere, even now. Ashla, bounding over to the bed and flopping down on it. Ashla, sorting through Adel's wardrobe to find an acceptable outfit for the day, mock criticizing every garment just for fun. Ashla, patting the cushion on the seat beside the window so they could giggle about everything and nothing.

I shouldn't have asked to go for a walk after the privy. We could have returned to the square and been escorted to safety together. Maybe it wouldn't have even happened at all.

She could practically see it in her mind, how changing that one decision might have completely altered the course of events. She pictured herself stepping out of the privy and walking back toward the music. Or, maybe if she hadn't even gone to the privy in the first place, none of this would have happened.

I should have picked a different dress. The memory of the sash burning to nothing gouged her soul.

The princess's bedroom had never felt so vast and hollow. The same hollowness resounded through her heart and mind, though she felt tiny in the middle of her wide bed as she lay there with her hands clasped on her stomach and her feet together.

A knock sounded at her door—three short raps that she didn't bother answering. They could assume she was asleep for all she cared. There was a short pause before the raps sounded again.

"Princess, Her Highness has instructed I enter whether I have your permission or not," an older woman's voice called through the door.

Adel only vaguely recognized the voice as one of her mother's ladies and decided she didn't much care in the same instant. Let her come in and do whatever she needed to do or say whatever she needed to say.

Sure enough, the door clicked open and she entered. Adel glanced at the gentle-looking woman as she crossed the bedroom on the way to her wardrobe in the far corner to her right. The sun kissed the woman's features, adding a softness to her wrinkles that only emphasized her gentle appearance. Adel watched her a few moments as she rummaged through the closet.

Finally, she stepped away with a plain, russet-red gown. "The Queen has summoned you to see her in the library, Princess. And right away, so we best not dally."

The thought of protesting crossed her mind briefly, but

another glance at the maid's demeanor made Adel reconsider. *She could well carry me, and probably would if I refused to go of my own accord.* She'd seen this woman move a heavy trunk all on her own without so much as a grunt.

Reluctantly, she sat up, which was effort enough in itself with how heavy her body felt. Her mind felt fuzzy, reminding her that she hadn't eaten since breakfast, and even then she'd only picked at her plate as she'd sat at the table by the window. The plate of breakfast pastries was long gone, or else she might have grabbed one or two before getting changed.

"Come now, Princess," the woman urged, draping the dress across the bed to help her out of her sleepwear.

With help, Adel was changed and presentable fairly quickly. Then began the journey through the halls toward the library. The smile she plastered on her face, though small and polite, felt painful, and as much as she wanted to stare at the carpeting along the floor, she forced herself to glance about the halls as if nothing were the matter.

How can I smile when she'll never smile again?

She let the smile fall away.

The walk to the library was excruciating. Even spying a pair of servants laughing together brought an ache to her chest and reminded her she walked alone. Why couldn't that be her?

Because you picked the wrong dress. Because you had to go for a walk. Because you thought only of yourself.

Her self-berating thoughts followed like a spectre all the way to the library, where her mother's lady guided her in and then disappeared somewhere into the shelves to leave them be.

Her mother was nervous—that much Adel could tell from stiff way she sat on the settee. As much as she was wrapped in her own turmoil, Adel hadn't missed the changes in her mother's behaviour since returning from the festival. Despite how calmly Queen Mela had ridden in the carriage after the Harvest Festival, in time that followed, she kept the royal guard close to her family, often skipping her daily walks across the grounds, and having many long, quiet, discussions with her husband, the king.

Adel was sure if she glanced over her shoulder now, a pair of guards would be positioned somewhere nearby.

Of all the changes, the queen not going on her daily walks across the castle grounds was the most telling to Adel. Her mother loved to be outside, breathing in the fresh air and basking in the sun. In the summer, the flower gardens became a staple lounging spot for her. She'd take a book or even a sketchpad and sit for hours at a time.

Bitterness roiled in the princess's gut at the thought of how the dahems, even as far away as they were, had affected her mother. She hated that they'd made her mother feel unsafe in her own kingdom, and potentially even her own castle. She hated that worry painted her mother's expression more often than not.

Worry and bitterness fought in Adel's own heart as well. It had been three weeks since they'd left Nithle, and she still hadn't received a letter from Arran. Her father had received one from King Alden, but he hadn't shared with her what he'd written about.

All it meant was she had very little idea of how things had progressed in Nithle since her argument with Arran. The only certainty was that there hadn't been any announcement regarding their courtship.

That's not important right now. It was, but it wasn't. *People's lives are at risk.*

With every gnaw of her own worries about the dangers in Nithle, she reminded herself Killer Ryla was there and if something terrible had happened, all the kingdoms would've been notified of it. Surely, her parents wouldn't keep that kind of news from her, right?

Then why hasn't Arran written to me? The question tasted of sorrow and irritation.

Even the familiar smell of books neatly shelved in rows and rows throughout the room couldn't calm Adel's thoughts as she stood in the library's entryway, staring across the room to where her mother sat on the large settee. Although the queen turned the pages of the book, Adel wasn't sure she was actually reading.

As she crossed the room, Mela looked up from the book, and by the time she set it aside, Adel was settling onto the smaller settee across from her. The princess adjusted her textured skirts, wondering if she should speak first or not. Her mother had been the one to call on her, but Adel wasn't even sure where to begin. Should she make small talk? Ask how she was enjoying the book?

The queen inhaled, her chest and shoulders rising before seeming to deflate as she let the breath out. "How have you been coping?"

Adel bit the inside of her lip, and her brow furrowed. "Most days are still difficult," she started. "It's like a grey cloud that follows along throughout the day, and then sometimes it suddenly bursts into a storm."

Her mother nodded knowingly. "As time passes, the grief will lessen. I promise."

It wasn't the first time she'd been told that since Ashla's death, but Adel made no comment.

Deep breath in. Deep breath out.

She kept her hazel eyes on her mother's blue ones, sensing there was more the queen wanted to say.

Sure enough, Mela picked up the conversation again. "A new lady-in-waiting has been chosen for you. Her name is Megnata. She's receiving instruction as we speak and should be with you in the next week or so."

The news felt like a punch to the gut. Adel opened and closed her mouth a few times, trying to find words for one of the many thoughts suddenly flying through her mind. She landed on, "A week? So soon?"

Mela's features softened sympathetically. "I know, love. I know there's still so much time needed for healing. Don't worry, in her initial trials, Megnata did brilliantly. You've missed enough of your lessons and duties, and having someone help with your day-to-day tasks can ease your mind to make space to work through the grief. You'll see."

No. I don't want *a new lady-in-waiting,* Adel protested silently, thinking about how Ashla would encourage her to push back against something she didn't want to do. Just like she had regarding the announcement of the courtship. Rather than do that, though, Adel swallowed.

"Okay, Mother."

"There's my girl." Mela smiled gently, but it quickly fell away as the queen shifted in her seat and straightened her back. "There was one other thing I wanted to speak with you about. It's about Arran."

Before she could stop herself, Adel interjected. "Has something else happened?"

"No," the queen immediately answered with a shake of her head.

The too-long pause afterward did nothing to slow Adel's heart, and the sinking sense that another blow was on its way overtook her.

"But just because something else hasn't happened yet

doesn't mean it won't. Nithle has become too dangerous. If we're being honest with ourselves, it always has been. We became complacent in the war's dormancy," Mela prefaced. Again, she paused, but only briefly this time. "I think it's time to choose another suitor."

The air left Adel's lungs, her stomach instantly in knots as frigidness ran through her veins. A jumbled array of thoughts crowded her mind. She broke her gaze to stare at the patterned carpet, trying to compose herself and prevent the tears that stung her eyes from falling.

This can't be happening! Why now? Something more must have happened. What did that letter say?

When Mela spoke next, her voice continued on soft and gentle. "I know this is hard, Adel, but sometimes these sorts of decisions have to be made, even when we don't like them. Your safety is one of the most important things to me, and then we have to consider the safety of our people."

Without looking up from the carpet, Adel asked, "What does Father say about this?" Her voice sounded small even to her. She wasn't sure that she'd even spoken aloud until she heard her mother sigh.

"Your father thinks it's too soon to make any such decision. We have to still consider Heta's alliance to Nithle and our friendship with the royal family," Mela began. "But that's why I wanted to speak with you about this. You know the dangers that await Nithle now. You know what could happen to Arran—and to you—should you decide to keep this courtship going."

Adel hated this, feeling numb under the weight of it all. Silence droned between them as she wrestled inwardly, and her eyes traced the colourful swirls of the carpet's pattern as if they'd bring some clarity. They didn't.

She wished suddenly for some of Ashla's bravery and spunk, but all that answered when she tried to summon these traits within herself were tears. She remained silent.

Finally, Mela let out another soft breath. "Think about it, Adel. Think about what you're willing to risk and what you're willing to lose."

What kind of choice is that? Adel's mind latched tightly onto the words. *Disappoint and worry Mother or break my own heart.*

CHAPTER

TWENTY

Darkness greeted Ryla as her eyes flew open.

A Killer's senses were always alert, which was why even the slumber she'd fallen into that evening in her chambers hadn't been enough to block out the hum of magic vibrating through the castle walls. Distant as it was, she could feel it.

Dahems.

Beyond the magic, her senses extended. Voices, muted by the bedroom door; creatures scurrying about and calling into the night, outside the window. Goosebumps rose across her flesh as she discarded the soft blankets and pressed bare feet to the stone floor.

In one quick motion, her sword was free of its sheath, which clattered to the floor beside the bed, and she flew to the door. The guards in the hall jumped as she threw it open, training their weapons on her before realizing who she was, even out of her usual attire. On the small table near the wall, the game of stones they'd been playing was forgotten. One of the group of five opened their mouths to say something, but she cut in.

"Get the royals to safe holds. Dahems are in the castle." Her words were quick—urgent orders given without the accompanying tone.

One of the guards looked around, as if the dahems should somehow be right there. His gaze reconnected with hers.

"How many?"

"Unknown."

"Alert the rest of the guard," the one who spoke ordered two of the group. "We'll get the prince." He motioned to himself and the remainder of the gathering.

Ryla tore down the hallway before the guards even reached the prince's door. The carpet fibres were rough under her bare feet as she ran in her underclothes—short, skin-tight leggings and a sleeveless top. Not the usual protection her battle attire offered, but there was no time. Her focus was on getting to the dahems before they got anywhere near the royal family. Especially Prince Arran.

Her senses latched on to the magical essences, using them to guide her through the multitude of hallways. All dahems had a magical energy signature, even if they didn't wield a particular power. It was a part of what made magic safer for them to use. Usually, it was calm and even, but among the essences she felt around her then was one much stronger. Jarring. It pulled her forward through the royal wing, where tapestries of past kings, queens, and royal children watched her fly by.

When she reached the large double doors that barred the royal wing from the rest of the castle, she slowed, listening for any sounds beyond. She placed a bare hand against the polished wood before pushing it outward, met by more stunned and confused guards.

"What's happening?" one got out before she could say anything.

"Dahems. The royals are already being taken to safety. Help anyone else." She moved past them without waiting for a response.

The next corridor she entered was much quieter, with

sconces fewer and farther in between casting flickering light across her vision and shadows across the floors and décor. When she came to a spiral staircase, she descended quickly in pitch darkness, relying on the way her feet planted on each step and her hand ran along the wall rather than sight. She didn't encounter anyone else.

Commotion sounded as she reached the next floor; she paused a moment, pressing against the wall to keep to the staircase's shadows. Metal on metal *tinged* and screeched, but it was the loud crack that she would normally associate with a thunderstorm that snared her attention. And just like a storm, the brilliance of the lightning flashed, casting harsh shadows throughout the hallway and revealing the front entrance staircase.

The Killer's steps became more cautious as she approached, using the darkness as a shield while waiting for any further sign of attack. She heard voices speaking in the sharp dahem tongue at the base of the stairs, but they were too far for even her advanced hearing to discern the actual words. The sounds of boot steps tramping up the stairs sufficed to clue her into their next move.

Two dahems ascended the stairs, only pausing a moment at the top to decide that one would go one way and the other would go the opposite direction. After a silent breath, she charged forward, her sword at the ready.

They both turned to her at the same time, and it was the older of the two dahems that was quickest to act, drawing and throwing a dagger in her direction with trained precision. Reflexes sharpened through years of her own training kept the flying blade from finding home in Ryla's chest. Instead, she felt it slice across her right shoulder, followed by warm blood running down her skin.

Ignoring the sting of the wound, she met the younger dahem's fighting staff. As her sword collided against the length of the weapon, her eyes flicked up quickly to the curved blade at its end. She noted the dahem smiled slightly, following her gaze, and she used his distracted arrogance as an opportunity to push forward and knee him in the stomach, then hit him in the side of the head with the hilt of her sword as he doubled over. His limp form went down like a sack of grain.

She parried against the older dahem who came at her quickly with fighting daggers. With her single blade parrying his dual attack, her sights fixated on the dahem's movements. She could tell this was a much more tenured fighter in Lavanai's army, and he landed a few more hits that she diverted away from her vitals and to her arms. But his movements were all upper body.

Ryla swung hard, pushing the dahem back and sweeping his legs. He shouted something she didn't understand as he fell, but her sword pierced through him, silencing anything else he might say before his body even hit the ground. She turned to finish the younger dahem off.

Another dahem charged up the stairs when she rounded on the entrance, and she pushed herself forward despite the blood dripping to her feet. She ran her sword through him without slowing, gaining enough momentum to take the stairs a few at a time, and then pushing forward again to leap the rest of the way down to where bodies of the guards lay by the open castle doors.

As she landed, another group of dahems was turning into the moonlit entryway, likely drawn by the sound of the commotion.

They're all returning here, she noted from within a new fray of attacks.

As natural to her as breathing, she knew where she needed to strike and parry and when. Even needing to reassess and pivot her method came with barely a thought. With grace and speed, she matched and felled the dahems, the bodies collecting around her.

Suddenly, a charge of electricity built in the air again—a magic so strong that it set her senses on high alert. She swung a fist at the dahem in front of her to knock it back and jumped into the air.

Lightning spider-webbed across the castle floor and leapt up after her, ensnaring her despite her efforts to avoid it. A sharp shock flashed through her entire body and projected her backward. She landed hard, skidding across the floor before coming to a stop. Sparks flew before her eyes when she opened them.

"This is how they send Killers to us?"

She recognized the laughing voice, even before her vision cleared to see Naxela's tall form ambling toward her. She mentally laboured to regain control of herself, but her body was slow to respond. It felt like every nerve was firing off at the same time, the pain only registering as a hindrance to her efforts to get back on her feet and fight.

My sword, she thought through the daze. Luckily, it seemed to have slid along with her as she registered its cool, wet metal against her leg.

Her sight was the first sense to come back in full, letting her bear witness to the carnage around her. Added to the guards' bodies were those of the rest of the dahems. Frozen in eternity, the dahems' shocked expressions told her they'd been no more expecting Naxela's assault than she had. She looked away from their lifeless gazes to Naxela, whose attention was fixed on her collapsed form. Even though his mace crackled with lightning, it was his eyes that revealed the biggest threat. The purity of the amber colour pooling through his irises and flooding his pupils was molten.

Lost.

His essence was deeply distorted. She had to end this and quickly. A human lost to magic was one matter; a dahem lost to it was entirely another.

"Look at you. Pathetic," he spat, swinging the weapon around carelessly in his hand. "The almighty, all-powerful Ryla: a bloody mess on the ground, immobilized by a spark of lightning. And they say we should fear you. Ha! What reason would *I* have to fear *you*?"

Ryla took a discreet but deep breath.

"They'll thank me for ending you, so we can focus on our true mission," he continued, raising the mace with both hands to bring it down on her.

She snapped into action, nudging her sword to her hand with a swift movement of her leg and forcing her body to roll out of the way. Chunks of stone floor flew up around her as his mace impacted, and she shielded her eyes with her arms. Any debris that made contact with her body was ignored, and she quickly shoved herself to her feet.

The dahem commander's expression shifted to shock as she charged at him, but he recovered quickly and met her attack with his mace. Although the strike sent reverberations through her body, she turned her blade so it lay flat against the weapon, fitting between its spikes. She put her palm against the slick blade and pushed as hard as she could muster, sending him off balance, then continued after him again without a moment's hesitation. The charge of magical energy was already crackling through the air again.

Act fast. Ryla's thought was calm despite the dire need

for urgency. It was only a matter of time before the magic overtook Naxela's mind and soul completely.

Naxela regained his footing and swung the mace toward her. She leapt sideways, leaving it to connect with the stone floor once again. The distinctive snap of the handle and loud crack of the mace head splitting met her ears. As it did, her attention flew to Naxela's face.

She knew dahems used weapons as conduits to hone their magic. Naxela's clattered to pieces on the stone floor.

The moment had come more quickly than she'd expected. He practically radiated magic now, his eyes completely overtaken by the molten amber, and the electricity sparking to life around his body. His full attention turned to her, and she knew that one of them was about to die.

The thought hadn't even fully formed in Ryla's mind when she charged at him. The castle and room faded as her focus fixed on the dahem. Every subtle muscle twitch revealed itself to her, and she could read exactly where he was going to go and what he was going to do. With her sword in hand, she poured all thought and instinct into her next act. She swung first upward through his outreaching arms, then brought her sword back down on an angle, beheading him and silencing his screams among the spray of blood.

The current unleashed a rush of sparks through her again, and it was only her trained poise that kept her from staggering entirely. Her breath left her, and she stood perfectly still as she held her mental walls firm. The magic hovered around her as it dissipated, a slow process because of its strength and volatility. How long she stood there, she wasn't sure, but she kept her senses alert as she waited for the magic to return to nature.

When it finally had, she cleaned off her sword on a piece of cloth ripped from the clothes of a fallen body. Righting herself again, blood streaked from her hand to her hair as she pushed loose strands from her face. Her breath came in spurts as the after effects of the currents of electricity still surged through her limbs.

Regardless of the charge running through her, she made her way up the stairs to the castle's north corridor. It was comparatively bare to other hallways, a row of windows looking out onto the castle grounds below, whitewashed by the moonlight. Just as she suspected, she eventually came across an alert guard.

The woman's expression quickly shifted from shielded to alarmed. "Killer Ryla!" The woman rushed forward in her thick leathers, looping her bow around her back in an easy motion. She opened her mouth to continue, but Ryla cut her off.

"The dahems are gone. The royals are safe to come out," she said. She could tell the woman warred with wanting to do what she could to attend to her. "Go."

The guard started, then nodded. "Thank you, High Protector. I'll send for the healer as well."

"The healer can wait." Ryla side-stepped the guard to continue on her path.

"Where are you going?" the guard called after her.

She didn't bother to answer.

Ryla's shoulder left a bloody smudge on the polished surface of the High Chamber's door as she pushed through. The torch in her hand, one she'd taken from just outside the room, chased away the darkness, and she fixed it into a sconce just inside. Frigid air embraced her as the door closed her in. Her feet crossed more carpeting leading to the far wall by the platform where the Keepers had sat weeks before.

She made her way behind the chairs to that same compartment she'd accessed not so long ago. She propped her sword against the wall, then got to work retrieving the Cherrywood box and amulet. A simple touch to the cool surface, then she returned the box to its hiding place, took her sword by the hilt, and made her way to stand before the chairs.

As she shifted, she felt pulls on the clotting and drying blood in the wounds, reopening some of them. The night's injuries would join the array of scars decorating her skin.

It didn't take long for three Keepers to materialize before her. As usual, their hoods hid their faces, and the single light source of the sconce didn't do anything to illuminate them any further. She could tell, however, they were assessing her.

"What's happened?" the one in the centre asked without preamble.

"Lavanai Commander Naxela was overtaken by his magic. He brought a group, not to target the Nithlean royals, but to hunt me."

The realization had dawned on her the moment the dahems had all returned to the front entryway to face her, only to have it confirmed by Naxela during his ramblings. She was certain his words were truth even in his madness.

She could sense the Keepers' discomfort. Dahems looking to fight Killers was a non-event, and that was precisely where their unease stemmed from—that she'd felt the need to report it. Even though they tried to stay as poised as a Killer, they couldn't hide their emotions.

When they didn't say anything, she continued, "I recommend an extraction to bring Prince Arran to safety. As long as I am their target, my duty to him is compromised."

"We will discuss this," the middle Keeper cut in, his tone even and firm despite any uncertainty or unease he felt.

Ryla understood the reason without any of them having to explain. *To extract him now would imply abandoning the kingdom.*

As the kingdom's only heir, Arran's life was more important than even he seemed to understand. Extracting him would ensure his safety until Lavanai could be taken care of, but the Keepers also needed to ensure it wouldn't compromise Nithle's faith in their protection of the kingdom overall.

"Thank you for this information, Killer Ryla. Keep watch over the prince and send for us again should anything else transpire," the Keeper said.

A small surge of magic filled the air before the three disappeared as quickly as they'd come, leaving her with nothing more than the chill of the room and the blood drying on her skin.

CHAPTER
TWENTY-TWO

Arran's heart had just barely slowed after being awoken, told he needed to get to safety, and rushed through the castle's winding secret passageways to safety. Now it sped up anew, accompanied by chills rushing down his spine. The water in the basin beside the stool where Ryla sat in the infirmary was reddish with blood, as was the rag Healer Dalam wrung out. The excess water plopped and splashed into the basin before he brought it back to Ryla's skin, dabbing away at blood, some of which was her own, judging by the wounds littering her arms and legs.

And what are those marks? They looked like the lightning he'd seen splitting the sky on stormy nights. But this was on her skin, red and raw, as if etched into her flesh from her feet up toward her knees.

Arran had only seen her fight once, and with the way she'd moved and parried against the dahems then, he'd taken her for an untouchable, dangerous warrior. Sitting here in the infirmary having her wounds examined and tended to, she looked almost like any injured fighter. Just another woman who'd been caught in battle.

His attention flicked to Ley to gauge his reaction, but if his heart had also started beating a little faster, the knight hid it well. Still, when Arran took a few cautious steps forward, Ley didn't join him.

As his gaze made its way back to Ryla, Arran noticed a large scrape and most of the hits had landed on her right arm—her non-dominant one. Her long, loose hair was draped over her left shoulder and out of the way of the healer's work. Arran knew the Killer well enough by now to know that the vast lack of injuries to her left side had been intentional. Nothing she did was without intention.

"Are you all right?" It was a silly question to ask her, but the anxiety that fluttered in his chest compelled him.

"Of course," she replied.

He noticed she assessed him the way he assessed her. For a moment, he couldn't understand why. She was the injured one. He'd been taken to safety and hadn't so much as heard dahems crashing through the castle.

The memories. He'd mentioned his triggers to her over their private sessions, so she knew that she was one of them. Yet, they hadn't even whispered in his mind just then.

He gave a small shake of his head to signal to her that they weren't an issue. He wasn't sure why, but that'd be something to figure out later. For now, he focused on her, still taken aback by the sight of her wounds. Seeing her like this seemed a reminder of her humanity—that is, until he looked into her eyes, devoid of all emotion. It was enough to show that her being injured wasn't so much a sign of humanity. It was more a sign of her mortality.

"You're certain you're okay, High Protector? What is the extent of your wounds?" he asked.

She glanced at Healer Dalam, who took it as a cue to answer the question. "Most are superficial," he began, drawing Arran's attention. He wrung out the rag again, then set it aside to pick up some instruments. "One or two are deeper and will need to be stitched closed. Some burns and inflammation that will need salve. There'll also be bruising, but overall, nothing of too much concern. If I may, Killer Ryla?" He held up the instruments: surgical thread, a needle, and needle clamps.

Ryla nodded. "Proceed."

Arran had so many questions about what had happened, how she'd gotten these wounds, and how the dahems had gotten into the castle at all, but he held them back. Now wasn't the time—assuming she'd actually share the full details of the battle at all.

"I'm indebted to you. It's thanks to you that my parents and I got enough warning to hide."

"The dahems weren't after you."

"Pardon?" He noticed even Healer Dalam paused in his work for a fraction of a second at her words. *If not us, then who were they after?*

That direction of conversation was interrupted, however, as his mother and father entered the infirmary and came to stand beside him. He saw they wanted to ask after her wellbeing the same as he had, but they stopped themselves.

His father's mind seemed to pivot easily. "Killer Ryla, what need was there to go to the High Chambers?" Despite trying to keep his voice even, Arran picked up an edge of anxiety in the king's tone.

That was among Arran's questions as well. A guard had mentioned she'd gone that way, and Huth, who had been dispatched after her, had confirmed that he'd organized servants to clean up the blood. Arran's eyes wandered, wondering if Huth lingered in the room, and found him standing at the ready along a far wall with that same servant Arran had almost collided with the other morning. She held a tray with a pot and some mugs in front of her; Huth must have asked her to prepare some tea or cider.

"I had business to discuss with the Keepers," Ryla said plainly.

"Is there anything we should be concerned about?" Shron asked as she looked the young woman over, a suppressed grimace touching her features.

"No," she replied.

"Of course. Surely, you must have been reporting this attack," Alden reasoned. He sounded a bit like he was trying to convince himself even as he looked to his queen.

Arran's sight shifted to where Commander Calar and his Second, Royal Knight Kein, stood to the side of the room along with Ley. The three men quietly discussed something, but Ley nudged them, ever attuned to his prince. Arran motioned for them to come forward, which they did and stood to his side.

Arran returned his attention to Ryla. "Killer Ryla." When she looked at him, he continued. "How many dahems were there?"

Alden put out a hand to stay the conversation. "Son, this can wait until she's more comfortable."

Ryla ignored the king. "Twenty at most. Led by Commander Naxela."

The image of the dahem who'd thrown him the night of the festival flashed through his mind again. He hadn't known the dahem's identity at the time, but Ryla had named him during one of their sessions, along with Commander Mithos. Other memories from the night commenced their whispering.

The water basin being emptied, Arran identified silently. *It's Healer Dalam, who's just finished tending to Killer Ryla's wounds, which I can see are wrapped in white bandages. The Killer's mark is inked into Ryla's left hand.* The whispers turned to more indistinct murmurs, so he pressed on. "Why such a small number?"

"Naxela was consumed by his magic," she supplied. "Those with him were likely loyal to him, eager for bloodshed, or both."

Knight Kein spoke for the first time, his gravelly voice punctuating his words. "I didn't know dahems could become lost."

"All beings who invite magic run the risk," Ryla explained, then added, as if anticipating the next question, "They're all dead."

Arran nodded. *That must be why Naxela didn't come after me and my parents.* Naxela must have fixated on the Killer in his magic-induced madness and ordered the others to do the same.

"What about his followers? Were they magic users as well?" he asked.

"No," Ryla replied.

He ran over these details in his head.

Calar thought aloud. "With Bunthle's destruction, I wouldn't doubt that a group that small could have passed around Lake Pol without being noticed. They may have even bypassed Thlent all together."

Arran nodded again, "I thought the same. I'd like to get confirmation though to make sure our people are safe. And a clearer idea of how they got into the castle at all."

"We'll send messengers first thing in the morning, Your Highness," Kein agreed with a firm nod that sent his longer, black hair tumbling around his high cheekbones.

An idea suddenly overcame Arran. "I'd like to go myself. I can check in on Thlent and then go to Bunthle to assess the situation firsthand."

Alden's stern voice interrupted. "Absolutely not."

Arran had almost forgotten his parents were there but turned to his father now. Concern unlike he'd ever seen was the most evident in the king's eyes and the way he held his body—rigid, but suggesting he wanted to act. When had he become so fearful? His mother's features held similar tension, brows drawn above her wide eyes.

"I'll have Killer Ryla and my escort with me," Arran reasoned. "It's my duty to ensure our defences are sound, and this will allow me to do that. I'll collect my information and then report back to you so we can discuss our next course of action."

Arran glanced at Ryla to see what she thought about it. Even as she connected with his gaze, however, she said nothing. She stood silently in the torchlight, the basin, stool, and Healer Dalam gone.

Another thought occurred to him. "And when we do return, I'd like to recommence my weapons training." He turned back to Calar and Kein. "Arrange something with the weapons master for me."

"It'll be done, Sire," Calar said with an affirmative nod.

"I should learn to properly protect myself," Arran continued as if needing to justify this sudden desire when he'd skirted his lessons in the past. "Killer Ryla won't always be around. I can't always rely on other people. I should at least know enough to get away or keep myself safe until others arrive."

"It's not a bad idea, Your Highness," Kein agreed. "I'm sure Ley can oversee the training."

"It'd be my pleasure." Ley nodded.

It was his father that Arran watched closely since he'd have the final say in the matter. He half wished Ryla would use her authority to help convince the king, but this had no bearing on her. Whether he got a grasp on weapons training or not, she would pursue her duty.

The king scratched at his stubbled jaw. "I will agree to the weapon's training," he ceded. "Speak with Veena to set it up."

"Yes, Your Highness," Calar said with a nod.

The king continued on, "As for venturing to Bunthle, a field knight will be suitable."

"Father, it's more important than ever that we show up for our people. In person. That'll truly demonstrate we're there to protect them and concerned after their wellbeing," Arran tried to reason.

"It's also more dangerous than ever for us. In order for us to protect our people, we need to be alive," Alden retorted.

"Killer Ryla will be with me. I can take as many guards as you like," Arran repeated in an effort to plead his case.

"No, Son. This is not up for discussion." With that, the king turned on his heel and left the infirmary. Knight Calar followed closely behind him.

The prince turned his attention to his mother, but Shron gave him a sympathetic look and shook her head. She closed the gap between them and placed her hands on his forearms where they hung at his sides.

"Listen to your father this time, dearest," she said softly. "Sending you to Bunthle would be walking you right toward the danger all of us, including the Union, are trying to protect you from."

Arran opened his mouth to say something more, but as he searched his mother's grey eyes, he saw all the love and concern she had for her only son. This was a lost battle. He set his jaw, let out a sigh, and nodded in defeat.

TWENTY-THREE

A rran felt more than a little conspicuous in his rich navy cloak, but it was the carriage he rode in and his surrounding entourage that really set him apart as they made their way through Nithle Proper later that morning. Killer Ryla sat across from him, once again in her full attire. Anyone would be hard pressed to know what had happened during the night as she gave no sign of any pain, even when a wheel hit an uneven part in the road.

Likewise, the village seemed to be getting on just fine, as he discovered from the few stops they'd made to question the people. No matter who was asked about how things were faring or if there were any concerns in the recent weeks, the response was always the same: nothing to report.

The people of Nithle Proper happily shared how it was nice to get back to normal even amidst repairs and rebuilds where the magical fire had scorched buildings and more guards milling about. Nithleans felt protected by the measures being taken.

They're none the wiser, he discovered as they wended their way down the bustling streets. *Good.*

A voice calling out from the crowd pulled Arran from his thoughts. "High Protector!"

Arran glanced Ryla's direction to see her looking out the window. When she didn't say anything and the voice called out again, he asked, "What is it? Is it safe?"

"Unclear," the Killer replied.

"Your Highness! Please, stop! I beg of you," the voice called again.

Arran leaned to the window himself now and saw a man trailing after his slow-moving carriage. He wondered what this middle-aged man wrapped in scarves and a heavy-looking coat would want with Ryla. Or even himself.

"Stop the carriage," Arran called out the window and the vehicle rolled to a halt while the guard instantly closed in around it. "Find out what the man wants."

"Of course, Your Highness," a knight said before dismounting to stride toward the man with another in step beside him.

The man's dirtied hands were clasped before him as he spoke with the knights. Arran thought he looked harmless enough, but he didn't recognize the man and given the calm state of the city in general, it was odd to have someone chase after them.

A crowd started to gather as the knights spoke with the man. The smell of horse and leathers pressed against the carriage as Ley drew his mount close to the window.

Keeping his voice low enough for Arran to hear, he offered, "We can tell him to request audience at the castle, Your Highness."

"Perhaps," Arran replied. "It looks like we may have word of what he wants, though."

One of the two knights that spoke to the man returned. "He says he has business with the High Protector. He'd like to thank her for helping his daughter."

That didn't give him much to work with, and Arran's brow furrowed as he looked again to Ryla. He was surprised to see her move from her seat toward the carriage door, which she opened herself before stepping out.

Trusting he was well protected, Arran let his curiosity lead him after her.

"Bring the man forward," Ryla instructed from where she stood perfectly still in the roadway as few steps away from the vehicle.

"Yes, High Protector."

Apart from whispers in the crowd, no one said anything as the man eagerly followed the knights. Getting a better look at him now, Arran pegged him as a farmer from his build and the dirtied boots that accompanied his dirtied hands. Probably from Thlent.

The man's gaze was reverent as he laid eyes on Ryla. "Thank you, High Protector! I travelled all this way to seek audience with most especially you, High Protector." He sank to one knee, head bowed. "You have my deepest gratitude. I am forever in your debt."

"You said Killer Ryla helped your daughter?" Arran asked, not unkindly.

"Yes, My Prince!" the man said without looking up. "The High Protector has brought my daughter back to me. I thought we had lost her forever to the magic, but our Esteemed Killer has brought her back!"

The words were piecing themselves together in Arran's head as another voice broke through the crowd.

"Father!"

A young woman now stood where the guard had originally blockaded the man, and the resemblance between the two of them was immediately apparent. From the heart shapes of their faces to the grey colours of their eyes to the turn of their mouths, they were practically gendered mirrors of one another. Her expression showed concern as she watched the display, and Arran nodded to the same knights as before, who went to retrieve her.

Her hurried steps brought her to them in what seemed only to be a few paces, and she curtseyed low in her plain, russet dress before crouching beside her father.

"Please forgive my father," she said, staring up at the royal and the Killer. "He just wanted so very much to thank you in person, High Protector. I must apologize for myself as well, for although I know you helped me, I don't much remember it."

"You dispelled magic from this woman," Arran said, stating more than asking and shifting his attention to Ryla.

"Yes." Her eyes swept across the same woman.

Something close to reverence struck Arran now, too. He couldn't quite put his finger on it, but he stared a moment longer just the same. Ryla looked no different as she stood among his people in the charcoal-coloured fabrics of her apparel, her long dark hair customarily tied back, brown eyes and facial expression as devoid of emotion as ever. Yet, something had shifted.

He broke his eyes away and turned his attention to the father and daughter before them. "Please rise," he said.

The daughter nodded, then helped her father as they both got to their feet. She held her father's hands in both of hers, as if she worried he might sink to a knee again.

"I, too, am grateful for Killer Ryla," Arran said, addressing the pair. "Her ability to help us, the people of Nithle, is unmatched. We are blessed to have her."

The man nodded vigorously. "Yes, My Prince. We are very, very blessed."

Arran took a step back, turning to address the crowd now. "Take heart, my people. The Union is with us."

Hope shone with the morning sun in that moment among the smattering of applause, cheers, and chatter that came to life at his words.

As they climbed back into the carriage and continued on their way, his thoughts hung on the idea of dispelling the magic. He wondered how it worked at its core. Of course, the basics of it were general knowledge—a Killer could push the magic from an individual, breaking the connection between it and its host. But the details of it were Union secrets. He didn't even bother to ask Ryla, knowing that she wouldn't respond.

If only we could dispel magic from dahems, he thought. Given their natural affinity to magic, however, it was generally assumed impossible. Not to mention the Union would have already taken that step if things were that simple.

As much as his excursion into Nithle Proper was giving him peace of mind that his people were safe and taken care of, he highly doubted that this was Ryla's purpose in taking him away from the protective castle walls. He doubted even more that she was suddenly going against the king's and queen's wishes for him to not go to Bunthle or even Thlent. Whatever her plan, the Killer hadn't revealed anything.

Ryla didn't speak again until the carriage rolled to another stop. She once again let herself out, but this time, waited at the door, watching him where he sat within. "Come this way."

The prince's eyes darted to her and then around them. "What's happening?"

"A lesson." Ryla waited for him to follow.

Anxiety bubbled in his gut. A lesson? Right here in the middle of Nithle Proper? Where everyone might see him come apart at the seams? That was exactly what he'd wanted to avoid.

Still, as he stared at Ryla, he knew he should trust her. She'd been nothing but helpful to this point. He took a deep breath, nodded, then shuffled along his seat to exit the carriage and follow her. The guard shifted around him without question.

He glanced around to situate himself, but rather than buildings, all he saw at first were watchful eyes. It felt like onlookers saw right through him and knew exactly what was going on.

Impossible, he chided himself. Besides Ryla, the only other person he'd mentioned his struggles to was Ley, and Ley was no gossip.

Tearing himself out of self-consciousness, Arran barely realized where Ryla had gotten them to stop before it was too late. He drew himself to a sharp stop as she halted in the city square and turned expectantly toward him. With the people milling about, he could clearly hear and see that this wasn't the night of the attack during the festival, but he couldn't bring himself to step forward. Irrationally, he worried that stepping forward would be stepping into that past moment directly.

Ryla's gaze shifted to Arran's right, where Ley stood, and the knight strode toward her. He saw their mouths moving but couldn't make out any of what they were saying among the sounds of the city or the chaos brewing in his mind. Even his eyes refused to focus well enough to read their lips. Whatever it was they said, Ley strode back toward him moments later.

The knight paused, resting a hand on Arran's shoulder and giving it a gentle squeeze. "You can do this, Arran."

He didn't have a chance to say anything in return; the knight moved on to convey some message to the rest of the guard.

Surveying the crowd, the prince could already see some of his people stop what they were doing to watch. Most had enough decency to look away when his gaze made its way to them, but a few held their open curiosity and waited for whatever was about to happen.

Arran looked to Ryla with a silent plea. *Not now. Not here.*

The way she continued to stare at him with her emotionless gaze seemed to hold a response. *Now. Here.*

He started and shook himself mentally. She couldn't read minds, and speaking with only thoughts wasn't possible, even with magic. Still, the conversation seemed to go on.

I can't do this.

You can. You must.

The cold air felt colder as Arran broke the stare to look up to the sky—the *pale* sky, the *cloudless* and *blue* sky of a fall day approaching winter. He steeled himself and brought his eyes back down to Ley this time. The knight waited patiently in his protective leathers and heavy cloak. An almost imperceptible nod and his dark gaze silently encouraged Arran again.

When Arran moved next, it was toward Ryla. The guard moved with him, some dispersing into the crowd, but allowing everyone to go about their business so long as they gave the prince and the Killer berth. He vaguely wondered what Ley had told them was happening. Then, he was standing before Ryla, almost eye to eye.

She wasted no time. "This is where you fell and nearly died."

The words hit him like a brick, eyebrows shooting up and his breath stopping in his chest. He dared glance around and found what she said to be true, the sights of the city's square around him now fading in and out with the sights of that night. A building off to his right, bricks bright with the sunlight, flashed to darkened shadows; chatter around him, light and casual, faded to dark, aggressive, fearful. A crack of thunder and flash of lightning—the blood of one of his people splattered across the ground because of his hesitation. Bile rose in his throat.

Connecting back to Ryla's gaze, he felt he wasn't seeing her at eye level, but looking up at her from the ground, trying to avoid being trampled as blood soaked into his clothes. The metallic smell of blood slammed into his nose. The dahem commander's voice began whispering into his thoughts.

"This will be one of the greatest challenges," Ryla of the present said, although Ryla of his memory remained unchanged, frozen instead at the first time he'd seen her. "Use the strategies I've taught you. Keep yourself here. Keep the memories away."

Her words were a lifeline he daren't let go of. *Keep yourself here*, he repeated to himself.

Being in the square again made his usual go-to choices difficult to use. The ground underneath was the same as that night, the positioning probably exactly the same as he didn't doubt her precision, people all about... The blue sky and the fact that people were walking instead of being held under threat of dahems wasn't enough. It was too raw here. Too real.

He could practically see Naxela swinging his mace at him and flinched, arms moving to protect himself from the vision.

"Naxela is dead," present Ryla's voice cut in again.

How she always understood where his mind was, he didn't know. Still, he forced his arms down to his sides, closing his hands into fists. He'd have to try something else. What was another strategy? It was hard to pull them out among the jumble of his thoughts and feelings, but one came forward.

I am Prince Arran of Nithle, he began. *I am seventeen years old. It is nearing noon. My guards, Ley, and I are in Nithle Proper standing freely. Killer Ryla stands before me, guiding me through fighting my memories. She killed Lavanai Commander Naxela, and I am safe from him.*

Still, his vision and mind fought him.

"It's not working," he lamented through gritted teeth. Even the bite of his nails into his palms wasn't doing anything to bring him out of it.

"What do you see?" Ryla asked.

It felt difficult to put to words, but he tried. "It's a battle between the memory and the present world. One moment, I see, hear, feel, even smell one, and the next moment, it'll be the other."

"Then it is, in fact, working."

Arran brought his gaze to hers again, studying her blank face as if it would reveal something to him. It didn't.

She continued, "Not too long ago, the memories reigned in these moments. Now, you can call the present into focus."

"But it won't *stay* in focus," Arran protested, trying to keep his voice low and his frustration from getting the better of him under so many scrutinizing eyes. His own stung with unshed tears.

"No. But this wasn't meant for you to conquer this place in one lesson. The memories are loudest and strongest here. It will take time. Repeated efforts. Do you understand?"

It was little comfort, but he nodded. He wanted to be rid of the fear that hummed through his body as he stood in the square. To be able to walk through life without these memories plaguing him.

"The lesson is over," she said.

Exhaustion fought with tension in Arran's body as they made their way back to the carriage. While his emotions were fried, the memories from the festival were still close, keeping his mind and body too alert. He rolled his shoulders as he climbed into the carriage first and settled back into his seat. Leaning his head back, he ran a hand through his curly hair and took several cleansing breaths.

"Protect the prince. Get him to the castle," Ryla said suddenly to, he assumed, Ley, and the distinct sound of the sword leaving its sheath followed.

His eyes flew open with a shot of panic.

CHAPTER

TWENTY-FOUR

B right grey melted to a brilliant shade of amber.
Concealment magic. Ryla had never seen this kind of
magic—it was said to have died out ages ago—but it was the
only explanation she could come up with for how an amber
pair of eyes had gone unnoticed by the Nithle people. More
importantly, how they'd gone unnoticed by her.

As much as she'd been focused on the prince, she'd kept her
senses and her sights on the crowd. She'd seen this man's face
in the masses gathered near the carriage, and he'd seemed as
human as the rest of them with his dark hair, soft features, and
lean build. Then, as they returned the carriage, she caught it.

The magic, a whisper on the air, suppressed. Subtle,
controlled. Powerful.

She'd barely sensed it at all. Had the dahem not been as
close as he was, Ryla was certain he would have gone unnoticed
among the crowd of onlookers.

A breath later, and she was in pursuit, sword drawn and
ready to strike. The dahem reacted with a jerk, grabbed a
woman nearby and shoved her toward Ryla. Dodging the
woman was a fluid motion—one step to the left, a slight twist
of her body to avoid the screaming, stumbling human, and
a hard push off against the stone of the street. The dahem
peeled through Nithle Proper's roads to get away.

Shrieks and shouts erupted around her as people jumped

out of the way and fled toward the buildings to escape from the commotion. Knights moved in to clear people away and form a barricade.

Abandoning any human behavioural pretence, the dahem used a burst of speed to crash through the human barrier. Ryla followed closely after him, leaping over fallen guards and knights to continue her chase.

The whistle of an arrow flying through the air snared her attention, and she ducked and slid across the ground as it streaked overhead and lodged itself in the dahem's thigh. Pushing herself up and back into a run, Ryla saw the dahem stumble ahead, but the arrow didn't otherwise seem to be affecting him. Still, she seized the opportunity to gain ground.

He rounded on her, the snap meeting her ears as he broke the shaft off the arrow and swung to stab her with it. She knocked his arm away with her right hand, then closed the distance between them, her face only inches from his as she drove her sword through his gut. He grunted and sputtered but still had enough strength despite his slim form to shove her back.

The force of it set her off balance. As she adjusted to regain her footing, the injured dahem propelled himself forward and landed a blow on her jaw. Wood cracked and snapped under Ryla's body crashing into a wagon behind her. Its frame jammed into her ribs and knocked the air from her lungs.

The dahem sprinted away while she regained her breath and got to her feet, then re-established her pursuit. The myriad of tall buildings was a blur at the speed they were going. Even the trail of blood the dahem left along the dirt and stones was nothing more than a streak in her periphery.

When the terrain below Ryla's feet changed from the city roadway to the rural dirt and gravel of Thlent, she saw the dahem snatch a lead from a nearby farmer and hoist himself in one fluid motion onto the horse's back. As the woman wearing farming trousers and a tunic fell to the ground with a scream, the dahem fought to control the horse for only a moment or two before he managed to rangle it into running submission. Ryla brought herself to a halt; she could not compete with the speed of a galloping horse. A few others, she guessed city guards, rushed to the fallen woman's aid.

With no scrap of cloth to wipe her sword, Ryla used her glove to clear away the blood coating the metal before sheathing the weapon. Eyes never leaving Thlent's fields, she then pulled off a glove and undid her jacket, her abdomen muscles clenching in protest against the cold air. A twinge from where she'd made impact with the wagon flared briefly.

She breathed in deep as she pressed and felt along her ribs. As far as she could tell from the tender points under her fingertips, the only damage would be bruising. She'd have to check her other wounds later to see if any had reopened.

By the time she returned to the castle, the shifting sun blanketed the guards outside its doors and down the stairs in shadow. Their forms sagged when they saw her, tension bleeding away like the dahem's blood had spilled to the ground. None asked questions as they parted for her to make way up the steps and push through the doors.

"Ryla!"

Relief painted Prince Arran's tone. He scrambled to his feet from where he'd been sitting on the stairs, blue eyes taking her in from head to toe in his approach. Still wrapped in his cloak, the navy fabric billowed behind him with his quick movements.

Knight Ley was only a step or two behind as he flexed his hand and dropped it from the hilt of his sword. "High

Protector, has the danger passed?"

"Yes," she replied. "He'll soon be dead."

"Why was that person a threat?" the knight continued his line of questioning.

"That was a dahem," she said and watched the pair don matching horrified expressions. "It was using a magic that conceal its eyes and suppress its essence. The magic is supposed to have died out."

"A dahem!" Arran made an effort to keep his voice low, but his words seemed to reverberate off the high ceilings and walls in the otherwise empty entryway. Apart from the three of them, there were only guards lining the wall and no one else. "How didn't you notice it earlier? Was it because of my lesson?"

Ryla shook her head just slightly. "It's a powerful magic. Usually, a magical presence extends further, and I can sense it at a greater distance. This kind of magic prevents that." The look that crossed Arran's face told her that he wasn't quite convinced, but she didn't have time to pacify him. She turned instead to Ley, "Have the guards find anyone who knew him, how long he was here, and what he was told. They saw him, so they should be able to describe him."

"Of course," Ley nodded. "Will you be questioning him while he's still alive? You said he'll be dead soon, but I'm assuming he's been captured?"

"He fled on horseback into Thlent, and he'll be making his way to Lavanai," she replied. "Even if he lives, he's been discovered and won't be foolish enough to return."

"Could there be more with that magic?" the knight asked next.

"I can't say for certain." Once, she would have said unlikely. There'd been no record of this kind of magic in a long time, but she couldn't rule this out as being the first sign of a resurgence of it and a new strategy by the dahems to get close to their targets.

The prince, who'd been watching the exchange silently to that point, chimed in. "Search the city. I'd say be discreet about it, but after this display, it won't be long before rumours fly."

"We'll have to make quick work of it," Ley agreed. "I'll see to it, Your Highness." He stepped away from them.

"In just a short time, you've destroyed any notion I had that Killers were untouchable."

Ryla shifted her sights from the knight's retreating form to Arran. She had no response to that, but she sensed the prince had more to say.

"First, you're bloodied and even burned. Now, I see a bruise forming along your jaw," he explained, gesturing toward what she assumed was the mark.

There was a minor throb where the dahem had struck her, but she didn't acknowledge it otherwise. It was superficial. "Killers have never been untouchable. We're trained to know where it's safe to get hit and how to manage the injuries."

"So you do feel pain." He titled his head slightly, eyes alight with interest.

"Not in the way you understand it, but yes. Without pain, we could be injured and never know it. We have to feel and understand pain to survive."

He seemed to consider her words, staring again at the mark on her face. She'd learned over her weeks watching over the young man that it was in his nature to try to understand everything. Even something as enigmatic as a Killer.

CHAPTER

TWENTY-FIVE

His blocks were clumsy. Arran could feel the rushing reverberations of the impact of the sword meeting his dueling daggers through his arms and into his core. It was one of the things he hated most about close combat—no matter how many times he practiced and regardless of which weapon he tried to use, he couldn't seem to get used to the feeling of his body vibrating. He tried to shift his grip to get a better feel for the daggers with their simple, leather-wrapped handles, but the effort only caused the blades to slip.

Luckily for him, Veena was highly skilled and had already anticipated he'd do this; the combat master shifted her weight to take a step back and withdraw the weight of her sword. Then she stood waiting for him to reset. She wasn't a patient woman, nor was she good at hiding that impatience, but she did her best to rein in pushing and scolding Nithle's only heir. Sometimes he wondered if he'd have better success at mastering her teachings if she didn't.

Her irritation invited disappointment within himself. This had been his idea, and he felt he had something to prove.

"Again," Veena commanded, the muscles on her arms and legs flexing under the leathers she wore.

They repeated the exercise several more times. It should have been simple—that much he knew—but he just couldn't seem to get the correct maneuvers. His less-dominant arm was slower and felt awkward as he twisted his wrist to get back into position. Even his dominant arm couldn't quite seem to get the flow of the movements. And then there were his feet, slipping on the gravel that made up part of the training area in an enclosure near the knights' quarters.

He'd gotten a decent grasp on archery and wasn't too bad with throwing daggers when we he was standing still, but he needed to at least gain some proficiency of close-range and movement-based fighting. He'd tried a number of weapons, even something as eccentric as the lone halberd that hung on the wall, but his body just didn't seem to have the coordination to make any of it work.

There was one blessing: so far the memories had been quiet despite the activity. He wasn't sure why but also wasn't about to argue it.

Still, he was frustrated, and those frustrations led to a few lucky forceful blows.

"Enough." Veena stepped back. With her long, light-coloured hair pulled back out of her face, the severity of her expression on her sharp features was crystal clear: She wasn't happy at all. "You need to focus! Do you think, if you're going to let your mind wander, you'll be able to defend yourself or your people? Do you think *she* lets her mind wander even for a second?"

She was pointing pretty aggressively at Ryla, who didn't so much as blink in response. If anything, he thought that Ryla probably agreed about the need to focus. Unlike Veena, however, he knew she wouldn't make the comparison between their fighting skills. In fact, she would discourage it.

"I'm not a Killer," he countered in annoyance, wiping sweat from his brow. He didn't even much care if he sounded a bit petulant. It would have at least been fairer, if only marginally, to compare him to Ley, who was observing the whole thing while leaning against a railing beside Ryla.

Veena's expression said it all: a verbal lashing was moments from being unleashed. He thought it ironic that he had two ends of the spectrum in the room watching him—one whose emotions were as easy to read as the winds and the other who didn't display any emotion at all. He wasn't sure which he preferred in that moment.

Whatever the full extent of the lashing was, Arran never found out. Instead, Veena snapped, "We'll pick this up later. And I expect you to be more prepared and focused next time." She held her hand out to take the daggers, jerking them away pretty harshly, and then spun on her heel to return them to where they belonged.

The prince sighed, suppressing a sudden pang of shame and trying not to let her wrath crawl under his skin. Shaking it was difficult, even while he undid and removed the leather bracers from his arms as he walked toward the storage cupboard. The smell of leather and wood practically assaulted him as he opened the double doors.

In his annoyance, he tossed the cuffs in haphazardly. "I'm a strategist, not a fighter," he mumbled to himself, next pulling the vest over his head and running a hand through his curls. They poked about haphazardly from the sweat.

"There's a role for each of us in war, Your Highness," Ley said from where he now stood beside his prince.

Arran glanced at him, noting the sincerity in the man's dark gaze. He sighed. "It's just frustrating when everyone expects me to be everything."

"The nature of your station, unfortunately," Ley noted with a lopsided, sympathetic smile. "Don't push yourself too hard, Arran. The skills will come with practice. We have to play to our strengths and realize there's no shame in relying on others to help us."

"Rely on others," Arran echoed distantly thinking of the letters his father had written to their allies in Heta, Piridet, and Veloth.

Ryla advising against attacking Lavanai head on had held them in their defensive positions, and strengthening their numbers was key. The Union's decree from their initial meeting had resulted in a number of new recruits who were already in training, but Arran knew his father worried it wasn't enough, and he couldn't blame him.

Seeking help from Veloth had been a bit of a shot in the dark given King Hadden's contentment with keeping to himself, but that there'd been no agreement to help yet from Heta and Piridet was troubling.

There must be something I can do. That dahem has caused unrest in Nithle Proper, Arran thought.

King Alden had ordered the city combed for other dahems possessing this magic. Short of having Ryla literally look at and be near every single person, Arran wasn't quite sure how effective their search was going to be. So far, the king had ordered that people be spoken to on an individual basis to see if there'd been anyone behaving suspiciously or even new people visiting the village. Any suspicious persons would be brought before Ryla for observation. Asking people to inform on each other left Arran with a feeling of unease. But right now, there seemed no other way to go about it.

The prince sighed heavily, closing the cupboard doors with a thud and wishing there were something more he could do for his people.

CHAPTER

TWENTY-SIX

Arran felt out of place sitting in the Assembly Chambers with only Ryla, Ley, and a smattering of royal guard lining the high walls. What sun did stream through the windows seemed to highlight the empty chairs beside him, where the king and queen would normally be seated. Instead, the cushioned chairs with stags carved into the tall, wooden backs were empty. His parents had been called away for other matters Arran wasn't privy to, but whatever they were, they took priority over convening with Lord Robyr of Wendur.

Despite the Union's order, Wendur hadn't sent any fighters or provided any resources to help Nithle's cause. The lord's son's conduct and potential treason, which Arran had mentioned to his father when he'd learned of the assembly, were also up for discussion. While he hadn't expected to have to take on both points of conversation himself, Arran was determined to have this meeting run smoothly.

You can do this, he told himself. It was a chance to prove he could at least do *something* with his position.

The doors creaked open to reveal an announcer. His chest expanded as he inhaled, then called across the expanse of the room with a booming voice. "Lord Davi of Wendur, Your Highness."

The prince blinked, brows furrowing. He turned a fraction in his chair to glance to where Ley stood to his left. His royal knight wore a similar expression for only a moment before giving an almost imperceptible shrug and then schooling his features.

"Admit him," Arran called back after a moment and the announcer bowed before disappearing through the doors again.

The young man strode into the room moments later, head held high and dressed in a long, dark jacket, belted at the waist, and equally dark trousers and footwear. His characteristically dishevelled hair had been combed neatly out of his face, leaving his light eyes appearing sharper than Arran has ever seen them.

The detail that struck him the most, however, was the embroidered galloping horse on the young lord's lapel rather than Nithle's stag. *Wendur's royal crest.* Arran hoped he was successful in keeping the surprise from his face.

"Lord Davi," he greeted over the clacking sound the young man's footwear made on the stone in his approach. "I had expected your father. I trust all is well with him?"

Davi's tone was cool, a small smile touching the corner of his mouth when he stopped and stood before where Arran sat. "He is, but he's entrusted me to convene and speak on his behalf."

Arran's jaw tightened, an uneasy feeling settling in his gut. *What possible reason is there to not attend an assembly with the king yourself?* He didn't want to jump to conclusions. Maybe Lord Robyr had also been called away on some matter, like the king had. Still, what could possibly trump meeting with the king and royal family if he was otherwise well?

The prince tried to swallow away his unease and tension, instead saying, "It seems he's preparing you for taking over as lord."

"That's right. The old man figures he won't live forever, so he may as well let me get started now." His reply was lighter this time, more conversational. His gaze flicked to Ryla. "High Protector." He bowed. "I hadn't expected you to concern yourself with such matters."

Arran peered over his right shoulder and up at her where she stood a pace or two away with her hand resting casually on the hilt of her sword. He spied the subtle shifts of her eyes as she took in the young lord but said nothing.

Arran offered an explanation. "She's my Union-appointed guardian. She goes where I go."

Davi's mouth quirked down this time, and he shifted on his feet. "I just want to ensure we're on even footing, and you're not going to use your human weapon to further attempt to strong arm Wendur into anything."

Tension bloomed anew within Arran. "Strong arm Wendur? Lord Davi, you do understand Wendur has an allegiance to Nithle regardless of the Union, correct?"

"Yes, yes. Wonderful Nithle came and rescued poor, broken Wendur after the kingdom fell. I've heard the stories. Been fed them since I was a child," Davi continued dismissively and even rolled his eyes. "Times have changed, Arran. A breach of the castle doors? A dahem spy in Nithle Proper? What makes you think you can protect any of us anymore? Especially since both of these incidents happened *after* her arrival." He gestured flippantly at Ryla. "You couldn't protect Bunthle. What's to say you can protect Wendur?"

"That's enough, Davi," Arran bit out, gritting his teeth. *How is this derailing so quickly?* His hands balled into fists on the arms of the chair, and he made a conscious effort to sit up and also lean forward. "These are trying times, but Nithle will uphold its duty to Wendur."

"By forcing us to fight in this battle? Give up our people to fight Lavanai?" Davi continued, eyes narrowing a fraction.

"When a kingdom goes to war, that means the whole kingdom stands together," Arran countered.

"Does it though?" The lord relaxed his posture just enough to run a hand through his hair before letting it fall back to his side. "The dahems are after you. Your family. Why should that implicate the rest of us? Hell, even the Union has put the Killer at *your* side."

"And I would be dead if they had not," countered Arran, relieved to find some firm ground to stand on. "Killer Ryla has protected Nithle and its people more than once since her arrival. I owe her and the Union my life."

A derisive chuckle left Lord Davi as he shook his head, eyeing Arran with a strange expression. "Perhaps the rumours are true after all."

Arran inhaled in an effort to keep himself calm. "What rumours might those be?"

"Please. You can't tell me you haven't heard them." Davi waited, but then his smile fell when Arran said nothing. "Come now. The fight with Princess Adel. Secret meetings with the Killer, many in your own chambers. The way you two are never separated. The way she's watchful over you."

Blood pounded into the prince's ears. The words fell around him, inviting anxiety, but never landed in any way that made sense. Who had been sharing this information outside the castle walls?

Davi dealt the blow. "Are you trying to court her, Your Highness?"

The pieces fell into place and practically shattered as they did.

"Mind your tongue!" Ley interjected sharply as he took a step forward. "Don't forget your place and who you're casting accusations against."

Davi held up his hands innocently and took a step backward. "I'm only asking questions. It's not as though I started these rumours."

Arran's mind whirled. "Of course I'm not trying to court her. She is my protector. The Union has sent her to assist us in this battle against Lavanai." He resisted looking over his shoulder at Ryla, worried it would somehow prove Davi right.

"That's the other thing," Davi said, changing pace. "If the Union is so grand and their Killers so powerful, why don't they send the whole lot of them to Lavanai and end this? Why do they continue to let Nithle fall under siege? Why do they allow us to continue to live in fear of these beasts? Why, when they do send help, is it only *one* Killer?"

"The Union has their reasons. Going directly to Lavanai would be suicide." But as the words left Arran's mouth, he knew they fell flat. He *knew* they were difficult to justify. Making an effort to cast the treasonous doubts from his mind, he tried to focus on regaining control of this conversation. Had to get Wendur back in line.

The young lord shook his head, not breaking eye contact with the prince. "I'm not convinced. I've been mulling over this for a long time, *Your Highness*. They present themselves as too powerful for any of this to continue on the way it is. They're lying to us. I'm sure of it. I want to talk some sense into you, especially after those rumours. I only hope I'm not too late."

Arran stared at him, searching his face for some semblance of the boy that he knew before all this. But all he could see was this hardened young man, set on fighting against him.

"Do you know why I don't have any siblings, Arran?"

Arran started, taken aback by this new line of questioning. "Your mother's last pregnancy failed. It was a tragedy, but I don't see—"

"That's the reason we fed to the people. The real reason is because *they* took the baby." Davi's tone was dark, with an expression on his face to match.

Arran knew who he meant but didn't understand his tone. "But—that's an honour. To have the Union choose your sibling is cause for celebration."

"An honour!" Davi choked out with a scoff. "It's no honour. They rip the child away from their parents before they can even hold them. It's as if the midwives just hand them off to the Keepers, as if they *know* they'll show up. I saw it happen with my own eyes. I was waiting outside the room with my nanny to welcome in the newest addition to the family, but then my mother's screams changed. I could tell this was different.

"I rushed into the room even as my nanny tried to hold me back. I was just in time to see Keepers disappear with the baby, then others started in on how we'd be condemned to death if we sought out the child."

Davi paused, but Arran couldn't get past the anger and pain etched into the young man's features. His story was so much like Ley's, but where Ley had held reverence, the young lord held so much ire in his tone.

"My mother has tried to end her life," he spat. "Repeatedly. They're not protecting us, Arran. They're using us as vessels to give them more human weapons like this one." He gestured to Ryla. "They *rob* us of our families and leave us with these scars. Some nights, I still hear the screams in my dreams. Some nights, the screams are real."

The revelation hung in the air and doused Arran like cold water. He forced down a shiver that threatened to creep up his spine. The young man's raw pain clawed at him.

Never had Arran heard such as story, and he suddenly

wondered if maybe the stories about his own mother weren't true. Was it really that she couldn't have more children or was she too heartbroken to try?

"Your Highness. Arran." Davi drew his attention again, his tone softer and more leveled now. He took a tentative step forward, well aware of the eyes watching his every movement. "You deserve to know the truth. I know you want the best for your people, so I beg you to consider my words."

Arran thought carefully, now daring to glance at Ryla out of the corner of his eye. But she wasn't paying him any mind. Her eyes, he saw, were trained on Davi alone.

The prince let out a steady breath. "You're right. I want the best for my people, and I'm deeply sorry your family has struggled with the Union choosing your sibling. I wish there were something I could do to offer you peace. But you're essentially asking me to denounce those who've protected my family for generations. You realize how insane that sounds, right?"

"You would have Wendur's support," Davi said soberly.

"What we're seeking is Wendur's support *in conjunction with* the Union. Not to stand against it." The hope that the conversation might finally get onto the course he wanted was barely a glimmer. Arran knew the only thing he'd be able to do at this point was try to prevent Davi from doing more damage. *But he's wearing that damned royal crest...*

"Wendur wants no part in this never-ending battle with Lavanai, even if that means we must stand on our own." Davi straightened his jacket, the silver buckle on the belt catching a spark of light. "I honestly hope you come to your senses, Arran. My father and I will be ready when you do, and we can truly consider how to bring this anguish to an end."

Arran gripped the lacquered wooden arms of the chair, trying to steady himself. His mind searched for anything he could say that might turn the situation around. Something to at least keep Wendur under Nithle's rule and protection. There was no way the city could stand against Lavanai on its own.

"Wendur is henceforth in exile."

All attention snapped to Ryla. She'd taken several steps forward, standing ahead of where Arran still sat in the chair. Her stance was relaxed but firm, hand still resting on the hilt of her blade.

She continued despite the hum of shock that filled the large room. "The Union will no longer come to your aid, and the city is at the mercy of Lavanai and all dahems."

The chill Arran had been suppressing before now raced through him. Her tone was so sure. Even. Final. When Arran returned his gaze to Davi, he caught the initial surprise on the young lord's face, but it quickly shifted to resignation.

"We're prepared for these consequences," Davi replied, wearing a wry smile as he rested his eyes on her. Arran tried to read what he might be thinking, but nothing revealed itself. When his attention returned to the prince, he said, "Consider my words."

The clack of his shoes followed the young lord out and beyond the groan of the Assembly Chambers' doors closing once again. The room felt hollow as not a single person spoke.

The churn of emotions Arran felt was enough to double him over, elbows resting on his knees and his hands linked behind his head. He didn't agree with Davi but also didn't want this for him, especially after hearing that story. Even if Wendur didn't want it, could they survive without the Union's protection?

"Your Highness." It was Ley, now crouched beside him and his hand a weight on the young man's back.

Ryla spoke again. "Nithle will not face consequences

for this."

Arran untangled his fingers from his curly hair and looked ahead to where she still stood, but now faced him. For once, *for damn once*, he wanted to see something in her gaze other than blankness. But there was still nothing in those brown pools.

He stood abruptly and took a step toward her, Ley's hand falling away as he did. "That's just grand, Ryla. It doesn't change the fact I've just severed off a piece of my kingdom."

"Arran!" The Royal Knight's protest had accompanied a quick scramble to his feet, and Arran could feel now as Ley gripped his arm to try to pull him back.

Ryla's gaze stayed steady on him, unthreatened by his approach and nearness. "Lords Davi and Robyr made their own decision."

"I forced their hand," Arran argued, eyes narrowed in his frustration. *Just another way I've failed my people.*

"They exposed themselves and nothing more," Ryla said plainly.

Chest heaving, he searched her features a moment longer. Even a breath away, he could no better understand or gain insight into her. More shockingly, his mind remained firmly in the present. Finally, he took a deep breath to try to calm himself. This would lead nowhere.

"Arran."

He heeded Ley's voice and another tug on his arm and distanced himself from the Killer. Worry knitted Ley's brow and created tension in his mouth. Seeing this, Arran forced the tightness from his body.

When the prince spoke again, his voice was calmer. "I'll have to inform my parents of what's happened as soon as possible."

"Of course," Ley replied with an uneasy nod.

A moment passed, then Ryla turned toward the door.

She'd taken only a few steps before Ley called after her. "Killer Ryla, is there something you need assistance with?"

"No. I'll be in the High Chambers," she replied without turning back.

Arran watched her retreating form and the way her hand continued to rest on her sword. *Off to inform the Keepers, no doubt.* He couldn't shake the self blame.

No matter how much her fire burned, it wouldn't burn from Mithos's mind the battered image of the spy, bleeding and slumped over the back of a horse. When the lookout had called to her to the fort's wall, she thought the description of the injured dahem was exaggerated, but no. She'd seen Killer Ryla's handiwork with her own two eyes.

Mithos spun, her swords following in arcs at her sides. More flames rippled to life across the training centre's dirt floors with her movements. They cast an orange glow that lit up the dark corners of the vast space, but only seemed to cast the high ceilings further into darkness until she stopped and pointed one of her twin blades to the heavens. The fire roared in its ascent but was quickly snuffed out as the commander called her magic back to her.

Her hand dropped to her side. *Commander,* she scoffed as her chest heaved from exertion. *The* only *commander.*

It wasn't bad enough the spy had died. He'd used his last breaths to report on Naxela's whereabouts; he'd been slain by Ryla in the middle of the night at Nithle castle. Of course, the spy hadn't had all the details of *why* Naxela had even been there, but after she spoke to others among the ranks, she'd pieced it together.

The fool just had to push too far and lose himself to his magic.

A number of his closest ranks were missing as well, no

doubt having gone with him on the suicide mission against the Killer.

He'd been doing so well... Or at least she'd thought he'd been doing well in his struggles to control the magic. Apparently, she'd been wrong.

It doesn't matter. It won't change things. Naxela was dead. Ryla probably knew or suspected Lavanai's intentions against her. Lord Jasim was second-guessing the use of magic. Again.

She wiped sweat from her face, only to feel the back of her hand tremble as it crossed her brow.

Pulling her hand away, she stared at its general location in the blackness as though it would admit why it shook. Not that she needed it to. *It's up to me now to continue the mission.*

She had no idea yet if she could even command alone, and the weight of Naxela's duties doubled her own. More ranks to oversee. More magic users to wrangle. Add to that taking on the responsibility of making sure none of those other magic users succumbed to the same fate as their commander, while allaying fears and keeping egos in check... Mithos released a heavy breath.

Captain Anxer had offered his consult. She knew it'd be smart to take him up on the offer given his history with Ryla and his experience in the army in general, but, for some reason, she felt pressured to handle it on her own.

Silence thrummed in her ears, accompanying the darkness of the training area. Torches remained unlit along the edges of the arena; she'd been too focused on finding release to the tension that seized her body and kept her awake long after everyone else had gone to sleep. Too focused on releasing the magic that made her feel restless.

It was hard to explain—she'd never felt it before—but it was as though she *had* to keep her body moving. Otherwise, the discomfort built below her skin and in her limbs.

The arena had been the safest place to come, devoid of others at this hour of the night and somewhere she could let her fire loose. If any those runes on the entryway were protective runes, she hoped they did their job.

Adjusting her grip on the hilts of her falchions, Mithos drew in a long breath, centred herself, and focused on a complex footwork drill to try to distract herself. She didn't call on her magic this time, settling for obscurity rather than fire to accompany her movements.

Keep your mettle.

She stepped, planting a foot firmly.

Hearten the ranks.

She pivoted and the dirt crunched under the ball of her foot.

Find the answers.

She shifted her weight and continued through the motions of the exercise. Her blades followed with whisper quietness, the movements feeling fluid and an easy extension of herself. The more she moved, the further her thoughts drifted away from the restlessness in her limbs and mind.

"Little Flame."

Mithos whirled, her blades immediately flying to the ready and igniting in flames. Through the dancing blaze, her wide eyes landed on Woxla. The trainer was dressed in a fitted set of dark trousers and tunic, long hair bound in a thick, single braid at his neck. A sympathetic smile crossed his features.

"Woxla," she breathed, shoulders sagging, fire extinguishing, and blades lowering.

"How long have you been in here?"

She thought a moment before countering with her own question, "What time is it?"

"Nearing dawn," he replied easily.

"Then longer than I thought. Several hours," she shrugged nonchalantly. Mithos shifted to the side, lifting a blade just a touch. Fire rippled down its length in a quick flare before flashing across the space to light a torch. The wood cracked loudly before the flame illuminated some of the area near them.

When she faced the trainer again, she saw him watching the torch.

"Good control, Commander." His amber gaze settled on hers a moment later. "Something on your mind?"

"Nothing." Mithos deflected, then paused. "Everything."

Woxla hummed a wordless response, crossing to the torch to lift it out of the sconce and light others along the wall. A warm glow cast over his battle-worn features as he did it. "It's unfortunate what happened to Naxela. It's also normal to be upset about it."

Mithos watched his easy movements as his boots scuffed through the dirt along the edge of the stone wall. She recognized the invite to open up. It wouldn't be the first time she'd opened up to Woxla.

When she'd first arrived in Lavanai, she'd been closed off and distrustful. Her parents and two older brothers had been slain fleeing a human attack on their small village to the north, leaving her to struggle to find her place. At first, she'd been sent to a keep for orphans in Icarsen, where she'd continued to dampen her magic. Somehow, her magic caught the interest of Lord Jasim, and despite her youth, he'd brought her into the ranks so she could work with the master of magic.

The same master of magic who waited patiently for her to speak now had broken through her emotional barriers. Barriers that felt like they were building back up as each moment ticked by.

"It feels like losing family again," Mithos finally admitted. "I'm so mad he let this happen…but I also know he wouldn't have done it intentionally and…it hurts." Clenching her fists, she felt the blades she was stilling holding onto, and quickly sheathed them. They snicked into place at her hips.

Woxla completed his round of lighting the torches and paused in front of Mithos. "I understand. Many of us are feeling similarly, Little Flame. It's hard to have someone who's a part of your everyday life suddenly not be there anymore, and harder still to know they succumbed to something awful. How do we move forward from that?"

"That's exactly my question," Mithos agreed.

Woxla stepped past her to retrieve a rake fastened against the wall just outside of the training area. Mithos joined him and took up a second one before they moved into the arena to rake the dirt back into place that she'd disturbed in her impromptu nighttime training session. The sound of the prongs scraping through it soothing her agitation.

"If only there were actually time to process any of this," Mithos commented as they worked. "I feel like the weight of the war is on my shoulders, even though I know it's not."

"No, it's not. However, you are right that there's not the amount of time we would like to mourn." Woxla's muscles flexed as he pulled the rake across the floor. "All we can do is work through it as best we can until we do have that time."

It wasn't the answer she'd hoped for, but Mithos knew even a master's magic couldn't touch time or speed up healing. Her chest constricted as she thought about the agitation still permeating her body.

Sorrow. It's sorrow, she told herself.

"Just remember you're not alone in this world, Little Flame. You've got me, Lord Jasim—all of us, really."

Mithos stopped mid-motion, peering up at Woxla. He stood with his rake upright, leaning with both hands folded at the top of the handle. Mithos straightened, connecting her gaze with Woxla's as she really considered his words.

A familiar warmth overtook her then. Family.

Unfortunately, fear was hot on its heels. *I can't lose any more of them.*

T he creak of the saddle reached Adel from across the arena
as Rynn hoisted himself from the wooden platform
to the back of the tall horse. The sound only added to the
atmosphere of the large barn where the smell of hay and horse
were strong enough to erode all others. Rynn adjusted how
he was sitting, then their trainer handed him the reins and
encouraged him to begin.

Adel had just finished her own portion of the lesson and
stood to the side now, leaning her elbows on the rail separating
the arena floor and the spectator area in her riding gear with
her dirty-blonde hair tied back out of her face. She grinned
as Rynn smiled at her while riding by at an easy pace, with
the trainer walking not far behind.

"Princess?"

Adel turned to Ashla's replacement. The princess knew it
wasn't fair to think of Megnata that way, but it pained her
to think of anyone but Ashla as her lady-in-waiting. It didn't
help either that Megnata was the complete opposite of Ashla
personality-wise. Whereas Ashla had been bright and full of
life, this woman seemed muted and reserved. Ready to serve,
but not ready to be a companion.

Even their appearances were starkly different. Ashla's shock
of red hair had been replaced by brunette. Green eyes were
replaced with brown. Megnata was shorter as well.

Adel had a feeling it'd been intentional. She wasn't sure if her mother was trying to ease the pain of Ashla's loss or erase the girl completely. She'd never have thought the latter before, but after her conversation with her in the library the other day, she couldn't help her suspicions.

"What is it, Megnata?" Adel asked without moving from her spot.

"There's a letter for you. The page just brought it." Megnata extended the folded parchment toward the princess.

"Thank you." Adel gave a small nod as she accepted the parchment from Megnata, who stepped back to give her privacy to read it. *Ashla would have tried to read it over my shoulder.*

Her heart hitched as she saw the seal. It was Arran's: the rack of a stag encircled by two rings rather than one, like the king's would have been. The letter suddenly felt heavier in her hands.

This was the first letter he'd sent her since their argument. The first she'd heard from him in weeks. She didn't know what to expect when she opened it.

Rumours that Megnata had overheard from gossips in the castle jumped into her mind unbidden. Somehow, some way, people in Heta were whispering about how Arran had stopped courting their princess to pursue the Killer. It was ridiculous. She felt Arran was sincere in trying to protect her even though he pushed her away. Besides, the Union wouldn't allow such a thing.

These self-reassurances didn't do much to ease the stabbing in her chest. It felt like everyone looked at her differently.

Adel's hazel gaze lifted only briefly to see how Rynn was getting along and saw he and the trainer were on the far side of the arena now, working on guiding the horse through obstacles. The look of deep concentration on his face almost made her laugh.

Returning her attention to the letter, she pulled at the seal, which gave way with a pop. She leaned with her forearms on the rail again and held the letter before her to begin reading.

Arran's familiar scrawl told news of the attack on the castle without going into too much detail. He also mentioned the dahem spy in Nithle and how it had resulted in a pretty public confrontation from Killer Ryla. This provoked a wave of unrest in the city, neighbours suddenly suspicious of their neighbours.

The thought that a dahem was in the village was bad enough, but the thought of a dahem having the power to hide in plain sight made her practically queasy. Luckily, the letter also mentioned finding the sympathizer who'd been giving the dahem board while he lurked through the city. The person had been sent to the dungeons, and King Alden was considering execution to make an example of them.

I am hopeful these words reach only you, Adel. I wish I could speak to you in person because there's so much I want to say. I've tried to put ink to paper but have failed with each attempt to convey what burns at my soul. So many thoughts run through my mind these days that I don't know how to sort through them all.

For now, suffice to say that I'm worried for my kingdom—for us all. We cannot possibly keep going like this.

My greatest wish is to protect you. I only hope I don't fail in that, too.

With love,

Arran

His voice seemed to float around her as she read the letter, and though she considered reading it a second time for that alone, she refolded the parchment and tucked it away in the pocket of her riding trousers. When she looked up this time, her brother was riding her way.

"Look how good I'm doing, Adel," Rynn said, bringing the horse to a stop in front of where she stood and peering down at her.

She smiled. "You're doing great. Soon you'll be outriding me." She was pretty sure he was already close. She'd always envied how he was one of those people that could master anything.

She reached out and patted the horse's neck. The animal craned to look back at her and nudged her shoulder.

"Was that a letter from Arran?" Rynn asked.

She rose a brow at her brother. "Shouldn't you be paying attention to your riding instead of watching what I'm doing?"

"A good rider can pay attention to what he's doing *and* his surroundings," the boy replied, lifting his chin in such a way that it sent his short, light brown hair tumbling backward.

Adel laughed. "I see you *are* paying attention to your lessons. Yes, it's a letter from Arran."

Rynn's bravado deflated to something more relaxed. "Are we going to visit him?"

"Maybe. I have to speak with Mother and Father first."

"I hope we can," Rynn continued, looking more pensive than a ten-year-old should. "You've been sad since the festival, and people are saying stupid things."

Mild amazement struck her at the words, but he encouraged the horse back into motion without waiting for a reply. Clearly she'd not been hiding the turmoil in her heart as well as she'd thought.

He's far more perceptive than I give him credit for, she mused. *I wonder what else he's noticed.*

Her real concern was whether he'd gotten wind of what their mother had said about breaking off her courtship with

Arran. If he had, he must be on Adel's side. The thought made her smile, but it disappeared quickly enough. Would their mother even allow her to go to Nithle? If she did, would she allow Adel and Arran a moment alone?

I have to try.

A del waited until after her brother's riding lesson was complete before looking for her parents. As anxious as she was to get it over with, she enjoyed the time with her brother. Riding was one of the few lessons they got to do together, or at least within a close timeframe, like today's. She fondly remembered the way her brother's face had lit up when they'd been told they'd be learning about horses together.

She'd changed out of her riding gear and into a heavy, violet dress, and then she and Rynn trekked toward the study. Rynn, who'd also changed and now wore an earth-coloured tunic and trousers, was supposed to meet with his tutor anyway, so she hoped her parents would be there, too.

"Isuh said today I'll be learning more about the Union," Rynn chattered as they walked down the expansive castle hallway.

"Is that so?" Adel asked. Children learned about the Union from a young age, but it was around Rynn's age that they started in on the more intricate details. "I'm sure he'll quiz you, so let's go over what you've learned so far."

"We talked about how the Union came during Great-Grandpapa's time when Lavanai started the war. The first Keeper and Killer saved us from being overrun. The kingdoms discussed it and accepted the Union's offer of protection, and the Union was founded after that. The Union building is far to the north, and we only ever see them when we really need to. They watch over us, and when we're in trouble, they'll send a Killer to protect us. Just like they did with Nithle at the festival," he told her with what she thought was pride for remembering everything.

"How long does it take for us to travel from Heta to the Union?" She knew, of course. These were the same lessons she'd had many years ago.

"Two weeks," he said after a brief moment's thought.

"Very good." She smiled.

His answering smile beamed back at her.

A servant pulled the study door open for them when they arrived and bowed to the young prince and Adel as she followed him through. Their small retinue of guards remained outside, but Megnata had followed them in and stopped a respectful distance away, yet close enough that Adel could call for her.

As she'd hoped, Adel saw her mother across the grand room standing by a table positioned beside a tall wall of books. Queen Mela was in discussion with the tutor, Isuh, while pointing at something on a parchment Isuh held between them and gesturing with the other hand at the same time. Rynn pulled out a chair to sit quietly at the table in front of them and watched his tutor expectantly.

Isuh, a man that Adel suspected wasn't that much older than herself, had taken over for his father, who'd taught her. And just as the two looked similar with their round features, light hair, and bespectacled eyes, the two had the same passion for guiding the Heta royal family through their tutelage.

Mela finally gave an approving nod, then fondly ran her hand over her son's head before approaching Adel. Her soft expression morphed to something more serious as she approached, and it remained as she stopped before her daughter with her hands clasped at her waist. The long sleeves of her cream and burgundy dress pooled around her wrists.

The silence between them gave Adel the sense her mother was waiting for her to speak first. "I received a letter from Arran." She spied the slightest of twitches on her mother's face but continued. "Nithle was attacked again, and they had a dahem spy hiding in the village."

The queen's light brows pinched with concern. "That's awful. Were any of them injured?"

Adel shook her head but reconsidered. "Some guards lost their lives. He wrote Killer Ryla protected them both times and killed the dahems."

"Thank the Union," she said, genuinely looking relieved. As much as the queen had reservations against her daughter marrying the prince, Adel knew she really did care for the Nithle family.

Adel deliberated her next words carefully. "I think it would be a good idea to visit Nithle. Remind people of our alliance and show our support to them."

Mela's expression darkened, eyes narrowing and features tightening. "Out of the question."

"Mother—" Adel tried, but the queen cut in again.

"We've just learned there has been another attack and a dahem spy. We'd be putting ourselves in danger to go there."

"This is *Nithle*, Mother. Heta's closest ally. We have to respond somehow," Adel argued but kept her voice as calm as possible. "It wouldn't reflect well on us to ignore them."

"We also need to quash these rumours," King Criph said, now joining the conversation as he entered the room. "You and Arran need to show people that your courtship is not impacted by a simple disagreement. We may also consider making the official announcement."

Adel winced. She was more concerned about making their relationship right for their own sakes, but she knew her father was right when he said the people needed to see it, too.

At least I'll get to see Arran. She allowed her heart to flutter.

That her father didn't seem to have the same reservations about the courtship as her mother was surprising. As she watched her parents now, she could plainly see the tension between them on this matter, and she sensed an argument brewing.

"Criph…" Mela gave him a hard look.

The king held up a hand. "No, we must do this. I received a letter from Alden today, and there are things he wants to speak with me about. Regardless, we need to show that our kingdoms still stand together. With these rumours and Wendur's exile, we can't leave things unchecked."

It'd been quite the surprise when the Keepers had made a brief visit to Heta to deliver the news about Wendur. Given that Heta had seen neither dahem attack nor magic-ailed human in decades, she couldn't fathom the last time the Keepers would have come to them.

Mela pitched her voice low, brow furrowing anew. "I'm not comfortable with this, Criph."

"We'll take our full guard, and then some," Criph said firmly. "We can't ignore this."

Adel saw her parents exchange a look that she didn't understand. They did that sometimes, where they seemed to communicate their inner thoughts by simply looking into each other's eyes with only the barest of movements signalling any body language. Whatever conversation transpired, she saw her mother surrendered.

The queen sighed heavily as her shoulders sagged. "Fine. I don't like this, but fine."

"Noted, My Queen." Criph pulled her toward him and gently brushed aside her long, blonde hair to kiss her temple. "I'll speak with the guard, and we'll be on our way first thing tomorrow."

"Rynn should come, too," Adel said suddenly. When her parents looked at her, she continued. "This would be a good political lesson for him, and I know he's been wanting to see Arran again."

Her father considered it a moment. "Yes, you're right."

"I want even more guard then," Mela said just as firmly as her husband had been previously.

"Of course," he agreed without hesitation. "My family will be protected."

"Good," the queen replied, then turned back to Adel with an unreadable expression. "We'll see you at dinner."

Adel nodded. She schooled her features to neutrality but felt hope stirring within her chest. Her parents stepped away, presumably to speak with Isuh and her brother, but she didn't wait around to find out. Instead, she turned on her heel and left the room.

"We're going to Nithle, Megnata," Adel said as the woman fell into step beside her. "Let's go to my room to prepare for the trip."

"Of course, Princess," Megnata replied agreeably.

Adel felt that pang of loss again, thinking of how Ashla would have replied differently. It was hard to decide if her friend would've been happy she'd have a chance to confront Arran or called her crazy for even considering the trip after all that had happened. Probably both.

Yet, none of these happened, and the only sound was two sets of footsteps, her own and Megnata's, echoing along the stone of the hallway.

CHAPTER
THIRTY

When the castle doors opened to admit King Criph and Queen Mela, followed by their two children, Arran tried to suppress the myriad of emotions rushing through him—eagerness, uncertainty, anxiety. It'd been hard enough to maintain decorum and not to rush to the front entrance when the page had announced the Heta royals' approach.

As much as he wanted to break away from where he stood with his parents to rush and sweep Adel into his arms, he held back. This was less about decorum and more that he wasn't sure if she'd welcome it, considering how they'd last parted. Still, the fact that she was here was a good sign, and a flicker of optimism found him when she smiled.

Attendants swarmed the royal family to take their overcoats and collect their trunks brought in from the carriage. As the doors closed behind them, a large retinue remained outside, speaking with Nithle's castle guards. Arran reassessed those in the entryway, and he took in the large party of royal knights and royal guard that stood close to Adel and her family and found places along the perimeter of the room.

With a nod from Alden, Knight Calar stepped forward to confer with Heta's lead royal knight, a strong woman who carried a spear in addition to the sword at her hip. As the commanders met, the royal families also came together. Adel and Rynn approached, and Arran saw the young boy's gaze lock on Ryla, who stood just to the side.

Taking a chance, Arran brought Adel in for a hug, inhaling her sweet scent and feeling the warmth of her body against his. That her arms held him just as tightly fanned the flame of optimism growing within.

"Thank you for coming," he said quietly, nuzzling into her neck.

She pulled back wordlessly, offering another small smile and bringing her hand to rest on the side of his face for just a moment. She let her hand fall away as her gaze shifted to the Killer. "Killer Ryla, it's a pleasure to see you again," Adel said. "I am grateful for your protection of Arran and his family."

Ryla said nothing, but Arran didn't get the sense that any of them had expected her to.

"This is my brother, Prince Rynn," Adel continued, placing a hand on the back of the young boy's shoulders.

"High Protector," he greeted. Even as he bowed, his wondering eyes never left her.

Ryla still didn't vocalize a reply but gave the prince a small nod of acknowledgement.

"Rynn." Criph pulled their attention. "How about you join me and your mother? I'm sure your sister and Arran have some catching up to do."

While the young prince walked quickly to his parents, Arran didn't miss the king's stern eyes locked on him and felt a sinking in his stomach. It was Queen Mela's guarded gaze that gave him bigger pause, however. Was this about the argument? Had the rumours reached Heta, too?

"Megnata, prepare my chambers for our stay," Adel said, drawing his attention away from the king and queen.

"Yes, Princess," the shorter woman replied before curtsying and heading to attend to her duties.

"Your new lady-in-waiting?" Arran asked as the rest of the room seemed to move about the entryway, save for the two of them, Ryla, Ley, and some of the Nithle and Heta guard.

Adel nodded, her expression tight while she took in their surroundings.

The need to say something swelled in his chest, but Arran couldn't find the right words to pierce the sudden heaviness around them. Before he could come up with anything, she composed herself and put on a smile.

"Let's walk," she said.

He noticed the smile didn't reach her eyes, and he tried to ignore the sinking in his stomach. "Anywhere you'd like."

He fell into step beside her as she walked the castle hallways. He heard the footsteps of the Killer, knights, and guards fall in behind them, but the retinue stayed a fair distance back. Still, the sound ricocheted off the walls, making it feel like they were right on their heels.

The continued silence between him and Adel made Arran even more anxious than he'd initially been feeling.

She must still be upset. He clenched and unclenched his jaw. He'd hoped against hope that the passing weeks and his letter would have helped make things clearer.

Just when the shadows were really beginning to take hold in his mind, Adel's voice finally broke the silence. "What happened to Wendur? We heard word of the exile."

Her voice was low enough, but Arran still felt the need to check around him to see who might be listening in. Apart from the guard that'd been in the room, Ley, Ryla, and his parents, the details of the conversation between Arran and Lord Davi had been kept quiet. All people needed to know was that Wendur's young lord had spoken out against the Union.

He cleared his throat. "Lord Robyr was supposed to meet

with Father, Mother, and me. Father and Mother got called away, so I alone went to meet him. Except, instead of Lord Robyr, Lord Davi showed up. From the start, something felt off. He wore Wendur's crest instead of Nithle's."

A stunned look crossed her features at that revelation.

"Then there were accusations of Nithle plotting to use the Killer to strengthen our alliance with the Union. He also tried to convince me to have Nithle abandon the Union all together... It was a mess. Ryla declared Wendur exiled at the end of it all." He paused a moment before continuing. "He told me that Lady Fyrah had another child after Davi, but that the Keepers took it."

Adel inhaled sharply. "But they always said..."

"I know."

"Why lie about that?"

Arran swallowed hard before recounting the next part. "He said it was no honour. That the Union tore their family apart and has caused them to suffer. His mother has tried to end her own life."

"That's terrible," Adel said quietly, her brow pinched as she took in the information.

He continued, "I let it get so out of control. Their exile is on me."

Adel's body held tension as she considered his words, but she surprised him. "If that's the way Lord Davi has been thinking, their exile would have happened eventually."

"Ryla said they simply exposed themselves."

Adel had the briefest of pauses. "She's right. Don't burden yourself with blame that's not yours. You can't always control what other people do. You can't save everyone."

He sighed. "I wish I could. Then I could protect my people. Maybe Ryla could be doing something greater for Nithle than being my constant shadow."

When Adel didn't reply, he glanced her way. There was a collection of unsaid words behind her gaze, fixed on the floor, and his brow knitted as he tried to puzzle out what they were.

Finally, he decided to simply ask. "What is it?"

He brought them to a halt and searched her face. The sun pouring through a few windows in the corridor caressed her soft features but did nothing to smooth out the tension around her eyes and mouth. She seemed to be mulling over whatever she was thinking about.

"Adel?"

She looked up at him. "There are rumours, Arran."

The simple words shot ice through his veins, and he sucked in a breath. It'd been foolish to hope the rumours wouldn't have reached her as well, even as far away as Heta was.

"I don't want to believe them," she said firmly, but refusing to meet his eyes. "And part of me doesn't. But with how we parted, with what you say Lord Davi accused you of, the rumours…the fact alone that you're referring to her without her title…"

Her distressed tone felt harder than any physical blow. Hearing it from Lord Davi, it'd been ludicrous. Seeing how Adel shrunk under it… His heart twisted watching her beautiful features contort as she tried to bring her emotions to heel. She was steeling herself against any potential hurt.

And he was the one hurting her.

"Adel," he repeated softly, placing his hands on her upper arms and willing her to look at him. It was only when her hazel eyes, glassed with suppressed emotion, met his blue that he continued. "There's no truth to any of it. Except, I suppose, that I've dropped her title. I hadn't even realized I'd done it, but it's not because I'm trying to court her or that I have feelings for her. I promise you that."

Her eyes searched his, but he could still read uncertainty behind them. He didn't know what he could say to quell her fears.

After a moment, he tried, "People like to talk and make things out of nothing."

"Private meetings in your chambers don't seem like nothing." Her voice was small; her gaze drifted from his.

He sucked in another breath, letting his hands fall away. "It's not nothing, but it's also not *that*." He paused, trying to find the words to explains. "Ever since the festival, I've been struggling with…memories. I know it doesn't make sense, but it's like reliving those moments in the square, and the real world fades away. Ryla—Killer Ryla—has been teaching me to master how to come out of those memories. So I can stay present. To keep myself here, as she would say."

Sympathy joined Adel's features, and she opened her mouth to say something, but Arran powered on.

"I know we don't agree on why I don't want you to stay in Nithle, but I promise you that it's not because I haven't wanted you by my side. The danger is closing in around us. It seems there's death and darkness everywhere I turn, and I want to protect you from it. I can't lose you."

Arran wasn't sure what to expect or how she'd react, but he hadn't expected her to rise to her toes and touch her lips to his. Warmth flooded through him, sweeping away the worries and fear upon contact. He pulled her to his body, kissing her in return as her hands came to rest on his chest. The moment came to an end too soon as she pulled back.

His blue eyes opened to meet her hazel. He was only vaguely aware of their retinue chatting down the hall from them as she brushed a curl away from his forehead. The delicate touch of her fingertips tracing down his face sent a thrill through him. He didn't move, afraid to shatter the moment.

"I love you, Arran," Adel began, letting her hand fall. "I want more than anything to be your queen. To be your safe place to fall when you're hurting so you don't have to face these horrors alone. But I need you to trust in me to stand with you. And I need to be able to trust in you."

The prince's heart simultaneously fluttered and plummeted. A cavern yawned between them as she stepped back, then walked toward the group of knights, guards, and the Killer. He turned to watch her, a sense of panic making home in his chest.

Am I going to lose her anyway?

THIRTY-ONE

Adel hadn't woken up that morning planning to stab herself in the heart, but that's exactly what it felt like she'd done. The way it raced and ached at the same time made it difficult to keep her pace and her breath steady as she traversed the corridors of Nithle castle. She couldn't help but feel that their entourage, servants, and any who passed were looking at her and could read exactly what had happened. Even though she and Arran walked beside each other now as if things were fine.

Things were anything but fine. Walking with Arran felt more ceremonious than anything, as if their pairing had been arranged rather than something they'd chosen. There would be more casualties in this than her heart.

She'd meant her words and her actions, which was what made it all the more difficult. It took so much effort to not reach out to him now and try to comfort him. Try to heal whatever was hurting within him and causing the memories, as he'd called them, to surface. She had no idea what that might be like, but she'd seen how much it pained him, potentially even embarrassed him, to reveal that to her.

Then there was the feeling of his lips on hers—the way he'd pulled her to him—and she craved it again. But she couldn't give herself to him if he was unwilling to see her as a true partner and trust her as she chose to trust him.

I believe him, she decided despite the unease she felt. *I don't fully understand dropping her title, but I believe him.*

Her decisions made her stomach, heart, and head ache indescribably, and the tension she'd caused between them was palpable.

She was certain his silence now was plagued by disquiet. Still, Adel held onto the hope Arran would say *something* despite the heavy blow she'd delivered. As much as she hadn't intended to say it, in the moment, it'd suddenly felt clear.

He's probably processing... She'd be lying if she said she didn't want him to react more readily to what she'd said—for his feelings for her to be so strong that he would, without hesitation, have a response that aligned with hers.

The longer the silence between them stretched on, the more disheartened she felt about the whole situation. Her thoughts had just begun venturing down the path of how much of a fool she was when Rynn seemed to pop out of nowhere.

"There you are!" he said.

"Here we are," Adel replied with as much of a smile as she could muster.

The young prince paused a moment, eyes travelling back and forth between the pair of them, but continued without pushing the matter. "Mother and Father said we should meet for the midday meal. They were going to send a page, but I said I'd get you."

Spying the small guard on Rynn's heels wearing her kingdom's colours confirmed Adel's thoughts that her parents wouldn't let him come by himself.

Arran chimed in beside her. "I suppose that means the meeting has concluded?"

The boy's hair flopped about as he gave a nod. "For now, anyway. King Alden was telling us that dahem spy had special magic…" he struggled for the word.

"Concealment magic," Arran supplied.

"Yes, that's it. Father said it's a good thing Killer Ryla was there to protect you," Rynn said to Arran.

"The Union gives us much to be grateful for," Adel said, then glanced back at the Killer.

Although still a fair distance away, Adel wasn't surprised to see the Killer watching them. Rynn and Arran continued to chat beside the princess, and she caught bits and pieces of how their parents had spoken about their long history of friendship and alliance, about how they were alarmed by Wendur's exile, and about the events that had happened since the festival.

Adel didn't know what she hoped to gain from staring at the Killer. Maybe a sense of understanding the situation, as if in staring she could absorb some of the woman's clarity or even see through the rumours that plagued her relationship. Instead, she was only met with the blank indifference.

With a sigh, Adel returned her attention to Arran and her brother. "We shouldn't keep our parents waiting," she said, cutting into their conversation. "I'm sure we can manage to walk and talk."

"You're right. I'll inform Ley and the others of what's happening," Arran offered, stepping away to do so.

Adel watched after him with another ache in her heart. A tug of her dress sleeve drew her attention, and Rynn waved her down to his level. She crouched, her dress pooling around her. "What is it, Rynn?" she asked.

"Did you two work it out?" he asked, which startled her. "Everyone was mentioning how you two had things to work out."

She smiled weakly. *Of course they were,* she thought to herself with annoyance. Even their own families were gossiping about them. "It's a little more complicated than that, Rynn."

Behind his blue-green eyes, he seemed to be trying to fit all the pieces together. "I don't want you to be sad. Should I talk to him?"

A genuine laugh escaped her, which surprised her as much as it did Rynn. "You're the best, little brother. Don't you worry about this. Whatever happens, I'll be okay."

He looked at her skeptically, his mouth contorted in a pensive expression.

Her heart warmed at his concern, and she placed her hands on his shoulders. "I promise."

"Okay," he ceded, still giving her a skeptical look. "Let's go eat!" he said next as Adel heard footsteps approach behind them.

She was surprised and grateful for his level of maturity, and she smiled at him again before giving his shoulders a squeeze and returning to her full height.

By the time they reached the dining hall, their parents were already there, gathering around the table. The heavenly smells of warm bread and hot soup greeted them, and Adel was certain she even smelled her favourite hot drink, made from local berries and syrups.

"Is this your doing, Arran?" she asked.

"I don't know what you're talking about," he replied, but the hint of a grin peeking through his melancholy gave him away.

It was a small gesture, but considering their tension, it meant a lot. Even if Nithle continued to be at war with Lavanai, even if they continued to break into the castle, these moments among that chaos would be enough.

Adel took the empty seat beside her mother at the grand table, and Rynn took the one beside their father. Arran sat across from her, with the Killer positioned a few feet behind him.

"Before we begin," Alden said from the head of the table, standing with his hands on his belt, "I'd like to take a moment to recognize Heta and Nithle's everlasting friendship." A smile adorned his aged features as he looked over Adel and her family. "No matter our peril, I know we can count on you."

Adel heard her father's chair shift across the stone floor now as he also stood. The gesture alone, she thought, showed the two men saw each other on equal ground, but something shifted in the atmosphere.

"Now more than ever, we must show we are here for each other, not just under the Union but as allied kingdoms," Criph said, his timbre and volume matching Alden's.

"Let us stand united as we face our challenges," Mela chimed in, also standing.

"And may we forever hold each other in our hearts," Shron continued from where she now stood beside her husband.

The Alliance Pact? Adel shuddered. She wondered what in their conversation Rynn had missed that had swayed their mother. *This is a giant leap from wanting me to sever ties with Arran.*

The words felt weighty, even as the kings and queens all regarded each other with reassurance and confidence. She couldn't fathom why they'd recite the Alliance Pact now of all times, nor could she shake the feeling that something was off. As she connected her gaze with Arran's, she got the sense he felt the same thing. She found herself looking just behind him to his ever-present shadow.

What do you think of all this, Killer Ryla? she thought, but the woman continued to stare at seemingly nothing, not so much as acknowledging Adel. This did nothing to allay her uneasiness.

Adel was pulled from her thoughts as a servant placed a bowl of the soup in front of her as well as a thick slice of bread. Their parents had already sat again, but she waited until they began to eat before starting into the meal herself. She held the cup warmed by the drink between her hands, then took a cautious sip to test its heat before drawing a larger gulp.

It wasn't until after the meal that Adel could privately reconnect with Arran again. Even then, it was only a stolen moment as they hung back while following their parents to a drawing room to relax after their meal. Their entourage of knights and guards, along with Killer Ryla, trailed just behind her and Arran.

"What do you think that was about?" Adel asked Arran, careful to keep her voice low.

"The Alliance Pact?" he asked, peering at her out of the corner of his eye.

Adel nodded, watching his features grow pensive.

"I have no idea. It was certainly odd," he said after a moment's pause.

"It almost seemed like a show for Killer Ryla," Adel continued. She still wasn't sure that was quite it, but worried what it would mean if it were.

"Except it predates the Union," Arran noted.

"I know…" Adel countered. "I just can't place what it is."

"Me neither," Arran agreed. He chuckled lightly. "I remember when I was younger, I'd always get it backwards and my tutor would get so cross. He'd say, 'The only heir to the Nithle throne *cannot possibly* get this wrong!'"

It felt wrong given the various sources of tension, but Adel giggled as he adopted a voice that she assumed was supposed to mimic his tutor's. It sounded ridiculous. "I can imagine.

Ashla used to think it was silly that I had to learn it. She said the *United* was already *united*, so what was the point in needing to know how to swear allegiance to those you were already allied with." Talking about Ashla still stung, but the lighter memory made Adel smile.

"I guess she never saw us expanding beyond our borders. Or anything like this." Arran gestured vaguely with his hand.

Adel opened her mouth to say something more, but closed it as a page approaching Alden and Shron halted the procession. The parchment in his hands had a royal seal on it, and although she couldn't make out the symbol on the seal, she could see the plum-coloured wax that held it closed.

"Piridet?" she asked.

Arran nodded tensely. "It looks like it."

Shron took the parchment, thanked the page, and they began walking again. Adel knew it wasn't her business, but she couldn't help but wonder what the letter was about.

CHAPTER

THIRTY-TWO

R yla positioned herself by the drawing room doors as they closed behind the group. That exact position gave her the best vantage point of the closer quarters if she were to need to act—she had full view of the collection of plush chairs where the royal families took their seats and first access to the door should someone try to enter. Her left hand relaxed on the top of the hilt of her sword while the right was rested atop the left.

Any comfort in the room resided in its temperature and the glow of lanterns that illuminated bookshelves and paintings lining the walls. Each of the Nithle and Heta families showed signs of tension with set jaws and rigid shoulders—even the young Prince Rynn could sense something was off. His eyes shifted from person to person as he got comfortable in the wingback chair beside his sister.

The recitation of the Alliance Pact was no more effective a mask than the concealment magic.

When she got settled into her seat, Shron broke the seal on the parchment, which tore as the wax pulled a small layer of the paper with it. She then unfolded it and leaned in to hold it between herself and Alden. The others waited patiently as they took in the message.

"This day is a day of alliances," Alden finally said, leaning away from the letter, which Shron passed across her husband to where her son was seated. "Piridet has written to assure us that it stands with Nithle during this difficult time."

"News of Wendur reached them," Arran said from where he sat. His eyes were still fixated on the page even as he spoke. "King Timith is sending fighters straight to Bunthle to strengthen our line there."

"That's wonderful news," Mela chimed in with a small smile.

"Why not send the fighters with the letter?" Adel asked with her hands folded on her skirts in her lap. "Wouldn't that make more sense, especially given Piridet is only a day or so from here?"

Arran shook his head, eyes landing on the princess. "It takes time to coordinate people and start them on their way. They have to consider supplies, travel arrangements...all of that on top of making sure Piridet remains protected. I have no doubt it was easier to send the messenger ahead with the news, and the fighters will come soon after," he explained gently. "It gives us time to prepare how we'd like to coordinate, too."

"Are we sending fighters too, Father?" Adel asked.

Although the question seemed innocent enough, the undercurrents didn't escape Ryla. There was unrest among the Heta royals. Not an immediate threat, but coupled with the earlier tensions, including those she'd seen while watching from a distance as Arran and Adel spoke, the Killer kept careful watch on the situation.

"We're still discussing Heta's contributions," Criph responded without really answering the question.

Sensible, the Killer thought. *He's being mindful of what he's committing his kingdom to.* When it came to the dahems, it could easily mean committing to death.

Despite her own assessment, Ryla saw Adel's lips purse together just slightly, but the princess quickly adopted a more neutral expression. Beside her, Arran's jaw tightened, but he didn't say anything. The tension rose only a fraction more, but it was noticeable.

"Of course," Alden said quickly as if to smooth it all over. "We need to carefully consider this so we're making smart choices and not simply jumping at what seems right. In any case," he took the outstretched parchment from his son, then refolded it along its creases, "we'll work out the details of convening with Piridet later."

"I'd like to be the one who meets with them, Father," Arran pushed the thread of conversation.

The tension mounted another step. "Son, you know how I feel about this. There's too much risk."

Ryla saw her charge square his shoulders, much like he had when he'd confronted her after Wendur's exile. His emotions were much more controlled this time.

Arran pressed on. "There's risk everywhere. In the castle. In Nithle Proper. Lavanai has invaded our space, and I can't hide within the castle walls forever."

"Sending you directly into the field, we may as well put a beacon on you," Alden argued.

Queen Shron placed a hand on her husband's arm, staying anything further he had to say. "Arran, consider the Union's wishes here. They've sent Killer Ryla to protect you expressly."

As it tended to do, Arran's gaze found her.

I cannot guide you here, Prince. She was not to interfere with matters unless they conflicted with the Union, such as the case with Wendur. But at present, nothing being said required her to assert her authority.

The young Prince Rynn's eyes landed on her, too, his curiosity washing over her. His sister's glance, however, strayed toward Arran's face. Trepidation was the princess's dominant emotion.

Arran's attention returned to his parents before he spoke again. "The Union said nothing of me being prisoner in my own castle. And if sending me as I am is a beacon, send me in disguise."

"Killer Ryla being by your side would give you away," Adel interjected now, her voice tight.

"Maybe Killer Ryla can be disguised as well," Rynn suggested. He shrank only slightly as all eyes rounded on him, and again he connected with the Killer's gaze, as if to draw strength. "Tutor Isuh told me a story of a Killer that did so before."

Ryla wasn't familiar with whatever instance he was referring to, but it could have been true. If it meant protecting their charge, a Killer would do just about anything.

"Rynn, let's not interfere," Mela said gently.

The clack of dishes reached Ryla from just outside the door, so it was no surprise to her when the door opened and a servant announced refreshments. Alden welcomed them in and the smell of berries and syrup filled the space as the cart with a large pot and cups rolled across the carpeted floor.

As the servant provided the royal families with their drinks, Shron pleasantly said, "We can discuss this more another time, Arran. Let's enjoy our company for now."

Conversation steered away from the looming danger and continued until the royal families excused themselves for the evening. Ryla waited for them to depart, leaving Arran and Adel as the last ones in the room. Even as Arran left through the door, Adel hung a pace back and stopped where the Killer stood, waiting to follow.

The princess swallowed, looking unsure of herself as she faced the warrior. "No matter what happens, please protect him."

Despite whatever had put the distance between the young royals, the princess's concern for the prince bled through her words. The Killer's reply came sure enough.

"As is my duty."

As Mithos crossed the Grand Hall toward the head table, she felt gazes fall on her. It wasn't often any of them saw the second in command in anything other than her casual or battle attire, but tonight she wore an elegant, deep plum-coloured gown. The way it sat just off her shoulders with the neckline straight below her collarbone softened her appearance. The sleeves delicately hugging her defined arms and the billowy flow of the gown's skirt served as reminders she was more than just a warrior.

While Lavanians in Icarsen were probably roaming the beautiful royal gardens, those at Yandana Fort gathered together in the hall for the end of season feast. Considering how many days she'd spent lately planning attacks and strategies with the dahem lord, she wondered if this would become a final feast for Yandana Fort. The room was bursting with Lavanai ranks, and she got the sense many of them were thinking the same as she was even as they smiled, laughed, and drank.

She brushed her dark, cropped hair across her forehead as she came to the table to stand beside Jasim, who was about to address the crowd. He'd likewise dressed for the occasion, his green overcoat sitting atop a cream-coloured, loose-fitting dress shirt that was tucked into his dark trousers. The shirt's high neckline accentuated his jaw, giving him a stately, almost regal look as he stood with his hands behind his back and feet shoulder width apart.

"Welcome." His commanding voice brought the room's attention to him. "Another season has passed, and we come together in celebration of each other. Our King has sent this message." He brought his hands around to the front, parchment at the ready, and began reading, "*My dearest people. I long for the day we can reunite and join in celebrating life and our community together. I have been keeping watch over you from afar and am proud of your work. I'm confident our efforts will be rewarded, and one day we will see peace. Know that we are with you in spirit.*"

There was light applause as Jasim folded the parchment and set it on the table behind him. As he'd read it, Mithos could practically hear her king's voice in the room even though it'd been years since she'd actually seen him. That was when she was chosen as a second in command alongside Naxela. They'd travelled to Icarsen for a formal introduction to the king so he could give them his blessing to uphold those positions.

She pictured the kind dahem with his dark eyes and prematurely greying hair. He was sharp and keen, and she felt as if he'd had the ability to assess her and Naxela from a single glance. It hadn't been a harsh gaze, but striking and exposing nonetheless. And when he'd spoken, his tone was that of gentle confidence. She'd never met anyone quite like him before.

I wonder what he thinks of Naxela's downfall.

Jasim's voice drew her back to the present. "Tonight, let us put the conflict aside and celebrate our royal family's safety. That *we* are still here and have made it this far."

The room applauded again as Jasim and Mithos rounded the table to take their seats. Plates filled up with the meat, vegetable, and fruit dishes that had been laid out for the choosing. For much of the produce, it would be the last opportunity to enjoy it until the warm weather returned. Very few fruits and vegetables survived the cold months, even in storage.

During the meal, Mithos chatted idly with the squad leaders, Captain Anxer, and Lord Jasim. Her eyes travelled occasionally to the décor set up for the evening: banners of blue with Lavanai's golden crest hung in the corners of the room. The whirling filigree framed a *torshid*, a creature of dahem lore that resembled a marten with larger pointed ears, three tails, and long claws. It was said if a *torshid* crossed someone's path, they'd be imbued with its wisdom, courage, and luck.

Perhaps one will cross our path sometime.

The commander let her attention drift to the large, freshly-stocked candle chandeliers setting the room in a brilliant glow. On the tables, flowers and other plants from the end of the season added a hint of fragrance among the hearty aroma of the meal.

Light music from a single musician, set up to their left, offered some ambiance to the setting. Mithos caught bits and pieces of the stringed instrument's tune and occasionally the sound of the musician's voice singing songs of celebration and their people. Mostly she tuned it out, until the notes of a familiar melody snared her attention.

A certain darkness shaping all these years.
An endlessness in raging battle's fears.
A crisis bleeding through the campaign,
In violence's wake, a terrible blood stain.

When the clouds disperse, destroying all we're seeing,
what can replace the purpose of our being?

When the night starts to fade, and the sun has left us blind,
the error will leave more than stains behind.

The captivating words snared her attention. Her eyes locked on the young singer who focused on his fingers plucking away at the strings of the lacquered instrument. Maybe it was the soft, pleasant cadence of his tenor tone. Maybe it was that the lyrics spoke to the end of the war.

She stood and excused herself from the table while the singer continued.

A certain craft that crumbles as it fails.
A shattering from that which we assail.
A certain clarity is seen in each one's eyes.
In verity, wonder what it is we'll decide.

The clouds dispersed and now we must rebuild,
Our purpose, at what cost has it been fulfilled?
The night has fled, and the sun leaves us blind.
Far more than stains have been left behind.

No one else batted an eye at the short tune, but it set Mithos's senses buzzing. The lyrics were speculation about what would happen to dahems when they finally defeated their enemies and could lay down their weapons. How after it all, Lavanai would still be there, although changed and needing to find themselves again.

She couldn't help but feel a bit silly. It was just a song. One she'd forgotten about, but not unfamiliar to her. Still, her itch for details that might sway their chances in defeating either Nithle or the Union drew her forward.

Leave no stone unturned.

The young dahem started when he looked up and saw Mithos standing over him. He scrambled to stand himself, nearly dropping his instrument in the process, and pushed his long bangs aside. "My apologies, Ma'am. I didn't see you there. Is there something I can play for you?"

"That song," Mithos said, taking a step closer to him. "That song you just played, tell me more about it."

He gave her a puzzled look. "What do you mean, Commander?"

"Where did the lyrics come from? Do we know anything more about them?" Mithos persisted, watching his reaction carefully.

The young dahem fidgeted, seeming unable to decide on how to hold his instrument. His light brows furrowed above his amber eyes.

There is *more,* she thought with a surge of excitement. She took a breath. *Calm down. Don't get ahead of yourself.*

"My father, he—he knows more than I do," the musician fumbled. "He'd normally be the one here, but he wanted me to have the chance to play for Lord Jasim. Said it was a great opportunity—which it is!" he clarified quickly.

She paid no mind to how flustered he was. "I'd like for your father to meet with me," Mithos replied. Seeing the boy stiffen, she thought she may have overdone her command and tried to soften the blow. "You've done nothing wrong, but I want to know more about this song. Is your father with you?"

The musician, like the market vendors, would have travelled to Yandana just for this special occasion. She hoped that he hadn't sent his son alone.

The young dahem nodded, his shoulders relaxing, if only a little.

"Great. Before you depart, bring your father to meet me with whatever information he has about that song. Tomorrow morning. There's a meeting room in the fort. An attendant will know where to lead you to find me." When she saw the dahem nod again, she made her way back to the table.

As she sat down, Jasim leaned over. "Everything all right?" he asked quietly, his eyes lingering on the dahem she'd been speaking with. The young musician settled back onto his seat and began strumming a new tune.

"Yes, My Lord. Another piece of my research," she explained and glanced over at him.

She could tell he puzzled over what sort of research might involve a musician and inwardly wished him not to ask questions for which she had no answers yet.

Finally, he nodded. "Give me an update when you can."

"Of course."

Mithos shielded her eyes against the rays of morning light streaming into the smaller meeting quarters situated near the war room in the fort. Apart from casting the room in a glowing haze, it brought the stacks of books and scrolls along the long table and in the corners of the room out of the shadows. The room had become something of a personal study for her over the weeks, and it was where she stored the texts she'd requested be sent from Icarsen for her research.

While she waited for her guests, she tidied up the space a bit, moving her notes and wells of ink to a smaller shelf along the far wall of the room. Before long, the knock came at the door.

"Enter," she called as she set the last of her items aside.

The door swung open with the slightest of whines, and in entered an elderly dahem along with the young musician she'd seen the night before. The unfamiliar dahem's appearance was well put together, with his tailored red tunic featuring ornamentation stitched in gold and a pair of dark trousers. His long, white hair was knotted at the back of his head.

"Commander," he greeted, his smile reaching the pale amber of his eyes. "It's an honour to meet you."

Noting the scroll of aged parchment the dahem carried, Mithos gestured toward the table, then said, "I appreciate you seeing me on such short notice."

"It's no trouble at all, and I'm happy to accommodate. When Jeet told me you had questions, I knew we had to chat as soon as possible," the dahem continued as he took a step toward the table.

"Hello again, Commander." Jeet greeted Mithos with a slight bow before following his father to the table.

"Hello, Jeet. Thank you for bringing your father to me."

"You're welcome," he replied, much more calmly than the previous night. "He'll be able to explain everything."

Mithos watched the older dahem with interest as he set the paper down with care and held out a hand to Jeet, who dropped some polished weights into his open palm. Every one of Mithos's senses tingled with anticipation again. She tried to bring her emotions to heel and made sure to keep her expression as casually interested or neutral as possible.

"What's your name?" Mithos asked as he began unrolling the parchment.

The dahem stopped mid-motion and turned toward her. The parchment rolled up on itself with an audible *thup*. Some of the excitement returned to his eyes as he peered at her. "Of course! My apologies, Commander. My name is Keretuw. You're welcome to call me Keret. Jeet is my son. You spoke with him just last night."

Mithos nodded, and he returned to his setup. Keret and Jeet finished setting weights on the edges of a piece of parchment, leaving the corners to curl around the stone objects.

"Thank you, my boy," Keret said with a smile to the young dahem. Keret gestured for Mithos to join him at the table as he said, "It's lucky I never travel without my parchments when I know certain songs will be performed. You just never know who might have questions about them."

The crinkles and small creases of the parchment spoke

to how much it'd been transported about, as did the words scrawled in fading ink. While she didn't quite understand why he'd bother carrying around parchments with lyrics, Mithos was thankful for the oddity in that moment. She let her eyes trail the words, as if seeing them rather than hearing them would reveal secrets.

"This song has been passed down through our family for many generations," Keret began.

"That's not uncommon," Mithos commented, still staring at the page.

"No, I suppose not. But this one in particular has been guarded by my family, though it's common enough that most every dahem knows it." Keret's tone took on a sobering, serious note. "What do you know of the piece, Commander?"

"It's a look beyond the war. Who will we be once we're victorious? What will it mean? How will we rebuild who we are as a people?" She stood straight now and looked at Keret, who watched her carefully. "The 'darkness' has shaped us, the 'raging battle' feels 'endless,' but after it all, there's more than just spilled blood. There's us. Given a new chance."

"Yes, yes, that's what they all think." There was almost a twinkle in Keret's pale eyes. "But the story that's been passed down with this parchment is very different. It's not about us dahems at all—it's about the Killers. What happens to them when they break the Union's hold."

Mithos's brows shot up, but she withheld her shock otherwise and allowed him to continue.

"We know of Killers as emotionless warriors trained to bring about our demise. They have no care for who they hurt and how. All that matters to them as the Union's tool is that we die. We're all told this from the time we can understand the conflict. But my ancestors knew a dahem who'd come across a Killer that was…changed."

"Changed?" she prompted him, maintaining a steady voice despite her surprise. "What do you mean? Changed how?"

He turned back to the page, and Mithos followed his lead even though she kept watch of him from the corner of her eye. His passion and conviction for this story were written all over her features. It had her heart racing.

"The dahem found a Killer who wasn't like the Killers we know. She wouldn't have thought the man a Killer at all, except for the Killer's mark on his hand and chest. His mind was broken, and he was overcome by all that he'd done under the Union's control," Keret said.

"You mean more than simply being completely devoted to them?" Mithos couldn't help but ask.

Keret nodded. "Exactly. The story hints that the Union has some way to control Killers, but something had happened with this one, and he couldn't cope with the change."

"The error…" Mithos trailed off, resisting the urge to reach out and touch the words on the page. Instead, she flexed her fingers at her side.

"That's what I feel is the 'something,' too. But we don't know what precisely it is. All we know is the dahem thought she could find a way to rehabilitate the Killer and hoped he would be sympathetic to our cause. Could you imagine having a warrior of that skill on our side?" Keret paused for impact. "The tale goes that one day while the Killer was deep in despair, she sang this to try to comfort them both. Like a mother might sing to a scared child."

"She wasn't able to convince the Killer to join us, was she?" Mithos asked.

"She never had the chance to try. The Union hunted their Killer, killing both him and the dahem who tried to help him.

All we have left is this story and this song." Keret gestured again to the parchment. "I've studied these lyrics since I was a child, fascinated by them as you are now."

"Why has no one ever brought this forward before?" she asked, looking at him again. "If this story is true, it proves there's a way to incapacitate Killers."

"What you just said is the very reason. '*If.*' The details here are too sparse. The song tells a story but doesn't give us anything concrete to work with. Even in my studies of what I've been told and what's been passed to me through my family, it's hard to prove any of it is more than a strange fire tale," Keret said somberly now. "But I can't help but wonder why anyone would make up such as story."

Mithos inhaled and let out a heavy sigh. She knew immediately that he was right and thought it probably the reason Jeet had been so uncomfortable with her asking about it.

"I'd like a copy of this." She gestured vaguely toward the lyrics. "Jeet, to your left is a fresh sheaf of parchment," she said, looking to where the youth had positioned himself across from them by the window.

"Not a problem, Commander." Keret took the proffered parchment and also the writing utensils his son handed him.

A short while later, she watched the young musician and his father walk away from the fort's main building. The sun had made its climb over the fort walls, shining down on the inner grounds.

The copied lyrics had been added to her pile of research, but what Keret had said wouldn't leave her mind. Whether the story was based on truth or simply a strange fantasy a dahem had conjured up, it promised the idea of a Killer much different than any they'd ever faced.

"Changed," she said quietly to herself. *A Killer with a*

shattered mind would be much easier to defeat.

She continued to think about it as she stood on the steps, trying to conceptualize how they might even go about doing that. She envisioned Ryla in her mind's eye, dead expression set, sword drawn, and body poised to act. Mithos studied the mental image.

Can we change you?

CHAPTER
THIRTY-FIVE

Maintaining appearances was not something Arran would have put at the top of his to-do list. Yet, in the activity-filled days that followed the Heta royals' arrival, the mounting tension between the Nithle and Heta families had him putting on a constant front. Between the meetings with lords and ladies and the speech given with Kings Alden and Criph standing side-by-side while Arran stood beside Adel with their mothers flanking them, it was too much.

The worst of it was the announcement of his courtship with Adel. What he'd pictured in his mind—an extravagant party, musicians, a celebration across their kingdoms—was far from the reality that transpired. Instead of a party, it was a declaration among the speeches. Instead of music, there was only the rustle of the autumn leaves scraping across the stonework of the outlook point. Celebrations felt muted despite the swirl of oranges and reds, lacking the heart he'd wanted, especially from himself and Adel.

Sure, they smiled and stood with her arm looped through his and his hand atop hers, but she'd never felt farther away from him. The kiss still burned on his lips, but it only served as a stark contrast to the coldness all around them.

Arran was grateful for the simple activity on the final day of their visit. Rynn had wanted to visit the market, and their parents had decided it might be a good opportunity to mingle with the people—as much as one could mingle with the people when followed by a large retinue of armed individuals ready to defend the royal bloodlines.

Nithle's prince kept a watchful eye for anything suspicious. Nothing looked amiss among the swaths of folks going about their day in warmer clothing of more muted navies and browns. They carried baskets of fruits and vegetables and other goods they'd purchased from the variety of vendors.

The buildings throughout the city were more shuttered than in the summer months, and much of the plant life along window sills and around buildings had wilted. Even the sky, grey as it was, added a sombre feeling to the excursion.

I'll take sombre over threatening, he thought.

He was on high alert within himself. So far, neither the cacophony of the crowd nor the fact that they were roaming around the city square sent his mind and memories into a tailspin. He attributed it to being so cognizant of everything around him, but also remembered the memory's powerful snare that day with Ryla despite doing the same.

His attention drifted occasionally in the Killer's direction to his left to see if she were about to spring into action. While her gaze was just as watchful as his own, he saw no cause for concern. He liked to think he'd gotten better at reading her. A sudden flick of her dark eyes or shift of how her hand rested on her sword hilt might be indication of something awry. But maybe the idea that he could understand her was only wishful thinking.

All the same, his grip remained firm on Adel's arm where it looped through his, as if that alone would shield her from whatever dangers might be about. She showed no sign of their disagreement to his people, instead smiling and leaning into him. The sting of that didn't ease up.

"Adel! Arran! Come look!" Rynn called from ahead of them.

The young prince had stopped at a woodworker's stand. Most of the wares were pieces of furniture with intricately carved patterns, including many with Nithle's crest. Along the front of the table, there were a few smaller items: toys, boxes, and other ornamental trinkets. As Arran approached with Adel, he got a better view of what Rynn had his hands on.

The square piece of light coloured wood looked large in his small hands with a nicely edged frame around the inner carvings. At the centre was the Union's sun-like crest, taking up most of the wood's surface with the four large spokes nearly touching the frame. Joining the Union's emblem were those of the four kingdoms: Nithle's stag, Heta's kestrel, Veloth's fish, and Piridet's fox.

Adel let go of Arran's arm to crouch by her brother. "It's lovely," she said with a smile. "Look at how precisely the lines and crests have been carved." She traced her fingers along the carvings as she spoke and Rynn nodded. "The woodworker did a wonderful job, didn't she?"

Rynn nodded again and looked to the woman standing behind the table. "Did you do these?"

"Yes, Young Prince," the middle-aged woman said with an appreciative grin. "Thank you for your kind words, Princess," she said to Adel this time. "Please, take what you like as my gift to Heta and your friendship to Nithle."

Adel smiled at the woodworker. "That's very gracious of you." She turned back to Rynn now. "Would you like to take this home?"

He nodded and held the carving to his chest, giving the woman a smile matching his sister's. "Thank you!"

Adel stood as Rynn walked ahead to show his parents his gift. The young prince's quick steps told Arran he wanted to run, but he held back his excitement, preserving his princely decorum. Or maybe it was just he was about that age where he wanted to prove to his parents he was a mature young man.

Adel continued to peruse the items on the table, and Arran noticed the appreciation of the work as she gently handled and examined the various pieces. The princess spoke easily with the woodworker, asking her about techniques and her craft overall. A small smile tugged at his lips. This was the young woman he had fallen in love with, full of life and intrigue. Showing kindness and respect to all who afforded it, regardless of station.

Eventually, she stepped away from the table without taking anything for herself but promised the woodworker she would return next time she visited Nithle. Adel retook Arran's arm, and they started down the street toward their parents. The process repeated a few times at different vendor stands throughout the excursion.

After spending a few hours weaving through the market, the group made its way back to the castle. The nearer to the castle and the Heta royal family's departure they drew, the more Arran felt the dissonance between them.

A single knight clad in silver armour at the castle steps was waiting for the group when they returned. He carried with him a purple pennant with silver trim and a leaping fox sewn into the sturdy fabric; the long staff it flew on rested on the ground by his feet. The man's helm was at his side rather than on his head, and he bowed at the sight of the royal families.

Knight Calar and Alden stepped forward, as did Arran. He realized after the first couple steps that Adel kept up with him, but he didn't protest.

"Your Highnesses," the Piridet knight greeted. "It is my pleasure to inform you that Princess Mihel is en route with our reinforcements."

"Mihel?" Arran heard himself say aloud. "That's unexpected."

He felt Adel's grip on his arm tighten just slightly, but otherwise she gave no indication of being affected by this revelation.

"The princess wanted to see to this personally given the gravity of the situation, Your Highness," the knight replied.

"This is great news," Alden said with a smile. "My son will convene with you shortly."

An attendant was called to fetch the carriage and the Hetaen royals' things. In the meantime, everyone moved into the castle entryway. No one seemed particularly keen to stand out in the autumn chill, and, besides that, with the arrival of the Piridet knight, preparations were in motion. Much of Arran's entourage disappeared into the castle to get ready.

Here we go, Arran thought with a weighty exhale.

He knew this moment was coming, but the reality of it crashed over him now. After days of arguing back and forth with his parents, they'd finally relented the day before and reluctantly agreed to allow him to meet with the Piridet forces after all. As much as he'd pushed for it, that his parents had actually agreed was still a shock.

The agreement wasn't without some compromise, though. In the end it meant disguising more than just himself and Ryla. There was also Ley and his royal guard, all of whom would be dressed down to look like any regular knights and fighters off to a new post.

Adel's voice came from where she continued to stand beside him, putting words to his thoughts. "It's really happening."

"So it seems," Arran replied, looking down at her.

A moment passed between them that washed away the rest

of the world. Arran felt as though a single breath would shatter it, and with the way Adel stared back at him, he was certain she felt the same. Worries of dahems and magic prickled at the surface. Worries of death whispered beyond perception. But warmth enveloped them, protecting them.

Adel was the first to speak, and Arran knew what she would say by the expression in her eyes.

"Arran… Please let me come with—"

"No," he interrupted her gently, shaking his head. "It's far too dangerous. I couldn't live with myself if anything happened to you."

He held his breath, his soul flinching at the disappointment and hurt in her face. Visions of how the last time he'd told her no like this flashed through his mind. Suddenly, she took his hand.

"I know things are…uncertain between us." Her voice was barely a whisper. "But you must come back to me."

Arran swallowed the lump of emotion as her words hit him. "I will."

"You'd better."

THIRTY-SIX

G iven the mix of field knights and fighters travelling on both foot and horseback with wagons in tow, it was a couple days of travelling before they reached the Piridetian encampment. The approaching night brought with it temperatures that left Arran feeling frozen in his nondescript leather armour, woolen head covering, and the scarf wrapped around his face. Despite the sound of crackling fires in the camp Piridet had constructed at the meeting point on the way to Bunthle, none of the warmth reached him. He hoped he'd be able to retire soon as he was sore from the long ride.

A knight led Arran and a portion of his disguised entourage to the heart of the encampment where a fire cast a glow across an open space at the centre of the tents. The welcomingly smoky scent wafted around them, and Arran spotted Mihel talking to someone, the princess's dark, braided hair disappearing into the fur that lined her fitted tan coat. She didn't notice the group approaching until the person she was speaking with gestured their way, at which point she turned. Her expression brightened upon seeing them.

She closed the distance between them in several steps, smiling wide. Word had been sent ahead to her that they'd be coming disguised, given the danger to Arran's life. "I'm glad you all made it safely." The temperatures and the way her breath hung in the air didn't seem to faze her, even though she'd left the comfort of the fire.

"Likewise," Arran said. "My family and I are grateful for Piridet's aid and to you for coming personally. You could have simply sent a commander on your behalf."

"Nonsense." She waved the suggestion away with her gloved hand. "My mother and father can handle Piridet without me. And, if anything, it'll give my younger siblings a better chance to get some practice in."

Arran wasn't sure what sort of practice she might be referring to but didn't see the need to ask.

"High Protector, I never did get a chance to thank you for intervening at the Harvest Festival. The Union's protection is a blessing in these hard times," Mihel said with a low bow.

Ryla acknowledged the princess with a small nod, but otherwise said nothing where she stood in a plain cloak that covered her attire. The garment's pooling hood cast a shadow over most of her face. It reminded Arran of the Keepers.

"I trust the rest of your group is getting settled in?" Mihel asked next.

Arran nodded. The group had parted ways when they entered the camp, the large collection of Nithle knights and guards dispersing to tend to the horses and supplies as well as find their quarters. "I imagine it'd be best to follow suit and rest before getting to talks of coordinating our forces," Arran said in hopes of moving the conversation along to get out of the chill air.

"Yes. I've worked out a night guard schedule to ensure the camp is secure for the time being. Come morning, we can discuss a new schedule that works for each of us, but for tonight, this'll do." Her tone had changed from its light, conversational nature to something focused and matter-of-fact.

"That's perfect," Arran said with a nod.

"Excellent. I'll have a knight show you to the tents we've left for you," Mihel said, motioning someone over and relaying the instruction. She then returned her attention to Arran and the Killer. "Should anything happen, my tent is here. Just send for me," Mihel said before they could step away. She gestured toward a moderately-sized structure, which, by design, lacked anything that would designate it as a royal's tent.

Another nod accompanied Arran's reply. "Noted. Send for me if something arises. Good night."

The knight led them just across the opening where the fire continued to burn and toward a few tents into the darkness. Arran knew this was to keep the royals close, but not close enough that they could easily be taken out. Ryla's and Ley's tents flanked his, and the other guards surrounded them.

As Arran entered the tent, he was greeted by a small warm light. The accommodations were mostly bare, but that was to be expected from a temporary encampment; it had a small lantern and heavy blankets draped across a decently-sized cot.

Arran mulled over the few times he'd stayed in a camp as he unbuckled, unlaced, and otherwise removed the leathers, taking it off piece by piece and setting it on the stand set up to the side. The more he took off, the more the cold bit at him, even through his heavy pants and tunic. After removing his boots, he quickly got under the heavy blankets, hoping to preserve what heat he did have.

Snuffing the light left him shivering in the kind of darkness that didn't change whether his eyes were open or closed.

"Considering the reports of how Lavanai attacked Bunthle, I'd like to set up guard detail all along the west side of Lake Pol as well as the north side."

Arran swept his hand across the map with his fingers touching the page lightly. It was weighted in place on a table set up in one of the camp's tents the next morning. "That would give us enough perspective to see every way the dahems might come at us."

Mihel, who'd wanted to discuss logistics of combining their forces before continuing their next stint of travel, pointed to the opposite end of the lake. "What if they were to come from the south side? Or if they even decided to cross it?"

"They've never crossed it," Arran said with a shake of his head. He brushed his curls off his forehead absently. "It leaves them too visible, and we could pick them off with archers once they got close enough. For all their physical speed, it doesn't help them in the water, so they don't have any advantage coming straight across."

"Seems odd to me—surely there must be dahems that can manipulate water with their magic," Mihel commented, her gaze trailing to Ryla.

Up until that point, the Killer had been standing across the table from them and watching silently. She now responded to Mihel's comment. "With the size of the lake, it would take much of their energy. But not outside of the realm of possibility."

"Something to consider, then." Mihel nodded resolutely.

Arran glanced at Ley, who stood near Ryla, hoping for some reinforcements of his thoughts, but judging from the thoughtful look on his face, he agreed with Mihel and Ryla. Arran conceded. "All right. As for coming from the south end, it's unlikely. It'd mean a longer journey for them with Yandana Fort being here." He pointed at the map again to where it sat near the northern-most point of the lake. "While I suppose we can't rule it out definitively, historically, they've never come that way to attack Nithle."

Turning his gaze to Mihel, Arran saw her nod. Her dark hair was pinned back out of her eyes, and the hard, focused look on her face surprised him. He was used to seeing her at formal events, which softened her appearance and demeanour. Here, he realized she matched him, perhaps even exceeded him, as she had the fighting prowess to accompany her strategist mindset.

Mihel picked up the conversation again. "With that in mind, it's probably best we distribute our numbers as you've mentioned. I can also send a few dozen of my fighters to join any lookouts. However, while I don't doubt what you've said about the south being an unlikely pathway for them, it would still be wise to guard for that possibility."

"We could use as many forces as possible wherever we establish a frontline," Arran countered. "We'll want to fortify it as best we can to stop the dahems at the pass, so to speak."

Mihel stood straight and looked him in the eye, her challenging gaze meeting his. "The dahems are already desperate enough because of Killer Ryla. I've heard how they put a spy right in Nithle Proper, so I have no doubt they're going to be looking for more blind spots to try to overcome you. I'm not saying put all of our forces there, but we should at least have enough to hold them off and have someone who can come sound the alarm to the main base."

"I think you should consider it, Your Highness," Ley chimed in now.

Arran broke Mihel's gaze to connect with Ley's. Arran had never had an official advisor but trusted Ley well enough to consider him one, and Ley knew when he could and should push back against Arran. It was something he liked about the man.

"You're right," Arran ceded and returned his attention to Mihel. "How many are you thinking?"

Mihel paused to calculate for a moment. "Maybe fifty. That should still give us enough to have Piridet fill in on the front and have the few dozen I mentioned at the other end."

"Choose twenty-five of your group, and I'll supply the other half," Arran said.

"Okay. We can refine the numbers later if needed," Mihel continued. "Where do you factor into this, High Protector?"

"I go where Prince Arran goes," Ryla replied. She seemed to catch something in Mihel's gaze that Arran didn't because she added, "These are my orders."

He was very familiar with the word "orders," but it seemed to carry a different weight when Ryla said it.

"Shall we discuss weapons?" he said to break the unease he felt and to urge the conversation on.

Mihel gave him a look that he couldn't quite read, but the conversation did indeed move on to weaponry.

It was around midday by the time the group finished working out the initial details of how to fit the Nithle and Piridet armies together once they reached Bunthle. Afterward, the two royals convened for a hot meal in the mess tent while the rest of the camp began packing to move along. Ryla was the only one who joined them, and she had situated herself near the door.

"We've heard all the stories, but I can't say I ever quite expected a Killer to be like her," Mihel said idly as they ate.

Arran glanced at Mihel as he chewed and saw the princess had her eyes locked on Ryla.

"And she does seem very honed in on you," Mihel added.

This elicited a sigh from Arran, and he swallowed his food before turning back to her. "The rumours?"

Mihel smirked and gave a subtle nod. "Word spreads fast through the United. Not that Piridet believed for a second that the Union would stand for that kind of thing, even if you were crazy enough to try it. Seeing the pair of you confirms it though: I can tell it's all nonsense. She couldn't be any more focused on the Union's mandates if she tried. And you, well, I know perhaps better than anyone how you feel about Adel, and I doubt that's changed."

He sighed again. "Now if only she would believe it."

"You're pushing her away, aren't you?"

He felt his heart lurch in his chest as the words surprised him. The feeling must have translated to his face because Mihel laughed.

"I was interested in you long enough to come to understand quite a bit about you, Arran," she explained gently.

"I'm trying to protect her from all this." He gestured vaguely around the tent with his spoon before scooping more of the hot food into his mouth.

"Of course you are. But why?" Mihel asked, then quickly rephrased when he made to speak. "Okay, I know. You don't want her to get hurt or to lose her, but why is that an inevitability for you?"

"You *do* understand Nithle has been at war with Lavanai for decades, right? You *do* remember what happened the night of the festival?" he stressed.

"That doesn't mean it's going to end badly. Adel can hold her own. Besides, in these sorts of situations, it's best to have people stand with you. That's why we're banding together, after all."

He turned away. All she said made sense, but still, the mere thought of losing Adel made Arran's stomach plummet and his chest tighten.

Mihel mused aloud between her own mouthfuls of the meal. "So, Wendur is exiled. Veloth probably wouldn't fight even if the dahems were on their borders. Has Heta promised any fighters?"

Arran was glad for the subject change, even if it were only minor. "No. King Criph doesn't seem to want to budge despite travelling all the way to Nithle to show their allegiance. Our parents even recited the Alliance Pact," Arran divulged.

Shock crossed the princess's expression as her brow furrowed. "That's...wow. I don't know what to make of that."

"Me neither, so I'm focusing on what I do know. You're here, we've worked out a plan, and hopefully it'll be enough to alleviate some of what Nithle has endured," Arran continued firmly.

"And what do you plan to do?" Mihel ventured next.

"What do you mean?"

"Are you going to stay with the frontline or return to the castle?" When he paused, she continued. "I'm not here to judge, Arran. We each have our strengths and have our places to be. I just need to know if I'm going to have an undercover prince and Killer in my midst moving forward."

He studied her. Her words rang true despite any initial defensiveness he felt. As much as he prided himself on being able to read people, he found himself surprised by Mihel. He was used to the immature girl of years past, the one whose jealousy would get the best of her when he and Adel were together. Maybe she'd been evolving all along and he'd failed to notice.

"My place is at the castle," he said. "We'll stay until I've had a chance to take stock of Bunthle and we're certain things are settled."

"Well, let's get to it then," Mihel said, standing and pushing away from the table.

As Arran stood, he saw Ryla shift near the door from the corner of his eye and suddenly became aware of her again. Her movement was subtle, and her expression was the same as always, but something about the set of her body was off.

"Ryla?" he asked, earning a look from Mihel that he didn't have time to think about.

Her brown eyes met his blue. "Dahems are coming."

CHAPTER

THIRTY-EIGHT

Wilting wildflowers and a tapestry of a fox standing at the edge of a forest sparsely decorated the small inn room. Given that Sirama was a small village on the outskirts of Piridet, the Heta royals could have beseeched the kingdom for some place more grand to rest their heads on their journey back to their own kingdom, but King Criph and Queen Mela had decided the inn would make do.

An untouched text laid open on the wooden table before Adel where she sat across from Rynn. The young prince dutifully turned the pages of his own book, but she couldn't seem to focus, no matter how many times her eyes ran over the words. Her thoughts were louder than the dark ink on the page, and her limbs tingled with restlessness.

By now, Arran would have reached the meeting point with Piridet, out in the open and away from the protective confines of Nithle castle. It had been hard to leave knowing he was potentially putting himself in danger and that she couldn't be there for him, but she tried to remind herself of the protective forces he'd be surrounded by.

Knight Ley is with him. His entourage. Killer Ryla, she told herself silently. *Even Mihel will be able to defend him. Thank the United that Piridet has stepped in.*

Still, she couldn't stop the thought that followed. *I wish I were with him, too.*

Adel shook herself mentally, allowing her sights to be snared by a guard doing his rounds. Darkness left the guard as mostly a silhouette passing by the curtained window.

The turning of another page in Rynn's book spurred her into movement, as if the motion had propelled her out of her seat. The princess felt her brother's gaze fall on her.

"What're you doing?" Rynn asked, pushing his chair back with a scrape across the worn wooden floor.

"I need to speak with Father." Even as the words left her mouth, she steeled herself against what she was about to do.

The doorknob's cold metal barely registered against her skin as she turned it and pulled the door open. A *thunk* behind her was followed by footsteps; she assumed Rynn was right behind her. Megnata had already been dismissed for the evening and was in her own quarters down the hall, so it was only the two siblings' and their guards' footsteps that travelled down the wide corridor to the chambers the king and queen shared.

Criph and Mela were equally guarded, and one of those guards knocked on the door as the royal children approached. By the time Adel and Rynn made it to the room, the door had already swung open to admit them.

As the door closed behind them, Adel took a deep breath where she'd paused just inside the room. It was similar to the one she and her brother shared, though slightly bigger with fresher flowers and more tapestries. The same sort of table was pushed off to the side of the room, and her parents sat in the chairs where it looked like they had been speaking quietly. The room also had a distinct smell of cinnamon, one of their mother's favourite scents.

Rynn stopped beside Adel almost protectively; maybe the restlessness she felt in her limbs reverberated to him. Her parents' expressions only projected curiosity and confusion.

Another deep breath. "I'd like to speak with Father alone."

Mela's brows pinched together, eyes flickering between her two children. "What is it, Adel?"

"It's okay," Criph told her with a gentle smile. "Can you take Rynn?"

Mela's gaze shifted to her husband, and a silent conversation passed between them. Adel noticed only subtle changes in their expressions—a crinkle of the eye, a quirk of the mouth, a tilt of the head—and none of it meant anything to her, but the couple seemed to understand each other perfectly. Eventually, the queen nodded and stood to herd their son. Rynn hesitated at first, but when Adel gave him a nod, he left with their mother, and the guards closed the door behind them.

Adel didn't waste a moment, using the nervous energy to drive her. "I need the truth. Why aren't we helping Nithle?" The king opened his mouth to respond, but she ploughed on before he could get a word out. "We just went and made this big show of our alliance. You all said the Alliance Pact. And yet…and yet it feels as though we're not going to do anything."

Criph's response came without pretense or preamble. "We're not."

Adel inhaled sharply. She studied his features, hoping that he was somehow trying to throw her off to calm her down. No matter how many times her eyes roamed his familiar face, she saw no hint of anything apart from the seriousness in his expression.

"That can't be true," she finally managed to say. Her voice sounded far away. "The alliance…"

The king's focus was locked on his daughter. "We can be allied with a kingdom and not agree with what it's doing. Just as we can care about people and not agree with what they're doing."

He'd barely moved in his chair, as if he weren't laying verbal blows and talking about betraying their closest ally. He was the picture of calmness and regality, the same as he'd looked only days before while giving an address to Nithle's people alongside King Alden.

Meanwhile, her mind was spinning out of control.

"That's ridiculous!" she spat. "We can't just abandon them."

"Adel—"

"We're just going to let them die? King Alden has been your friend since childhood! Lavanai's forces wiped out another village! Invaded the castle! We almost died witnessing their assault on the kingdom. Ashla *did die*!" The words tumbled out of her mouth, and she couldn't seem to stop them.

"Adel!"

Her father's sharp tone was enough to bring her to a halt. Her chest heaved, and she realized she was shaking. There was more ready to burst from her, but she forced her mouth to stay closed.

His expression and tone had an edge of strain when he spoke again, lines on his face appearing deeper than she'd ever seen them. "You don't understand. I was hoping this conversation could wait."

"What's to understand? We're *abandoning* them!" she repeated.

Frustration and weariness joined the strain, and Adel got the sense he was collecting his thoughts. Again, she wanted to say more but waited. Maybe she would get a proper explanation after all.

It was the king's turn to take a deep breath. "Alden becomes more and more like his father and grandfather each day," Criph said, his tone quieter now. He broke eye contact just briefly to stare at his hands before looking at her again. "When we were kids, he promised that wouldn't happen. That he would set things right."

Adel searched her father's eyes for some clue as to what he was going on about. All she saw was a king that looked simultaneously more aged from the weight of what he was saying and younger as his thoughts pulled him back in time.

When he didn't continue, Adel prodded gently. "What do you mean?"

Another heavy breath. "The war."

"What about it?"

"Nithle initiated the war with Lavanai."

Her jaw fell, but her father held up a hand, holding back her words.

"There has never been amicability between our people and the dahems, but there used to be something resembling peace. They didn't bother us. We didn't bother them. But King Gerge, Alden's grandfather, feared the dahems' powers. He feared they would come after him and his people once they fully realized the advantage they had over humans.

"So, he attacked them first. He and a faction of his closest followers plotted and carried out a secret attack. When Lavanai retaliated, he used that to gain favour from his people to begin the war. He spun a story. Said Lavanai was dangerous and finally coming after them with their magic. He used his lie to breed fear into the Nithlean people, and by extension, the rest of the United. He said the dahems needed to be kept in check, or all humans would die.

"Lavanai's king came to Nithle to make peace, and Gerge had him captured and executed. There was no going back after that, and Gerge guarded his secret closely."

The air hummed in the silence that followed the story. It hadn't done anything to calm her racing thoughts; if anything, it spun them more wildly out of control.

"How do you know this?" Adel's voice was barely a whisper, as though it were being smothered by what Criph had just shared. If this were true…

"Each Nithle royal passes the truth down to the next generation. When Alden and his brothers and sister learned of it, he shared it with me even though he was effectively risking his neck." He paused again. "He was mortified. He'd always seen his father as a hero. This shattered everything he knew, and, even though he wasn't first in line for the throne, he vowed he would bring an end to the conflict. He didn't want to admit the truth, but he wanted to find some way to bring an end to the fighting."

The king's shoulders heaved with another sigh. "I don't know when things changed. He never shared that with me. Maybe it was when his siblings each died in battle, and he had to take the throne. Maybe it was when Arran was born, and they learned Shron could have no other children. Maybe he's fearful Arran will be killed by the dahems."

He licked his lips as he sifted through his thoughts again, eyes seeming to see somewhere beyond the physical world even as he stared at his daughter. "I tried to remind him what he had set out to do. Of his promise. Of my promise to do anything I could to help our kingdoms find peace again. He's at the point of no return. Thinks there's no other way. He's planning to launch an attack on Lavanai directly—despite the Killer's advisement against it."

Does Arran know? Was he keeping such a horrible secret from her? What if his insistence on protecting her was to shield her from the lie and the suicide mission his father was planning?

Adel found her voice again. "We have to stop them! We

can show them there's another way."

"No. Now is the time to protect my family and my people. Alden isn't going to give up. I spent the better part of our trip and even the weeks leading up to it trying to convince him otherwise. I need to plan to protect *us* from the consequences of his decisions. Things have changed, and so, too, have many of our contingency plans. We will never abandon Nithle, but—"

"But we have!" Adel snapped again.

The strain in Criph's expression disappeared as it hardened anew. His tone held a warning when he spoke. "You have no idea what you're talking about."

She ignored what he said, latching instead onto another thought as it came to her. "And how does the Union fit into all of this?"

"Their part of the story remains unchanged."

Yet, something whispered to her that the Union must know of the truth. *What if they know the truth and still can't stop Lavanai?* The thought made her stomach drop. Could the dahems really be that powerful? Aloud, she said, "We have to help Nithle."

"Enough!" Criph snapped, his knuckles turning white where he gripped the arms of the chair. "Don't let your heart lead you blindly."

The words slapped her, the tingles rippling out in sudden shock and rage like she'd never felt before. "You think that's what this is about? That I only want to help because I love Arran?"

Her father said nothing for a fraction of a second too long.

Heat rose in her cheeks. "How dare you! There is more to me than a girl in love. I know the cost of this war, and if there's something we can do to stop it, I'm going to do it!"

Not waiting for his response, Adel stormed from the room

and down the hall at a run. She barely registered that the guards were no longer posted outside the door.

Her feet led her not back to her shared quarters with her brother, but to a room she remembered seeing an attendant come out of earlier. No one would look for her here—at least not at first. As she leaned against the closed door to catch her breath, she took in the supplies and clothing for groundskeepers as well as another door across the small room. The smell of dirt, dampness, and old leathers filled her senses as her chest heaved.

She stared at the space around her for what felt an eternity as she tried to stop the hurting in her heart and the chaos in her mind. *How can I help? What can I do?*

Fury burned her blood, and resentment chased close behind. So many people were telling her what to do—Arran, her mother, now her father—and just expecting her to submit and go along with it all. No longer. She couldn't bring herself to care about the consequences she would face for this.

I have to return to Nithle.

Whether Arran knew the secret or not, no matter how much he pushed her away, she knew with complete certainty that she needed to return to him. To be by his side and fight with him—whatever that meant at this point. Maybe King Alden was right. Maybe there was no other way now. But she'd be there for it.

Adel pushed herself forward, knowing she had to act quickly. The guards would be searching for her once her parents realized she hadn't gone back to her room, and she wanted to be far away from here by the time that happened.

She crossed to where groundskeepers' clothing hung along the wall, quickly shedding her light evening dress to pull on a pair of too-large worker's pants and a baggy tunic. The boots were the only things that fit even close to right, but even they were still roomy. Making her way to the other door, she plucked a coat from where it hung along the wall. The heavy material was a soft hide lined with what felt like wool, and when she slipped her arms through and pulled the hood up, it hung well past her waist and hands and almost covered her eyes. The ensemble would be enough to conceal her identity.

Caution bade her open the door slowly and peek through the crack before venturing out. Beyond was another narrow room with a fire crackling away where she couldn't see. A soft orange glow warmed the space, but no one said anything. The room seemed empty.

Giving it one more second to be sure, she collected her thoughts, then darted out toward what she hoped was a door leading outside. When she peered through its window to situate herself, she indeed saw the outdoors and, thankfully, no guards. She needed to act quickly before they came back.

The air nipped at her as she slipped across the inn's grounds to where she had seen the stables. If people here were on the same sort of schedule as her stable hands in Heta, there wouldn't be anyone about right now. It was a lot to bank on, but she had no other choice.

Luckily, the stables were empty except for the horses. The place smelled of hay and the animals, who stirred from her nervous energy as she went stall to stall to find her family's crest. Finally, she found the kestrel on a blanket hanging just outside a stall door.

Thank goodness for lessons, she thought as she took the sturdy blanket and entered the stall. The thought of lessons reminded her of one person she'd be leaving behind. *I'm sorry, Rynn.*

She draped the blanket across the stallion's back, and his nostrils flared to capture her scent, but otherwise, he let her go about the rest of the saddling and bridling process without protest.

Finally, she lifted the reins over the horse's head so the loop rested over the saddle horn, and then she grasped them just under the horse's chin to guide him out of the stall. The clop of his hooves seemed excessively loud on the stone floor, and she tensed with each step they took, but no one came their way even as her heart hammered. After pushing the stable doors open, she hoisted herself into the saddle, which creaked as she settled in, and urged the animal into motion.

He took off like a bolt of lightning. Adel wasn't sure if she heard shouting behind her or if it was her imagination, but she took off toward Nithle without looking back.

In spite of the adrenaline and anger propelling her along, a smile curved Adel's lips as the wind pulled at the hood and overly-large clothes. A new strength and determination had awoken inside of her.

If only Ashla could see me now.

The camp was abuzz with energy as a flurry of motion erupted around Ryla. At her word, Arran and Mihel had spurred their people into action, and even as a scout came rushing in on horseback with confirmation that dahems had been spotted coming quickly, no one was still. Arran and Mihel doled out orders while attendants strapped on their armour.

Ryla was alert to all going on, but her main focus was on Arran, who stood as still as his nervous energy would allow for the leathers to be tied tightly around his body. The fact that she could sense them meant the dahems were too close for him to make an escape back to Nithle Proper and the safety of the castle.

She thought as well of his lessons with the strict weapons master and the progress he'd been making with the bow and even dueling daggers, both of which he carried with him now.

Not ready. Progress was good, but this was real battle, not a master class.

She'd have to protect him by some other means.

As Arran tightened the last piece of his leathers with the Ley's help, Ryla stepped toward them. The knight immediately gave her his attention.

"We must get the prince to safety," she said and he nodded in agreement.

"What? No! I can help fight." Even as he said it, the tension in his jaw and shoulders belied his verbal bravado.

"Listen to Killer Ryla, Arran," Mihel bit out as she adjusted the protection around her neck and then drew her sword. "Your desire to fight is commendable, but you've done what you can. Now, for the sake of your kingdom, follow her to safety."

"What was the point of putting all this on then?" he asked with annoyance as he motioned up and down his body to the various pieces of protective gear.

"To keep you alive," Ryla said, reconnecting her gaze with Ley's. The knight gave her another nod.

"Be reasonable, Arran," Ley said gently. "Princess Mihel can handle things here and will send word for more fighters. We need to make sure you're safe."

Ryla caught the prince's eye again. His blues bore into her browns with something akin to betrayal crossing his features, but it had no effect on her.

She pressed on. "We're wasting time."

The prince inhaled. "Fine. Let's go."

A collection of guard moved in a wave as Arran, Ley, and Ryla shifted away from the oncoming dahem forces through the remaining tents and bundled wagons ready for departure. Laboured breathing and fast feet didn't take them far before the sounds of battle sounded in the air. Cries of effort and pain tangled in an indiscernible mess among the clash of weapons and twang of bows. With each step, the conflict sounded more distant.

As the rest of the group continued along the cold-hardened ground, Prince Arran came to a grinding halt, nearly tripping over his own feet in the process. Ryla rounded on him. The telltale signs of a mind consumed with past horrors was written in his blank stare and tensing facial muscles.

"Arran!" Ley called before bringing the rest of the group

to a stop and rushing back to surround him. "We have to keep moving."

Ryla ignored the knight, knowing they had a very small window within which to act.

"Arran," she commanded in her emotionless way. "Look at me."

When he didn't, she took it a step further, grabbing hold of his upper arms hard enough to make the leathers creak. Still nothing. She punched him in the face.

He staggered, a long, slow blink following as he registered the world around him again and a red mark bloomed along his cheekbone. Many in the entourage had gasped, but Ley seemed to understand what was happening and stopped anyone from stepping forward by holding out an arm.

Ryla addressed Arran now as he stared at her. "Hang on to that pain and stay in the present."

The next moment, one of the guards shouted, "Your Highness!"

The whoosh of fire drowned out Arran's protests as Ryla shoved him hard in the direction of his guards, who were backing away at the same time. The Killer took several paces backward as the flames climbed to an eight-foot wall around her.

I'm the target, she thought as she registered Mithos's magical essence amid the heat pouring down around her. *Just like with Naxela.* He'd warned her as much.

She turned away from the wall of flames when she sensed unfamiliar magic users. A group of eight, garbed in full Lavanian battle leathers, formed a perimeter along the edge of the blaze, seemingly unaffected by the heat as she stepped into the middle. The flame's light cast shadows across their features and set their amber eyes aglow.

They're after something.

If they were after her life, it would have made more sense to let the fire consume her. It felt calm and controlled, leading Ryla to believe Mithos was still in command of her faculties. The dahem could smother her with her magical fire without a second thought. That she didn't meant there was another strategy at play that Ryla didn't have time to figure out.

The options, of which there were very few, flipped through Ryla's mind. She had to fight the dahems to get outside the ring of fire, certainly—but would she push by those watching her, slay them herself, or sacrifice them to their commander's magic?

All thought of Arran and Nithle fled her.

She would do whatever it took to stay alive.

Ryla became perfectly still, using every sense she could—from sight to sensing magic—to predict how the group might attack. These dahems were well-trained, barely even communicating in glances to each other. Every tiny movement meant something; every tensing muscle or hum of magic was a warning.

Leaping into the air, Ryla avoided the lightning strike that crackled across the ground toward her. This lightning didn't touch her, and for the brief moment she was in the air, she twisted to scan what the others might do next. One of the dahems protected the rest of the group from the electric charge by bringing the ground up to form a shield. As she landed, the force of it slamming into her legs, the electricity fizzled out and the earthly barrier crumbled. She propelled herself toward the group.

The dahem grunted as her shoulder connected with its chest with enough force to send it flying through the flames to the other side. The high-pitched scream was brief before it was swallowed by the roar of the fire.

Another dahem that charged from her left narrowly missed Ryla's sword when she thrust it forward, leaving it to spear the air instead. She adjusted her stance and balance, striking again, this time hitting the target while debilitating another. Before she could give the finishing blow, the hum of magic rose again, and the earth burst up from underneath her feet. Her efforts to jump away were ineffective as another chunk of the ground shot up, slammed into her legs, and sent her rolling across the ground.

Ryla used the motion to her advantage, twisting into a position that allowed her to get partially upright and dig into the ground to slow her down and avoid the flames. By the time she came to a stop, she had one knee against the terrain, the opposite foot dug into the earth with that knee close to her chest. Her palms lay flat for extra balance, but balance was a secondary concern.

Brown eyes darted across the ground, halting when they came to her sword, at which point she pushed her body into action. The switch in her mind from attacking the dahems to retrieving her sword was nearly subconscious. Words she'd heard often in her training from many a Keeper surfaced in her mind: *never relinquish your weapon.*

No doubt as mindful of her movements as she was theirs, another surge of earth magic rippled along the ground and sent the weapon skidding out of the flaming circle before she could get to it.

Her eyes locked on where it had skidded through the wall of fire, and she surged forward, prepared to take on whatever injury necessary.

Get the sword. Get out of the dahems' reach, her mind commanded.

She danced around another surge of lightning, which

was quickly followed by another piece of hard ground flying up in front of her. Adjusting her footing, she decided to try another way through the flames. She'd worry about closing the gap between her and her weapon once on the other side.

Mid-movement, her form seized.

Each of Ryla's senses failed. The world disappeared, became impossibly silent and devoid of scents and the touch of nature. Even the roar and motion of the flames snuffed out and stilled. She felt both outside of and trapped within her body. A void swallowed her whole.

The sensation of a bowstring snapping reverberated through her entire body. Suddenly, she couldn't breathe.

Thousands of faces flashed through her mind in such a rapid succession she couldn't recognize them. The flying images were accompanied by blood and screams and more screams and more screams.

And then she realized one of the screams was her own.

And the world crashed back into place with the entirety of existence slamming into her at full force.

Her heart beat too quickly. Her mind raced. Her body trembled.

Somehow, a question flit through her mind among the chaos. *Is this death?*

The pain blooming in her lungs and rawness of her throat told her this was all real and she was alive.

The rest of her senses trickled back, but too slowly. She had no idea where the dahems were, if the fire still burned around her, how much time had passed. Nothing. As her thoughts scrambled to right themselves, only one word resounded within her. It begged to be called into existence, so she opened her mouth.

"*Cizeth!*"

Gold light erupted from around her, bringing with it more screams as it doused the terrain.

To Ryla, it felt like warmth—a blanket wrapping around her, protecting and comforting her as the images of death and chaos continued on in her mind. She'd never heard the word she had called out, but she knew it unleashed the light and called it to her.

Sharp pain jolted through her body, starting with her knees as she collapsed to the ground and fell forward onto her stomach. The light began to fade all too soon, and the weight of reality burrowed into her again. She closed her eyes to try to block out the chaos. Somewhere amidst the noise, she heard a call for retreat and voices calling to their commander.

"High Protector!"

To whom the voice belonged, she didn't know. It sounded both near and far, potentially right at her side or across the field.

"She's shaking," another voice chimed in.

"*Shaking?*" A third voice, dripping with disbelief. A pause. "Someone get a healer!"

"No need." A fourth voice. The only one that registered any sort of familiarity and commanded Ryla's attention. "Get up, Ryla." The Keeper's voice was distinctly close, like its owner might crawl inside her mind. She might welcome it.

"Esteemed Keepers, something's happened to her," the third voice tried to explain with thick desperation. "We'll get the healer to examine her right away."

"She *will stand* on her *own*."

The duty to obey the Keeper chipped away at some of the mayhem, faces and voices fading if only slightly. Still, she couldn't move or open her eyes. Not that keeping her eyes sealed helped much. Apart from the faces, screams, and blood, a tumult of feeling ripped through her. One she recognized very easily but had never experienced herself: panic.

Her gloved hands balled into fists where they rested on the ground near her head. Overwhelming was too small a word.

On top of everything else, she became distinctly aware that magic was pulling toward her. Not the slow, controlled pull she was used to when inviting the magic to her to draw it from others. No. This was fast. Sharp. Aggressive.

It'll devour me.

Somehow, through everything, she heard a laugh.

"Shut up, dahem!" someone snapped. "You're lucky we don't execute you right on the spot. The princess will want to have a word with you."

Princess? Aren't we in the middle of a battle? Hasn't it only been a few moments since the golden light vanished?

"It doesn't matter if you kill me," the dahem got out between chortles. "We've ruined *her*."

Ryla's body responded in a flurry of rage and a need to know what the dahem was mouthing off about. In a few swift movements, she located and grabbed her sword, threw a human to the side, and had the laughing dahem pinned to the ground. She blinked a few times as she stared down at him. It felt like her eyes were burning.

"Explain." There was a dangerous edge to Ryla's voice that she didn't recognize.

The dahem stopped laughing, and out of the corner of her eye, Ryla saw the Keepers block others from intervening. That they even wanted to intervene annoyed her. Who were they to try to stop her? *Can they feel the chaos, too?* she wondered. Suppressing it for the moment, she returned her full attention to the dahem.

"Speak!"

She leaned in, her weight applying more pressure to the

dahem's chest under her hand and bringing her sword's blade to his neck.

"When Mithos told us of the story of rendering a Killer incapacitated, I didn't believe it. Now though… Well, you're not incapacitated, but you're *changed*."

Her eyes searched his face for further meaning, but all she saw as he lapsed into another chortle was the crinkle around his eyes. And his burned skin. Severely burned, she saw, now that she truly looked at him.

"The flames…" Ryla barely uttered.

The chortling stopped. "The light."

She inhaled, brow furrowing. Without letting up the pressure, she glanced around. The dishevelled remnants of the camp and bodies littered the ground around them. All dahem, she thought, from their essences. Shifting her gaze to the humans, she could see they were unharmed, even that fool of a Nithlean prince.

Why didn't he run?

She didn't have time to make sense of it.

The dahem, tones now sober, brought her attention back to him. "You're still dangerous, certainly. But you'll be of no help to those at the castle now."

"What did he say?"

Ryla didn't need to look to recognize Arran's voice.

"There's an attack on the castle, too," Ryla reasoned aloud for Arran's benefit. The dahem's grin told her all she needed to know. "They're as good as dead."

"Mind still as sharp as ever," the dahem chided.

Ryla tossed her sword to the side and slugged the dahem across the face. The physical exertion felt good even as her knuckles smarted where they'd connected. The dahem fell silent but for a groan, and, with that, she stood and motioned for no one in particular to collect him.

It finally clicked in her mind: *Mihel is the princess that'll want to speak with him.*

As the dahem, who seemed to have lost his desire to laugh, was dragged off, she collected her sword, wiped it, and rammed it into its sheath with such force that she heard a click and felt the tug at her waist.

"Ryla!" Arran called to her, his voice drawing nearer. It sounded too like he shoved his way through some people. "We have to get to the castle and—"

He came up short in motion and sentence when she whirled on him. His eyes widened and his dark brows shot up. Shock and horror—not uncommon reactions to seeing a Killer sometimes, but this was something else. Even the first time he'd seen her, he hadn't looked at her like this.

"What is it?" she snapped. Part of her wondered if he could see her eyes burning as she felt the continuous sting.

"Your eyes..."

Maybe he can, she mused.

"...are streaked gold..."

Ice shot through her limbs, and she whipped around to find the Keepers.

I'm tainted. She couldn't bring herself to vocalize the reality. *The magic pulling toward me. I didn't have my mental blockers up. But I didn't invite it.*

She saw for the first time there were six Keepers, each with their faces in shadows. Even still, she could see the tension in their shoulders and caught the shift of hoods as though they glanced at each other. One stepped forward a few paces, and she recognized him immediately from his essence. His magical signature. The gravity of the Keeper's ability to use even some magic struck her as it never had. She also had a distinct sense that if they were to pull back their hoods, their eyes, too, would have at least flecks of gold littered throughout their irises.

"What happened to me?" Even as she asked it, something within her responded. *That word called it to me. I* did *invite it.*

The Keepers said nothing as she stared at them. Not a single one of them was shocked by what had happened. Not a single one of them was concerned about the magic.

They've seen this happen before. She tried to swallow away the tightness in her throat. A new thought jumped into her mind. *The magic has been here all along.*

As if they could see the recognition cross her expression, the Keepers closed the gap.

"Report," the Keeper that had originally spoken commanded of one of the others.

"Too many. Many are gone," another Keeper said briefly.

The words were too vague to register any particular meaning to Ryla, and the first Keeper didn't give her mind time to catch up.

"We must go," he said.

"Go? What's going on here?" Arran's voice broke through again. His tone was frantic, and he moved onto the next thought before they could respond to or ignore him. "If what the dahem said is true, we need to get back to the castle. I need your help, Ryla."

A pinch twisted in Ryla's chest that she didn't understand. "I can't help you now, Arran." She couldn't look at him but felt his gaze boring into her. She suppressed the desire to hide from not only his gaze, but all the eyes she felt on her.

"Of course you can. You're changed. Anyone can see that, but you're still a Killer. You're still as fast and strong as you always were," he persisted, his voice strained and desperate.

"Ryla will not be returning to Nithle," the Keeper said,

his voice firm. "We will return to the Union immediately."

"What are you talking about?"

Ryla grit her teeth to bite back telling the prince to mind his place.

"Come, Ryla." The Keeper turned the icy tone on her.

She took a step to follow them, feeling too aware of her body.

"Ryla!" Arran called out.

"Arran!" A new voice that sounded like Ley; Ryla knew he would stop the young man from putting himself in harm's way with the Union.

"There's nothing more I can do for you, Arran." She struggled to keep her voice even. She still wouldn't look at him. "Go protect your people."

A final step toward the Keepers, and the land and people around her disappeared with a swell of magic.

CHAPTER

FORTY

The steady throb pulsating in Arran's cheek was all that permeated the feeling of unreality wrapped tightly around him. That and the aching in his legs from sprinting through the camp.

It all happened so fast. One moment, he'd been fleeing the dahems with his heart in his throat and Ley and Ryla, along with the rest of his guard, racing with him. The next, the clamour of war had vibrated through the air to dance over his skin, and that touch had dragged him into the most powerful memory yet.

The battleground and the sea of tents had faded before him, replaced by the square in Nithle Proper. What started out as simple sparks of the festival's playmakers turned into a flash of lightning and a crack of thunder. His indecision, his *uselessness*, had ended a life. Again. Again and again and again.

Just as forcefully, Ryla had wrenched him back to reality before a wall of flames seemed to swallow her whole. Panic had nestled into his chest then. He'd barely heard Ley trying to urge him on.

"Your Highness?" A voice outside the unreality. It barely made a crack.

Arran's gaze connected with Ley's. The man looked haggard with dirt and blood splatted on his face and armour. Concern etched his features with furrowed brows, a tight jaw, and tense shoulders.

Yet, all Arran felt like he could see was the dancing flames and the swell of the dahem army. Arran had needed to act. He'd focused on the pain in his cheek, just as Ryla had instructed, and did what he could to defend himself and fight back. Among the melee, the small, dark-haired dahem had continued to shout orders as she controlled her magically-formed blaze. At least, he assumed they were orders given the commanding tone of her flowing language and how others snapped into action.

Mithos. That's her name.

Suddenly, there'd been an explosion like none he'd felt or seen before. As a child, Arran had been outside on the castle grounds when the old blacksmith's forge had exploded, and the explosion from the battlefield had reminded him of that. Except the forge exploding felt miniscule in comparison.

It was so bright. He squinted as he relived it in his memories. *And her eyes...*

He could still picture Ryla's eyes: gold-streaked and full of ire. And her features, usually blank, hardened to match. It was like seeing an entirely different person, the most horrifying part of it being the presence of magic where there'd been none before.

What happened in the flames? What did the dahems do to her?

Arran had no idea if there was any precedence of magic being forced upon someone else, but he'd also never heard of magic overtaking someone this quickly either. His mind raced with the possibilities.

"Arran."

He saw Ley's mouth move, but his brain was slow to connect the sound of the voice to its owner.

Ground yourself in the pain, Arran told himself as he focused on the throb below his eye again.

"They took her." The words came out quick and short as he scanned the scene around them. More bodies than he dared count. Knights and fielders shifting through the carnage to find any still alive. Screams of pain from somewhere nearby sent a group running in that direction.

Ley let out a breath that didn't sound the least bit relieved. "They did. We have to trust the Keepers know what they're doing. They'll help Killer Ryla and then return to us."

"How can you be so sure?" Arran didn't like that he heard Davi in his own question. What if the young lord had been right all along? His stomach dropped as panic blasted through the numbness and diluted the pain. "We have to return to the castle! My parents—that dahem said they attacked the castle as well. We have to help them." The prince turned frantically. "Someone fetch me a horse!"

Ley's hands planted firmly on Arran's shoulders even as footsteps rushed off. "Hang on, Your Highness. We need to assess the situation here before we go running off to—"

"Let Mihel handle the situation here," Arran demanded sharply as he stared at him hard. "She'll know how to handle this better than I ever could. Someone can inform her where we've gone."

"Think logically, Arran. It's too dangerous to go rushing into things. Not with what's just happened."

"To *hell* with logic right now!" His lungs strained for air, shoulders heaving to try to renew the supply. He barely had enough to say, "*Please, Ley.*"

"Commander Calar and the rest of the Royal Knights will…" Ley trailed off as his eyes darted back and forth between Arran's. There must have been something there that compelled him because he let out another heavy breath, dropping his hands. "We'll take as many with us as we can. We have no idea what we'll face out there."

Arran swallowed and nodded. "Thank you."

"I have a sense you'd go whether I agreed or not. My duty is to protect you, Arran. And if this is your will, then I shall follow."

Arran wasn't sure he'd ever experienced the depth of gratitude he felt for Ley just then. He thought to vocalize it, but Ley had already turned away to give his own orders and gather a group to return with them to the castle. The moment gave Arran the opportunity to take in his surroundings again.

Forcing himself to see past the blood and the bodies, Arran took in the sights of the battered and collapsed tents as well as those wagons that had been prepared to leave, now upturned. Food, supplies, furniture, dishes, and many other things, strewn across the ground. Healers and others moved around them to get to those who needed aid.

Finally, hooves approached. Arran was momentarily surprised that the horses weren't more skittish with all that was happening around them, but he remembered they were battle-trained animals. As if to agree with his silent realization, one of them let out a huff and tossed its head. As it did, the prince noticed the leather shaffron running down the horse's face and peytral covering its chest, the material nearly the same colour as the beast's bay coat.

Ley came to stand beside Arran again. "I've gathered a group of thirty-five, Your Highness."

"Good." Arran nearly choked on the word, the panic still bubbling within. In an effort to ease the building inner tension, he stepped toward the horses. "Let's move out."

The creak of leather barding joined the rest of the din as Arran and his company hauled themselves into saddles.

Arran's aching legs protested, but he forced himself to ignore it this time.

I can't stop until I've reached my parents, he told himself.

They're as good as dead, Ryla's cold words echoed in his mind.

"Move out!" Arran called to the company as he urged the horse forward. Thundering hooves crossed the plain.

Others watched the group depart, but Arran trusted Mihel would be able to handle things in the camp while he went to the castle. Realistically, he didn't know what he and a group of a thirty-five would accomplish against a company of dahems, but he had to know that his parents were safe.

She's wrong, he told himself firmly, gripping the reins tighter. The sinking feeling in his gut reminded him Ryla had never been wrong before. *This time, she is.*

CHAPTER

FORTY-ONE

Wind pushed at Ryla's body and nipped the bare skin on her face. It cooled her eyes, which still felt like they were burning, and she wondered absently as she stared at the Union stronghold if all Tainted felt this. None had ever complained of it, although most never had words for her.

You've been touched, too. The words of the tainted Nithlean girl surfaced unbidden in her mind.

Touched by magic... Ryla thought now. It hadn't been nonsense after all.

The magical transportation from Nithle to the Union grounds had felt almost as different as her eyes did. The swell of magic was stronger, more present somehow, but it didn't pull toward her like the magic on the battlefield had. Whatever magic the Keepers had and used, there was some sort of block. She wasn't sure whether the block protected her from the magic or the magic from her.

Watchtowers stood at intervals around the otherwise open Union grounds, and while they had always been occupied, Ryla had never seen them this active. There were five Keepers to a tower: three at the base, working magic to keep an invisible force field in place, and two at the top of the platform, vigilantly watching those who came close.

The number of Keepers in each tower wasn't the only unorthodox thing about the scene. After any other mission,

Keepers would transport Killers directly into the stronghold, the main hall acting as both a physical and magical entryway. There, she'd receive word on whether she had another task to complete or whether she would return to the training routine that occupied all Killers when they weren't on duty.

Instead, Ryla and the six Keepers accompanying her stood and waited in silence to cross the force field. Despite the wind, Ryla noticed their hoods didn't budge and their faces remained in shadow. None seemed to pay her any attention, but she wasn't so naïve as to think their awareness wasn't keen.

After several long minutes, a shift in the magical essence signaled the removal of the magical barrier. Several minutes more brought the group across the empty plains toward the formidable, single-storey building after crossing the between the watchtowers. The stronghold's dark, stone face stood starkly against the grey sky—a sight Ryla had seen many times. That it stood unchanged despite the change coursing through her brought her comfort.

Entering the building revealed a wide, rounded space devoid of any decoration or person. Even the few other Killers she knew the Union had were nowhere to be seen, and she couldn't sense them either. Without warning, her mind wandered back to Lord Davi and his story of his taken sibling. Did that person still live? Had she met this Killer?

It doesn't matter. She banished the thought from her head.

Her mind became annoyingly preoccupied with questions of where the Keepers were leading her and for what purpose as they travelled the hallways. She tried focusing on the way their footsteps ricocheted and the smell of the torches lighting the windowless walls. These only helped marginally to keep her mind off the questions she didn't want or need to think about. The Keepers were her guardians. There was no sense in questioning them. No need to.

They finally stopped at the end of a hall where a lone set of double doors hung from ornate-looking hinges. Ryla's brow furrowed at the frivolity of it among the otherwise unadorned building. She'd never been in this wing before and couldn't fathom what might be behind the door.

One of the Keepers broke off from the group and entered the room without a word. The others, Ryla suddenly noticed, stood in something of a cluster around her. That she hadn't noticed their formation earlier startled her, and a sinking feeling gripped her core.

Pay attention, she scolded herself. Her jaw clenched.

One of the two doors opened again, and the Keeper motioned for Ryla to enter. She stepped across the threshold and was immediately closed in without the other Keepers.

"It's been years since a Killer has broken."

The smooth male voice drew Ryla's attention in a snap. The ceiling's skylight illuminated a man who, surely, was a Keeper, although she'd never before seen one dressed as he was. Rather than heavy robes, he wore simple tan slacks and a white short-sleeved shirt with a dark fabric belt around the waist. More fascinating were the tattoos that marked the backs of his hands and inner elbows. The dark, thick lines were shapes she wasn't familiar with but reminded her of the sloping *S* shapes of the Killer's marks.

The man approached her with interest, his eyes fixed on her as he had a slight forward lean in his posture. His hands were clasped before him, as if to stop himself from reaching out to touch her.

Ryla was equally interested. There was no magical essence coming from him the way it did other Keepers, and when she caught sight of his light-coloured eyes, she didn't see any signs of gold.

"Come this way." The man ushered her across the sizable room to one of the work spaces, which had a table, tall stool, and many healer's instruments.

Ryla trailed him as he unclasped his hands and ran one through his short, blond hair. She perched wordlessly on the stool, taking in more of her surroundings. The skylight she'd noticed earlier let in light that made even far recesses of the room feel bright. It smelled cleaner than most rooms, and that, coupled with the instruments, made her confident this Keeper was some sort of healer. He wasn't the usual healer that tended to Killers, though.

"Yes, many years indeed since there's been a breaking. And certainly we've never seen it in one of your calibre before, so I can imagine how deeply the effects are running."

This Keeper talked too much. His words summoned questions she didn't want to consider and feelings she didn't want to feel. She didn't need to know any of this. These were all distractions.

She felt a knot in her core and held back from saying anything, watching this Keeper as he watched her.

"I can see the questions in your eyes," he said, which startled her, even with his gentle tone.

How? The question leapt to her mind without invitation alongside the unbidden spike of anxiety in her chest.

"It's okay to ask them," he encouraged with the same gentle tone.

She glanced over her shoulder at the Keeper who'd entered the room before and stood even now at the door.

The man before her chuckled good-naturedly. "Don't worry about them. They know the circumstances are different. We need to assess where you are."

It still didn't feel right, but she let loose one of the first questions on her tongue. "What is this magic?"

"It's called *Cevrla*," he replied easily, the word rolling off his tongue with a foreigner's accent.

"Soul binding." She recognized the old language; the same as the words she'd say at a Passing Ceremony. She'd never heard the word *Cevrla* before, but it translated seamlessly in her mind, as if the magic were properly introducing itself to her.

"Yes." The healer grinned now, pleased by the development.

"How does it work?" Ryla asked next, although the pieces were already starting to fall into place internally. Again, it was as though the magic spoke to her.

"*Cevrla* is an old, powerful magic. Centuries ago, Keepers learned that this magic could be invited by humans and bound to their very essence. And weaponized in a different way than elemental magic. It's a guarded ritual that I don't even know the intricate details of, but once it's complete, the magic and the human host effectively become one.

"However, *Cevrla* is as volatile as it is powerful. It even has the ability to invite other magics, but when bound to one person, it calms and can be controlled. That same calm permeates the host's soul, making them as you were—measured, calculating…"

"Emotionless," Ryla cut in, the word barely a whisper as it left her mouth.

The man gave a slow nod. "The younger the host, the more readily and safely the magic takes to them. Because it can be calmed, its dangerous effects are slower acting. It provides us with powerful, level-headed fighters who aren't distracted by emotion and perfectly honed on their duty. The training from Keepers solidifies this, which is why even now you fight with human nature."

Ryla swallowed, considering what he'd just shared. She hesitated before continuing. "What of the word *Cizeth*? What is that?" It didn't translate, but even as she said it now, the magic stirred in her, a hum or tingle in her veins.

The healer tilted his head just slightly, brows coming together. "I've never heard it. No other broken one has mentioned it. Did you hear this word?"

"Something like that," she replied at first. She couldn't explain it, but she had this sense she should keep the next words to herself. She pushed through anyway; she had a duty to report. "When it—the breaking—happened, it was a word that came to my mind, and when I called it out, there was a golden light."

"Most interesting," the healer said as he picked up something to take notes on from the table. "This seems a new development. I'll have to do research."

Ryla's gaze fixated on the writing instrument as it wiggled back and forth while he wrote. There was still something else missing. "If this magic is so perfect, how does this happen?"

The writing paused, and the healer looked up at her, eyes alive with intrigue. "That's the caveat. As you know, a weapon acts as a conduit so the magic will be more concentrated and controlled. We call it a Channel. It is imprinted to you."

The rest fell into place for Ryla. "But this Channel becomes a gateway to *Cevrla*, and when someone else touches it, it turns the magic chaotic." She touched the hilt of her sword, the Keepers' orders to never let another touch her blade coming to mind. Without a doubt, she knew that what was happening to her was because someone else touched her sword.

The man paused before speaking again, considering his words. He set his writing aside and fully faced Ryla. "It doesn't *turn* it chaotic. It *unleashes* the chaos. We don't know for certain, but we hypothesize that the touch of another disturbs the magic in a way that it perceives it as a threat, and then *Cevrla* devours the soul in an attempt to protect it. Remember, *Cevrla* is volatile. And it's now consuming you."

Ryla's glance flicked to a mirror across the room. Even at the distance she sat from it, she could see the gold in her eyes, the brown already barely visible. The burning sensation also lingered.

"I'm still a human, and like other humans, my body cannot handle magic. Yet, it's held this powerful magic for this long…" she thought aloud, gaze falling back to the healer. "When you say this magic is consuming me and devouring my soul…"

"I mean, just like any other human, it will end you."

CHAPTER

FORTY-TWO

The examination left Ryla no more at ease than when she'd walked into the room. Even with the knowledge she now had, it didn't serve any purpose. It didn't *fix* anything. The healer let on as much as he did because, ultimately, this magic was going to kill her. Or the Keepers would kill her when she became lost.

That death was her fate wasn't what held the tension in her body and the knot in her stomach; death was always an inevitable future for Killers. This was different.

"Your sword, Ryla."

The words startled her as she stepped from the room and faced the five Keepers with the sixth behind her. She stared incredulously at the shadowed face of the Keeper directly in front of her, trying again to see past the shroud to the features beneath. She saw nothing; all the same, she got the distinct sense she was being met with an expectant stare.

"No," she responded confidently. *This is a test.*

"You must surrender your sword. This is to protect us all," the Keeper said firmly.

Ryla's eyes narrowed, and she squared her shoulders. "The Killer's Code—"

"No longer applies to you."

The words hit her like bricks, and she almost physically staggered. It must have shown on her face.

"The magic will corrupt your mind just as any human. Your weapon has always been your greatest tool, and we can't risk allowing you to keep it."

Her sense of duty warred with the new chaos of emotions running through her. Worry clutched her chest at the thought of giving up her sword, as if she were cutting off her arm rather than handing over forged metal. Not to mention what she had just learned from the healer: that the weapon was a Channel that helped her control the magic to some degree.

What'll happen when I surrender it? Isn't that dangerous, too?

With knitted brows, she realized her breathing laboured and her heart hammered. Could she simply hand over her sword to the Keepers?

Of course you can, she admonished herself. *These are Keepers. Do not disobey.*

Ryla reached around her waist, unfastening the belt with fingers that shook despite their familiarity with the task. She hesitated a moment with it in her hands, worried about someone touching it. Her eyes locked on the sheath and cloth belt hanging around her hands, and she wrapped it around the hilt and sheath as best she could, hoping to both fasten it in place and prevent others from coming into contact with the hilt or blade. She wasn't sure this would even be enough.

When she looked up, she was met with a Keeper's outstretched hands and arms covered in a parchment-coloured cloth. Ryla placed the sword gently on the cloth, and she had barely let go before the Keeper swiftly wrapped it up and turned away.

They don't want to touch it either. It brought her some comfort as her eyes trained on the Keeper's back. As the sword got further away, she could have sworn the chaos in her grew stronger, but she didn't know how much of that was only because she expected it to.

"Come, Ryla," another Keeper beckoned.

As she followed, the remaining Keepers fell into the same formation again. She felt she was being corralled, like an errant animal being brought in from pasture.

The corridors they traversed were just as plain as the others but for large paintings of the kingdoms' crests every once in a while. As they walked by Nithle's stag, Ryla wondered what would become of them. She was certain the castle was in ruins, which would leave Arran to pick up the pieces. To figure out how to move on. She felt the same clenching in her core she had back on the battlefield when she couldn't look at him.

Guilt? Failure? Shame? She tested each of these to see if they would bring to light what the feeling was. It only left her wondering if it might be a mix of all three.

The longer they walked, the more aware Ryla became that the Keepers were leading her to another area of the stronghold she'd never been. The walls were somehow even barer than any other part of the building. When they stopped, they stood in front of a pristine, lacquered door.

Beyond, she felt the echoes of old magic, and it drew to her. It was like back on the battlefield, although this time she realized the magic pulling toward her was being absorbed by *Cevrla*. She wondered if this would hasten her demise.

The Keeper at the fore reached into their robes to produce an old-looking key and unlock the door. Despite its pristine façade, as soon as the door swung open, Ryla knew what this room was. It looked nearly exactly the same as any other room where those overrun by magic were held.

"We will gather you when the Collective is ready," the Keeper said coolly.

Ryla again looked at the shadowed face, both understanding

and not understanding the words and the situation. Her chest tightened anew.

You are tainted. You need to be contained to prevent hurting others.

With a deep breath, Ryla forced her feet to move, crossing the threshold of the small room. It was devoid of anything, leaving no means to make a weapon or method of escape.

The door closed behind her with a resounding thud, and darkness swallowed her whole. She knew she needed to accept her situation. The only way she was getting out was if someone opened the door for her.

Alone and without her sword, her thoughts unleashed themselves with a vengeance. The dahem's laugh filled her mind first, followed quickly by carnage and blood. All the things she'd blocked out without a thought now plagued her and demanded she feel something for them.

More guilt? Remorse? Horror? She wasn't sure which it was. Or should be.

She turned in the direction of the door, as if hoping someone would come back and open it. It remained closed.

Her breathing was too loud, and her legs were unsteady under her weight. She backed up until she bumped into a wall; she got the sense it was cold, even though none of it permeated her clothes. She slid down until she sat on the floor, brought her knees to her chest, and buried her head in her arms.

CHAPTER

FORTY-THREE

Y andana's infirmary was thick with emotion, most notably
dismay and pain. The emotional barrage coupled with
the sight of dahems with various injuries, including many
burns of some sort, was almost enough to barrel Jasim over.
As it was, he found himself holding his breath in an effort to
keep his composure.

Even if he hadn't have recognized some of those being
tended to throughout the infirmary, that he was looking
down at Mithos laid out on one of the beds was enough to
say this was the team she'd led in their attack. Remarkably,
she seemed untouched compared to the others. There wasn't
so much as a scuff on her battle leathers. No burns marred
her skin, which worried him more. The commander's eyes
were closed, and she didn't move.

Spying the slow rise and fall of her chest tamped down on
his anxiety some, but still, he wiped his palms on his thighs as
he gingerly placed his thumb on one of Mithos's eyelids; she
didn't respond to his touch, and his hand hesitated a moment
before pulling it back.

Amber irises alone. A sigh of relief escaped him. *This isn't
her doing.* "What happened?" he bit out more forcefully
than intended. He released her eyelid and pushed up to his
full height.

The healer attending to Mithos jumped slightly. "I'm not

sure, My Lord. She was brought to me this way. Reportedly, she was complaining of her eyes burning before she lost consciousness."

"It didn't look as though there were any signs of injury to her eyes." Jasim shook his head. "Has anyone else complained of burning eyes?"

The dahem nodded. "Plenty. But they all had other burns to go along with it. Commander Mithos is the only one who looks like she doesn't have any physical injuries."

Jasim swept his gaze across the room again. Several of his ranks watched the exchange. He took a deep breath and again addressed the dahem attending to Mithos. "I want to know the moment she's awake and strong enough to talk."

"Of course, Sire," the tall dahem responded with a sharp nod.

Despite the weight of the room, Jasim spent a bit more time checking on the rest of the group. His hope was that someone would have insight into what had happened, but all he got were bits and pieces of what *might* have happened.

One claimed Mithos lost control of her fire. Another said a magic user had betrayed them. Really, as horrible and disappointing as that second claim was to think about, it held a ring of truth when Jasim considered it. Not that he'd be able to interrogate any of the other magic users Mithos had taken, considering they'd all been killed.

As he turned to leave the infirmary, Jasim caught a passing porter by the arm. "When you're done delivering those items, find me someone who can fully explain what happened and bring them to me."

The porter seemed to tighten his clutch on the loose cloths and handle of the bucket of water he carried, but he nodded just the same. "Yes, My Lord!" He scurried off.

"Kurisha!" Jasim shouted next, seeing the dahem in question cross an open area several feet away. He closed the space between them to meet where Kurisha had paused mid-step. "Let me know as soon as Captain Anxer and his group return from Nithle castle. I want reports to learn if they encountered anything like this," he said as he gestured generally about them.

Kurisha nodded, ever the dutiful page. The young dahem scratched something down on the stack of small parchment sheets in his hand. Jasim didn't take offense to the fact he didn't offer any sort of verbal acknowledgement.

The page walked off, leaving Jasim alone with his troubled thoughts.

CHAPTER
FORTY-FOUR

After waiting anxiously into the night and the better part of the next day without word of what had become of Captain Anxer's group, Jasim sent out a small group for reconnaissance. Given the state of affairs, he was expecting the worst and hoping for the best—a situation that he never liked to be in.

Equally stressful was Mithos's state. It hadn't declined since the group had returned to Yandana Fort several days ago, but it wasn't improving either. Jasim ordered a watch be kept over her at all times.

The dahem lord was pouring over plans and choppy reports with his advisors in the war room when the team he'd sent to Nithle returned around midday, four days after they'd left. Immediately, he tried to read their expressions to prepare himself for what kind of disaster they may have seen, but he saw no such terror in their countenances.

"Lord Jasim, sir," one of the dahems greeted, extending a parchment to him.

The small sheaf of parchment crinkled when he took it. His brow furrowed as he looked it over, not sure he could believe his eyes. There were no words, only two seals: Alden's seal, but also Anxer's. Alden's seal, he noticed immediately, looked like a quill had been run through it on an angle, marring the stag's antlers in the wax.

"Does this mean what I presume it means?" Jasim asked, turning his gaze back to the team leader.

The dahem nodded. "Captain Anxer has overtaken Nithle Proper, including the castle. The king 'n queen are dead 'n the Nithleans have fled the city. It's ours," the dahem reported with an air of reverent disbelief in his voice.

Jasim's heart raced. *Ours.* He glanced between each of the other reconnaissance team members. None of them disputed what the leader said, and he didn't think it was because they were hiding something.

"And what of Prince Arran and Nithle's other forces?" It was one of the missing pieces he was hoping Mithos would be able to fill in eventually. All he'd heard so far was that no one had seen him.

"We're still unsure where the prince is, but the cap'n confirmed he wasn't at the castle. He suspects he's at the encampment, which has moved into Thlent. But, apart from a few scouts 'n smaller groups looking for weak spots, the cap'n says they've not made a move on the castle," the dahem reported.

"Why not just have their magic-using ally attack Anxer's group the same way they did Mithos's?" Jasim wondered aloud, letting the parchment fall to the table. He noticed one of the silent advisors picked it up immediately, probably looking for forgery or some form of trickery.

"We asked him about that. No sign of any magic users 'mong the humans," the dahem said with a shake of the head.

"Perhaps they died after all," Jasim mused.

"I doubt that."

Jasim's attention snapped toward the door and the voice, both surprised and elated to see Mithos standing. Alive and awake, she wore loose-fitting patient's garb that threatened to swallow her small frame whole. She took a few steps forward, but her eyes seemed unfocused.

Not unfocused, the dahem lord realized. *Unseeing.*

Indeed, she had someone leading her through the doorway even as she reached out her hands to feel her way around and avoid crashing into furniture. Without waiting for an order, one of the advisors got a seat for her. Her movements were unsure as she crossed the room with the help of the other dahem, and she seemed to be trying to determine where everyone and everything was in the war room with the way she tilted her head at the sounds of other movements.

Jasim had so much to ask, so many details of the battle he wanted to know, but he held back, leaving her space to orient herself and elaborate on what she meant.

Mithos situated herself in the chair and then turned slightly toward Jasim as she spoke, as if she at least knew where he was. "Given her skills and that power, I'd wager she yet lives. Ryla was their magic user."

The room erupted into a chorus of shock and protests. Claims of it being impossible and nonsense.

"Enough!" Jasim barked at the advisors and others who were murmuring at his second's words. His own head spun at the thought of it. "Explain, Mithos. Was she so…desperate," the word didn't feel right, but he persisted, "that she called this magic to her in battle?"

Mithos shook her head slowly, her dark bangs crossing in front of her eyes. She brushed them away as she said, "No. I feel it's been there all along. It felt the same as mine feels in me—in tune, as if the magic and the host are united. I don't know that she even knew herself. That *anyone* knew. But I saw it with my own eyes. *Felt* it in my body."

She paused, as if realizing the gravity of the statement as it left her mouth. "My magic users and I had her surrounded and were attacking her from all angles." She continued to recount how she'd seen through her flames as Ryla remained on the defensive, how her sword was knocked from her hands. "I grabbed it, and the moment I did, I felt this surge of magic and the Killer called out some word I'd never heard before. With it came golden light, the likes of which I've never seen or experienced."

Jasim tried to envision the scene even as he struggled to believe that a Killer could have such magic and not know about it.

"Are you certain your injury hasn't left you confused, Commander?" one of the advisors asked gently, although Jasim could still hear the thick layer of skepticism in his voice. He shot the dahem a look, and to his credit, the advisor's shoulders hunched just slightly.

"I'm not suffering a head injury," retorted Mithos, turning toward the voice. Jasim was impressed she was able to keep her tone even. "I saw and felt the magic." She faced Jasim again, and he watched her intently. "This magic is meant to kill us. Except for me, those closest to the attack are dead. I've already checked with the healers. I don't know how I survived it. Her power coursed through me like an inferno. There aren't supposed to be survivors of that attack, I'm sure of it, and yet, here I am."

It was all Jasim could to do suppress the chill that overtook him.

Mithos continued, unseeing eyes still locked on Jasim, just as they might have been during any other report. "Where is Ryla now?"

Jasim directed his attention to the reconnaissance leader.

The dahem replied, "There's been no sign of her. The cap'n assumes she's near the prince wherever he is."

Mithos's brow furrowed, as if considering the statement against something in her own mind. Finally, she said, "There's a bard song with a hidden alternative story. It tells of a Killer who'd broken free of the Union's control and suffered for it."

"The Union punished the Killer?" Jasim found himself asking.

"No. Well, yes. But what I mean is they suffered mentally before the Union hunted down the Killer and the dahem who helped him." She shook her head. "There's no proof of its veracity. But, supposing there's any truth…perhaps we are seeing it unravel anew. This revelation of magic, the scream I heard from Ryla… If this is the change Killers face, I bet the Union hunts their own warriors to conceal this weakness."

An advisor jumped in again. "It's a *bard song*, Commander. I know it helps to look for meaning when these things happen, for an explanation, but—"

"This isn't an attempt to find meaning, Halfa," Mithos countered sharply, eyes narrowing and nose crinkling in annoyance. "It's an attempt to piece together what's happened. Regardless of whether the story has a lick of truth, I don't see the Union standing idly by after a magical attack such as that—especially from one of their own."

The advisor continued unaffected. "It's quite the leap to pit an unfounded tale against realities that we still don't have full explanations—or even details—for. We don't know for certain that it was the Killer who used the magic."

"I *do* know for sure," spat Mithos. "That is the *one* detail I know with perfect certainty."

Halfa huffed and turned to Jasim. "My Lord, with all due respect, we need to be reasonable about this."

When the dahem lord glanced at his advisor this time, Jasim saw his pleading eyes. His bias against Mithos's position aside, Jasim knew his advisor was right. He couldn't get swept up in one possibility of Ryla's fate while the others hadn't been disproven.

Jasim took a breath to centre himself. "We will consider all possible scenarios, including that Ryla may still be alive and changed. If she wasn't the magic user, she may be alive anyway. It's as Mithos says, the Union will need to react to this level of magic, regardless of its source. We can't deny there was magic of some sort at play."

Halfa's mouth pressed into a thin line, but he said nothing, especially when Jasim gave him a hard look.

Mithos spoke again, the picture of calm. "The truth of the narrative notwithstanding, we have to decide our next course quickly."

"My Lord, we can't be distracted by this business of magic and the Killer. It makes far more sense for us to focus our efforts on Nithle. Tale or no tale, the Union would have sent another Killer now if they were going to do so. With Nithle's weakened state—" Halfa persisted.

Mithos interjected. "The Union is weakened as well. They should have done something more by this point. At the very least reacted to their Killer's magic."

Halfa shifted but kept his head aloft. "Perhaps they consider it a lost cause. We've nearly wiped out the entire kingdom."

"Nithle is essentially the founding grounds of the Union. I highly doubt they'd surrender it so easily," Mithos countered.

Jasim was content to listen to the pair banter. Generally, it helped him think and find a clear course of action, but in this case, both of them made sense. It was too good an opportunity to pass up on fully conquering Nithle, but if the Union had truly been weakened as well...

"My Lord?"

Although it was Halfa that had spoken again, looking around the room told Jasim everyone waited for his decision. The parchment with Alden's marred seal snared his attention again.

We need to make sure, he told himself. "We need to investigate both of these situations. We need to find out for sure where Prince Arran is and if he yet lives. I'll send word to Captain Anxer to find him. Additionally, I want a team formed to do reconnaissance on the Union."

"I'd like to be part of that second team, My Lord," Mithos said.

"I seriously doubt the healers have given you approval," Jasim said sternly, glancing at the aide who was standing near the wall, ready to help Mithos when needed.

"I may be blind, but my mind is sound," she snapped back in a tone he hadn't been expecting. Her hands gripped together in her lap, shoulders square and rigid now. "I know it doesn't make any sense, but what I do know may be useful if we come up against anything else on Union grounds."

Jasim stared at her unseeing, amber eyes that, despite everything, still held the same intensity and assuredness they always had. He felt something akin to pity for her state but knew he couldn't let feeling bad for his commander lead his decision.

He had to tread carefully.

"Take time to get situated. To eat," Jasim said finally. "Once you have, we'll meet back here to discuss what steps we'll take next."

"Thank you, My Lord," Mithos ceded without hesitation, leaning forward in her seat as if to bow.

Jasim motioned for the aide to help Mithos depart, and he also dismissed the reconnaissance team to be at the ready for when his missive to Captain Anxer was prepared. Only the dahem lord and his advisors remained.

He pre-emptively dismissed their protests. "I'm not interested."

Still, Halfa picked up where he'd left off. Fabric from his loose pants swished as he rounded the table to stand across from Jasim in what seemed to be an effort to force face-to-face communication. "I'm not sure it's wise to be putting so much attention on the Union, Sire. It makes no sense. A bard song? A Killer having magic?"

"It doesn't hurt to be cautious," Jasim said, turning to re-examine the parchments strewn across the table he'd been looking at previously.

"If I may say so, My Lord, you seem to be approaching this with more than caution. Don't let what happened with Lord Lamis cloud your judgement. A Killer having or calling magic to them is unfounded and goes against their nature," the advisor continued.

Jasim leaned back in his chair, flabbergasted by Halfa's audacity. "This has nothing to do with my brother. There is much that doesn't make sense when it comes to the Union and Killers. It doesn't make sense for humans to be as strong and as fast as Killers are. It doesn't make sense for anyone to behave like Killers do. I'm not confident we're going to get all of the answers we seek, but this could be something.

"Whether the magic was called to Ryla in that moment or somehow lived in her all along doesn't make a difference to me. The fact of the matter is I believe Mithos's account of sensing the Killer use magic. Magic that dealt death and damage to our people. I've never before seen burns and injuries like those I've witnessed since their return. Never. I'm not risking our people just because you think what my commander is saying doesn't make sense."

The advisors exchanged glances, but none of them challenged him. He wasn't sure if it was simply because of his steadfastness or something else. Whatever it was, he was relieved to cease arguing. He had more important things to worry about.

Like the possibility that Ryla was more dangerous than they had ever imagined.

CHAPTER
FORTY-FIVE

Adel's heart hadn't stopped pounding since she'd spoken to the fleeing Nithlean refugees. At first, it had just been the peoples of Thlent and Nithle Proper she'd come across, sharing horrific stories of an army of dahems marching into the heart of the kingdom. They'd caused destruction as they chased people out of their homes and demanded the surrender of the Nithlean rulers.

It wasn't until she encountered refugees from the castle, however, that the horror truly set in. One servant told her how Lavanai's forces had fought through the defenses of Nithle castle's outer wall, then there was the banging on the doors before they broke through them, too. The blood of servants, pages, guards, and knights splattered the castle corridors. Tapestries burned. The king and queen were dead.

The king and queen are dead. The servant's words echoed over and over in Adel's mind. She could still picture the tears streaming down the older woman's face and hear the way her voice shattered.

Lavanai had overtaken Nithle castle and Nithle Proper but many had managed to flee. No one had any news about Sothle and Wendur. And despite Nithle and Piridet armies gathering in Thlent to try to retake the castle, no one could tell Adel whether Arran yet lived.

She'd had to fight down the bile as she thanked the people

for what they could tell her and encouraged them to go to Piridet and Heta for safety.

The horse Adel had taken walked at an easy gait now as Heta's princess continued on her way, resisting the urge to send the horse tearing across the plains so she could find out if Arran was still alive.

Crop-bare fields on either side of her path left her feeling exposed, although the over-large clothes still hung on her back. Not a being was in sight along the frost-coated grounds of Nithle's outer territory, but she couldn't help the tension that seized her limbs. She was ready to bolt at any hint of danger. When she finally came upon the Piridetian pennant and Nithlean flag, she urged the horse into a gallop.

The motion, and she was sure eventually the hoof-falls across the terrain, attracted attention to her, and some fighters got into line with arrows and swords, waiting for order to take her down. A knight turned, presumably to call for someone, and a moment later, Adel saw Mihel step forward, her intricately designed armour gleaming in the afternoon sun. Adel could tell her fellow princess was trying to figure out who was approaching, and that's when it dawned on Adel the cloak's hood still concealed her face.

Holding tightly to the reins with one hand, she tugged gently to get the horse to slow its pace, then quickly reached up to loosen the rope holding the hood in place and pushed it back. A shiver threatened to overtake her as the cold air suddenly hit her skin. Mihel started barking orders at the others, and those around her lowered their weapons.

Mihel stepped forward once Adel was close, looking up at her with lowered brows and tight eyes. "Adel! What are you doing here?"

"I couldn't stand by as my kingdom did nothing," she

replied, sliding off the horse and handing the reins to someone waiting to take them. "Especially not after what I learned from my father. And then all those refugees... What happened here, Mihel?" She was too afraid to ask the real question on her mind: *Where is Arran?*

Mihel stared at her incredulously, but it only took a moment for her to snap back to action and motion for Adel to follow. A retinue of knights, guards, and fighters closed in tight behind them. Adel eyed them but fell into step with Mihel.

"From the reports I've gathered, both the castle and the encampment where Arran and I met up were attacked simultaneously. Killer Ryla sensed the dahems before even our scouts gave warning. She took Arran to flee the battle, and I led the rest of our fighters against Lavanai's assault," Mihel explained as they walked toward a collection of tents.

Adel paid as close attention as she could, to their surroundings as well as what Mihel was saying. Both were a challenge with her mind spinning as fast as it was, and really what she was listening for was any details that would tell her what had happened to Arran.

"Lavanai brought magic users who targeted Arran and Killer Ryla. I don't know the specifics of what happened as I was elsewhere, but Arran was there and says Killer Ryla shoved him out of the way of the magic before they surrounded the Killer. The next thing they knew, there was a scream and a bright golden light that killed the dahems closest to it and severely injured those farther away. Even where I was, I saw the flash. I still don't know that I believe this next part myself, but Arran says he saw it with his own eyes."

Adel's heart skipped. *Says*, she thought and swallowed the lump in her throat. *She said 'says.' He must be alive!*

Mihel peered at Adel now, even as she continued walking.

"Killer Ryla had changed. Less emotionless and more human. But, even more concerning, her eyes were gold-streaked."

Adel's mouth popped open. "The same as the Tainted?"

Mihel nodded. "Apparently."

Adel rushed on before Mihel could say anything else. "Where is she now?"

"The Killer is gone. The Union retrieved her. Between that and hearing about the attack on Nithle Proper, Arran took off with a retinue before I even had full scope of the situation. Then when I was finally able to make it here…"

The tension and depth of the situation became more palpable as the words sunk in. The amount of guard suddenly made sense, as did their reaction to her approach. Without the protection Killer Ryla offered, they were at a disadvantage.

Adel's jaw clenched as they stopped, surrounded by tents. When she looked at Mihel, she suddenly saw the other princess in a way she hadn't seen her before. She was used to the softness the dresses brought her. Now, the young woman she saw before her was all warrior. The tightness of the princess's features, the darkness around her eyes, the scrapes along her skin that Adel only just noticed told her all she needed to know about what she'd missed since leaving Nithle.

They've been through hell. Even that felt like too light of a descriptor.

When Mihel continued her account of the situation, it sounded much less like a report. "He's not in a good place, Adel. When I reached him, I was honestly afraid he'd lost his will to live. Knight Ley told me that despite Killer Ryla's… powers, whatever that was, and the fact that we're alive, he sees that battle as a loss. And then when he learned of the king's and queen's deaths, it got even worse. His grief is strong, and no one has been able to reach him."

"Knight Ley?" Adel ventured, wringing her fingers together as she locked eyes with Mihel's dark ones.

The other princess shook her head. "Not even him. Knight Ley has barely left Arran's tent, keeping watch outside and waiting. We haven't seen Arran in days."

The ache grew within Adel, and she found herself looking through the sea of tents to try to determine which was his. *I need to go to him.* She needed to be there with him.

"When I saw it was you riding up, I felt hope for the first time since any of this happened," Mihel continued. "If anyone can reach him, it's going to be you. Come."

Adel followed Mihel the rest of the way through the maze of tents, and she finally spotted Knight Ley. He looked haggard, and she realized he'd lost a lot, too: his king and queen, his fellow Royal Knights, his home. She bit her lip to fight against the lump that formed in her throat and threatened to unleash tears.

Later, she told herself firmly. *You can cry later.*

As she approached, Ley's expression became a mix of relief and confusion. "Princess Adel." He looked around her. "Where is your guard? Where is your army?"

"I came by myself," she said, watching his eyes widen. "I wish I could say I had my kingdom to stand with yours, but it is only me."

Ley was pensive a moment, then shook his head. "You're more than welcome here, Princess."

"I'm so sorry, Knight Ley," she said gently. *This could have all been prevented.* Those were words she held back, knowing they wouldn't undo what had happened.

"You five stay here with the princess," Mihel said behind them, and Adel peered over her shoulder, watching five of the fighters disappear into the rows of tents. Mihel caught Adel's gaze. "It's best to keep them as inconspicuous as possible, just in case."

Adel nodded in understanding but couldn't help the wandering of her eyes through the tents and even into the clear, cloudless sky, as if there might be an attack from above.

"If you need me, send for me," the other princess said, glancing between Adel and the tent Ley stood in front of before disappearing with the remainder of her guard.

Adel returned her attention to the coarse tent material and tried to calm the rapid beating of her heart. She'd been so keen on seeing him, but now this close to where he was, she was nervous to do so.

What if I can't reach him?

"Princess." Knight Ley drew her attention. The sorrow was a thick aura around him, but the steadiness of his poise didn't waver. "I beg of you..."

Heart wrenching, Adel steeled herself and pushed through the tent flap. It was just as cold within as it was outside, and mostly dark but for a single candle that had been lit to the left. The small flame flickered as the tent flap closed behind her, but it didn't go out, outlining the profile of a figure beside it.

Her breath caught in her chest at the sight of him, hunched over, seated on the edge of his cot. The candlelight was just enough to outline his unseeing stare and shattered expression. The fact that he didn't even look up at the sound of someone coming into the tent would have been alarming, but for the fact that she was also well acquainted with grief.

What she'd learned from her father weighed heavily on her mind. Would it help or hinder him? Should she tell him?

No, her thoughts responded sharply. *At least, not yet. It won't be a spark to spur him through his grief. It'll push him farther into it.*

Would her being there make any difference? Mihel seemed to think so, and Ley seemed hopeful. Even if it was only to bring some life back into him, she knew she had to try.

"Arran," she said gently as she took a step forward. Her boots scuffed slightly on the dirt, but neither her voice nor her movement stirred him. "Arran."

Still nothing. She inhaled deeply, afraid she would startle him but also needing to get him to respond. When she was directly in front of him, she crouched, the cloak pooling around her as she did.

It distressed her to see his handsome features so pained. His eyes continued to see nothing, until all at once they found her, coming into focus in a flash.

"Adel!" his voice croaked.

He gave her no time to reply, pulling her to him, which resulted in a sort of half crouch as he held her tightly to his chest. She struggled to keep balance but managed to wrap her arms around him in return. The relief finally washed through her.

With her head against his chest, she could hear his breathing—the kind that held back sobs. She shifted them so she was sitting on his lap with her arm around his shoulders and his head against her collarbone.

"Let it out, Arran," she said softly, running a hand down the back of his head and neck soothingly.

The strangled sound that escaped him was one she never wanted to hear again. It was so heavy with grief it brought tears to her own eyes, and although she tilted her head back to stop her own sorrow from escaping, tears burned her cheeks. His body shook as he gripped her, but she stayed the course with her gentle movements in an effort to bring even a little bit of comfort to him. At the very least she hoped her touch would reassure him that she was there. That he didn't have to go through this alone.

She had no idea how long they sat like that, but Arran continued to cling to her, and she stayed where she was, even when it got uncomfortable. His cries faded, as if he had nothing left to give, but the fierceness with which he held her persisted. She knew this grief would not pass quickly, if ever.

"They're gone... It's over..." His voice was barely a whisper and rough from the crying.

"It's not over as long as we're still here," Adel countered softly. "Your people are safe. You're still alive."

"They've taken my kingdom. They took my parents. They took Ryla," Arran fought weakly.

"I know," Adel said, her own voice catching. She cleared her throat. "I know, Arran. But we're still here. Piridet still stands with you. I'm sure we can find more allies." When she thought about what she knew, she wasn't sure the latter of those was true. Still, she tried to build him back up.

"And Heta?" he asked uncertainly.

She paused and took a breath. "I came alone."

Her heart jumped into her throat when he quickly pulled away from her and then gripped her arms with bruising force. She hadn't expected him to move that quickly or with that much strength.

"You came by *yourself*? Are you *insane*?" he hissed.

He was angry. Oh, was he angry. The candle flickered away beside them, and she could see the fierce gleam in his glassed blue eyes. The anxiousness tightened her chest again, even as she focused on steadying her breathing before speaking.

Adel's reply came slow and firm. "It wasn't wise, but it was necessary. I made it here unharmed, and I'd do it again if I had to."

His narrowed gaze pierced like ice, but she could tell he had nothing to fight her with. His grip on her arms loosened. She hated the thought that it might be all this tragedy that finally stopped him from pushing her away.

"I need to be here with you, Arran. Now more than ever. Within a span of days, so many things have changed in our world," she said, maintaining the firmness while softening the edge of her voice. "We can get through all this together."

He was searching her eyes. For what, she didn't know, but for something. The lost and uncertain look in his gaze unsettled her.

This is the grief, she reminded herself. *Grief makes everything feel unclear. Grief leads you to seek for hope and strength and answers in others until you can regain it in yourself.*

Memories of the depths of her own grief in the wake of Ashla's death slammed into her; some days it still felt like that. This was still raw for him.

Is this how I behaved?

A lot of what had happened during that time was a blur, with minutes seeping into hours into days. Adel knew she'd had the luxury of time and space to process her grief.

Arran didn't. Wouldn't.

Although she didn't know the current state of the war and how frequently the dahems were attacking this encampment, she couldn't see this going any way but escalation. It was just as she'd said—so many things had changed in their world in just a few short days, and each of them only knew parts of it. She couldn't help but come back to wondering how her knowledge of the origins of the war would change the course of things.

There was the very real possibility it would obliterate Arran completely.

CHAPTER

FORTY-SIX

Ryla felt their eyes on her. People staring was not a new experience by any means, but she was more aware of them than ever. Not anxious, annoyed, or even self-conscious. Just *aware*. Before, it would have been a recognition on her periphery. Now, it was a distinct consciousness of the fact.

Let them watch me. Let them see who I am. Who I'm becoming.

Realization had struck her while sitting in that pitch dark room with nothing but her thoughts: it wasn't the magic that made her who she was. A whisper had broken through the disorder in her mind, reminding her she was more than the magic. Whether that whisper was her own conjuring or something else, she didn't know. It didn't matter. She held onto it.

The Union had trained her to be what she was, not just physically, but mentally and emotionally, too. Especially emotionally. Sadness, joy, fear, curiosity, even anger—all had been stunted based on calculated instruction from childhood. The Keepers had never allowed these things. Once, she would have said they'd been stripped away, but clearly they still existed. Whatever the case, it had allowed her to *thrive* in her duty.

She'd only lost control because of the volatility of the magic coursing through her body. That might cause anyone else to crumble, but she was no ordinary person. She would bring this to the heel. She'd prove to the Union she was still a valuable asset. Still *capable* of her duty and worthy of the code they said no longer applied to her.

The unfamiliar room she stood in was large enough for nearly one hundred people to sit comfortably, yet she wagered there were no more than fifty Keepers milling about within the plain walls. Despite the organization's power, it didn't have the numbers she knew the United expected. More Keepers weren't necessary, or for the United to know their true numbers.

Even the number of Killers wasn't vast. Although, given that she still hadn't seen or even sensed any of the others, she wondered if there were any other Killers on site at all. Part of her craved for any hint of them. She thought it might be to feel some semblance of familiarity within the shifting world around her. If she were being honest with herself, she wanted to see what their magic felt like.

Have they sent the others away? Ryla wondered as she watched the unhooded Keepers around her.

The usually drawn fabric sat in pools around their shoulders and revealed first and foremost that she'd been right: there were varying degrees of gold in their eyes. Mild compared to her own state, but still there.

She found herself taking in their features over and over again. Strangers by appearance, yet most of them felt familiar to her in essence. She had no idea what to feel *for* them though. Among the swirl of emotions, she thought she should feel *something*—they'd been her caretakers since her birth—but there was little more than quiet curiosity.

Do they feel anything for me? She exhaled, long and low, mentally pushing the question away from her.

To distract herself, she turned her attention to her sword, the most familiar thing in the room. It sat on a table several feet to her right with a Keeper standing guard beside it.

Instinct told her to retrieve it, but she held herself where she was, straight-faced and unmoving. The fact that she was able to hold herself despite everything gave her a sense of what she assumed was pride.

Feel it. Let it pass, she told herself. It was how she'd decided to process and handle each emotion she encountered. Some were easier to let pass than others, their foreignness feeling stuck to her ribs.

The quiet conversation between the Keepers died as another man entered from a door along the side of the rounded room. He wore an intricately designed shirt and trousers, and the light fabric had silver stitching all over, hanging somewhat loosely on his body.

Ryla's eyes trailed him. As she tracked his easy gait, she knew she'd never come into contact with this person. This man gave off no magical essence, and his eyes didn't have any hint of gold to speak of, their bright blues practically shining like un-muddied water under a sparkling sun and cloudless sky. His short, blond hair was combed back out of his face, though still hung loosely. If Keepers had some sort of king or lord, this man must have been it, she determined.

He assessed her just as she did him. Those clear eyes of his broke their connected gaze, scanning over her body before returning to her face. What he thought of her as she stood there in her usual charcoal attire, it was hard to conclude. The sharp features of his long face were as blank as a non-Killer could manage.

A few moments more, and he shifted to address the Keepers. "It is an unfortunate situation we find ourselves in." His voice was rich and carried with little effort, commanding the attention of the room. "Not only do we have a compromised Killer, but also witnesses. Many."

Her brow furrowed only slightly before she scolded herself for not having considered the witnesses and the impact they had on the situation. *Enough.*

With this internal battle of her mind, it wasn't difficult for her to understand why the Union did what it did—what it had done to *her.* She'd never had to concentrate on paying attention and gathering the details. Never had to keep herself in check in order to be able to function. All of these distractions would have only served to get people killed, including herself. She'd always known this, of course, but to experience it was to truly understand the depths of it.

How does anyone survive this?

The man continued. "This unfortunate situation is also quite unique. Not only in the fact that we have witnesses—humans and dahems alike—but Ryla's condition is unlike anything we've seen before. There is no question *Cevrla* was disrupted, yet it has not fractured her as it has her predecessors. She is not lost despite the gold of her eyes."

There was a shift in the atmosphere as the man positioned himself in the middle of the head of the room with his hands clasped behind his back. He seemed to command the space more now. Even Ryla found herself hanging onto his every word.

"We must act quickly to prevent all involved—dahem and human alike—from sharing whatever information they've garnered, but especially Lavanai. Our usual efforts of sending a retrieval group won't do as there are far more witnesses than we're accustomed to. We'll need to consider different methods," he said, and he twisted his body in such a way that his gaze landed on Ryla again. "Perhaps we could use her as our hunter."

The room immediately erupted into a hum of murmurs, some of which Ryla's keen hearing was able to pick up. They had concerns about what the statement meant for the human witnesses. Concerns about her volatility in the field and the risk it'd mean.

While she'd expected to feel good about the prospect of returning to her duties, Ryla instead felt unease, which was only enhanced by the Keepers' rumblings. What he proposed wasn't being a line of defence who would deal death where necessary. It was delivering death forthright.

It brought to mind the countless times people asked why the Union simply didn't attack Lavanai. The countless times when she told others to do so would be their death.

I told Alden as much. But this Keeper isn't suggesting I go into the heart of Lavanai, is he?

Surely he meant only to go after those who'd stayed in the United's territory. Only those who'd survived her magic.

A thought suddenly occurred to her. *Did Mithos survive?*

Ryla combed through her memories, searching for Mithos's essence along the way. The more she pursued it, the more the memory pulled at her, threatening to drag her in. She started to pull herself back to the present when something snagged her.

It's there.

The roar of Mithos's flames erupted to life around her.

She was back at the encampment, watching the flames shift but the other magic users remained motionless. It was like the entire memory was in tableau except for the dancing fire, and the hum of magic that vibrated in the space around her.

Several distinct magical essences pulled toward her, but there was one, a strong one, that wasn't wending its way in her direction. Rather, a sort of tug of war transpired between what she now identified as *Cevrla* and Mithos's magic.

Golden light consumed her, and she blinked away the altered memory, the hum of apprehension still as present as it had been a moment ago.

She did survive. I'm sure of it.

Ryla grounded herself by looking at the man, gauging his reaction. He seemed perfectly calm as he surveyed the room, chin high and sure. Apart from the tilt of his chin, the way he watched them was familiar to her. This man was no Killer, but there was something about him that signaled to her he'd been as primed for his role as she'd been for hers.

Among the din, it occurred to her that the Union didn't seem to have a plan in place for this worst case scenario.

Her breath caught. *It's never been this catastrophic. He's going against normal protocol.*

None of the Keepers had been troubled about the situation until he'd mentioned using her. He'd said usually a group would seek out the witnesses. She wagered that would have been a group of Keepers, perhaps those with a stronger affinity to magic. She realized now this meeting had probably been as much for deciding who was to go as it was for announcing her fate, if not more so. The other Keepers had already known what would happen to her. Or at least they'd thought they had.

"Why should we risk ourselves?" the white-garbed man spoke again, the timbre of his voice bringing the rest to silence. "We have a Killer who, despite what's happened, is still composed and functioning. Her fate has always been death. There will be other Killers, but only if we continue to stand and hold our ground. Only if we protect our ways.

"The United will not survive without the Union. We *cannot* abandon them, and our best chance at continuing to serve them is to remain strong and quash this *now*…with *her*."

Ryla's thoughts interjected, unbidden. *Cannot abandon them, yet I'm certain Alden and Shron have been killed.* She mentally shook herself. *Death is a consequence of war. They were not abandoned.*

Beyond her thoughts, the Keepers seemed to consider the man's words. While they did, Ryla wondered what would become of the human witnesses. Would she face Arran as foe rather than guardian? Considering what the man had just said about protecting the kingdoms, she thought not, but she also couldn't see how they fit into this lead Keeper's plans yet.

"High Keeper Raynold," someone from the crowd spoke, their voice firm.

It was a voice Ryla recognized, and she had a surreal moment of putting a face to not only the magic, but the voice. She almost couldn't connect the rough vocal tone to the shorter woman with the dark complexion and dark, curly hair. The light in the room caught the small flecks of gold in her eyes.

Raynold, Ryla committed the name to memory, even as she took in the woman's appearance. She'd never heard the term High Keeper before, but it confirmed her assumptions this was the man in charge.

"You may speak," he said.

The woman stood. "With all respect, this isn't a wise plan. I understand your reason, but we cannot risk this. To send her back into the line of duty in any capacity is to risk more witnesses. Ryla has proven an exception, I agree, but I do not think she could avoid this nor do I think her unique enough to annihilate the entire Lavanian army," the Keeper concluded.

Ryla knew just as those nodding around her did that this Keeper was right. But the High Keeper was also right: the United needed them. Her time in Nithle had shown her that the kingdoms were more fractured than ever. The Union and Killers needed to protect these people, to bring them back together, and in order to continue doing that, *Cevrla* needed to be kept a secret.

What Lavanai would do with this knowledge…

"And what do you suggest?" the High Keeper asked. "Ryla's magic is powerful. Harnessing magic in this way has long been the Union's goal, and this would be the perfect opportunity to test it."

"Ryla's magic *is* powerful, but given that we have witnesses, it may not be as perfect as we thought since memories should have been altered and dahems should have been killed. The other possibility is that there was someone else with powerful magic that shielded against *Cevrla*," the female Keeper replied.

The thought struck Ryla. *Mithos. Did her flames dilute my magic's effectiveness?*

Before Ryla could really latch onto the thought, the Keeper continued. "I know we must act quickly, High Keeper, but we must also continue to be reasonable in our approach. Under different circumstances, one with only a few or no witnesses, we could put Ryla's magic to the test to grow it as a weapon, but this is much too risky."

"You make a good point," Raynold ceded. "Still, we find ourselves in a difficult situation."

"What about the other Union strongholds?" someone else asked.

"Only as a last resort," Raynold replied firmly.

Knowledge of other Union strongholds wasn't a secret from Ryla or, she assumed, the other Killers. All the same, she had no other knowledge of them, how they operated, or where precisely they were located. Although she'd never needed to know about them, she was curious now.

Even more curious, however, was that the High Keeper didn't want to call on them except as a last resort. Her instinct told her to use all resources to confront a situation if necessary, and what better than another Union that might know how to approach this?

Feel it. Let it pass, Ryla reminded herself. *Do not question.* The words leapt out from her memory and seemed to echo around her.

Her first lessons had been lessons of trust. Trust the Keepers. Trust the Union. As those who trained and took care of Killers, they had the wisdom to navigate the bigger picture, and Killers could rely on that wisdom to survive. To trust in their decisions meant her mind would be clearer for the task at hand.

She closed her eyes and took a breath in an effort to stave off her thoughts and the memories they conjured. The words repeated in her mind. *Do not question.*

FORTY-SEVEN

Arran took a shuddering breath. Even as he did, it barely felt like the air entered his lungs. It was as though his ribcage was bound and couldn't expand enough to allow the air in. And then there was the throbbing in his temples that wouldn't go away.

This was the first time he'd made any sort of significant movement in… He wasn't sure how long. Every moment felt like a slow crawl toward completing even the most mundane of tasks.

Currently, he had his hands planted on a table as he hunched to stare down at the small wash basin. The tent was dark enough that he couldn't quite make out all the details in the water's reflection, but with what he could see, he didn't recognize the person staring back at him. Sallow eyes and complexion beneath a growth of unkempt facial hair. His curls looked to be in knots.

Consciously thinking about having to move was a new and challenging experience. He had to will his body to respond to what would normally be an automatic communication between it and his mind. Then, once it finally did respond, everything felt sluggish and heavy, as if the ground wanted to swallow him whole.

I wish it would. He squeezed his eyes shut, forcing himself to counter the negative thought. *If it did, I wouldn't have*

Adel. She came for me. A modicum of inner warmth pierced through the tightness in his chest and fought against the weight threatening to drag him out of existence.

He eventually made his hands obey and managed to splash water on his face and run his hands through his tangled curls. The cold water and cool air sent a shiver through him that he both felt and didn't feel. It felt outside of him. He wasn't sure he felt present at all.

But he was trying.

And that was at least something.

Or so Adel told him, and he was taking her word for it and leaning on her in a way he had never expected to need to. The guilt he felt contended with the rest of his internal bedlam. How many times had he pushed her away only to cling to her now?

His heart ached. When he could exist beyond a single moment, he'd make it up to her. For now, he had to focus on picking up the rough towel to dry off his face and stop the water from dripping from his hair, eyelashes, and skin.

Exiting the tent, he blinked away the brightness of the grey sky. It took a moment for his eyes to adjust to even see Ley, ever loyal, standing just outside of the tent.

"Your Highness," the knight greeted breathily.

Arran could see the strain in Ley's features: tired eyes, taut expression, and that perceptible sense of making an effort to hold oneself in place. Arran felt a pang of guilt again. Had Ley had anyone to grieve with?

While all the menial tasks had felt like they'd taken eons, Arran found wrapping this man in a hug took very little effort at all. Absently, he wondered if he'd ever hugged Ley. In this moment, station disappeared. Arran felt the tightness of Ley's grasp on him and the weight of their new mutual reality.

They parted with strained expressions, but no tears. Arran got the sense that Ley was at the same point as he was—where he'd cried all he could for a while.

Ley's voice cracked when he spoke. "I'm glad to see you, Arran."

"I'm glad to see you, too," Arran replied, the sluggish feeling returning as he directed his body to pivot and take in his surroundings.

All that met him was a sea of tall white and brown tents that blended together. It was very quiet. He wasn't sure what he'd expected; maybe the chaos of war that echoed in his mind or the chatter of whoever still survived. But he hadn't expected this absolute stillness where even nature seemed to be holding its breath.

"Princess Mihel called for the daily convening almost an hour ago," Ley explained, seeming to sense Arran's confusion.

An hour? the prince thought. *Am I truly moving that slowly?* He didn't doubt Ley, but it didn't feel right somehow. He shook himself mentally. "Take me to them."

As they began walking, some other members of his guard emerged from between the tents. They fell into step without saying a word, and Arran forced himself to not check for Ryla. She'd become such a constant in his days that her absence was a void.

Her final words to him echoed in his mind. *There's nothing more I can do for you, Arran.*

The gold streaking her eyes was just as startling as the other changes: her words, her tone, her overall demeanour. The taint of magic wasn't something he'd been prepared for, nor did it make sense to him. The aggressiveness of the magic in Ryla was startling... Yet she wasn't behaving as someone lost would. Different, yes, but not beyond knowing herself.

Arran chased the image from his mind, trying to focus instead on where Ley lead him. Eventually, they came upon a larger tent, Nithle's and Piridet's flags dancing weakly atop it in the small breeze.

The goal was to enter unnoticed, but before he could fathom any stealth, the opening tent flap drew attention to him and his party. He felt eyes turning towards him from among the small gathering of knights and generals where they stood huddled around the table with Mihel and Adel at the centre.

His attention zeroed in on Adel—her soft features, warm eyes, comforting presence. He needed to go to her.

Her brow furrowed as she looked his way, and she shifted just slightly, as if she were about to approach, but Mihel stopped talking and her eyes fell on him. Any who weren't already looking at him turned to see what had snared her attention.

"Your Highness!" some of the Nithleans exclaimed.

They exchanged glances among themselves, seemingly torn between rushing forward and remaining in place. Ley stepped in front of him, as if shielding the prince from his own people. The thought left a sour taste in his mouth, but he needed space. He was grateful to his knight.

Crossing the tent through the crowd was a bit of a blur, but he finally made it past people and their softly spoken greetings and gratitude to where Mihel and Adel stood. He took up a spot at the table beside Adel. Her presence was an immediate salve.

"Are you okay enough to be doing this?" Mihel leaned in and asked as quietly as she did gently.

He nodded. Or he thought he did. He wasn't sure, so he ended up saying, "Yes. I need to be here. I can't promise I'll be of much use, but I need to be here."

Mihel gave her own nod, and the look of respect and understanding in her dark eyes put him a bit more at ease. He shifted his attention to Adel, who awarded him a small supportive smile.

Mihel stood straight now, addressing the room. "I think it's safe to say we're all heartened to see Prince Arran here with us. It has been an incredibly difficult time for Nithle, and we will continue to stand together."

Part of him expected a recitation of the Alliance Pact, the way his parents and Adel's had done at dinner. *How long ago was that?* he wondered. It felt both recent and a hundred years in the past.

But no one said a word of the pact. There was a quiet murmuring of agreement with Mihel's statement, then everyone simply readjusted to peer over the table, which was where he forced his eyes to focus now. At first, it simply looked like a scattering of aged papers and wooden figures, but then things came more into focus, and he recognized the etchings and the figures. It took a lot of effort, but Arran tried to tap into his strategist brain to bring back some normalcy and make sense of the locations of the figures on the page.

He surmised the larger group of figurines must be the very encampment in which he stood. They were many kilometers away from the castle; somewhere on the outskirts of Thlent as far as he could tell. Lavanai had overtaken the castle. He seemed to remember hearing something about that.

How did my people get out? he asked no one. He wasn't sure he could get the words to come out even if he wanted to.

He vaguely remembered talks of people escaping, perhaps even being let go. Then there were whispered memories of sending them to Piridet for safety and talk of sending word to Sothle and Wendur in the southwest to get to safety, too.

Did someone suggest sending them to Veloth? He couldn't quite remember.

Apart from the encampment, he noticed the positioning of wooden figures along the lake and other pathways dahems might use to come from Lavanai to Nithle, much in the same formations he and Mihel had talked about before all...this.

Adel's voice cut through his sluggish thoughts, "Mihel has done a really great job of coordinating everything."

He realized then as well that Mihel had resumed speaking with the knights and general; he'd missed every word of it. "Numbers?" he asked, not sure at first if his voice was as much of a whisper as hers. Since no one else reacted, he figured he was okay.

"What was that?" Adel asked him.

"What are our numbers?" he managed to ask. "We're stretched too thin."

Even out of the corner of his eye, he saw Adel's expression confirm his fears. He had no idea how few they were in numbers now, but considering the two points of attack Lavanai had laid on them, he wasn't optimistic.

"Mihel sent a messenger along with the refugees to her father for more support," Adel explained. "We haven't heard back yet, but a single messenger is all she cares to risk right now."

He nodded—or thought he did—again. This time he didn't have any words to go with it, but internally agreed with the Piridetian princess's judgement. Especially until he had a better sense of how many people they were working with. He tried to force himself to pay attention.

"Knight Eridan, Knight Feon. Give me a status update," Mihel said.

He wasn't sure if the princess had overheard or suspected

their conversation and asked the question for his benefit, or if this was a general part of the daily meeting.

Focus on the stats, Arran, he told himself as he stood straighter and turned his attention to the two knights.

Knight Eridan was a tall man with wavy, dark hair tied back in a few braids. His expression was severe, and Arran was sure he'd seen him before the attack, although he couldn't quite place when. He wasn't surprised when it was Eridan who started.

"After the initial attack, Piridet's numbers were reduced by about a third. Since then, we've lost a few dozen more to their injuries. Most survivors are prepared to fight, pending the healer's approval where necessary."

Knight Feon followed by saying, "Our numbers are very similar, with heavier losses from the castle. Under orders of Knight Kein, all forces that could be spared have been rerouted here. A few hundred of our people left with the refugees to offer protection where they could, but some of those were facing more severe injuries."

Feon paused, looking first at Mihel, who nodded for him to continue, and then to Arran. Arran didn't like the look in the man's eyes and felt he had to brace himself.

"Sire, there are fourteen field knights remaining, eight royal guard, and two royal knights," he said.

The curse left Arran's lips before he could hold it back. Already, his mind was conjuring up images of the slaughter that must have taken place at the castle, and he pictured how the royal guard and knights must have fallen protecting his parents. As he stood there in the tent, the echoes of turmoil reverberated around him. Oddly, it was the complete silence of the others in the tent that brought him back from it before he slipped too far or thought of Ryla's instructions. Their eyes on him were enough to make him feel too seen, too exposed.

His gaze shifted across those closest to him. Ley would be one of the remaining royal knights. His eyes came to rest on the other: Royal Knight Kein, one of the men who would've been at his parents' sides. When their eyes connected, Arran could see the weariness in them, but the knight still managed a nod. Arran had so many questions for this man he wasn't sure he dared to ask. Not just now, but ever.

Arran wondered which of them had taken Calar's place as the Royal Commander, and a stab of panic pierced him when he realized he had to decide. It was supposed to be the royal family that chose, right? He wasn't sure he had the wherewithal to make that kind of decision and looked away as if the knight were already silently asking him to make a choice.

The unease in his mind was flitting about again, edging back toward images of bedlam and slaughter.

We've still got forces to work with, he told himself firmly in an effort to not get lost in it. *We're still here.*

His inner pep talk and stab at reassurance didn't amount to much.

How much of what remains standing is because of Ryla?

It wasn't until he heard Mihel dismiss the others and the tent began to clear out that he felt the weight lift a little, and even then, it wasn't enough. Once the rest of the gathering had filed out of the tent, it was only Mihel, Adel, Ley, Kein, Eridan, and himself that remained.

Arran took a deep breath before asking the question that had been lingering in his thoughts since the attack itself. "What happened?

Mihel shifting something on the table brought Arran back to the present. "The dahems came in two fronts: one sent to the castle and the other to us. Our people held them off, but we suspect Lavanai was planning something for you and Killer Ryla from the start."

Arran actually felt his nod this time; he was sure of it. "More likely her. There was an attack weeks ago during the night. She had told me they were targeting her. Not in as many words, but I feel that's what she meant. I'd thought it'd just been because the leading dahem was Lost and deranged, but now I wonder…"

He felt more than he saw those around him have a collective moment of shock and horror, and he realized that he hadn't even told Adel what he'd just mentioned.

"Why did no one else know of this?" Ley asked sharply.

Arran regarded him evenly, not wanting to fight the man but knowing he had to say something. "Just as I said, the dahem was lost. Ryla…Killer Ryla killed him. I thought it was the end of it, and that if she'd been concerned, she would have mentioned it more widely."

Mihel's tone was critical. "If the dahems were targeting the High Protector, that's not a good thing. You should have told someone about it and had her sent away—"

He ran a hand down his face, feeling both the stubble that had grown in along his jaw and the weariness in his chest in equal measure. "Considering the Union didn't take her away when they found out, I didn't think there was much to worry about. And far be it from me to question their judgement."

"I'm sure if they had foreseen what was going to happen, then they would have taken her," Mihel countered.

"I don't think anyone could have foreseen this," Adel noted as she took a nearby stool and sat at the table. She leaned on it with her arms crossed in front of her.

Mihel let out a gruff sigh. "You're probably right. It all just seems clear to us now because we're on the other side of the disaster." She took a calming breath before continuing. "Anyway, after the Keepers took her and my party regrouped, we followed after you as soon as possible. We directed those fleeing to Piridet and sent word to Sothle and Wendur to evacuate to Veloth."

So that all did happen. It was slightly reassuring that his memories weren't completely muddled.

Mihel continued, "By the time I'd arrived, you'd already learned of your parents' deaths..."

Arran's jaw tightened until it ached, and no one said anything for a long moment. His eyes lingered on where his castle sat on the map. He vaguely remembered it now, but it felt far away. Like it had happened to someone else, not him.

When Arran, Ley, and the rest of those who'd joined them made it to Thlent, the villagers were already in the process of moving out with wagons full of whatever they could take with them. Nithle Proper was equally in pandemonium, and although at first they'd tried to venture into the city, as soon as they saw the fires and destruction, Ley forced them to turn around and hold in Thlent.

One of their party continued on to try to gather information, but before that fielder even returned, those who'd escaped the castle crossed their paths. They'd been heartened to see their prince alive, but heartbroken to report the fall of their king and queen.

I collapsed. Another faraway memory. He wasn't sure if he preferred this type of memory over the all-consuming ones.

"Knight Kein," Mihel prompted, pulling Arran from his inner musings.

"Yes, Princess," the man's gravelly voice entered the conversation. "Lavanai attacked Nithle castle with a large force after barrelling through Thlent and the city. As soon as we saw sign of them, Commander Calar ordered the royal knights and guard to arms and to take the king and queen to safety."

The prince's brow pinched together as he listened to and watched the man speak. The tightness in his chest swelled.

"Somehow, they still found us among the secret passageways and in the safe room in the wing by the kitchens. We suspect they tortured some poor soul along the way to get the information. Your Highness…" Kein stopped a moment. When he spoke again, his voice was thick. "Your parents both fought bravely, as did everyone protecting them. It is with the deepest regret I say I failed to save them, and I barely fled with my life to ensure you, at least, still lived."

Silence fell over the tent again, and Arran leaned on the table now, bracing himself with his palms. He shut his eyes tightly as the words speared him. How long he stood there with his head hung, he couldn't say. He wanted to offer Kein some comfort and say he hadn't failed, but those were not the words that he eventually summoned as he opened his eyes to stare at the grain of the tabletop.

"All this death and destruction. *For what?* What threat do we pose to Lavanai that they can't let us be? They seem to have no interest in controlling us. Just annihilating us. Why?"

"I know why."

Arran whirled on Adel.

His eyes searched her beautiful face as he wondered if he dared for that to be true. He was met with a mix of anxiety and a heavy burden in her features. Dread wrapped him in a dooming embrace.

CHAPTER

FORTY-EIGHT

A del's heart hammered away in her chest and blood
thumped in her ears as she held eye contact with Arran.
Terror. That was how she would describe the emotion she
saw, and she hated that she'd put it there. Any doubt she held
about him knowing the secrets of his family's past flittered
away. This wasn't the kind of terror of being caught; this was
the kind of terror of bracing for further devastation.

Her only wish was for a more private setting.

I'm going to shatter him anew...

Mihel broke the long bout of silence. "Adel. Please explain."

She finally pulled her gaze from Arran's and stared at her
hands gripping her arms where they leaned on the table. The
tension was already causing some cramping, and she flexed
her fingers. She tried to remember exactly what her father
had told her and the best way to relay that information to
her expectant audience.

"The Nithle royal family initiated the war," she heard
herself say unceremoniously, but she couldn't stop now. "There
was a time when dahems and humans weren't attacking each
other, but King Gerge was afraid of their magic anyway and
launched a secret attack that caused Lavanai to retaliate. The
king used the retaliation as propaganda, spreading the lie that
the dahems attacked first and needed to be stopped or else all
humans would be in danger. When the dahem king came to

Nithle afterward, it wasn't in an attack, it was to make peace, and the royal family had him executed…"

She worried she'd left out details and spoken too quickly for any of them to understand. Her chest heaved slightly, as if she'd run around the tent instead of spoken. She'd stared at her arms the entire time, unable to bear the looks that undoubtedly crossed their faces. Unable to see how it impacted Arran.

"Who told you this?" Ley demanded after only a moment's hesitation that she figured was probably due to shock. His tone was nothing short of appalled.

"My father," she replied.

"And where did he hear these lies?" Ley continued harshly.

Although she cowered slightly, Adel didn't take it personally. "King Alden."

The name compelled her to peer up at Arran now. Maybe it wasn't even the name, but Arran's continued silence. He looked numb, and she had to take a breath before continuing.

"My father said the story gets passed down through the generations, and when King Alden learned it, he told my father since they were best friends. At first, King Alden wanted to change things. End the war and put a stop to all this, but…"

"Then he got scared. Just like everyone else," Mihel conjectured, tapping her lower lip absently. "I think it'd be safe to say that it was when Shron became pregnant. Probably became worse still when they realized there'd only be one heir to the throne."

Adel nodded, feeling certain her father had mentioned something of the same.

Kein spoke now. "King Alden did become more nervous when the queen was pregnant, but we attributed it to first-time fatherhood and then the increased attacks once Lavanai learned of the prince's conception. As for when we learned there would only be one heir…that would cause anyone in their position to panic."

Still, Ley protested, his tone again sharp. "Continuing the war has put them in more danger than stopping it would have."

"Father said King Alden didn't want to reveal the truth of it," Adel said, watching Ley now. She felt bad for him, knowing this was shaking the foundation of everything he stood for. "He hadn't figured out a way to end things without doing that. Or, at the very least, he started to believe that it was impossible. My father refused to send aid because he said King Alden was no longer planning to stop the war. In fact, he was planning to attack Lavanai against Killer Ryla's advice."

The knight shook his head. "None of this makes sense. He wouldn't go against Killer Ryla's wishes, and he could have called for a peace treaty."

"It could make sense."

Adel jumped at Arran's voice. His features were littered with all of the pain of the situation. He stepped around the table now, closer to the group.

Arran continued, "Spikes in attacks have consistently corresponded with births, coronations, courtships—various incidents that would advance the kingdom. Think about it. We were going to announce our courtship at the Harvest Festival, and they attacked before we even could.

"My father probably didn't have things figured out and would try *anything* at that point. Declaring a peace treaty wouldn't have worked because of the deep-seated fear and hatred between dahems and humans. People would have thought he was crazy or trying to save the throne while not caring about anyone else."

The prince and his knight were locked in a stare down, and Adel could clearly see the tension between them. The usual smiles and genuine care had been replaced with tight and severe expressions, challenging one another.

"There's no reason for King Criph to lie," Arran continued, his voice low but firm. "And it explains so many things. Like why Lavanai has such a singular focus on Nithle when they could attack and overtake other kingdoms. Proximity alone doesn't explain it when they could also target Veloth from the south. I don't think my father was a bad man, Ley. I can't speak for my grandfather or great-grandfather, but my father, at least, seemed to want to make things right. He was just out of his depth."

Adel wasn't quite sure what the emotion that swelled in her was—maybe pride? Before she could figure it out, she heard the tent flap shift and peered past Arran to see a Piridetian field knight poke his head in.

"Princess Mihel," the knight called.

"What is it?" she asked as everyone else in the tent turned to him, even Arran and Ley.

"The Heta banner approaches," the knight replied, causing Adel's chest to constrict.

Mihel glanced her way, but then returned her attention to her knight. "Are we sure it's them?"

The knight nodded. "A scout saw King Criph leading the group. About fifty accompany him."

She nodded. "I'll come to meet him. Gather a party together."

"Tell Knight Feon to gather my guard as well," Arran added.

The knight gave another nod before disappearing through the flap, and Adel stood, unsure if her suddenly wobbly legs would hold her.

Father? He's come to force me home. Mother's probably furious, her thoughts raced. She swallowed the anxiety bursting within as the consequences of her actions rode on the camp.

Mihel reconnected with Adel's gaze. "It looks like your father has finally come for you, Adel."

Her response came quick and sure. "I'm not going anywhere."

A hint of a grin graced Mihel's lips. "I know. Just prepare yourself."

Despite her mental preparation as they trekked through the camp surrounded by their guard, when Adel saw the kestrel banner flying and her father standing in his armour beside his horse with the group of fifty riders behind him, she felt her resolve waver. It reminded her of the time when she and Ashla had snuck into the kitchen in the middle of the night when they were nine to have a "baking" party. Mostly, it had ended up in a giant mess, and although it had only been the kitchen master and the king and queen there to reprimand them, it had felt like a whole battalion.

You're not a child anymore, Adel told herself silently and made a concerted effort to square her shoulders and walk taller with each step she took.

When Arran laced his fingers through hers, she realized the action must have been more obvious than she'd intended. But then she looked at him, and he wore a small, supportive grin. The simple gesture gave her strength.

I can do this. She squeezed his hand before facing her father.

At first, she only caught glimpses of him through the shoulders of the guard surrounding them, but as the guard stepped away to present the royal trio, she saw the look of scrutiny on his face. He assessed what exactly he was coming upon, and then his expression shifted to pained as the three royal children approached. There wasn't a doubt in her mind he'd learned from the refugees, like she had, what happened at the castle, yet as his eyes passed through those around them, she wondered who he was looking for.

It dawned on her. *Killer Ryla.*

His gaze continued to shift, and there was a flicker of relief when it fell back to her after surveying the rest of the group, but the look hardened over.

"Welcome, King Criph," Mihel was the first to speak, drawing his attention. "You'll have to forgive us for making you wait and for our caution. These are trying times."

"So, it's true then?" the king asked, doing away with any niceties.

Mihel looked at Arran at this point, and he nodded as his grip on Adel's hand tightened. As Adel watched him, she wasn't sure he'd be able to get any words past his fixed jaw.

"Yes," he said, then cleared his throat and spoke with more volume. "My parents have been killed. Nithle has fallen."

Adel held her breath. She was certain this was the first time he'd vocalized that reality, and she worried it might wreck him all over again. Despite his eyes glassing over, however, he remained firm and held his gaze with her father.

Her attention trailed back to King Criph, and she was shocked by the pain she saw reflected in the tightness of his eyes and the slump of his shoulders. She hadn't factored this into how reuniting with him would transpire. She pictured him angry, furious even, and demanding for her to return to Heta.

She bit her lip. *Of course. Alden was his best friend.*

A wave of shame hit her. Only her fear of his potential ire over her actions stayed her from going to him.

"I know what my father told you about my family. About Nithle. About this war," Arran spoke again, and this time it was Adel that gripped his hand a little tighter.

"Do you understand, then, why I couldn't stand with

him?" Criph asked, his features hardening again despite the thickness of his voice.

Adel steadied her breath, unsure how this would go.

"I do," Arran responded without hesitation. "I understand how fear has driven each of us, and I'd like the opportunity to speak with you about it."

The king sized up the prince, as though deciding whether some test had been met and passed. "Then we shall convene."

Arran turned slightly to the left, never letting go of Adel's hand. "Knight Feon."

"Yes, Your Highness?" the man answered immediately.

"See to it that our friends are taken care of while the king and I speak," Arran said in a tone that reminded Adel more of his old self.

"Of course, Sire," Feon replied with a slight bow before turning to his people to give direction.

"Let me know if I can be of any assistance to either of you," Mihel offered as people began to move around them. "In the meantime, I'll ensure our line is held and send for you if necessary."

"Thank you," Arran said with a nod.

It was odd, after all of these days, to see Mihel deferring to Arran instead of taking charge of the situation, but Adel realized the princess was falling back into the role she'd been called for. This was still Nithle's battle, and Piridet was a support. She'd stepped in when they'd needed someone to take charge, and she'd held them together, but there was a distinct difference between filling in and taking over. It gave Adel a new level of respect for her fellow princess.

Yet, she wasn't sure where she fit in with each of these moving parts.

As if to answer her uncertainties, Arran said, "I need you

with me, Adel."

Warmth spread through her, and when she looked into his blue eyes, she saw the silent plea for her there. But would her father allow it?

It doesn't matter if he will or not, Adel told herself. *Arran won't have it any other way.* Aloud she replied, "Of course."

Criph made no comment about their exchange. He simply gestured for them to lead the way, so they began the trek back into the maze of tents.

Arran leaned close to her, his voice quiet as he spoke and his breath brushing against her ear and cheek. "Take us back to where the meeting was earlier."

She peeked at him out of the corner of her eye, her brow furrowing slightly.

"I'm not familiar with the layout yet," Arran explained just as quietly. "And I don't quite remember the way we just came."

His embarrassment hit her hard. Now wasn't a good time to discuss it, but she made a mental note to bring it up later since she didn't want him to feel bad about that kind of thing. She released his hand at that point and hooked her arm through his.

While she was slightly surprised Arran hadn't asked Knight Ley or Kein, both of whom kept pace on either side of them, to take the lead, she replied with a subtle nod. Arran afforded her a small smile.

Although on some level a tent was a tent was a tent to her, Adel had a fairly good sense of how to navigate this camp, which is something she wouldn't have expected when she'd ridden up on horseback. Though she mostly stayed with Arran and attended the daily meetings, Mihel had made a point to show her the entire camp, just in case. The "just in case" part wasn't something she was keen on thinking about or putting words to, but she understood.

The group was silent, which seemed to amplify the rest of the sounds around them. A small shift of the breeze rustling against a tent or even the subtle scraping of her father's armour sounded as clear as day to her, and a time or two she worried her own breathing was too loud.

Relief trickled in when they reached the tent. As they entered, Arran and Ley exchanged some sort of glance, but the knight stayed outside to stand post along with Kein and other members of the Nithlean and Hetaen retinue. Only she, her father, and Arran entered, and Arran took over the lead now, purposefully leading them to the table with the map. The fact that he'd wanted to come here at all rather than a tent with more comfortable seating hadn't escaped her perception, but she wasn't quite sure what he had planned for her father or this conversation.

They got situated around the table, and then Arran started.

"I can't pretend to know why my father never told me about Nithle's true involvement in the war, but I can say I want to bring the war to an end." His tone was thick and heavy, but there was no waver in his words.

"Your father once said he wanted to stop this war, too. That he was tired of death on both sides of the battle, but then it seemed that death was all he could see," Criph said carefully as he loosened his armour. His hazel eyes traced the map but also flicked up to Arran. "As things have progressed...I knew he'd abandoned any promise he'd once made to stop the war peacefully. I tried once more to convince him when we last visited."

"This war has taken everything from me," Arran replied, then corrected himself as he glanced at Adel. "Almost everything. It has taken my parents. My kingdom. It even took the Killer."

Criph's eyebrows shot up. "The Killer is dead?"

"No. But something happened to her that has left her tainted, and the Union took her," Arran explained. Before King Criph could say anything more, Arran continued. "It makes sense to me that my father didn't know how to peacefully end this war. Not without having our people and the rest of the kingdoms turn on him. Even if Veloth, Piridet, and Heta haven't been involved with Lavanai the same way we have, there's been enough fear spread and enough damage done that it would've been difficult to side with Nithle. But I have nothing like that to lose. They've already taken my kingdom."

A warning note sounded in Criph's next words. "The kingdoms may see you as weak. They may see you as surrendering instead of making peace, *especially* because of all you've lost."

Arran paused, and the silence was palpable. Adel watched them both, these men she loved, with intense interest, not seeing any need to interject as they spoke. She agreed with her father about the appearance of surrender and tried to work through the complexity of the situation. If they continued to wage war with Lavanai, there was the risk of it continuing perpetually, but trying to make peace with them would be difficult for people to accept.

"You're right that this is where your father got stuck. I never held that against him because this isn't an easy situation to navigate," Criph said, his tone softened. There was no challenge now; if anything, it was almost paternal.

"And what if we admitted to the truth?" Arran asked.

Criph sighed. "I doubt anyone will believe the truth at this point."

"Even if you were to corroborate it?" Arran continued.

"Suppose then they did believe it; it could sabotage your

chance at ever being king or ever regaining your kingdom. It may even turn the other kingdoms against Heta since I held this knowledge," Criph said carefully, his eyes locked on Arran now.

"People's lives are more important to me than having a throne," Arran replied just as evenly.

"That's noble, Arran. I have a responsibility to my kingdom. It's a big risk to stop one war and potentially invite another," Criph added.

Arran collected his thoughts. "The way I see it, you're risking war falling on your kingdom regardless. Even if I were to die in battle without ever uttering a word of this to anyone else, I don't see this ending. Lavanai might target Heta next since you're our closest ally and because of my relationship with Adel. They may worry your next move would be to seek revenge. They may already be thinking that. And the United haven't exactly shown much unity. I doubt Nithle's fall would suddenly inspire them."

Fear trickled its way in as Adel sat on the hard stool listening to their back and forth. Nithle falling and the talk of her own kingdom being at war? Things were quickly careening toward a no-win situation…

"Arran's right," she finally chimed in, and both men turned their attention to where she sat at the table. The weight of their gazes slammed into her, but she held herself. "Well, to clarify, you're both right about the risks of war, but I think what Arran says about Lavanai coming after Heta is more likely to happen. We don't know for certain that the other kingdoms would turn on us if you said you knew about Nithle's secret, too. It could have been the shock of the revelation, but Mihel didn't make any comment about it."

"Mihel doesn't speak for Piridet," Criph reminded her.

"No, but it does show that not everyone will have a negative reaction," Adel continued.

"Even if all the royal families reacted favourably, we'd have our people to contend with. This will cause unrest among them," Criph countered.

"There's always unrest, isn't there?" Adel continued. "I don't think we can say it's been an even slate of peace among our people."

"That's true. However, we risk our people turning on us," the king said with a slow shake of his head. "The possibility they'll lose confidence in our decision-making and try to overthrow us is very real."

Adel fell silent, again seeing her father's point, but she didn't want to let go of the idea that things might turn out in their favour. No one said a word for several moments.

Criph sighed, breaking the silence. "Alden spent a good portion of his life going back and forth like this. We can't expect to make this kind of decision in a snap. We need time."

"We don't have time," Arran countered. "With all due respect, Your Majesty, I can't see Lavanai sitting on this much longer. I'd wager the only reason they haven't done anything yet is because they're tending to their wounded, just as we are. But they'll come for us sooner rather than later. They know they've weakened us and have brought my kingdom to its knees. We need to act quickly before they deal the final blow."

Criph regarded Arran evenly. "Then what do you propose we do?"

Adel fixed her eyes on Arran, and when their eyes met she saw in them all the uncertainty she felt closing in around her.

CHAPTER

FORTY-NINE

T he sword laid out on a sheaf of cloth atop a table snared Ryla's attention. It was hers, without a doubt, remnants of the magic still whispering around the blade in that haze she could see.

Can all magic users see this? she wondered. She thought of all the times Repelling when she'd seen hazes of magic. She'd thought it was the technique that allowed her to see it, but now she wondered if it wasn't more than that.

Her mind didn't linger on the question, instead warring internally with the need to approach the weapon. Despite the weeks of training that had passed in this same way, the draw to her sword lingered. Perhaps this was some of the sentimentality and emotional security of an object she'd seen in others. She didn't dare ask about it.

Regardless of what emotions she was feeling, the Keepers wouldn't let her touch the weapon. The vivid memories that transported her back to the battlefield reminded Ryla that she didn't need her sword to summon the magic even the Keepers seemed to fear. In fact, it hadn't been until her blade was out of her grasp that she'd been able to use it.

Yet, despite their fear of it being used against them, the Keepers wanted to try to harness that magic again.

A man paced back and forth before her in the expansive stone-walled training room hidden in the lower level of the

Union stronghold. His tight black trousers and sleeveless black top set him apart from the other Keepers. He, like the healer who'd told Ryla about *Cevrla*, had tattoos marking his skin; she could see the unfamiliar swirls on the palms of his hands and at the base of his hairline along his neck. His apprentice, observing from beside her sword, wore a similar outfit and bore the same markings. The young man's ever-watchful eyes, however, didn't show any hints of the gold that his master's did.

This Keeper taught the other Keepers how to use their magic, but even with his instruction, Ryla wasn't making any progress. As much as she could practically feel the magic burning beneath her skin, she couldn't do anything with it, no matter what method she tried to use. Even that word *Cizeth* hadn't called the golden light again.

"If not for your eyes and being a Killer, I wouldn't think you had any magic in you at all," the Keeper said, his enunciation of 'at all' blending the words together.

She studied the Keeper's face, lined with age and frustration. She didn't fault him his irritation.

This man knew how to bestow *Cevrla* onto a Killer—had admitted to having a role in it. She'd asked him about the procedure, including how a newborn could even invite magic or have it passed to them, but he'd refused to impart any information. She'd argued that in understanding it more, she might better control it, but he hadn't budged.

What Ryla could discern was that none of the Keepers, including this man, could understand why *Cevrla* hadn't fully devoured her soul yet. She was still of sound mind and the magic hadn't completely returned to its chaotic state. Still, she'd made no progress, despite the High Keeper's insistence they continue to try to harness it.

"All right. Again," the Keeper said, stopping before her,

looking up so one golden gaze met the other. "Put yourself on the battlefield, feel how it felt, harness *Cevrla*."

Her instincts balked at this newest exercise, protesting the very idea of putting her mind in danger by returning to the moment her world completely shattered and shifted. The Keeper theorized Ryla needed to tap into her soul in order for *Cevrla* to properly respond again.

Ryla took a breath, ignored the protesting self-preservation, and delved into her own mind to allow the moment to consume her. The flames erupted around her in her mind's eye—but the scene that emerged pulled her farther back in her memories.

The fire snuffed from her vision, but her skin burned where day-old ink still healed. The bandage around her left hand, across her chest, and covering her half-shaved head protected the symbol newly marked into her flesh in those three places. Still, she could feel the pull as she tightened her grip on her sword.

This younger version of Ryla, just about six, easily ignored the fire on her skin to instead focus on the movements she'd just been taught by the weapons' master. Her sword, big compared to her smaller body, slashed through the air and twisted in her grip as she faced imaginary enemies in front of and behind her. Breath, steady in her chest, elicited flowing footwork as her body moved.

"Repeat. Faster," the weapons' master of her memories told her from where they stood, draped in their cloak just out of her line of vision.

Young Ryla repeated the exercise, following the same foot patterns, swings of her sword, and breathing techniques she'd been taught. The child moved fluidly around the room like a noble might move through a ballroom dance. The sound of the blade cutting air and her boot steps were the only accompaniment to this battle dance.

The ache in her limbs went ignored as the lesson continued, engraving the movements into her muscle memory while training those same muscles to extend past their limits. Endure beyond them.

A tingle of energy prickled under her skin, something the Ryla of present recognized as the magic weaving through her. Somehow, it strengthened her, gave her speed, and eased any protest from her body. Young Ryla had thought it was simply the training at work. Present Ryla could now see her experience tainted by the magic she'd been oblivious to.

As the burning sensation of her eyes blurred the memory and brought her back to the present, she had no idea how much time had passed.

Regardless, it hadn't changed the look of frustration practically etched into the Keeper's features. The apprentice hadn't moved from where he stood by her sword. It seemed that nothing had changed around her despite the roiling feeling in her gut.

Before she could be asked about her vision or voluntarily report on it, movement caught her eye. The door to the training room opened silently to reveal the main Keeper who'd collected her from Nithle. She still hadn't been given his name.

All it took was looking at him, and she knew her fate had been decided. She was either about to walk to her death or back to battle.

CHAPTER

FIFTY

Reports of the volleys of arrows raining down on the Nithlean, Piridetian, and Hetaen fighters doused the very small hope that the dahems occupying Nithle Proper had been somehow incapacitated.

If only Ryla's magic had reached here, maybe then it could have saved... Arran shook his head, stopping the thoughts in their tracks before they took him out of the moment.

Arran, Criph, and Adel kept to the tent where maps were strewn across the table with figures changing positions at each report that came in from the field knights and commanders. As it was, the figures representing Lavanai lined the border of Nithle Proper and Thlent some distance from where the human army figures stood almost in the heart of Thlent. Long-range weapons were Lavanai's primary choice of attack, but there were a few battalions that clashed with the humans on foot.

Mihel brought the latest news herself, saying they hadn't lost any ground to the dahems, although they hadn't gained any either. She stood in the tent with her hair swept back in a tight braid and her armour spattered in dirt and, Arran thought, probably blood. Her features were harder than he'd seen before.

As his eyes locked on the splattering of blood across the warrior princess's shoulder plate, his thoughts churned in his mind. There were some things that just weren't making sense to him.

"Mihel," he said, standing straight and looking at her from across the table. "In your opinion, would these dahems have been able to overthrow Nithle?"

She thought on it only a moment. "It's hard to say. Certainly, there's a mix of skill levels we're facing. I don't doubt some of them are probably the original lot that took over the castle. There's no sense in completely leaving taken lands unprotected, but many of these dahems are less skilled than we would have expected."

Arran nodded as he thought on it.

Adel seemed to be thinking aloud as she said, "Do they think that little of us that they're not even worried about sending their best fighters?"

"It's more likely that they're planning something," Arran realized, running through their numbers in his head. Even with three days of battle, they hadn't lost many and still had a fairly strong line. "Like they're holding them in the castle for some reason while this group meets us in battle." He paused again, his eyes moving around the tent, but not really taking anything in as his brow furrowed. "They're keeping us occupied, maybe."

"That could well be the case," Criph spoke now. "I'm not sure we're in a position to try to confirm that, though. We don't have the capacity to break off and find out what they might be up to."

"The king is right," Mihel agreed. "Even with these weaker dahems, it's still a fierce fight, and we need to focus here to stay alive—to have *any* chance of looking beyond this battlefield."

There'd been no word or action from the Union since they'd taken Ryla. No word on how they felt about what was going on. No word on what they were going to do to help.

No way to even try to contact the Union to find out. Arran thought briefly of the High Chambers and the amulet they could use to request audience with the Union.

If they're smart, they'll be ignoring all calls from Nithle right now, he thought. He wouldn't have been surprised if the dahem fighters had ransacked the castle to look for anything they could use against the Union.

Whatever they were up to, he knew Criph and Mihel were right: they needed to focus on what was in front of them before they'd be able to consider anything else.

"We need to shift from the defensive to the offensive," he said after some thought. "They've been forcing us to respond. We need to make *them* respond to *us* now. We're still on Nithlean territory. We've gotten a sense of how they're fighting and what level of fighters we're up against, so I'm confident we could come up with a plan. *Even* with the numbers we have," he added as he saw Criph open his mouth to speak. Arran felt something surging in him as he said the words. Adrenaline? Fear maybe?

The opening tent flap stopped any further words on his tongue, and he looked toward the entrance to see his new Royal Commander, Kein, enter the tent. Everyone straightened, the atmosphere shifting noticeably.

"I'm sorry, Your Highnesses," the man apologized, giving a slight bow even as his chest heaved, as though he had run all the way to the tent.

"What's going on?" Arran asked, his eyes searching the man's features for clues. He saw only confusion and uncertainty, which immediately set him on edge.

"Some of Lavanai's army is withdrawing and heading northward," Kein puffed out.

"Northward?" Adel asked from beside Arran, and there

was no mistaking the tension in her voice.

"Has anyone been able to find out why?" Mihel bit out.

Kein shook his head, his long hair falling into his eyes before he pushed it back. "No one is engaging them right now. We sent a scout as close as we dared so we could overhear what was going on as their groups began moving out, but the dahems were of course speaking in their own language. The scout said there was one word that he kept hearing that seemed to trigger something in them."

"What was it, Kein?" Arran asked, feeling his chest tightening. He didn't know any of the dahem language, but instinct told him he needed to know what they'd said.

"*Strala*… No, that wasn't it. *Yasta*-something," Kein tried the syllables out on his tongue, but couldn't seem to recall the exact syllables.

Still, it triggered something in Arran, too.

"*Yastalai*?" he asked, and he could feel all the eyes in the room on him again.

"Yes, that's it," Kein said confidently. "Yah-stah-leye." Even repeating the word back, the syllables didn't seem comfortable.

"You've heard this word before?" Criph asked.

It was only conjecture. No one had actually confirmed what the word had meant. Still, it brought Arran back to the village square, the mace arcing over his head. He felt confident in its meaning somehow.

"Killer," he breathed out. "It means Killer."

CHAPTER

FIFTY-ONE

"How do you know it means Killer?"

The question had come from her father, but Adel tasted it on her own tongue as well. Hope and anxiety warred within her as she tracked Arran's movements when he began to pace the length of the wooden table. His agitation did nothing to calm her. What if he was wrong? Even more, what if he was *right*?

Adel could tell Arran's mind was working as quickly as her thrumming heart when he said, "That night, at the Harvest Festival, the dahems shouted it just before Killer Ryla entered the fray."

"Did you ask her about it? Confirm the translation with her afterward?" Mihel asked from where she still stood since entering the tent.

"No." He seemed to read the same uncertainty in Mihel's features that Adel did because he continued. "I know, it sounds crazy to be so certain without confirmation, but I am."

The hesitancy on everyone else's faces while Arran's features held steadfast and pleading for someone to believe him encouraged Adel to swallow down her anxiousness. "Suppose you're right, Arran. What do we *do* with that information? Does it mean the Union is back? Have they sent another Killer? Are they nearby?"

"With the way Commander Kein says the dahems are

moving out, I can't help but wonder if there is a Killer nearby. We could follow them," Arran suggested, his eyes now fixated on the map and the figures still set up in clusters on it. "Kein, come show me where the reports are showing their movement."

"Yes, Your Highness," he said with a nod and approached the table.

Mihel stepped forward as well and asked, "Hold on, follow them? To what end?" She leaned over the table anyway to watch where Kein pointed on the roads leading away from Nithle castle

"She's right, Arran," Criph started. "Rather than follow them, this could be an opportunity to reclaim Nithle castle if they completely vacate it."

"Reclaim the castle?" Arran looked up at the king with bewilderment. "To echo Mihel's question, to what end? Retaking the castle doesn't accomplish anything."

"Of course it does. It means you've taken your kingdom back and gives your people a place to return to. I know they're safely away from this chaos right now, but don't forget about them," Criph said, his incredulity matching Arran's dumbfounded expression.

"I haven't forgotten about them," Arran said defensively.

The king continued, "It also prevents the dahems from expanding their empire."

"Or we follow the dahems and help this new Killer defeat them once and for all," Arran countered. "That'll be just as effective, if not more so, in preventing the expansion of Lavanai's empire."

Criph shook his head. "Until their king learns of what happens and sends additional forces. We'd be risking an awful lot on *if* a Killer is even there. Maybe it's a ruse and we were *intended* to hear it. You're not thinking straight right now."

Adel could see that plainly, too. This wasn't the same composed strategist she'd seen in the past, where there was confidence and reason in Arran's decisions. This was frenetic. Probably some mix of his lingering grief and desperation for a solution to the chaos her father mentioned. She ached to reach out to him, to offer him some sense of peace among the storm.

Look at me, Arran. Maybe if he just looked at her, she could slow down both of their racing hearts and minds.

Still, his eyes were fixated on her father, her father's on Arran's. Mihel still studied the map weighted to the large table as if it would reveal something. The tent felt altogether hollow and suffocating among the low light brought on by the lanterns placed throughout it.

A thought suddenly came to Adel that she hoped would serve both Arran's and her father's ideas. "Is there any possibility of dividing and addressing both of these things? What if some stay to retake the castle and the rest track the dahems to find out what's happening?"

Mihel's sharp gaze flicked to Adel, her features hard and pensive. "If we knew more, such as how far they were travelling, we could consider it more readily."

"If we're going to divide our forces, I'd much rather most of us track the dahems and the rest travel to Veloth," Arran said. "Reinforcements are much more important than protecting an empty castle."

For the first time, everyone seemed to consider Arran's words as more than just reactionary suggestions. To Adel, it felt like a physical shift in the tent's atmosphere that she couldn't put words to.

"It's not the worst idea." Criph ran a hand over his balding head. "Although convincing King Hadden of anything will be trying, if we did succeed in soliciting their help, then we'll have additional forces regardless. Whether that means defending Nithle castle or reuniting our forces for whatever the situation is at that point."

If, if, if, if. Adel felt like she would go mad over all these if statements and uncertainty. How could anyone be expected to operate like this? How could they know what the right decision was when they were being pulled so many different ways?

She stared at the map without really taking in any of what the ink strokes actually meant. She just needed *something* to look at while everyone spun in their *if* circles.

Mihel huffed a breath. "We need to decide on this quickly. Every minute we stand here talking, the dahems could be getting farther away. I'm not concerned about tracking them, but they have the advantage of speed and we don't want the gap to get too wide."

"Criph, Adel, I'd like you two to go to Veloth," Arran announced.

Adel's attention snapped up as the air stole from her lungs. "What?" Surely, she hadn't heard him right.

Arran's gaze snared her. Gone was the frenetic energy, and in its place the steady strategist she'd been hoping for earlier. His resolve almost scared her. "King Hadden is more likely to listen to your father than he is any of us, especially me. And you, Adel, have a chance of getting through to Nea, Jase, and Rold. You can bring Heta's guard with you while Mihel and I lead our forces northward. It makes the most sense."

When she turned her attention to her father, she saw him nodding along silently from where he'd taken a seat at the table. Looking Mihel's direction afforded her a similar reaction. When Adel had suggested dividing their forces, she hadn't meant like this.

"You can do it, Adel. There's no one I trust more for this mission," Arran said, his voice steady and reassuring.

It didn't ease the knot in her stomach.

CHAPTER

FIFTY-TWO

None of the tension had left Adel's body by the time they returned to their tent just over an hour later. The meager cot creaked under her weight as she sat down while Arran fastened the tent door closed from the inside, the fabric ties *wisping* across each other as he did. Over the weeks she'd been in the camp, she'd gotten used to the smell of dirt and canvas, but the scents suddenly overwhelmed her. Even the cold air seemed to seep particularly deep into her bones.

"I don't want to be separated from you again," Adel said as the cot sank and creaked again beside her. "Not with all that's happened. With all that *could* happen."

Arran took one of her hands in his, threading their fingers. His touch didn't quite ground her but was a tether she didn't ever want to let go of.

His voice was thick as he responded. "Nor I you, but we need to act. We can't wait to see which flag flies back at us when an army returns to Nithle."

"I know. And I see your reasoning with sending me and my father to Veloth. It's just..." Her words lodged in her throat, eyes stinging as they fixated on the plain canvas wall ahead of her. "You'll be charging headlong into battle against the dahems. Whether the Union has returned or not... We both know the consequences of that."

"I'll come back to you."

"How can you be so sure?"

"I'll be well protected. You'll be well protected."

She wished his conviction was strong enough to allay her fears. "Being well protected doesn't guarantee anyone's safety." Her voice was small.

Ashla and his parents had all be under the protection of Royal Knights. Even with Royal Knights Ley and Kein alongside Mihel's forces, Adel couldn't help but worry if it would be enough. And, as much as Arran had told her Ryla said there wasn't anything more she could do, she hadn't really believed the Union would do nothing until they hadn't shown up when the fighting started again.

Her mind raced toward situations where what they had wasn't enough. Where magic flashed before her eyes and weapons splashed human blood across the ground.

And Arran wasn't a fighter. Even if he were, the dahems had done enough damage to scare even the Union away, if only temporarily. What hope did the rest of them have?

His conviction held. "I have to believe it will. I won't be able to go on if I don't."

Adel drew her eyes from the canvas to his face now. Despite his conviction, she could read the fear all over his features—his brows knitted, his lips pressed into a thin line, and his strong jaw set firmly. He'd been staring at their joined hands but now met her gaze. His sharp blue eyes were glassed with unshed tears.

Pulling her hand free, Adel threw her arms around his neck, nestling into his shoulder and inhaling his scent, mixed as it was with leathers and sweat. His arms around her midsection held her just as tightly.

Adel forced back a sob. "I can't lose you."

"And you think I can stand to lose you?" She felt his head

shake. "We've both lost too much already. If I lost someone else I love, I couldn't bear it."

"Your Highnesses," Ley's voice called from outside the tent. "It's time."

As they parted, Arran's hands rested with a tremble on her cheeks, and then he brought his lips to hers. With every second of the kiss, she made an effort to memorize their softness, the way butterflies loosed in her stomach, but mostly how it cut through her chilled bones with incredible warmth. The way it made every ounce of trouble she felt fade to nothing.

Her eyes fluttered open as he withdrew again. In his gaze, she saw the depth of his love for her.

"I promise we'll see each other again," he vowed.

Ashla had said something similar. She'd also held her face in her hands. Adel had never seen her again.

"Okay."

She chose to believe this time was different. She had to.

CHAPTER

FIFTY-THREE

F lourish or fall. There was no more time for pursuing a magic that flowed through her but wouldn't respond. Ryla had known, even as the Keepers left her in the small opening among the copse of trees near where Lavanai's forces had set up camp, that they'd be watching. Somehow, they always had eyes on everything, no matter how far away. And Ryla was certain they were nowhere near her now. Certain they'd extracted themselves and any remaining Killers from the United just as she'd recommended they do with Nithle's only heir.

Without being able to tap into the magic, the Killer had no idea how she was going to correct this situation with the witnesses, so she focused on what she did know how to do: kill dahems.

Once Lavanai's forces had gotten over the initial shock of her presence and golden-eyed gaze, and once she'd shaken the invasive sensation of their stares, they collided.

As she fought now, she could feel the pulse of magic throughout her body, but it didn't emerge. Blood sprayed across Ryla's neck as she felled another dahem. The warmth of it felt equally familiar and as perverse on her skin as the blood in the memories that wouldn't leave her alone. Yet, she knew she couldn't stop.

She leapt backward and away from the group that charged

her, boots skidding on the gravel and dirt of the pathway. Her free hand extended to the ground as she held her sword-hand to the side to keep balance. The stones poked at her palm through the glove as she grabbed and threw a handful in the dahems' faces, causing them to recoil and swipe at their eyes. It was enough for her to move in and end them.

More Lavanian fighters came as their bodies fell, but Ryla also began to feel a shift in the atmosphere, like something stirring within her. She could only identify it as *Cevrla* responding to something, but her mind was too distracted to identify what. That is, until she saw Mithos step through the crowd, accompanied by two other dahems. The one, she recognized as Lord Jasim. The other she wrote off as unimportant.

The impact that followed her gap in concentration sent Ryla flying before her body slammed face-down on the ground several feet away. Her lungs ached for air, and she gasped in as much as she could as she pushed herself onto her elbows to see a new opponent charging at her. Winded, she spun so she was on her back and able to kick up at the attacker. Her feet connected with the dahem's abdomen, knocking it back and opening up the opportunity to jump back to her feet and run it through with her sword.

Distractions, she thought vehemently as she continued to suck air back into her lungs. Her eyes roamed the group around her, but everyone seemed to have paused.

The essence of the magic in the air was just as it had been that day *Cevrla* ignited and Mithos's fire burned around her. Ryla's gaze honed in on Mithos's eyes, and despite the distance between them, she thought they looked duller. It reminded her of the eyes of the Lost after their magic had burned through them completely. But unlike the Lost, Ryla sensed the magic still lingered within Lavanai's commander.

What is she doing here? Ryla realized her eyes weren't just dull, but unseeing. The shorter dahem looked around in a way that suggested she was trying to gain her bearings more from sound than sight. *It doesn't make sense.*

Her thoughts suddenly returned to wondering if Mithos's powers had diluted her own magic. *If I kill Mithos, will the witnesses be purged of the knowledge of what happened?*

It was a long shot, but the only one she had.

She didn't wait for some answer from nature, instead charging toward Mithos at full speed.

In a burst of motion, Ryla saw Mithos get pulled away into the trees even as she protested. The dahem lord stepped into place to block the path to her, and still others fell into place in front of him. Her sword connected sharply with their weapons as she barreled through and knocked the dahems out of the way, trails of blood in her wake. Not for a second was her focus on her target broken, even when she came face-to-face with Lavanai's Lord Jasim.

The conviction in his amber eyes laid bare his rancour toward her—how she'd killed his brother. His brother had shared the same stature and the same eye shape and amber shade. If she wasn't mistaken, the blade that currently clashed with her own was his brother's as well.

As if to confirm it, her mind swept her back to that battlefield, the warmth of summer wrapping her in its embrace. Ryla's smaller stature was up against the full-grown dahem lord, Lamis, who indeed wielded the same sword. The dahem may have towered over her youthful form, but she used the difference to her advantage at every instinctual step she took.

It's cold, not warm. I face Jasim, not Lamis. He doesn't have his brother's magic, Ryla narrated to herself, shattering the memory. It hadn't quite overtaken her, but it had been doing what it could to sink in its claws. Her renewed focus had her pushing back against Jasim's attacks.

When Jasim freed a hand from his hilt to reach for his belt, Ryla was already moving to evade him. The dagger he'd grabbed narrowly missed the space between her shoulder and her neck. Instead, it scratched the thick fabric along her left arm without managing to break though. She used that fraction of a second where his balance shifted to shove him hard and throw him off kilter.

The dahem lord stumbled before regaining his footing, looking neither impressed nor shocked by her actions, only adjusting his grip on both weapons. Why the others weren't stepping in, she didn't know. Was it some mark of respect to their general? Was there some unspoken order holding them back?

Jasim came at her this time, his sword directed lower, as if he were trying to draw her down to it. Before he could dip it too low, Ryla slid her own blade underneath, entangled it in hers with a spin of her arm, pulled it toward herself, and trapped Jasim's forearm against her side. Before he could make use of his dagger, she crashed a fist into his cheek. The impact of it resounded through her knuckles and wrist while her arm's grip loosened just enough that the contact sent Jasim reeling backward again.

He was quick to right his balance, not even bothering to wipe the blood trailing down his lip as he stared her down. She used the pause to locate Mithos, whom she knew was still around if only from the familiar hum of magic that tugged against her own. Sure enough, there was a cluster of dahems protecting and encircling her in a way that almost suggested they were trying to hide her. She picked up what sounded like protests and commands from the group. They may as well have put their banner atop her head.

It was Ryla that moved first this time, intending to rush Jasim and either cut him down or throw him to the ground to get to Mithos. She anticipated that killing the dahem lord would most certainly spur the others into action, so she needed to be quick about it.

Step.

Step.

Step.

Her long strides, strength, and a distinct feeling of magical enhancement pushed her forward, and she crossed the distance between them before swinging her blade. It seemed Jasim was taking moves from her own strategy as he tried to capture her arm the way she had done his. He hadn't gotten hold as well as she had, and there was a physical struggle between them as the warning bells went off in Ryla's head.

Don't let anyone else touch your sword. At the same time, her mind argued, *Maybe this is what needs to happen to correct the situation.*

Jasim tossed his own sword and the dagger aside, which earned a chorus of protests from the other dahems and caused some to lurch forward. He bit back at them with words that Ryla didn't understand, but the harsh tone was clear: stay back.

She watched his face, reading it and his body as well as she could to discern his next move. He shoved her this time with strength that forced her half a step back. The dahem lord's speed almost seemed to increase as he came at her now and managed to capture her blade between his gloved hands.

Her muscles tightened on instinct, bracing for the fallout. There was a beat where she and Jasim simply stared at each other, amber eyes meeting gold-stained ones, as if both of them expected something to happen.

There was no golden light.

No screams.

No sensations of blood.

No feeling of a bowstring snapping.

It was just…nothing.

A breath of time was all it took for Ryla to wrench the sword from his grasp. She was sure by the snag of fabric and the cry of pain that at least one of Jasim's gloves had torn through to skin from the motion. A string of curses as he doubled over and clutched the hand to his abdomen was confirmation enough.

As she'd expected, the forces surged toward her now in a wave, and she let instinct take over before they could do the same to her. The first opponent was a dahem with a halberd, swinging low to take out her legs. The weapon was just low and slow enough that she was able to plant a booted foot to pin it to the ground while she shifted to run the dahem through. With her sword in his chest, she spied over his shoulder and to where the trees thickened as the group that had Mithos was on the move.

Frustration coursed through her before she could stop it, and the distraction earned her a body-check. A spray of blood followed as Ryla's sword dragged through the first dahem's chest cavity before wrenching free, never leaving her hand.

But for the fact that there were now other dahems crowding around, she probably would have been sent sprawling across the ground again. Instead, she met a wall of bodies bracing themselves for impact. She pushed herself off of them and regained her balance.

As she entered into the fray, she felt Mithos's magic growing more distant, but the pull was ever present. Even with this delay, she wasn't worried about finding her again. And with the way Ryla's senses were firing and her thoughts about destroying Mithos, she knew it wasn't a question but a necessity.

She would find her.

CHAPTER

FIFTY-FOUR

The leaves rustled along the spider-webbing tree branches in the gentle nighttime breeze. Fatigue bit down to Ryla's bones, which was why she'd disappeared among the chaotic fray of clashing metal and limbs when the sun began to dip on the horizon. Lavanai's forces had combed through the wooded area she'd stolen into to hunt her down until all became cloaked in darkness.

They hadn't given up entirely. Through the branches and foliage from the limb she perched on, Ryla could see the groups collected among the tress, probably watching and listening for movement from her while they chatted idly in their sharp language. Otherwise, it seemed the entire army had come to a standstill.

Ryla had always been told dahems were just as attuned to her essence as she was to theirs, but watching them now, she wasn't so sure that was true. Still, there was always the possibility it was a ruse to lure her into a false sense of security.

They wouldn't be foolish enough to think I'd fall for that, she thought derisively. *They must truly have no inkling of where I am.*

The pull of magic she felt made Mithos feel only a whisper away although she was well beyond Ryla's sightline. She hadn't felt the magic when she first arrived, but now that she'd caught wind of it, it wouldn't leave her alone.

She has to know that I could pinpoint her in a storm, Ryla thought as her eyes traced guard lining the trees. *That she even dared come near me is ridiculous.*

Sensing dahem essences was one of the earliest skills she'd learned, but this was something new. It was something visceral that drew her to Lavanai's commander.

Does she feel it, too?

Ryla remained unmoving for some time, leaning against the trunk of the tree while balancing on the sturdiest limb she'd been able to find. Her stomach rumbled inaudibly as the smells of meat and vegetables wafted her way, but she couldn't risk finding anything to eat herself. She focused instead on what she could do: stay almost perfectly still except for the rise and fall of her chest.

It was harder to ignore things like a sudden itch, but the Killer found she was still able to settle into stillness. If anything, it was her wandering mind that bothered her. Unimportant sounds—crickets, other night insects and creatures—competed with those she did want to be mindful of, like the dahem guard.

She allowed no more than her eyes to move. The shade of the tree and the distance between her and any light sources should have sufficed to hide any glimmer that might catch her eyes, but she made sure to hood or avert her gaze as much as possible. In moments where dahems stepped a bit farther away from her, she would relax and knead her muscles.

Time stretched on, the darkness falling more deeply as some of the camp retired for the night. Even the guard nearby thinned out, giving her more opportunity to move and loosen up. She moved as silently as ever, pushing away from the trunk of the tree and carefully crossing to a neighbouring one with lower branches before quietly dropping to the ground. She held position and her breath when she landed, waiting for any movement that might spring at her out of the darkness.

None came.

Continuing her silent movements, the Killer wandered away from the camp despite it becoming even harder and harder to see. Peering up toward the sky only brought vague shapes of branches and leaves and the effortless flight of an owl.

She let out a breath, feeling her shoulders sag before she pulled them square.

Focus on the mission. I need to get to Mithos. She closed her eyes and opened her senses. *Still feel her.*

She held onto that feeling, blocking out everything else as best she could, and wended her way through the trees and the darkness. The dahem camp was fairly expansive, tents and wagons and their horses littered throughout the forest. Mithos herself was buried within it somewhere. There was no doubt she was getting closer though as the magic hummed out more with each step.

That stronger hum of magic made her footsteps more cautious, just in case Mithos could indeed sense her as well. She made it well around the camp when an influx of dahem energy snared her attention. She pulled up short and pushed herself into the darkness as the group moved in and a collection of night watch met them to talk.

What they were saying, she couldn't make out from where she pressed herself against the trunk of a tree and strained to listen. Their tones sounded excited at first, then annoyed, before levelling out to confidence.

The Keepers said they were waiting for the rest of their contingent before continuing their pursuit north, Ryla reviewed silently. *This must be that contingent. Then, they march on the Union.*

How the Keepers knew that was the dahems' course, she had no idea.

It doesn't matter. Do not question. Stay focused.

Returning to her pursuit of Mithos turned into a waiting game as she wanted the dahems to settle. Yet, instead of the new group of dahems adding to the collection of canvas tents, they moved about and seemed to be preparing. The passing time began inviting light to the sky.

Damn it. Annoyance coursed through Ryla as she retreated farther into the trees while there was still enough shadow cast by the branches above her.

Suddenly, someone she thought might be a messenger rushed up from the south, and it wasn't long before a large group of dahems broke off to respond to whatever was going on. The dahems' tones were sharp and commanding as they called each other to action. This time, Ryla made out the words for human and army. Nithle was also on their tongues, and instinct spurred her to move.

Fools, her thoughts bit out. *Although, this could be an opportunity to find Mithos while the rest respond to the human army.*

Her mind raced as it warred between her duties, new and old. Was her priority the witnesses or Nithle's only heir? Handling the witnesses was a less sure venture—an attempt to correct the situation that may or may not pan out. Nithle's prince, she knew she could protect.

You were relieved of your duties to him, she argued silently, watching as more dahems donned their battle leathers and gathered their weapons to move southward. *But the Union has always protected Nithle at all costs.*

Another group moved out. Her jaw clenched and her muscles tensed. *Damn that prince.*

Using the clamour around her to disguise her own sounds and movements, she took off in the same direction.

The clash of weapons and shouts grew louder and louder,

especially as the copse of trees thinned around her. Soon, she came to a space where the trees were fewer and farther in between and the armies collided in a melee of weapons, fighters on foot, and horses squealing and groaning in the early morning air as their riders steered them through the shifting bodies.

There were more humans than she'd expected, and she caught glimpses of the Nithlean and Piridetian crests on their armour. Mihel snared her gaze as the princess charged at a group of dahems with a sword while flanked by guards. The dahems were quick, but Mihel was skilled, and Ryla trusted the princess's abilities.

Her eyes wove through the commotion, searching for the dark curls, blue eyes, and fumbling form of Nithle's prince. No doubt Mihel would have told him to stay back, but Ryla knew, if he hadn't completely collapsed in on himself, he'd have refused to stay behind after everything that had happened.

Sure enough, she found him alongside Ley as they defended themselves against a pair of dahems. Grief pulled at the edges of Arran's hardened features as he used what little proficiency he'd learned with duelling daggers against one dahem. Ley put himself between his prince and a second dahem's blade. Metal cried against metal, but the dahem was stronger, pushing Ley's weapon away before knocking him aside. Arran disengaged and shouted for Ley, then took a step backward and seemed to consider his next move.

Her eyes flitted to the other humans, trying to separate themselves from their foes to protect Arran.

They're not fast enough.

She returned her attention to the dahems, seeing how they danced around him and struck, but without seeming to have an intent to kill.

They could have killed him by now. They want me to act.

Despite recognizing the lure for what it was, her body, and maybe even the magic within her, hummed with the need to move. She drew her sword in a flash.

Mere breaths brought her across the terrain to the prince. She thrust her sword in the space between the prince and the dahem to block the blade intent on slashing Arran. The impact vibrated in her bones and muscles, but she held firm before pulling her sword upward to throw the dahem off balance.

She trained her sights on the attacker, keeping the other dahem close in her periphery. Apart from watching to anticipate their next moves, she noticed they didn't appear the least bit surprised by her presence.

"You're here."

She ignored Arran's amazed words. She ran one dahem through and silenced the other just as it started to call to its fellows.

There was no time to waste. She turned to Arran, who wore a stunned expression as their eyes connected. His gaze danced between her golden-hued eyes. She wondered vaguely if there was any of her natural eye colour left at this point and what it would mean for her if there weren't. Would she be like the Lost? So far, she wasn't even like the Tainted.

No time for that, she told herself sharply. She wanted to prepare herself and others for what might happen, but there were more pressing matters. "Get out of here, all of you," Ryla snapped at Arran.

He recovered quickly enough. "We're here to help. Whatever Lavanai's goal is now, we're here to stop it."

"They have their sights set on the Union," she retorted, watching as Ley dragged himself to his feet with the help of another knight. Her attention returned to Arran before he could react. "But the Union is gone. If you were smart, the United would follow their example."

"What?" Arran looked as though she'd struck him. "Has Lavanai already succeeded? Why are you here?"

More forces charged at them, and Ryla met their attacks without answering the prince. Body after body fell again. Human reinforcements joined the fray, pushing back Lavanai's fighters as best they could. Ryla continued her efforts, staying within reach of the prince to get back to him and protect him.

A quick scuff of feet behind her drew Ryla's attention and the swing of her sword, but the assailant caught her wrist effortlessly. A bone-crushing grip held fast over her glove. Her eyes widened when they connected with the attacker's. Dark. Not the eyes of a dahem at all, but a human. Memories tugged at her, flashing through the faces of those she'd encountered in Nithle, and a memory surfaced clearly.

Her eyes widened. *A servant?*

She remembered her collecting the breakfast dishes from her chambers at Nithle castle, and again in the infirmary with the pot of tea standing beside Huth. The woman had unassuming, soft features, gaze usually cast downward, and shoulders typically hunched in meek deference.

Why does she fight at Lavanai's side?

A small smirk crossed the woman's darker complexion, the shadows cast from the morning light making the expression somehow more menacing. She was dressed very differently than Ryla had ever seen. Gone was the servant's garb of skirts and a blouse, replaced by leathers that protected her lithe form. Still, her face was the same.

The steel grip on her wrist did more than simply send pain receptors off in Ryla's mind. *There's something more here.*

When Ryla gave another sharp pull of her arm to free her

wrist, the woman gripped harder and threw a punch into her side at what seemed like lightning speed. The wind flew from Ryla's lungs, and she doubled over with her wrist still trapped in the woman's grasp.

The Killer tried to ignore the throb blooming along her ribs, taking the opportunity to use her lower position to the ground as leverage. She relaxed her legs to drag the woman to the ground with her, and the woman stumbled but was quick to recover her footing and keep control of the situation. She yanked at Ryla's arm, forcing her to stand again. Ryla grit her teeth through the jarring pain.

The woman's attention shifted momentarily around them. Ryla could hear shouts and was almost certain she heard Arran ordering fighters to her aid, but there may as well have been no one but the Killer and this human on the battlefield in that moment.

The speed, the strength, the maneuvering... she thought as she continued assessing the woman in the seconds that passed. *A rogue Killer? Or someone like me who's betrayed us.*

But the woman's eyes didn't have a hint of gold. In fact, Ryla didn't sense any magic emanating from her.

"Killers aren't so powerful after all," the woman said, speaking to herself. She had a melodic voice that seemed to slow somehow as it crossed Ryla's ears.

The image of the woman in front of her remained unchanged, the darker skin and long, dark hair just the same. Yet, a hint of amber seemed to glimmer across her eyes—then the veneer vanished completely.

"Concealment magic," Ryla hissed.

The woman's expression faltered. Ryla used it as an opportunity to haul her to the ground, then quickly shifted her sword to her free hand. The dahem regained her focus and let go of the Killer's wrist to roll out of harm's way. As the dahem scrambled away, Ryla closed the gap between them, tossing her sword back to her dominant hand and driving it through the dahem's thigh. The cry of pain resounded as Ryla pushed her forward onto her stomach, her sword pinning her to the ground where it still lodged in her leg.

Keeping one hand firmly on the hilt of her sword, Ryla crouched at the dahem's side. Ryla saw through narrowed eyes the grit teeth and pinched expression on her features. She resisted the questions running through her head, like how long had the dahem been in the castle, what other damage had she done undetected, and why hadn't she just murdered the royals in their sleep.

Ryla could guess at some of the other damage done. This dahem had probably been how Lavanai was getting its information, such as knowing when she and Arran would be away from the castle to launch their attack from two fronts.

What bothered her the most was how she hadn't been able to sense this dahem at all. Even now, the magic was hidden from her despite the amber shining in her unmasked eyes. What power did this dahem have to prevent the ruse from failing as soon as Ryla laid eyes on her? What power did she have that she could hide her magic?

"A sympathizer?" Arran's voice came from beside her.

He was out of breath, and when she glanced up at him for a fraction of a second, Ryla saw he had a small trickle of blood trailing from his sweaty hairline down his dirtied skin. It didn't look serious enough to be concerned about.

"A dahem with concealment magic," she corrected and saw the revelation hit him immediately.

"But she was in the castle…" he said breathily.

"I know."

"She served you. You've seen her and been around her."
Disbelief laced through his every word.

"*I know*," Ryla stressed, which earned her a chuckle from
the dahem through her pain.

Anger flared in Ryla's chest, and she twisted the sword,
earning another cry from the pinned dahem. Ryla was the
one to glance around now to see if any were coming to the
dahem's aid, but the others didn't seem to be bothered.

Arran cried out, too, the sound a mix of grief and rage that
pierced the air as he slammed a dagger through the dahem's
back, silencing her permanently. Ryla considered him from
where she crouched. The wild look in his wide eyes was made all
the more harrowing because of the blood and the dirt on him.

"If not for this dahem, my kingdom might still be standing," he said after a moment, the wild look not leaving his
face as he pieced together the same conclusion she had arrived
at. He didn't even attempt to meet the Killer's watchful gaze.

"There's no need for an explanation," Ryla said, knowing
he sought her pardon, as if his actions could've offended or
alarmed her.

She rose to her feet and wrenched their weapons free from
the dahem's body. After wiping the gore from his blade, she
extended it to him hilt first, but he still wouldn't meet her gaze.

"Arran." The command in her voice finally prompted him
to look at her.

The muscles in his face were tight, his pupils blown out.
She'd seen this kind of expression enough times.

"I've ended more lives than many armies. This death is
nothing to me."

Even as she said this, and he took the blade, the images
of blood and carnage returned to her mind. Wiping her own
blade clean and focusing on the present details seemed to

accomplish nothing. She wondered if she ought to even fight it.

Arran's voice broke through the images in her head. "But you're a Killer," he said.

"And you're a prince fighting for his life and kingdom," she retorted.

He watched her carefully. She got the distinct sense that he was just as thrown off by her mannerisms and tone as she still was. It looked as though he might say something else, but Ley and some other knights finally broke through the throng of dahems to get to him.

"Arran! Are you all right?" the royal knight asked, worrying over the prince as a parent might their child.

"I'm fine," Arran said unconvincingly and tried to redirect the conversation. "How are we faring?"

"Princess Mihel and the Piridetian forces are holding up. They've moved to the westernmost edge of Lavanai's forces, and she's still trying to pierce through from what I'm told. The dahems are pulling back here, so Commander Kein has ordered everyone regroup. He'll await your counsel for further action, of course," Ley explained. He spared Ryla a glance, hiding any reaction he might have had to her presence and appearance, before his gaze returned to Arran. "Still no word about Heta or Veloth."

Ryla wasn't aware how any dynamics might have changed between the United but felt it was better this way. She was about to remind Arran they should use this opportunity to leave, but the words never left her mouth.

Instead, she looked away from the group, that familiar pull overtaking her again now that other distractions were gone. She turned, seeing Lavanai was indeed pulling back, as Ley had said. There was a smaller group still in range, assessing what she and the humans might do. She took a step forward.

"Ryla?"

It was Arran that had called after her, but at this point she wasn't paying him much mind now that things were calming. *I should refocus on Mithos.*

She only stopped because Arran, followed closely by Ley, rounded her to block her path. Whatever look matched the annoyance she felt caused the prince to start, but he held his ground and stared back at her.

"Come with us while we pull back for a while. Both sides clearly need to regroup. Even Killers need to rest, right?" His tone was firm, but inviting. Even now, he deferred to her.

She held his gaze, weighing her options. She could rest again before pursuing Mithos; it would give her time to recuperate the strength and energy spent fighting on the prince's behalf. As much as the magic continued to needle at her senses, she couldn't fault the reasoning and knew, impaired vision or not, she couldn't underestimate Mithos. Ryla needed to be at full strength before facing her.

As for the dahems, they might send a small group to the north…

It doesn't matter, she reminded herself. *The Union is gone. They'll come back here afterward for the report. I gave the Keepers the time they needed to disappear.* The air stirred around her in a gentle, albeit cold, breeze.

"Fine," she yielded curtly.

Something that might have been a relieved smile briefly crossed Arran's features, and he looked at Ley who only nodded while at least part of his attention remained on Ryla. The knight didn't trust her anymore. She couldn't fault that reasoning either.

A human with golden-stained eyes was never safe.

CHAPTER
FIFTY-FIVE

"Are you sure we can trust her, Sire?"

Arran lifted his head from where he sat on the stool in his tent to Ley, standing a short distance away. The knight's shoulders were squared, back rigid, and hands within quick reach of his sword, as if he expected someone to come ripping through the tent.

The healer pressed a hot compress to the prince's shoulder, which sent another wave of goosebumps crawling across his skin, as if the first wave from the cold air's assault wasn't enough. The old injury from the Harvest Festival throbbed more than slightly after all the activity of these couple of days, including riding hard to catch up with the dahems. Now jumping headlong into battle had really aggravated the old injury.

He'd had no intentions of being on the sidelines at this point though. This was do or die.

Adel's plea to be careful remained close to his heart, neighbouring the ache as he thought about her and her father venturing to Veloth for further aid. Arran was grateful she understood his need to follow the dahems north to find out why they were talking about Killers.

It meant abandoning Nithle castle to the dahems that remained... But the castle be damned. His people were safe, and he'd needed to make sure the rest of the United remained protected, too. Whatever services he could offer to the Killer, he was prepared to do so.

He hadn't expected the Killer to be Ryla.

As it was, she'd been given a private tent, where she'd retired soon after they returned to where they could set up camp. The question now was how they would all proceed.

"She rushed into battle to protect me, Ley," Arran finally replied. "No one can deny that she's different, but she *still* came to my aid. I have no reason not to trust her."

"She's tainted, Arran," Ley pressed. "For all we know, she's well on her way to being lost. I hear you. Believe me, I hear you, but magic is dangerous. The fact that we can see the changes in her, including the physical impact on her eyes, says that she's no more immune to it than anyone else. And the fact that it overcame her so quickly is alarming."

"If it comes to it, then we do what we have to and end her life." The bitter thought made his stomach turn.

Ley shook his head, brows pinching together. "We wouldn't have a hope in the world if she becomes lost. Her mind is wandering. If you hadn't stopped her, she would have gone running off after the dahems. I'm surprised she even listened to you at all."

Arran didn't have a retort for that. He'd noticed the same thing. Somehow, pausing for the moment would benefit her, and then she would…do whatever it was she was doing. Something about it—all of it—made him uneasy. It was like meeting her anew and adjusting to a different breed of foreignness. He didn't know whether to attribute that to what she was or the magic that so clearly stained her eyes.

But she's still not like the other Tainted… He didn't know how or why, but the magic wasn't impacting her the same way. He was sure of it.

The prince sighed heavily and rolled his shoulder just a little as the healer removed the heat from it. The sharp scent of the herbs and ointments lingered in the air as moisture clung to his skin. He gave the man his thanks before dismissing him from the tent, trusting the healer to keep the conversation to himself. Arran stood as the healer left and pulled a heavy tunic over his head against the cold. The fabric scratched his skin, designed more for durability during travel than comfort.

"I'm not sending her away, Ley." Arran took the reins of the conversation. "She said the Union is gone and all the kingdoms should leave, too."

Ley's brows shot up. "Gone? What does that mean?"

"She didn't elaborate. She only said the Union was gone and the dahems were after them. I'm not sure if that means they've already succeeded in destroying the Union or something else."

"We need to know more," Ley insisted.

Arran nodded. "I agree, but I don't think we're going to get anything out of her right now, especially if her mind is wandering as you say."

The knight shifted uncharacteristically from foot to foot. "We can't afford to wait. Her magic leaves us with many risks, and we can't be sure of when Lavanai will re-engage."

Arran sighed, running a hand through his curls, fingers catching on a few knots along the way. "I know. But we also have to consider their need to navigate the changing situation as much as ours. How long until Kein and Mihel are ready for us?"

"Probably another hour. That should give them enough time to gather the reports," Ley noted.

Arran nodded again. "Rest while you can, Ley. You took some heavy blows in the battle. More than I did. I know the healer cleared you, but we've got to take advantage of these moments."

The knight offered a gentle smile now. "I'll be fine, but I appreciate your concern. There will be a guard outside this tent until I return."

Arran watched the tent flap fall back into place at Ley's departure, and although he hoped the man would take his advice and rest, he knew that he wouldn't be too far.

Anxiety gnawed at Arran. As much as he'd committed himself to whatever result this battle brought, he wanted to make it out alive. Yet, he wasn't sure if he was fully prepared.

I was lucky today. He worried at the inside of his lip. *The memories dissipated quickly.*

The sounds of battle had awoken them, throwing him back to trying to escape with Ryla, the explosion that rocked the earth, and most especially the night of the Harvest Festival. Having to quickly run through Ryla's instruction to snap out of it was a challenge he'd barely been ready for, and apprehension gripped him at the thought of it potentially not working next time.

He'd promised himself, Ley, and Adel that if the memories became too much, he'd take himself out of the fight, if only for the safety of those around him. He wouldn't allow ignoring his limits to stain his hands with the blood of those who'd protect him.

A sudden gust of wind pressed against the side of the tent, and the canvas bowed in slightly. The thick fabric held while a shiver rattled Arran's bones. He walked toward the tent entrance as the wind died away and stepped out. The guards looked at him, but he didn't pay them any mind, squinting against the bright, although now overcast, sky.

A storm? he wondered and surveyed the camp. Many were taking care to secure tents. The sound of metal meeting metal rung out as mallets crashed against tent pegs.

His roaming eyes paused, heart jolting as he noticed a lone figure standing in an area devoid of tents that people were now decidedly avoiding.

Maybe Ley is right...

Ryla faced the direction they'd parted ways with the dahems, but he had no idea why or what would be occupying her thoughts. Her sword was still sheathed, but her frame was firm as she stood with her back to him. Despite his arguments to Ley, her presence spoke more of danger than protection now.

A human tainted by magic. He wondered again about the depth of that. Was this strange behaviour part of that? She didn't turn his direction, but he could clearly picture the gold that had overtaken her eyes as if he was staring into them.

He wondered how long she'd been standing there when snow began to drift down from the grey sky. She didn't seem to notice it.

CHAPTER

FIFTY-SIX

"The Killer is making people uncomfortable, Your Highness."

Those words, or some variation of them, had been relayed to Arran at least ten times as he crossed the camp to meet with Mihel and Kein. Knights felt it was their duty to let the prince know, on behalf of the fielders, of the camp atmosphere. He thanked them for sharing their concerns.

He masked his worries with appreciative nods and a calm exterior. He'd meant what he'd said to Ley about not wanting to send her away. It wasn't just a matter of her abilities—her presence was a beacon of familiarity among his newly uncertain world.

Ley remained silent beside Arran through all of it. It seemed that despite his reservations, he wasn't about to reopen that conversation and delve into the matter more than he already had. Even when Arran glanced over at the man, his expression was neutral, showing no sign of his thoughts.

A light dusting of snow drifted across the ground now, and Arran watched the flakes dance while lost in his thoughts. It was the time of the year for snow to begin to take purchase across the kingdoms, and they'd have to adapt as best they could.

The meeting tent was within sight several yards away, but Arran stopped in his tracks. Ley only took one step more before stopping as well and turning to his prince.

"What is it?" Ley asked with a hint of concern mixed in the questioning of his voice.

"I'm going to talk to Ryla," Arran declared, pivoting and striding off with purpose. He only had a vague idea of which tent she'd been given on the northern edge of the camp, but he felt that with the attitude everyone was feeling toward her, whatever tent she'd been put up in would be easy enough to find.

"I don't think that's a good idea, Your Highness," Ley called as he quickly caught up with the few steps the young prince had taken.

"Because she's unstable, right?" Arran said with a little more frustration than he'd intended.

Ley didn't flinch. Instead, his tone was just as firm. "Yes. The Tainted are people we lock away for their safety *and* ours. Were we back at the castle, I'd be recommending we do the same with Killer Ryla."

"Back at the castle? Look at where we are, Ley." He spread his arms wide, twisting from side to side, before dropping them back to his sides. "We're on a battlefield. What happens at the castle doesn't apply here, and I'm really starting to think that a lot of things I once knew don't apply at all. I *know* what magic can do to humans. I've seen it. But something is different, and I intend to find out what. And you agreed with me that we need to understand what the situation is with the Union," Arran stated sharply. Ley opened his mouth to say something more, but Arran continued before the knight could speak. "I'm *going* to talk to her."

Ley was quiet a moment, jaw set, as if considering his words and what to do. Finally, he said, "I'm not leaving your side or letting my guard down."

"I wouldn't expect you to," Arran replied, then added,

"Thank you."

Ryla's tent may as well have had the Union crest stitched into every side. There were some fighters who seemed to have taken up post for their comrades, and they carefully watched what would otherwise be a nondescript tent as if it were about to catch flames or explode out at them. Several eyed Arran and Ley as they approached, but none of them made to speak with or stop them.

The prince paused at the tent flap, noting that Ley took a moment to steel himself for whatever was about to happen by taking a breath and squaring his shoulders. Strangely, Arran felt calm, even as he adjusted his cloak.

"Ryla?" he called, trying to balance being loud enough to hear without drawing more attention than was already on them.

He was rewarded by the sounds of something being set down on a table, and then she pulled back the flap. There was no attempt to hide on her part. The complete stoicism of her nature may have been altered, but it seemed to Arran she wasn't bothered by the watchful gazes around her.

"I'd like to speak with you," Arran told her, and she motioned for him and Ley to enter.

The sound he'd heard had been a cup, which he saw her retrieve and drink from. It was an odd experience, if only because he'd never seen her consume anything. Still, Killers needed to eat and sleep, although the untouched cot set up in the middle of the tent away from the walls suggested that she hadn't done any of the latter yet.

Anyone else might have insisted he sit, but she didn't offer any such pleasantries. If anything, he might have insisted *she* sit.

Does that hierarchy even still apply? he wondered.

What did it mean now if the Union truly was gone? The United would have no one to answer to anymore. The thoughts suddenly weighed on him since he didn't know a world without the Union—no one alive did.

He watched as she placed the cup back on the small table and turned to him, waiting for him to speak. He really took her in at that moment, resisting the nagging fear her golden eyes triggered in him. She looked so much the same: the same odd clothes, the same binding of her hair at the base of her neck, the same sureness of how she held herself. His eyes darted to where her sword was strapped to her right hip, but she didn't seem interested in drawing it.

This is nothing like the Tainted. Nothing like the corruption of magic I've seen in others and learned about.

Words were leaden on his tongue as he suddenly wondered what the Union being gone meant for Ryla. Even if the United didn't know a world without the Union, at least they had their people, but Ryla...her entire existence revolved around this organization that had abandoned all of them. Had abandoned *her.*

"Has Lavanai destroyed the Union? Are the Keepers returning?" he finally managed.

"Lavanai hasn't yet reached the Union. The Keepers left. I can't say whether they will return," she replied, her tone even, but not in the same way it had been when they'd first met. It was more intentionally so than natural.

"Are they returning for *you?*" he asked next. Part of him didn't care if the Union ever came back for the United. But Killers were the Union's creation. Their responsibility.

"My life was forfeit the second I was tainted," she said matter-of-factly.

His stomach dropped. He had a lot of questions about that, too, but his reply took another direction. "Meaning they're leaving you to die."

"Of course." Something in his expression seemed to prompt her to continue. "What did you think happened to Killers who were past their use?"

"I…" Arran struggled for words. He'd never even thought of it. "You're a human."

She shook her head. "I'm a weapon. A tool for their end. That is my duty."

He inhaled, nails biting into fisted hands at his sides, if only because he didn't know what else to do with them. He didn't like the idea of the next question, but it begged to be asked.

"Would they have killed you?"

"That was the other option, yes. This situation is more unique than is standard," she said.

When she didn't carry on, he asked. "Meaning?"

"It's none of your concern." Her expression gave nothing away.

He was taken aback, blood suddenly boiling. "None of my concern? Whatever is left of my kingdom is actively waging war against Lavanai, and somehow you're still involved with this battle. It seems like it's a lot of my concern."

"You take care of your battle, and I'll take care of mine," she said dismissively. All that was missing was a wave of her hand, like a lady shooing away someone beneath her station.

Arran's eyes narrowed, and he noticed her own features harden in anticipation of the confrontation. He thought he heard Ley shift beside him, but the knight made no move otherwise.

"My entire camp is unnerved by your presence," Arran said with an edge to his voice.

"I'm aware."

"They're worried you're no different than any other tainted human. They're worried that you're going to be lost to your magic," he continued. "But the magic in you seems different somehow. There's no denying you've been tainted, but you're not unhinged like other humans with eyes as gold as yours."

"Observation is one of your strong suits," Ryla replied evasively.

The questions came rolling out of him in a rush. "What's different about you? Or the magic within you? Was it always there? Did you invite it in that battle? Why risk it?"

Silence stretched between them, only the wind outside and the shifting of the tent fabric in its wake filling the space. Arran continued to watch her, chest rising and falling a bit heavier than he'd expected, but she didn't so much as shift her gaze. He sighed, closing his eyes briefly to compose himself and slow his racing heart. When he opened them again, she hadn't moved.

"Let me help you, Ryla," he tried, his tone much softer now.

She considered him for only a fraction of a second. "I told you, my life is forfeit."

"I don't accept that," he replied firmly.

"That's the difference between regular humans and Killers. Even now," she began humourlessly. "I can accept the reality staring me in the face."

"Is that reality or are you surrendering?" Arran challenged without thought. He heard Ley shift again and knew the knight thought he was straying into unsafe territory.

A wry smile crossed Ryla's features, which startled him. He wondered if it felt weird to her.

"I can assure you that no matter how bleak and how much you don't like it, this is reality, not submission."

He held firm. "I choose to disagree."

"As is your wont."

He knew a stalemate when he saw one. That didn't make

him any less uncomfortable with what Ryla said. There had to be a future for her beyond the Union.

Just because she can't see it doesn't mean it doesn't exist.

He continued watching her just as she watched him. Even now, he knew he couldn't read her completely, although it was easier to discern more of what used to be hidden by her emotionlessness. He could see in her golden eyes that she fully believed what she said. The magic wasn't touching her mind—at least not to any great extent—and he could see it clearly now that he looked right at her.

Still, he wouldn't accept this was it for her.

CHAPTER

FIFTY-SEVEN

Not a soul stopped Ryla as she left the Nithlean and Piridetian camp despite the late afternoon bustle. Given their attitude and apprehension toward her, she wasn't surprised. Once revered, now feared. All because her brown eyes had shifted to gold. The fear of magic kept them alive in all other circumstances; why should *her* gold-stained eyes be any different to them?

Each step across the snowy terrain toward the Lavanian encampment left her with the sense that Mithos approached her as well. The way their magic called to each other had gotten to the point that Ryla could no longer ignore it.

It seems she can no more resist it than I.

The magic, she was certain, was keeping her awake. Although she'd rested her body, her mind wouldn't succumb, and sleep had evaded her all afternoon. Despite the lack of sleep, her mind felt sound, and she was unworried.

The trek led to an empty field. She could see the far treeline of the deciduous forest that bordered Lavanai and the unclaimed lands in the far distance, the brown, gold, and red leaves hanging on somehow against the changing season. Behind her, she knew the human camp was out of sight. Grey sky painted the hard terrain a dusty brown among the few flakes that had taken purchase from the earlier snowfall.

The magic thrummed at her across the field, especially as

her sights locked on Mithos standing by herself across the way. Ryla was both surprised and not surprised to see her alone. Mithos's damaged eyesight should have been a hindrance, but she appeared to walk without any difficulties.

How much is the magic guiding her?

While she'd half expected to see the haze of magic hover about, just as she'd seen around her own sword, there was nothing but the contrast of the commander's worn leather armour and dark hair as Ryla stared across at her. Still, she could feel the magic.

Now's my chance. The chance to find out how killing Mithos might solve this issue of the witnesses. The chance to fulfill her final duty to the Union before meeting her own end.

The smooth scrape of her sword leaving its sheath met her ears and her pace accelerated. Magic spiked within to send waves down her limbs and furnish her Killer speed. Snow fluffed up as her boots tamped across the terrain.

Mithos was only a fraction of a second behind in breaking into a run and drawing her weapons, the twin falchions resting in her hands just as naturally as Ryla's sword rested in hers. The Killer and the dahem quickly came together in a way that made the metal of their weapons ring out, and they both grunted from the impact.

Somehow, it felt like a shockwave of magic meeting magic, even though Ryla still couldn't summon the golden light.

Pure gold eyes connected with dimmed amber for only a brief moment before the pair were a flurry of motion. Ryla was curious what Mithos's goal was in this fight but did her best to shove the distracting thoughts from her mind. If there was ever a time she needed her perfect Killer focus and stoicism, it was now. Although she'd never get that back in its purity, she had to emulate it as best she could.

She focused on Mithos's movements. Slightly clumsier than they once might have been, Ryla could tell Mithos was relying heavily on her other senses to detect, predict, and counter the Killer's attacks. Still, the commander was far more skilled than any human and probably most dahems. Once she'd had more practice, Ryla was certain Mithos would be a master anew.

She won't live that long.

Not a word was uttered between them as the fight dragged on. The silence was filled by the sounds of attacking, parrying, dodging, and recovering, and even the usual hum of magic had amplified after that initial shockwave. If there was one thing Ryla became assured of as they battled, it was that Mithos's magic was powerful and felt like a counterpoint to her own.

Ryla's mind wandered at this realization. *Does Cevrla come to dahems naturally? Is that why they can wield magic without consequence like I did, but, when their connection is disrupted, their eyes dim instead of shine? Does it not consume them, but rather fade away? How does it differ from what happened to Naxela?*

She hadn't considered it before, but now wanted—no, *needed*—to know if she wasn't the only broken one on this battlefield. Her soul practically cried out for someone to relate to. Mithos hadn't summoned her fire yet, relying only on the physical battle of their swords.

Draw it out.

It would mean pushing Mithos to the point where she'd have no choice but to use it.

Ryla renewed her efforts to take advantage of the dahem's damaged eyesight, first knocking her off balance with an initial hit and then attacking her from as many directions as she could. Even then, Mithos kept up, blocking the assaults each time, even if barely.

Sweeping Mithos's legs from under her while she was busy blocking an attack from Ryla's sword challenged the Killer's own balance, but proved effective. It landed the dahem on her side and sent one of the twin blades sliding several feet away with the scrape of rocks and dirt. Ryla planted her boot on the hand that held Mithos's other sword, pinning it to the ground, then pointed her own blade so it just touched under the dahem's chin.

Mithos inhaled at the touch of the cold metal, and both warriors paused in that moment, chests rising and falling as they sucked in air. Neither of them made a sound, even their breathing barely audible. Mithos's smaller form tensed, but there was no particular stirring of magic that Ryla sensed with the action. It was an ideal time to unleash the fire. Send it blazing through the falchion to engulf her boot and fly up her leg to the rest of the Killer's body.

A slight shift in Mithos's expression told Ryla all she needed to know.

"It broke you, too."

The whispered utterance hung in the colder air as the temperature dropped from the wearing day.

Whether Mithos heard the words or not, Ryla had no idea, but the dahem kicked her feet to knock the Killer away. Ryla stumbled as Mithos's boots connected with her legs, and she ended up on the ground herself but rolled into a crouch. It cheered her that some of her fighting reflexes were still intact, even as her legs throbbed from the impact.

The dahem was already charging at her again, leaving one falchion abandoned in the snow. Ryla had just enough time to duck and roll out of the way of the blade to bring herself to her feet many paces away. She noticed a small trickle of blood under Mithos's chin. She didn't recall her sword nicking the skin, but it must have.

Suddenly, the small trickle of blood brought on memories of flowing blood, accompanied by the screams, which then all dissolved into walls of fire. Ryla staggered as reality unexpectedly distorted and reshaped around her to the point that she wasn't sure that what she was seeing wasn't real.

I'm in an open field, sky overcast in the fading afternoon. I'm battling Commander Mithos of Lavanai, she pulled the words from the chaotic images flashing through her mind.

The lightning strike, the shifting ground, the amber dahem eyes reflecting the flames. Knocked to the ground, sword falling away.

Her eyes are dull. There's snow on the ground.

A bowstring snapping within her. Golden light coming to the call of *Cizeth*.

The light in her memory faded, bringing her back to the battlefield with Mithos, who was rushing at her again.

Ryla snapped back into battle readiness and narrowly block the falchion.

The second one plunged into her chest.

It felt like flames pouring into her then, igniting a pain unlike any she'd ever known except to witness it. It immobilized her. The falchion acted as a stopper, locking her breath in her chest, and she choked for air. Her thoughts scattered and screamed loudly before falling absolutely silent.

A golden embrace enveloped her from the inside out. This magic was familiar to her, a comfort even as her chest burned. *Cevrla* entangled with the burn from the blade, bringing about a numbness that felt like relief, but also so, so cold.

Her gaze shifted from the grey sky that she hadn't even realized she was staring at. Her eyes connected briefly with Mithos's before her lids slowly tumbled like the snowflakes that melted as they landed softly on her skin.

I can accept the reality staring me in the face.

The thought drifted around her, as if said by someone else.

CHAPTER

FIFTY-EIGHT

Mithos's chest heaved. When her blade had first entered Ryla's chest, the world had opened up for her again. Despite the darkening sky, she could see the young woman's pure golden eyes staring wide with shock and pain. Pain that traced through the Killer's features. Whatever magic Ryla had been given burned through her in a flash of gold that brought a dull brown to her irises. Her features relaxed. Mithos watched as her eyes began to close.

And, as Ryla's eyes closed, so too did Mithos's vision haze over again, and the weight of the Killer's limp body brought her to her knees as the falchion, still lodged in her chest, dragged her to the ground after her. The Killer's sword fell gracelessly with a *thunk*.

Breaking for the second blade had been a gamble. Mithos hadn't known if it'd been a ruse, but the moments had ticked on and there'd been no sounds of movement from the Killer.

Mithos had thought of simply running up to her right then and using one blade to end it, but she hadn't known how long she had. She'd figured at least if the stillness broke while running to her fallen blade, she might have a chance to regain the second falchion and fight back. With only seconds to decide, she'd scrambled to her feet to break for the fallen blade.

The element of surprise had worked in her favour.

Mithos hadn't imagined it would end like this—part of

her had started to think it would never end at all—and yet, here they were.

There was no fanfare, no protest.

Just life and death.

One of the most skilled warriors she'd ever faced was dead.

And she'd been the one to steal life from her.

It broke you, too.

They'd been barely audible, but Mithos had heard Ryla's words. She hadn't expected the words to chill her blood, but realization dawned on her with their impact. The fire she'd once mastered wasn't coming. Whatever had happened to Ryla the day that changed the Killer had also affected her, and not just her sight, but her magic.

Time felt like it slowed as Mithos's knees and legs grew cold from kneeling in the accumulating snow. She shuddered as the cold mixed with the sweat she'd built up during the battle. Her leathers felt heavy and like ice, which scared her to some degree.

It broke you, too.

Her magic's fire typically kept her body running warm, but it had been fading. The dropping temperatures had been biting at her more and more, and now... Now she felt downright frigid.

Has my magic left me?

When she finally pulled her falchion from Ryla's chest, she was certain a great deal of time had passed. She guessed it was heading into the night now as it got colder and colder, but she couldn't tell for sure.

Forlornness occupied Mithos's chest and thoughts. There was no one there to mourn this death. Ending Ryla's life felt like the end of an era, or at least the beginning of hope for her and her people, but it wasn't an accomplishment.

She let the blades rest at her sides on the freezing ground. The pull of magic had brought her here; now there was a hollowness in its wake. She wasn't fully sure where *here* was or how to get back to the camp, so she was at the mercy of whoever found her. She could only hope that it'd be Lavanai's army.

They'll come, she thought without worry.

She wasn't even sure how she'd gotten away without being stopped by the others in the camp. Ufrala, her guide, had gone to get something to eat, assured by Mithos's words that she wouldn't be needed for a while and could take time to herself. Yet, there were many dahems who surely would have seen her, many who could have stopped her and asked what was happening or if she needed help.

We can attempt to piece it together later.

Whatever the circumstance, she'd made it out of her camp without being stopped, just as Ryla had seemingly made it out of hers. She was only marginally surprised that the prince hadn't followed Ryla, considering the reports of how Ryla had entered the fray to save him yet again. Even changed, she still carried out her duties as if nothing had happened.

No, that's not right. She knew very well something had happened.

The words echoed in her mind again. *It broke you, too.*

She definitely knew.

She thought of that bard song. She'd read the words enough times that she could probably recite them. Ryla's situation seemed different. Every time she'd gone over the words and their potential alternative meaning, Mithos had pictured an incapacitated Killer, overwrought with burdens of their existence. There was no way that person would have been able to fight, let alone with enough skill to nearly end a dahem life. Mithos was well aware as soon as she'd felt the tip of the blade under her chin that Ryla could have ended her there.

And yet...she hadn't. She'd still been measured and in full control.

Or at least nearly full control, Mithos corrected, thinking of the stillness the Killer had lapsed into.

Mithos gingerly reached out her hand until it connected with the fabric of the Killer's attire. She wasn't entirely sure why she did it, but part of her wondered if it was an effort to solidify reality or make sure that she wasn't alone. Sure enough, Ryla's body remained, the sturdy fabric of the Killer's clothes rough under her icy fingertips.

Time dragged on, but also seemed to fly. Had hours passed? Minutes? She had no idea. The wind was a cruel companion that reminded her the fire still hadn't returned within her. Otherwise, it was so, so quiet. Not even the sounds of animals came to life around her.

The quiet finally gave way to the shift of armour and weapons. The steady thump of hooves was a warning thunder.

She couldn't take the chance that this was friends approaching. Mithos felt for the hilts of her falchions, the snow nipping at her bare, stiff hands as she grasped them. Although she couldn't quite see, she looked in the direction of the oncoming force.

How long until they see her? she thought, supposing the group might be human.

Her grip tightened on the hilts of her swords.

CHAPTER

FIFTY-NINE

Arran's decision to pursue Ryla tested loyalties. While some had been content for the Killer to venture off by herself, someone had reported it to him before dawn the next morning when she hadn't returned. The prince was annoyed they'd let it happen and couldn't just let her disappear.

She's not going to stare reality in the face alone, he thought to himself as he rode alongside Ley at the front of the group of about twenty-five that accompanied him.

Arran was balancing the fine line of trust with his people. They might lose faith in him entirely as they questioned his judgement with this endeavour or, more favourably, they could come to trust him completely if this turned out well. He hoped they took it as a sign that he wouldn't leave anyone behind, no matter their circumstance.

Ley stopped his mount and pointed his gloved hand across the open, snow-covered field. "What's that?"

Arran paused and glanced at his knight, then followed his gesture to where there were two figures, still shadows in the dawning light, far into the wide open space. Both were on the ground, one on their knees and the other laying in front of the first. The one kneeling seemed smaller in stature with short, dark hair. For the one laying on the ground, it was harder to tell with the way the snow had started to build up, but they were unmoving.

The prince's chest tightened, and his feet squeezed his horse's sides of their own volition.

"Arran!" Ley called after him as the prince's horse took off at a trot.

Hooves took up the same pace behind him, creating a low rumble and clanking of armour. Ley's horse was quicker, and he caught up with Arran easily.

"Don't let your emotions overwhelm you!" Ley cautioned, riding up beside him. "We can't go running headlong into this. We have no idea who or what awaits us."

Arran ignored him at first, his attention on the forms in case any further detail became apparent as he drew closer. With only a vague sense of the direction Ryla had gone, it took them hours to even find this place. It *had* to be her.

He saw the figure who was kneeling rise to their feet, their body locking into a defensive posture with a sword in each hand.

Just as this happened, Ley cut him off, turning in front of him, which caused Arran's horse to come up short with a neigh and a few stomps in protest. The rest of the group came to a halt as well while a sweeping sound of some dismounting and then weapons being drawn cut through the air. A smaller portion of the group fighters came up beside the prince and the royal knight, bows up and arrows nocked into place, ready to fly at a moment's notice.

Arran didn't look at Ley, but he knew the man's dark gaze was locked on him as he blocked the way. He got the sense Ley would tackle him from his horse's back should he try to proceed further. His eyes widened as they focused on the scene while peering over Ley's shoulder.

It wasn't just the cold air biting at his throat and lungs as his chest heaved from adrenaline that froze him from the inside out.

"No… How?" Arran breathed out, his grip on the reins tightening.

Mithos. It had to be her given her dark hair, smaller stature, and dual blades in her hands as if extensions of herself. Something was off about Lavanai's commander, as if she was only guessing where they were, but he didn't discount the danger she presented.

But that means…

Sure enough, it was Ryla who lay at Mithos's feet, blood staining the snow around her crumpled, lifeless body. Despite the distance between them, he was sure it was her.

She was right. It was a sight Arran never thought he'd see. Even as that moment eons ago in the infirmary had reminded him of her mortality, it'd been difficult to believe she could ever actually fall.

Dread and sorrow swept him up. It took everything not to crumble to the ground. The sounds became muffled around him, although he was certain Ley was giving orders despite not moving from where he stood in front of Arran. A moment later, one of the knight's hands planted on his shoulder, giving him a jolt.

"Stay with me, Arran," Ley said, speaking much more gently now from where he'd sidled up beside him again.

His eyes flicked to Ley, focusing on the man's concerned expression and features. The rise and fall of Arran's chest was too fast, and it felt like a physical effort to stop his body from collapsing in on itself. This wasn't like fighting his memories. Focusing on the here and now and the world around him would only reignite the horrors.

"She's dead." The words fell out of his mouth without his consent. Even to his own muffled hearing, they sounded flat.

Forlorn, maybe. But mostly flat.

"Yes," Ley replied evenly, his tone still gentle but commanding. His dark-eyed gaze searched Arran's, as if making sure he was present. "We're still here."

We're still here.

The words held an impact he wasn't expecting, echoes of every time he'd faced them adding to their truth. He'd said them himself. Adel had said them. And now Ley. It must mean something if they kept coming up, right? This reminder from different sources couldn't be a coincidence, could it?

A flash of Ryla's bloodied, lifeless body entered his mind again, with the other memories tumbling along after it. The first time she'd stopped Naxela's mace from crushing him, bringing a new hope to him and his people as the dahems died and fled in her wake. The way she held herself with complete assurance in her abilities. The bloodied vision of her being tended to by Healer Dalam. The first time he'd seen the streaks of gold in her eyes and heard emotion in her voice. The conversation just hours before this, and the wry smile as she spoke of accepting her reality.

"This is the reality I'm faced with," Arran said quietly.

Ley's brows knitted together, and Arran wasn't quite sure if the knight hadn't heard him or if he merely didn't recognize the echo of Ryla's words.

Despite the heaviness in his body and the chaos in his mind, Arran steeled himself and gave Ley a slight nod before swinging his leg over and dismounting. The man stared at him a moment longer before joining him. The fighters in their armour with the stag of his kingdom on the shoulder plates still stood or sat astride their horses, many with bows and arrows ready for fire, their eyes trained on the sights before them. Behind them, those with swords and other weapons were also at the ready, waiting for the command, their expressions firm.

Ley supplied some additional information. "I've sent someone to alert Commander Kein and Princess Mihel. From what we can see, it appears to be Lavanai Commander Mithos alone, but we can't be too sure there aren't others somewhere or on their way."

The dahem hadn't moved, her rigid stance keeping her own weapons at the ready. Doing what he could to ignore the body on the ground and the tightness in his chest, Arran scanned the field and didn't see anyone else.

Has she not attacked because she's alone?

He considered the number of archers they'd brought before speaking. "We could end her. The fact that she hasn't come at us yet means she's on the defensive for some reason. Our group might cause her some trouble, but it shouldn't be enough that she would worry about us, and even if it were, why not run away by now?"

"I was wondering the same," Ley agreed with a nod. "However, it could be some sort of trap to unleash her magic on us."

"No," Arran continued. "I really feel something isn't right here. Like she's stuck where she is for some reason, and maybe she can't even use her magic. Look at the terrain—there's no sign of fire damage."

"The snow may be covering it," Ley reasoned.

"Perhaps. All the same, why not unleash her magic by now? Maybe before…" He tripped over the swell of sorrow again and elected to rephrase. "Maybe Ryla was able to stunt Mithos's magic somehow. Maybe she even did it the day everything changed. By all reports, Mithos should be just as dead as the others impacted by whatever Ryla's magic was."

Ley inhaled, his scruffy jaw tight. "That's a lot of conjecture for our small group."

"We don't have time to wait for Mihel and the others," Arran glanced at the horse standing quietly beside him and thought about how long it'd taken them to arm themselves, gather mounts, and then reach the field. Mihel would certainly bring a larger group. "By then, the rest of Lavanai's army could be here, and we'll have lost the chance to take out their commander."

Ley sighed now, his breath a small puff as it left his mouth, but nodded in resignation. "Our choices aren't great. It's your decision, Your Highness."

The tightness in Arran's chest squeezed harder, fury blooming from the grief. He wished suddenly he had his own bow and arrows with him to take aim at the dahem standing across the field from him. To hamper Lavanai's army by eliminating their commander would only be a small comeuppance for the damage they'd done to him and his kingdom, but it'd be something.

But the bow and quiver sat in his tent, forgotten during the quick gathering of forces to track Ryla. He daren't get close enough for close combat with his daggers, and while he considered taking a bow from one of the fighters at his side, he knew he'd have to make do with being the one to issue the command.

He took a sobering breath that didn't touch the burning tension in his body. "Release!" he called loudly enough for the archers to hear him.

The group acted in two waves, the first letting loose their nocked arrows. They flew through the air, some arcing higher while others soared directly at Mithos. The moment seemed to slow. Arran held his breath. She'd only have a few seconds to react to the barrage of arrows before the second set came her way.

Regardless of what stayed her from charging or running away, the dahem rapidly adjusted her grip on her blades to block and knock away arrows. She dodged others she didn't block, leaving them to pierce the ground or skitter across it at her feet.

The second wave of arrows were already streaking through the air, and his heart jolted as she continued her defensive maneuvers. Then the dahem cried out and fell to one knee, an arrow lodged in her thigh as another grazed her shoulder enough to split the leather of her battle attire and draw blood.

The grimace on Mithos's face was clear even from where they stood. Arran watched with focused, narrowed eyes, waiting for her to react in some way. Even an injured dahem was a dangerous one, so she couldn't be discounted yet. She pressed at her leg without dropping the falchion, ignoring her shoulder completely as she partially doubled over.

The fact that she wasn't incinerating them with fire or even trying to flee solidified his belief that something was amiss with Lavanai's commander.

"She should have burned those arrows to nothing," Ley commented beside him with wondering tones.

"And yet, she didn't," Arran agreed, then followed up with, "Nock!"

There was another sweep of motion as the archers brought their weapons back to the ready. This was their chance to take out one of Lavanai's best fighters.

Tit for tat, Arran thought to himself bitterly, again forcing his eyes to stay on her and not trail to the body on the ground.

Mithos made to stand, her leg collapsing under her a few times as the blood flowed freely from the wound in her thigh. Her steel-coloured pant leg now looked black as the blood seeped into it and trailed down to the snow at her feet. She drove one blade into the ground to push herself to her feet, favouring the injured leg even as she wrenched the blade free and balanced.

Arran couldn't imagine what she was planning to do. The leg couldn't even support her to get to her feet. He imagined the arrow may have hit an artery with the way it bled freely and the fact that she made no attempt to remove it.

The prince found his eyes shift to the blood in the snow again, which brought his gaze back to Ryla's body and the aged blood around her. For some reason, in that moment, he needed to be sure her form hadn't been hit by the foray of arrows. While a few arrows had landed around her, her body was miraculously untouched. The relief was a small bit of salve.

Still, the ache returned to his chest. His teeth clenched, and he jerked his eyes away from the Killer back to the dahem. Mithos seemed to stare back at them, waiting for her own reality to come to her now. He took a deep breath. He was ready to deliver it.

"Release!"

CHAPTER

SIXTY

I t'd been years since Adel had visited Veloth. It felt different crossing through Veloth Proper on horseback rather than tucked away in a carriage. The open air gave a different perspective of the clusters of buildings leading up to the seashore where she knew docks and many boats made fishing, the kingdom's main source of trade, possible.

The stone and rock buildings had withstood the water's wrath during many a storm season. She remembered when she was a kid thinking the sea was always challenging Veloth for its keep, so it unleashed fierce winds and cold rain on them often. Ashla had always fuelled that imagination, saying there was a colony of sea dahems on an unseen island, and they were protecting their home with their water magic. It had taken Adel much reassurance from her mother that sea dahems didn't exist.

Her brow furrowed now at the thought, and she pulled her coat tighter as a gust of wind pushed through the village at her company. The gust brought with it a strong smell of salt and the water plants that lurked below the sea's surface and undoubtedly washed up on shore.

"It's cold here," Adel commented. Her breath hung in the air as if anyone needed proof of it.

Her father nodded his agreement wordlessly, then signaled with his hand for one of the riders beside them to go on ahead.

The Heta banner streamed from the sturdy wooden pole the rider carried as her horse proceeded at a lope. That left the rest of their entourage, made up of the remaining riders that had come to Nithle with her father, to move forward at a slower pace.

She took in the village again as the group moved forward.

Did Nithle's people make it here safely? she wondered. As she stared into the crowds, she didn't see anyone with the stag crest or any garb that would signal their Nithlean heritage, but maybe that was intentional, in order to hide them. *It'd make sense.*

People of all ages looked like they might cast off into the sea at a moment's notice with their more practical dress. They wore heavy garments that could probably repel water while keeping them warm. Equally warm-looking hats were snug against their heads, resting across their foreheads, covering their ears, and touching the napes of their necks. Adel suddenly wished she had one.

I'll have to ask Nea, she thought to herself, knowing Veloth's princess would know where to procure such a hat. It'd go nicely with the borrowed groundskeeper's garb she once again sported.

People watched them as they traversed the sprawling streets toward the large castle positioned along the waterfront. One edge of it skirted a sheer drop into the water below. Like Nithle castle, it rested atop a hill but looked more imposing against the grey sky with its sharp architecture and pointed spires. Several green flags with the silver crest of a leaping fish adorned the immediate pathway to the castle grounds, and Adel saw her rider waiting near the steps with Heta's pennant now planted firmly at her feet while it continued to flap in the wind.

A number of attendants came out to greet the group and helped the princess and king dismount before stable hands took their horses, while still others tended to the entourage. Criph waited until his lead of royal knights, Knight Britta, accompanied them. The woman had a sword, like all Heta's knights, but her weapon of choice, a spear, was firmly in her grasp at her side. She quietly spoke to another of the entourage, and the man joined them while the others prepared to station themselves outside the castle.

Indoors wasn't much warmer, but Adel hoped for a fire wherever they would meet with King Hadden. Another hope she had was that his children would be there, which might lend more strength to their cause and convince the king to act.

They were led to a large chamber that made Adel think of throne rooms. They had faded in popularity over the years, but it appeared as though Hadden upheld this tradition. The princess was distracted from the breadth and high ceilings of the room by the large fish that hung on the wall behind the throne. It looked as long as her father was tall and thrice as wide, its opalescent scales glistening in the flickering light emitted by the three massive chandeliers.

A subtle nudge from the butt of Britta's spear against Adel's calf told her that she was staring. She took a few quick steps to catch up with her father, shifting her mindset to the task at hand.

Not a soul waited for them, which made her wonder whether the king would grant them audience at all. Her curiosity was answered only moments later when Hadden and the three royal children entered the room, the king taking the chair while the two princes and the princess stood to the right of him. She connected with each of their lighter gazes, but Nea held her attention the longest. It was as though she silently questioned what was going on, and her round features were pulled in a pained expression. Adel wasn't sure what sort of body language she could use to communicate the reason they'd come.

"Criph," Hadden said, his voice clear and ringing out across the room. The older man sat tall in the high-back, ornate chair, with one leg crossed over the other. His hand casually straightened the knee-length tunic across his trousers. "It's been quite some time."

Adel didn't think the king cowardly, but she knew there was more bravado in him than actual calmness over the situation. Everything about his appearance was composed, from his put-together outfit to the long, neat braid of his greying hair to his body language. Adel was certain King Hadden was also carefully choosing his words.

"Yes, it has, Hadden," Criph responded noncommittally.

"Terrible what's happened to Nithle. You can imagine our shock when the people of Wendur and Sothle arrived here and our sadness given their tidings. My condolences, Princess," Veloth's king continued, his expression sympathetic.

As relieved as she was to learn Wendur and Sothle had made it here, Adel's brow furrowed. "Condolences?" Was he expressing condolences over what he thought was her losing the chance to rule over a kingdom since Nithle had been overrun?

"Of course. I know better than anyone what it's like to lose your partner to dahems." Sorrow etched his features and his voice caught.

It was like a lightning bolt of recognition. The king's condolences, Nea's pained expression. When Adel looked at Rold and Jase, she could see even they wore similar looks of sympathy. Clearly the shape of the story had changed.

"Arran lives," she declared, watching Nea's dark eyebrows

shoot up as the princes exchanged a look of relief.

"King Alden and Queen Shron have been killed," Criph clarified beside her, his voice sombre. "But Adel is right. Prince Arran is very much alive and is, at this moment, leading an army to fight Lavanai."

It was Hadden's turn for his eyebrows to raise in surprise. "By himself? That's a foolhardy task!"

"Piridet stands with him. As does Heta," Criph replied firmly.

Warmth flooded through Adel, and she resisted giving her father a smile. *Thank you, Father.*

"So the kingdoms are waging active war with Lavanai now? What hope do we have against them seeing as the Killer failed? Or is that part also untrue?" Hadden challenged, looking slightly more uncomfortable now. He seemed to be piecing together why they were there.

"No, that part is true. Killer Ryla was…compromised in the attack, and the Union removed her," Criph replied. He was now the one choosing his words carefully.

Adel held her breath, wondering if word of Ryla's gold-streaked eyes had reached this far. She couldn't see how it wouldn't. Yet none of the Veloth royals seemed aware of it—at the very least, they made no comment or reaction.

Criph continued quickly. "Her fall is precisely why we must stand together now. We don't know Lavanai's full intentions, but it seems they're confident enough to try to overthrow the United. They broke through Nithle's army, killed the king and queen, and thwarted a Killer. If the positions were reversed, it seems to me this would be the perfect opportunity to attack."

"And what of the Union in all this?" Hadden held his voice steady. "Are they sending further aid?"

Adel bit her lip. "We've not heard from them since Killer

Ryla was taken."

Hadden shook his head. "If the Union isn't intervening, there's no hope for any of us."

"We have strength if we stand together," Adel countered. She saw the siblings whispering among themselves at this point and wished she could hear their discussion.

Hadden's composure was slipping, his suddenly fidgety hands and small facial tics giving him away where he sat before them. He seemed oblivious to his children convening beside him, or maybe he just didn't care.

"Hadden, I understand your fears. We all saw how impacted you were by Lelleth's death," Criph said gently, although even then the words seemed to lance the man. "It's time to take a stand against Lavanai and ensure this doesn't happen to anyone else. Just because Veloth has avoided most of this doesn't guarantee your safety, the safety of your kingdom, or the safety of your children."

There was a pregnant pause, broken only by the sound of the wind pressing against the windows of the large chamber. It reminded Adel that there wasn't any fire lit in here after all; even Rold, Jase, and Nea wore warm tunics to brace against the cold. Yet, Adel felt heated by the intensity of the atmosphere.

"Father." It was Jase who spoke, his heavy boots *thunking* across the stone floor as he stepped forward. The eldest of the three siblings, he stood tall with his shoulders firmly set. His dark brown hair was combed out of his face. Once his father looked at him, he spoke again. "We have to be a unified front. Regardless of how exaggerated what we've heard is, it's a miracle that Arran yet lives, and Adel is right. We need to do something now so that this doesn't happen to more of us."

"If Mother were alive, she'd want us to do this," Nea asserted, her tone firm and even. "This is the exact sort of thing she was trying to stop. She died trying to gather any information on the dahems so we wouldn't have to continue this battle forever. The United is truly coming together now, and we should stand with them."

Nea issued Adel a small nod, her curls bouncing slightly from the effort. It told Adel all she needed to know: Nea and her brothers would support the cause, even if their father refused. How many in Veloth's army would be loyal to the children over their father, she wasn't sure, but any help was better than none.

"My children, you don't know what you're saying," Hadden protested, his voice more uneasy than angry, even though he squared his shoulders and held his chin up.

"We *do* know what we're saying, Father," Jase retorted.

Rold picked up where his brother left off. "You've tried to shelter us, but we've been paying attention to what's happening across the United. We were at the Harvest Festival when Lavanai attacked. Nea's right: Mother wouldn't have us sit idly by, and there's nothing you can say to convince me otherwise."

Adel was surprised by Rold's steadfastness. The youngest of the children, he was typically more reserved, like herself. Yet, she saw a maturity and confidence in his soft, teenage features that she hadn't before and felt a kinship to him given her own recent step outside of reticence.

Jase laid it out plainly. "We're doing this with or without you, Father."

"It would be easier *with* you though," Nea added, receiving nods of agreement from her brothers.

The king's mouth fell agape as he stared at his children. Adel glanced at her own father, who'd been silent for the last several minutes. He stood at her side watching the situation as she was, his posture relaxed but steady. She found her eyes tracing the design of their kingdom's crest on his sleeve, the patch of burgundy and silver standing out against the darker colour of his heavier jacket.

"King Criph, Adel, could you please give us some time with our father?" Nea asked.

"Of course," Criph responded with an inclination of his head.

Nea offered a small smile. "Thank you. An attendant will take you somewhere warm to wait."

CHAPTER

SIXTY-ONE

The steady flame heated Adel's skin as she and her father waited in a lavish room with plush seating, a handsome fireplace, and tapestries showcasing Veloth's artistry. Along the far wall, there was a line of sculptures: a spoked sun, a fish, a stag, a kestrel, and a fox. She couldn't tell what the sculptures were made of, but the white material looked durable and even elegant.

Adel and her father sat in comfortable silence as they waited on Veloth's decision. This was the first moment alone since their argument in Sirama's inn, but Criph wasn't taking the opportunity discuss it. She sensed he wanted to, but she knew her father would want to do it when they were in a completely private setting. Preferably, within their own castle walls.

When someone did come, Adel was surprised to see Nea's warm expression greeting them and not a page. The Velothian princess walked in confidently, and although her presence was warm, Adel knew better than to take her expression at face value. When she wanted to, Nea could school her emotions or misdirect.

"My brothers and I appreciate your patience as we spoke with our father. Rold, Jase, and my father would like to speak with you now, King Criph," Nea said easily. "I have someone waiting to take you to them."

Criph nodded wordlessly as he rose from his seat and

made his way toward the door, where Knight Britta now stood as she'd been waiting outside the room. Once they left, Nea closed the door and crossed the space to sit beside Adel on the divan by the fire. She arranged her tunic's skirt as she sat, half-turned to Adel with one leg resting sideways on the cushions.

Adel watched her fellow princess, unsure how to even broach whatever conversation they were about to have, but Nea saved her the trouble.

"We convinced Father to have Veloth join the battle. I'll admit, he's still so afraid—and honestly, we are, too, given the horror stories we've heard from the refugees." Nea paused, seeming to collect her thoughts. "I feel terribly for making him do this, but it's now or never. We can't afford to wait around and hope the dahems pass us by if the rest of the United falls."

Shock was the first thing Adel felt, but it was followed closely by relief. "Thank you, Nea. I heard the stories myself, and I'm afraid, too. There's so much that's gone wrong already, and there's no telling what else we'll face. But I agree with you. We have to take a stand."

"My brothers and I have long wanted to, and we've been trying to come up with a plan in the background. It's unfortunate that we've had to wait for this kind of situation to finally convince Father, but hopefully it's not too late for everyone," Nea said without taking her eyes from Adel.

Nea was a few years older than her anyway, but Adel felt she could really see it now in the set of her expression.

Maybe it's just the maturity that comes with carrying a weight...and death, Adel thought. She wondered if she and Arran looked older, too. "So what happens now? Or is that what they're discussing?"

"That's what they're discussing. Not that I don't want us to be a part of that, but I noticed that you, Princess, don't have proper armour. Does Arran care that little for you that he wouldn't send you off with armour?" she said with a half grin. "I'm teasing. I know things are hectic right now, so it's lucky you came to Veloth. While the men are chatting, you and I can visit the armory and get you fitted."

Adel raised a brow. "Do we have time for that?" She knew sport armour could be crafted in a few hours, but she'd always been under the impression crafting armour for battle was a longer endeavour.

"Our armour is different. Should be ready in a day." Nea beamed. "It was something Mother started years before she died, and over time, we've perfected it."

Adel couldn't help but smile, warmed by the way Nea spoke about her mother. It made her wonder how her own mother was doing, and Rynn, too. Her father had sent a messenger with word of their current situation, but that'd probably only add to the worry.

As if Nea could sense the change in her line of thoughts, she asked, "How are you doing, truly?"

"It's…it's a lot to take in and digest. I don't think I've had a chance to process all of these changes yet. Even with losing Ashla. Then, when I returned to Nithle, the king and queen were already dead, and I was pretty sure I would lose Arran, too. Thankfully, he wasn't injured—at least, not physically," Adel said, looking at the fire again.

"I get it," Nea replied. "Losing Mother nearly destroyed us all. Rold and I didn't leave our rooms for days, and even after we did, it was a long time before we really functioned again."

Adel nodded knowingly. *I'm not the only one to go through that then.*

Nea continued, "We've all felt the ripple effects of it since. Losing both his parents in one day… I'm sure Arran was—*is*—emotionally devastated. It's hard to move forward."

Adel watched the way the flames danced and lit up the bricks of the fireplace in a soft orange glow.

"He's lucky to have you, Adel."

Brow knitted, her attention drifted back to Nea.

The other princess's expression was soft. "I'd wager you had a big role in that first little while, and the fact that he's now off to battle Lavanai is no small feat."

"He has Mihel with him. I know that's lending him strength," Adel said.

Nea shook her head with a small smile. "Mihel is a force to be reckoned with, but she's never been *his* force. That's been you. Don't sell yourself short."

"I'm not meaning to," Adel replied. "But I can't take all the credit, either."

Nea regarded her a moment, then smiled again and stood. "Well, all the credit, partial credit, he's lucky to have you. No one should have to deal with death alone."

A pang of sadness hit her then. She'd processed Ashla's passing mostly by herself. From the way Arran had embraced her at the Passing Ceremony, Adel knew he'd been trying his best to be there and that pushing her away was to prevent more tragedy, but it wasn't what she'd needed from him. She decided that after all this, they'd have to learn how to be there for each other in the ways they needed it, not with misguided attempts to protect one another.

Taking a deep breath, Adel stood, too, almost eye to eye with Nea.

"Ready to get some of the best armour you'll ever own?" Nea was back to beaming.

Adel smiled in return. "Lead the way."

CHAPTER

SIXTY-TWO

T hrough the searing pain and the blur of red and white around her, Mithos heard the call across the field to unleash another assault of arrows. With the state of her leg—sopped in her own blood and barely agreeing to move, let alone hold her weight—she knew this could be the end of her.

Burn, Mithos begged her powers. She hadn't had to use words to summon the flames since the first days of learning to control it after setting the yard on fire.

A fraction of a second had passed since the call for the assault. The collective twang of bowstrings competed against her wildly beating heart. Both were so loud in her ears.

Burn!

It was her only chance, otherwise, she'd be joining Ryla. The whistle of arrows cut through the air and her focus, and although she faced the direction they were coming from, it was all an unfocused jumble.

Burn...

There wasn't even the slightest stirring in her. No familiar ripple of heat.

It broke you, too.
BURN!

CHAPTER
SIXTY-THREE

A rran shielded his eyes, and he felt someone, probably
Ley, covering his body with their own as an explosion
of flames roared from across the open field. The screams of
horses were barely audible as they fled. The heat radiated over
Arran's body, reminding him of being close to a fire in camp and
having a gust of wind blow. It was too hot but didn't actually
burn, so he got a sense that the flames didn't reach them.

It only lasted a moment before the heat retreated, the bitter
cold snapping back into place, and he shivered violently. The
person shifted off of him, and Arran opened his eyes to look
around. From first glance at his company, it didn't appear
anyone was injured, but the horses had fled and he could tell
from everyone's wide eyes and slack jaws they were stunned.

"Are you okay, Arran?" Ley's voice drew his attention.

The prince could see the concern in his knight's expression
as dark eyes searched his face.

"Yeah," Arran said, a little less confidently than he'd
intended. His gaze was drawn past Ley to the field, and his
eyes widened as his mouth fell slightly agape.

Where there had been snow directly in front of Mithos,
there was now scorched ground and smoke rising from the
char. The char gave way to slush and eventually to snow where
Arran and his group stood. After the initial shock of the sight,
the prince's eyes snapped to where Mithos had been along

with Ryla's body.

He wasn't sure why he was relieved to see Ryla's body still there since it was just that: a body. All the same, relief was what he felt when he saw it was still where it had been moments before, as if nothing had happened. Except something had happened, and Mithos's body now lay beside hers, slumped onto its side and looking just as lifeless.

"Is she dead?" someone asked from beside him.

"Only one way to find out," Arran replied.

Ley interjected sternly. "We should wait for Mihel and the others."

Arran glanced at him. "By then, Mithos could be back on her feet and launching flames at us. Clearly, I was wrong about her not being able to use her magic. Even if that was in desperation, we can't count on it not happening again."

"Exactly. We can't risk moving forward, having her awaken, and then scorching us to ash," Ley countered.

Arran thought on it a moment. He wanted to get closer to ensure the blow was final, but it was indeed a risk. "You're right. We'll fire another round of arrows first." The prince swung around to address his archers. "Who among you has the truest aim?"

An older man stepped forward without challenge. "I do, Your Highness."

Arran regarded him, taking in his long beard, sharp eyes, and sturdy frame. "Do you have a clear enough shot of the commander's body to pierce her heart?"

The man paced slightly to the right, tilting his head each way to assess the situation before him. Finally, he turned back to his prince. "Yes, Your Highness."

"Nock and take aim," Arran ordered.

Wordlessly, the man got into position, adjusting where

he stood only once to ensure his aim.

"Ready, Your Highness," the archer said.

"Re—"

An arrow's whistle cut through Arran's command, and his archer cried out, stumbling to the side. Arran cursed, whirling in the direction the arrow had come from to see a sizeable group charging on foot in their direction. From their speed and the fact that they were attacking, he could only assume it was Lavanai's forces swiftly closing the distance.

"Ley!" Arran bit out.

"I see them!"

"Everyone fall in. Fire at will!" Arran commanded without turning to his fighters.

The dahems kept coming without slowing, even as some among them fell. Arran's heart hammered against his ribs, and he felt himself being pulled backwards as the ranks enveloped him, leaving them as a wall of protection.

No! Arran thought.

He broke away from the fighters as the sounds of forces colliding rang out across the otherwise silent field. His hands went to his belt, grasping at his dueling daggers and freeing them of their sheaths as he pushed through his guards.

I have to help.

He summoned Veena's lessons on using dueling daggers to his mind. As a sword came arcing toward him, he caught it with one dagger while using the other to stab at the dahem. His aim was sloppy, and the dagger missed, giving the dahem the opportunity to push him back and swing again. He ducked low, slashing one of the daggers out at the dahem's ankles, feeling the bite of the blade into the fabric of their trousers where there was a gap in the leathers. The dahem screamed, and Arran stabbed at them again while they were distracted, hitting home this time.

He quickly pushed himself to his full height. *That was lucky.*

The fighting continued on for several minutes as Arran pressed closer to his guard so they could band together and combine their strengths. Still, he was jostled about and had several near misses as well as true hits that careened off the plates of his armour.

"Your Highness, no!" someone called out.

Even as Arran heard the voice, he felt himself taken off balance and pulled backward, his weapons falling to the ground as his arms suddenly pinned to his sides and his back slammed against another's torso. His feet lifted off the ground as he was pulled away from the fray. Fear iced his veins as he felt a cold blade press to his throat, and he was certain if he swallowed, it would slice his skin.

Ley's panicked expression met his as the knight shouted orders at the others, but Arran barely registered Ley's words over the voice shouting near his ear. The voice was commanding, the dahem language ringing powerfully.

The same powerful voice rang out in Arran's own language next. "Stand down or the last of Nithle dies," it ordered.

Arran's eyes widened as he fought to grasp what had just happened. His group stared on in horror, and he saw the dahem forces move to encircle them all.

He felt compelled to look to where Mithos and Ryla's bodies were but didn't dare turn his head. Out of his periphery, he spied a trio of dahems making their way to the bodies, and when they reached them, one checked Ryla and the other, Mithos. They looked at each other before one ran partway back and shouted to the dahem holding him. He only caught a few words that meant anything to him: Mithos, *Yastalai*, and Jasim.

His blood went cold again. Lord Jasim.

"I won't give another warning," Jasim growled. "Drop your weapons or he dies."

"Don't!" Arran chanced to say. He wasn't sure where the word came from, only knowing they shouldn't surrender just for his life. If that meant he had to die in the fight, it meant he had to die. His parents had died. Even Ryla had died. People died, but that didn't mean the cause had to end.

Ley and the others paused, caught between motion and uncertainty. The fighters looked to the knights for guidance, and the knights to the royal knight. Ley's gaze was firmly on Arran and the dahem holding him. The subtle movements of his strained, dark eyes as he tried to avoid such a heavy price didn't escape the prince.

While his group pressed in on the humans, Jasim spoke at a volume only the two of them could hear. "I don't think you understand what's at stake here, Prince Arran."

"You're Lord Jasim of Lavanai. My parents are dead. Killer Ryla is dead. I am the last of my kingdom and my line," Arran laid it out while he watched Ley and the others lower their weapons.

"You're familiar with the elements, but you don't seem to understand their weight," Jasim continued.

"The Union will send another," Arran continued. He wasn't sure how much Lavanai knew about the state of the Union, but he'd test his bluff.

Jasim gave a derisive chuckle. "I don't think they will. Surely, they would have acted by now. They know we're coming for them."

With how tightly Jasim held him, Arran wasn't sure he could shudder even if he wanted to. "Even if the Union falls, even if Nithle falls, the United will fight. We're done with this war and will bring it to an end," Arran said confidently despite the ice in his limbs.

For the first time, he knew what it meant to face his death and for it to not mean the end. Did he want to die? No. He didn't want to leave his people behind. Ley. Adel… His heart twisted hard. But if he had to, he would face death knowing that, now that they knew the truth, others wouldn't stop trying to bring the war to an end, whatever that might look like.

Jasim continued at the same volume. "The Union *will* fall. And then *we* will end this war. I assure you that our people are equally tired of this fighting."

The words struck Arran. Could the dahems really be tired of this as well? Regardless of what triggered the war, he'd assumed Lavanai sought vengeance if nothing else at this point.

Arran dared swallow. The blade at his throat nipped at his skin. Nervous energy welled in his chest. "I know now why the war started. The real reason I mean. I know what Nithle… what my family did and kept from me all these years."

Jasim's form stiffened and his grip tightened, as if just as struck by Arran's words as Arran had been by his. There was a heavy pause, everyone seeming to wait for something to happen. Arran connected with Ley's gaze again, hoping to tell him silently to not make a move even though a moment before he'd had wanted them to fight.

Ley's concern and frustration were starkly apparent, as was his confusion as to what was going on, but he didn't budge from where he held his arm out to hold back the others. The rest of the group waited with bated breath, some facing the scene with their prince and the dahem lord, while others faced the dahems surrounding them.

"And what do you plan to do with this information, Prince Arran?" Jasim asked carefully, his accent somehow thickening with the weight of the words.

Arran paused. There hadn't been enough time to decide what to do with the revelation Adel had brought or how to approach ending the war with Lavanai. And then there was the ire he felt over the death of his parents, of Ryla, and even of Ashla, still tasting fresh and bitter on his tongue.

Yet despite all this, suddenly the answer felt clear.

Is it possible? he thought, as almost simultaneously he said, "I plan for peace."

Jasim chuckled again. "With Lavanai? That's quite the thing to say, considering you've stormed after my army and tried to kill my commander."

She's alive then, Arran thought as he moved only his eyes. The dahems tended to her leg wound now, but Mithos didn't seem conscious at all. "She killed Ryla."

Another chuckle. "You can't have peace with Lavanai and still protect or avenge the very ones that exist to annihilate us."

The sobering words resurfaced the idea of his world without the Union.

"You're right." He paused. "I can't pretend that I've gone about this the right way or that I fully understand everything. I assure you my goal is peace, even if I have no idea what that looks like or how to attain it."

Jasim hesitated again but didn't release Arran or remove the blade from his neck. "After all that's happened, you're willing to throw down your arms?"

Arran swallowed, feeling that nip of the dahem lord's blade once more.

"Yes... Are you?"

CHAPTER

SIXTY-FOUR

F or all he shouldn't, for all the words could be a ploy to
lure him into a false sense of security before enacting
revenge, Lord Jasim of Lavanai believed Prince Arran of Nithle.
Maybe it was the slight tremble in the young man's body or the
tone of his voice, but there was something about this heir to a
dark secret saying he'd put down his weapons that rang true.

Yes, Jasim thought wearily in response to Arran turning
his own question back at him. But for the fact that his hands
were occupied, he would have run one over his face. Instead,
he said, "It's not my decision to make."

King Ottel would be intrigued by this development,
certainly, and he'd want Jasim's advice regarding it, so Jasim
knew he had to tread carefully. Not only would it be a matter
of ensuring the prince was telling the truth, it was also a matter
of how the other kingdoms would react—including Lavanai.
He knew this couldn't count as Nithle surrendering to them;
Arran wouldn't agree to that. This had to be a mutual truce.

"Contact your king, then," Arran offered, his voice even
despite his body's tremble.

Jasim was impressed by the prince's comportment. "Until
then, we're at a standstill."

"We don't attack you, you don't attack us," Arran agreed,
and Jasim got the sense he would have nodded if not for the
dagger to his throat.

He paused again, considering the situation. The years of battle flashed through his mind, as did the thought of ending Arran right here and now. It would only take a small movement of his wrist to slit his neck, and the Nithle line would be gone forever.

But then the war would continue, as they knew it would. That was a next course of events they were prepared for—but now, with the potential for peace, the future wasn't so clear cut.

"If you call upon the Union—" Jasim began.

"The Union is gone."

The dahem lord wasn't sure if he was more taken aback by being interrupted or by the statement itself, especially given what Arran had said only moments ago about another coming.

"Repeat that." His heart picked up its pace.

"The Union is gone," Arran said again. "Ryla told me. Whatever happened to her... They fled."

Again, Jasim believed him. Part of it was because the words reportedly came from Ryla, and he'd seen the change in her first hand. The gold of her eyes had struck fear in him on the battlefield, her danger amplified by the threat of the magic powerful enough to change her eyes, but not stay her skill. She'd still been fast and precise. Still dangerous. His injured hand suddenly ached.

He glanced to where her body lay, wondering how Mithos had succeeded in ending her life; the three who'd gone to Mithos and Ryla had said the Killer had a wound to her chest. Jasim trusted Mithos's abilities, but with how he'd struggled against the Killer himself, it amazed him that Mithos had dealt the finishing blow.

Mostly blind and magicless, she still succeeded. No, that wasn't right. Her magic was there now, if only a whisper of it. It *had* been gone though, he was sure of it. It was part of what had taken them so long to find her despite searching through the night. Until there'd been a burst of it all at once. And now, it was building anew. He didn't know what to make of it.

Jasim breathed out, shifting his focus back to Arran. "That changes a lot." How much it would change was the real question. *If both Nithle and the Union were gone, would the other kingdoms surrender? Maybe it* is *as simple as ending this boy...*

King Ottel had always trusted Jasim to make whatever decision was needed on the battlefield, but this reached beyond the battlefield. Yet, it was a prime opportunity to bring Nithle's chapter in history to a close. The dahem lord ruminated for several long moments disturbed only by the quiet sounds of nature as no one else dared move.

Jasim finally focused on the royal knight and the rest of the band that accompanied them. When he spoke, his words were still for Arran. "We will proceed. Tell them what's going on, and I'll release you."

Without hesitation, Arran said, "Drop or put down your weapons. You are not to attack the dahems—Lord Jasim and his group or the rest of their army."

"Your Highness!" the knight protested.

"Trust me, Ley," Arran said firmly.

The fear in the man's eyes was plain, but the knight still yielded to the prince and put his sword away. The man looked at Jasim, as if to try to gauge his intentions, but the dahem lord was certain he gave nothing away. He'd have preferred if Ley had dropped the sword instead, but he'd accept this. The knight broke his gaze to give the others stern looks; they followed suit, completely sheathing, shouldering, or dropping their weapons.

Once they'd each done so, Jasim turned to his own company, speaking to them now in their language. "Do the same.

Weapons away. Do not attack this group or other humans," he said, watching the shock replace what had a moment before been satisfaction at the turn of events. "Do it."

Like the human army, the dahems reluctantly stowed their weapons. Then, and only then, did Jasim remove his blade from the prince's neck and release his grip on him. While he fastened the dagger in the sheath at his waist, Arran turned to him, a move that Jasim thought bold, if not brave.

There were a few red marks along the prince's throat. He could see some courage in the young man's blue eyes, but more, he saw determination among the mix of emotions brewing just below the surface. Jasim could relate to the complex feelings.

In an attempt to ignore them, he said, "We'll return to our camp. I'll contact our king. I imagine you have more forces coming?" The dahem lord continued to watch the prince carefully—his form shook, but only slightly, even as he schooled his expression to meet the lord's gaze.

"There will be more fighters from Piridet and some from Heta. While I've sent people to Veloth, I have no idea if they will support us," Arran told him, his voice held even.

Jasim wasn't sure whether this candor was a gesture of trust or stupidity, but he immediately rethought the notion of stupidity. He didn't think the prince was stupid. Maybe it was naïveté that had prompted him to share the information, but not stupidity. The dahem donned a wry grin.

"Potentially every kingdom," he mused aloud. *Even if we don't come to an agreement, I at least know who to expect now.*

Recruiting the help of the other human kingdoms was smart. He did mental math on the number of forces he had left, then guessed what the rest of the human armies might have in their ranks. Nithle and Piridet would have the most, followed by Heta, then Veloth.

Lavanai would need to prepare, especially if King Ottel were to join them. Jasim considered telling him to stay in Icarsen but also knew making a show of peace would be solidified by the presence of Lavanai's king. It left him feeling on edge.

Arran's voice broke through his internal reverie. "We'll keep watch for them. Head them off and inform them of what's going on. We'll do what we can to stop them from attacking."

"That's quite the task," Jasim told him.

"I know," he replied.

Jasim was pleased that Arran didn't try to minimize the situation or make some sort of promise he couldn't keep.

"It may be some time before we get word from our king," Jasim warned next.

"Then we wait."

He regarded the prince, then glanced around the scene again. Both of their groups waited with bated breath for what would happen next. His trio near Ryla's body and Mithos waited to move their commander. He hoped they'd been able to stop the bleeding. They'd said nothing else since their original report about the gushing wound in her leg, slowed only because the commander had been smart enough to leave the arrow where it was.

Out of the corner of his eye, he saw Arran follow his gaze and guessed at the prince's thoughts.

"Do with Ryla's body what you will," Jasim offered and saw the prince's brow furrow. "I have reason enough to begrudge her—many dahems do—but she was only following her orders and had very little say in it. Although, at the end of it all, I wonder..." He brought his attention back to Arran now without finishing the thought.

Arran's eyes met Jasim's again. "Is there—"

Jasim shook his head. His tone was a little sharper when he spoke, "There is no magic in the world that can restore life to the dead, boy. And if there were, she's one person I wouldn't bring back."

The prince's expression fell before he reined it in, clenching his jaw. He inhaled deeply, then nodded resolutely.

The dahem lord carried on. "I'll send for you when I have word from King Ottel."

Jasim looked back toward those with Mithos and, when he got their attention, gestured for them to collect and move her. They carefully hoisted up her small frame and weapons, then began walking in the direction of their camp. When he turned to the rest of those who'd come with him, he pointed at two and motioned for them to go help; even if they only acted as extra guard, he'd be content. Finally, he signalled for the others to leave the humans and join him, which they did with only slight hesitation.

Before turning away himself, Jasim looked pointedly at the young man once more. "If even one person comes after us, this is null."

Arran held his gaze firmly. "Consider the feeling mutual."

"Then we're in agreement," Jasim said with a curt nod.

Without waiting for any further response, Jasim turned from the group, presenting them with his first test: to not literally stab him in the back. He didn't quite pause but didn't rush away either. He heard no movement behind him.

Though facing forward, he focused on them for only a few moments longer, then made his way to fall into step with the dahems tending to Mithos. Only one of them carried her now, small thing that she was. Her form was limp in the dahem's arms, but Jasim could still see the movement of her chest. It was rising and falling too quickly for his liking.

"Report," he commanded sharply.

"She's unconscious, My Lord," a dahem not carrying Mithos replied. "She's lost a lot of blood, but we were able to tourniquet the wound. Her breathing is laboured, but there isn't any sign at present she won't survive. We won't know what happened until she wakes up."

Jasim nodded brusquely. "Take her to the healer as quickly as possible and monitor her. When she wakes up, I want to be notified."

"Of course, Sire," the dahem replied, then nudged the one carrying Mithos to move more quickly.

The dahem took a moment to adjust his grip, then nodded to the other, and they took off together with the rest of the group in tow.

Jasim watched as the small group went and resisted the urge to look over his shoulder, curious about what the prince and the band of humans were doing. A voice in the back of his head said it would be smarter to look back just to be sure, but he wanted to show his steadfastness in what he'd said.

To distract himself, he started mentally drafting the letter to King Ottel: a dead Killer, the Union vacated, and a ceasefire with Nithle. It was a lot for even Jasim to take in. He wondered which the king would find most interesting.

CHAPTER

SIXTY-FIVE

I nstinct told Arran to keep his eyes on Jasim and his group until they disappeared from sight. No one with him moved, not even Ley. The cold seeped into his thick coat, and his breath puffed out before him as he considered the very real situation he'd just put them in: trusting the dahems. Could it even be done?

In the moment, it had made perfect sense. How better to stop the fighting than to literally ask for it?

Now, he had to consider the aftermath of it. All the stories from his childhood crept into his mind. Warnings of dahems beyond the kingdom borders. Tales of dahems capturing and torturing young children simply because they were cruel.

Then there were the memories of everything that had happened since the Harvest Festival. People scrambling in the village square, worry over where Adel was, running and hiding, capture, the innocent dying, the fast-moving form of the Killer breaking through the crowd, Ashla's death…

Outside of the memories, his eyes came into focus on Ryla's body, still untouched and motionless. When he crouched to gather his daggers, then stepped toward her, everyone else seemed to take it as a cue it was safe to move again. Some tended to the wounded, including the archer who'd been struck in the side by Lavanai's arrow.

"Why did they leave her to us, Ley?" Arran asked aloud

as the knight met his uncertain pace.

"They ended her life," Ley replied without sugar coating. "I guess even their nature tells them to stop at death."

Arran thought a moment as they drew closer to her. "I wonder about what we've been told of their nature. I know," he added, noticing Ley open his mouth to respond. "But with what just happened… He could have very easily killed me and been done with it. They could have killed the rest of you and no one would have been the wiser until Mihel and Kein found our bodies. If dahems really are these creatures hell-bent on destruction, why not just go through with it?"

Ley sighed. "I can't say. I see your reasoning, but this whole thing has left me uneasy, and I'm certain others feel the same."

The prince steeled his jaw, knowing Ley was right. If they'd been questioning his judgement before, they were going to think he'd lost his senses now. He wished he could hear some of Ley's optimism at the moment but knew better than to expect or even ask for it, given the course of events.

The one person he truly wanted to talk it over with was in Veloth. At least, he hoped Adel had made it to the southern kingdom safely. He trusted their allies enough to keep her safe while she was there, but he worried about the journey itself. He would just have to hope that no news meant good news.

As Arran looked upon Ryla's fallen body, he got the sense she hadn't been disturbed. Maybe it was the somewhat awkward angle of her legs or the way strands of hair shifted across her motionless features in the subtle breeze. Maybe it was the way her hand, even in death, loosely gripped her sword, which lay covered in snow at her side.

His eyes eventually found the darkness of the fabric in her sternum, and his brow furrowed at the tear in the fabric that revealed the wound to her chest.

"It doesn't feel right," Arran commented to Ley. Ley didn't say anything, so Arran continued. "Killers are our protectors. It feels like they shouldn't die."

When Ley responded, his voice was barely audible. "Everyone dies."

"I know. But it still feels unimaginable," Arran persisted.

A thought occurred to him. A long shot, but now that he'd thought it, he had to check. He rounded to her left side and crouched by her sword, where he lost himself for a moment in the blood on the blade. It shone a rusty, brownish red through the white flecks of snow under the continuously lightening sky. He closed his eyes against the scenes of battle that came rushing to his mind.

Opening them again, Arran reached for her arm.

"What are you doing?" Ley asked.

The prince didn't reply, instead gingerly removing the sword from her grasp, placing it to his side before peeling back her glove. It felt improper to touch her body. He wasn't sure what brought the knots to his stomach more: feeling he was disturbing the dead or severely disrespecting the hierarchy, but he had to know. When the glove finally gave way enough to reveal the mark on the back of her hand, he had his answer.

He took a deep breath and hung his head with closed eyes. Hot liquid burned at his lash line. He pressed the back of his hand to his mouth, inhaling the scent of the soft leather gloves. *It's truly her. She and the Union are truly gone.* The thought left him feeling hollow. Pulling the glove back over her hand, he asked, "Who can carry her?"

There was a sort of shuffling behind him, presumably Ley turning to order someone to help. A large fielder came up on the right side of the body, folding the Killer's arms over her chest before lifting her. It wasn't just that Arran thought the

Killer deserved a better burial spot than some random field, it was also a matter of not having any proper tools to dig with.

As he stood, her sword in his hand, Arran looked at Ley, who eyed him carefully and with a touch of concern. Arran said nothing, turning to observe his people, curious if any of the distrust he was expecting would be evident in their countenances, but there was no sign of it. Even as they made the journey back to camp, no one said a word. He wasn't sure whether or not to take that as a good sign.

CHAPTER

SIXTY-SIX

The dancing flames left Arran feeling as heavy as the blanket of the night sky that fell by evening. They hadn't stoked as large a fire as a true Passing Ceremony would have—this was more of a fire to keep anyone nearby warm—but it would do. He realized a Killer didn't have a treasured possession to burn and release their soul from the world anyway.

The closest thing to a treasured possession Ryla had would probably have been her sword, but there was no sense trying to fuel a fire hot enough for that. Mihel had suggested giving the weapon to the company blacksmith, but the idea didn't sit well. If it couldn't be destroyed as a part of a Passing Ceremony, Arran wanted the sword to remain intact.

What was it Ryla had done at the Passing Ceremony? She'd thrown dirt and leaves, that was it. Would that mean anything to her?

The Killer's body had been buried just outside the camp without much formality. As much as it went against custom to do things so flagrantly, it felt fitting to the Killer's nature. They lived, they fought, they died. Simple. Unceremonious.

They face realities, Arran thought to himself, watching the shifting reds and oranges. The words she'd said, or at least their translation, sprung to mind. *Be free of life's burdens.*

Killers didn't have family to mourn them, or friends even. Well, that might not be true. He thought back to Lord

Davi and his parents; they were still mourning, even without knowing if their loved one was alive or dead.

I'm mourning her. The words family and friend didn't fit Arran's relationship with her quite right, and he wondered if others protected by Killers felt as attached to them as he had to Ryla. Maybe.

He wasn't sure how long he stood there. Eventually, Ley came to collect him to meet with Mihel. Arran had no doubt the princess, and even others in camp, had already gotten wind of the deal he'd made with Lord Jasim; that was the kind of news that would spread like wildfire.

As he and Ley walked into the tent, warmth folded around Arran and the smell of burning wood from a small fire filled his senses. He loosened his cloak slightly but didn't remove it.

Mihel sat at the table, leaning forward and speaking quietly to Eridan. His expression was mostly even, but the tension in his shoulders gave away his true feelings. The princess was more composed, but Arran got a strong sense she was also unsettled by what she'd heard. They both looked his way as he and Ley took up spots across from them at the table.

Mihel cut to the chase. "Making a deal with Lavanai is not something I would have expected. Even considering all our conversations and what we know from Adel and her father… It's a bold move, Arran."

"That's assuming what we've heard is true," Eridan said, as if trying to give Arran a way out of the situation.

"It's true," Arran replied without any preamble. He realized how weary he sounded then, even to himself. He felt like he sunk into the wooden bench. "I made a deal with Lord Jasim to stop the fighting so we can talk peace. I don't expect everyone to be happy with it, but it's the decision I made."

"Then why aren't we talking to him right now?" Eridan

chimed in again.

"Because," Mihel interjected before Arran could reply, "he's just a *lord*. We'd need to speak with the *king* to achieve inter-kingdom peace—if their king even wants to entertain this sort of thing. He's not been seen for years, so we don't really have any idea of what sort of being he is or how he might want to approach this." She had a pensive look on her face as she spoke.

Arran nodded. "There's a lot of uncertainty, I'll admit. But it's a chance to bring an end to this, and I don't know about you all, but I'd love to know a life beyond fear of war with Lavanai. Especially now with the Union gone."

"So they *are* for sure gone, then?" Mihel asked curiously.

After his visit to the Killer in her tent, Arran had relayed the conversation to Mihel, who'd seemed rather perturbed by the news. Even now, her curiosity only thinly veiled the concern she felt about it.

"Our only way to confirm would be to go to the Union itself. It does seem to be the case, though. If ever there were a time to send help, it'd be now." Arran paused, still watching the princess. "It's going to take adjusting to."

Her furrowed brow and bit lip relaxed into appreciation for his understanding; then she schooled her expression. "Whether the Union's gone or not, we'll have to deal with it when we find out. What are our next moves? Apart from waiting to hear from Jasim and somehow explaining this situation to our people without an uprising."

Arran felt a wry grin tug at his lips. "I imagine we'll have to wait for our reinforcements to arrive. Have we heard anything from Adel or King Criph? Do we know if Veloth is coming with them?"

Mihel shook her head. "Still nothing on that front.

Realistically, they should have already made it *to* Veloth, so it's a matter of, like you said, waiting. I'm sure they'll send a messenger to let us know what to expect before they arrive."

Arran moved to his next thought. "Are you going to write your father?"

"I'll have to," she replied nonchalantly. "I don't have the authority to make this kind of decision for my kingdom."

"How do you think he'll react?" the prince continued tentatively. As much as Mihel handled everything well, he wasn't sure King Timith would be as calm. The man was an interesting individual, and Arran had always felt the way he carried and made himself hard to read was intentional. He didn't see the king as volatile, but he knew the man kept his opinions close to his chest.

"Honestly, it's hard to say," she said with a slight shrug. There seemed to be more to her thoughts than that, but when she continued, she said, "All the same, my kingdom's additional fighters should be arriving any day now. In the interim, let's figure out how we're going to address our people and convince those we've called upon to stand down."

Arran nodded, the heaviness returning to his chest. The conversation with Mihel—her ready acceptance of the situation—had lifted some of the worry he'd felt over the decision he'd made. But now, the possibility of having made everyone his enemy was palpable.

The only thing he could do was wait to see if that possibility would transform into reality.

Although he didn't expect Ley would betray him, he knew the knight was uncomfortable with the turn of events. With his biggest support so uneasy, he couldn't help but think things didn't bode well for him.

Was this how my parents felt all the time? Arran wondered.

Despite all his studies and all his training, nothing had prepared him for this. His mother and father had never divulged how the weight of rule impacted them. They acknowledged there were tough decisions and that not everyone would agree, but the true emotional toll was never a topic of discussion.

The anger he felt over their decision to keep things from him grew with each passing day. It was difficult to reconcile with the sadness and grief he still felt over their deaths. He considered talking to Adel about it when she arrived.

If we'll even have a spare moment.

Arran realized the princess and two knights were watching him in his introspection, and he hoped he hadn't gotten lost in his thoughts for too long. He shook himself mentally and adjusted how he was sitting to stir his mind. It seemed to help, as he had a thought.

"Something we can do to ease everyone into the idea is maintain our perimeter guard. It'll ensure we're not left unprotected and demonstrate to the dahems that we're not letting our guard down. I'm sure Lavanai will understand if we approach the situation with caution. They'll probably do the same." He wasn't sure what he would say to his people yet, but at least he could come up with a plan of what to do.

"Fair," Mihel agreed. "We can review what we have in place and make any necessary changes. Eridan, go find Commander Kein or at the very least Knight Feon so we can do that."

"Of course, Your Highness," the knight said without question, placing his large hands on the table to push himself up and keep balance as he lifted his legs, one after the other, over the bench.

After the knight was through the tent flap and out of earshot, Mihel trained her gaze back on Arran.

"He's not overly happy with all this," she explained. "But

Eridan is loyal to me and won't do anything to jeopardize the situation."

Arran glanced at Ley out of the corner of his eye, but Ley was watching Mihel.

The princess continued, "This is an unprecedented situation, so I'm hopeful people will at least be willing to hear you out. I'm going to be honest, I'm not sure where I sit yet, but I'm open to seeing where this goes. It would be nice to not have to have the war in the back of my mind all the time."

She fell silent just a moment, her delicate features trained on the grain of the table. Arran sensed she had more to say, however, and waited patiently for her to continue. Finally, her eyes lifted anew.

"In Piridet, we've always had this lingering worry of if Nithle falls, what happens to the rest of us? How should we prepare? I know people won't want to let go for a long time, but to have some semblance of being at peace... That's not a chance I'm willing to pass up."

CHAPTER
SIXTY-SEVEN

Adel's new armour made only the lightest of sounds, like water tinkling on metal, as she dismounted from her horse. The tightly-knit mail's mobility astounded her. It didn't have any of the weight of other mail she'd seen. Even now, she could picture the armourer working away on weaving the metal links together. The process had looked no different than any other process she'd seen, but the armourer was working much more quickly.

Nea had showed her how the pattern of the mail links and the kind of metal used was what made it unique and so lightweight despite the tight knit. Because of its lightness, she'd doubted its protective qualities at first, but Nea had performed a few test hits on a dummy wearing the mail and the links hadn't so much as buckled.

Adel straightened her new pant legs—another gift from Nea—which had bunched from riding, and then adjusted the wool-lined cloak around her shoulders. It was colder here; the air even *smelled* cold somehow. She didn't think they could be farther north than Heta, but the air was different.

Passing the horse's reins to an attendant, Adel gave the animal an appreciative stroke down the length of its face before she joined her father, King Hadden, and Prince Jase in walking through the collection of tents, led by a guide. Their knights trailed closely, Knight Britta pretty much in step beside Adel. She was curious that the woman wasn't walking with her father, but for all she knew, Britta had been told to stay with her.

Despite her conversation with Nea, Adel was amazed that the situation, or perhaps whatever the siblings had said to King Hadden, had struck him so profoundly as to convince him to leave his kingdom, actively seek out battle with Lavanai, and place his two younger children in charge in his absence. The man held his head high, but she could see his caution in the way he'd been looking around their entire trip, keeping his guard close to him and wearing the much heavier, more traditional Velothian armour.

It was later into the evening by that point, so the camp was relatively quiet and it was difficult to read the atmosphere. Something felt off, which set her on edge, but she couldn't place what it was.

Her thoughts worried at her, stomach knotting. *What's happened here? Is everyone safe? Arran?*

The group's torchlights sent shadows across the tents, and a few heads poked out in response. Some stared longer than others, and she wondered if it was because they'd noticed the Veloth crest among them. Regardless of how long they stared, she couldn't get any sense of what was going on.

The group paused just outside of a larger tent near the middle of the encampment. Someone announced them, and then they were admitted into the canvas quarters. All but two of their knights remained outside, joining the post around the tent, Adel assumed. Britta and a Veloth royal knight she couldn't remember the name of joined them inside.

Entering the tent invited warmth and an array of different people, but she was only concerned with finding one. Her eyes strayed to the head of the table, finding Arran standing beside a chair there. The tension in her shoulders melted into a swell of emotion that brought happy tears to her eyes.

He's safe. Yet, she couldn't help but notice he did look older. Dark shadows had collected under his eyes and there was a hardness to them that she wasn't quite familiar with.

As she removed her cloak, she peered around the rest of the tent to take in who else was there. She spied Mihel, who gave her a slight nod of acknowledgement, which she returned before moving her gaze along. A tall woman stood beside Mihel, her dark hair in a thick, loose braid hung over her right shoulder. She had sharp features and dark eyes, but her look wasn't severe. Piridet's fox crest was stylistically embroidered into the deep purple of her overcoat across the left side of the chest up to the shoulder.

Beside her was a gangly teen boy who hadn't come into his height yet. His hair was just as dark, but his eyes were a lighter shade of hazel. His posture reminded Adel of how Arran would stand when addressing people, although the boy bore the severity that was missing from the woman beside him. His overcoat had the same embroidered crest.

Criph broke the silent wonderment. "Queen Diah, Prince Cavrin. What a surprise."

"Likewise. Well, we'd been warned you'd be arriving, Criph, but is this truly King Hadden or have you found a doppelganger?" the woman, Queen Diah, asked, her voice light and curious. Her eyes locked on the greying man, as if he would disappear if she were to look away.

"It's me," Hadden confirmed. "My children convinced me it's time to join this fight against Lavanai."

Adel caught a subtle shift in Arran's expression she didn't think anyone else would've noticed. It was the slightest of tension around his eyes and a small tilt of his chin. She tried to stay a wash of anxiety. How had things progressed since they'd been apart? The camp seemed secure. The one unexpected thing about it was that it looked like they'd settled here, as if this were a new frontline. She wondered why they'd stay in one place when Lavanai was on the move.

"Let's sit and talk," Mihel spoke now, gesturing to the long table lined with benches.

As they each situated themselves at the table, Adel sat across from Arran. She would have preferred to sit beside him so she could both be near him and have a whispered conversation, but she settled for this. His eyes were on her as she adjusted her tunic, one of his brows raising just slightly. At first, she was confused and took a quick glance at herself to see what he might be looking at, then remembered she'd taken off her cloak, so the mail was showing.

She laughed lightly, feeling a bit self-conscious for some reason. "Nea had me fitted."

"It looks good on you," Arran replied with a small smile.

Adel smiled unbidden, and warmth spread through her chest where anxiety still lingered. She didn't have time to say anything else as everyone finally settled in.

"Arran, I think you should give them a summary of events," Mihel prompted.

His gaze stayed with Adel a moment longer before his smile vanished, and he was back to being the head of his kingdom.

The head of his kingdom, Adel's thoughts echoed on themselves, as if realizing it for the first time. The weight on his shoulders was suddenly glaringly obvious, and she was troubled she'd been too distracted to notice it earlier.

Arran took a breath, lacing his hands on the table before him as if to anchor himself. "A lot has changed since we left Nithle. We clashed with Lavanai on a battleground slightly north from this camp. We hadn't expected to come across them here and figured we'd be trailing them, but they'd been held up in their own journey by Killer Ryla."

There were a few inhales and raised brows, but no one stopped him. Adel felt her own heart quicken. Her eyes shifted around the tent to see if the High Protector was standing silent vigil in a corner somewhere, but there was no sign of her. Her attention returned to Arran, brows pinched.

"Even after what happened in my kingdom, even with her eyes showing all signs of magic, she performed with the same skill and was clear of mind."

Adel stole a glance at Hadden, seeing if his reaction to the news of a tainted Killer was the same as when they'd shared it with him back in Veloth. As much as Adel had wanted to withhold the information for fear Hadden would use it as an excuse to hide, she knew her father had been right to tell him. The man needed to know *all* the details of what he was getting into, including how dire things had become because of what had happened with Killer Ryla.

To his credit, Hadden didn't so much as flinch at the mention of it this time, but he was intently focused on Arran.

Nithle's prince continued, "She returned to camp with us briefly, but then disappeared. We tracked her down, but by then, she'd…she'd already been killed by Lavanai's Commander Mithos."

Adel felt as though her own sharp intake of breath pierced her. *Killed!* She couldn't imagine the dark-clothed warrior being defeated. She'd exuded strength at all turns. Even though she'd never seen her in battle, Adel pictured a force to be reckoned with, like a storm crashing through a village. *Did the change in her make her vulnerable?*

Through her initial shock, the princess realized Arran had

paused and was staring without seeing. *Stay with me, Arran,* Adel thought, worried he was reliving the scene and getting lost to his memories.

Another breath, and Arran picked the story up again. "We almost succeeded in killing Mithos, but Lord Jasim and a band of his army intervened. He would have killed me, and honestly I would have let him because I knew others would continue the war where I failed, but there was another way out."

"Surrender?" Hadden accused, followed by an almost imperceptible twitch on one side of his mouth.

"Armistice," Arran said pointedly.

While the word made Adel freeze, she heard the uncomfortable shifting—felt it even, as the bench moved beneath her.

Still, Arran persisted. "The dahems, at least Lord Jasim and his forces, want this fight no more than the rest of us. We've agreed to lay down our weapons, and he's writing his king to learn if he will entertain a peace treaty."

Hadden was quick to react. "Just like that? Everyone— *dahems*—agreed to stop fighting just like that?" His voice was even, but Adel could tell it was the same airs he'd put on in his own castle.

"It's been over a week, and there have been no further attacks," Mihel supplied confidently. "As you saw, we've maintained our guard stationed around the camp as a precaution. We're not approaching this lightly."

Hadden shook his head and leaned forward. "That you're approaching it at all borders on insane."

"And what of the Union?" Prince Jase spoke for the first time since walking into the tent. "How will the Union feel about this peace treaty with the very people that have been our enemies forever? The very people they protect us from?"

"Before her death, Killer Ryla told me the Union has gone.

They've abandoned us," Arran explained gravely.

"Abandoned?" Adel couldn't stop the word from escaping her mouth. She felt suddenly very cold. *They wouldn't truly do that, would they?*

Arran met her gaze again. "I don't have all the details, but my best estimation is whatever happened to her left the Union vulnerable, so they've retreated."

"They just left us to fend for ourselves against the dahems?" Jase asked, his tone appalled and features drawn tight.

"It's a heavy blow to take, but that would seem to be the case." Diah spoke now, her light and curious tone from earlier having transformed into even contemplation. "It leaves us in an interesting position, and, from what I gather, Lavanai's Lord Jasim feels the same way. The Union has been with us since Lavanai and Nithle went to war. They've been our protectors and guided us through the difficult times with the dahems. It's not easy for me to think they'll no longer have that role for us, and I don't know what our future looks like. Yet, I can't overlook them simply turning away from *us* as it became difficult for *them*."

Hadden leaned into his protest, fists gripped on the table. "The Union leaving shows us the true danger of the situation! If something happened that so gravely impacted them, what hope is there for us? The war began because the dahems used their power against Nithle."

"The war began on a lie," Arran interjected again, staring firmly at Hadden. "My great-grandfather was afraid of the dahems' magical abilities although they'd never been used against him. He orchestrated the whole thing to look as though the dahems delivered the first blow, but it was *my* kingdom that started the war."

"Did Lord Jasim tell you this?" The fearful edge in Hadden's voice was more evident now.

"I told him this," Adel said, her tone steady as she leaned forward to look at the man seated on the other side of her father. She could see the king had started fidgeting with the end of his braid, although he paused for a fraction of a second at her words, his mouth agape.

"And I'm the one who told her," Criph said just as steadily. When Hadden's gaze shifted to him, he continued. "Nithle has kept this secret since the beginning. Alden shared it with me when we were younger. He wanted to find a way to break the cycle with Lavanai but never could. He intended to march on Lavanai."

Diah's eyes flashed. "Was that the true intention of his letter to us? Not to have us stand in defense but trick us into dangerous territory?"

Criph shook his head. "I can't say for sure what his intentions were with entreating Piridet. Given the conversations I had with him before the end, however, it very well may have been."

Eyes fell on Arran.

The young man also shook his head. "I can no more say my father's intentions than King Criph can. All I know is my father had mentioned such a plan and Killer Ryla advised against it. He shared nothing further with me about it."

Heta's king turned his attention to Arran. "Regardless of Alden's intentions, what you propose is the first time we're seeing steps to end this war, but you know what we spoke about before, Arran."

Arran nodded soberly, his chest rising and falling with a breath. "I'm already seeing what we spoke of among this camp. Even at this table. Not everyone agrees on peace with Lavanai. Our history is stained, and the enmity runs deep. I can't guarantee Lavanai's king will even agree to it—but it's an opportunity to end this without any more bloodshed."

"Which is why I've agreed to support Nithle," Diah spoke up. "When Timith and I agreed I'd join Cavrin and our army to provide support for Mihel and Arran, I had no idea this is what I'd be walking into. But I'm making this decision for my kingdom, and now it's time for you two to decide for yours." She looked between Criph and Hadden and came to rest on Criph. "I'm sure Mela would understand whatever decision you make."

Adel wondered about that. She could only hope her mother would understand, or at least try to. If this could remove the danger from the equation, there'd be no reason to worry about her safety anymore.

There was a pause, everyone seeming to fall into thought, and everything hit Adel at once in the silence. Killer Ryla was dead. The Union had abandoned them. Arran and Lord Jasim had made a deal. The weight of these events pressed on her.

"Heta will stand with Nithle," Criph said after a silence. "We've a hard road ahead of us, and this won't be an easy treaty, but, it's as Arran and Diah have said: it's an opportunity to end the war with no further bloodshed and repair the rift between kingdoms."

"I want no part of this," Hadden bit out.

"Father…" Jase's tone was plaintive.

Veloth's king continued without so much as looking at his son. "Have you all lost your minds? Have we all forgotten what the dahems have done?"

"No one is forgetting anything, Hadden," Criph said with a shake of his head.

"They killed Lelleth!" Hadden raged and brought a fist down atop the table, making Adel jump.

"And they killed my parents," Arran said in such a way that it commanded Hadden's attention. "A treaty won't erase the past. It won't wash away the spilled blood on either side. They've killed people we love, and I'm sure we've killed people they love. This isn't an effort to forget any of that. It's a promise there will be no more of it moving forward. It's an acknowledgement that we see where we've each gone wrong and are taking strides to do better and be better."

Pride. That was the word for what Adel felt in that moment. The warmth of it was quickly sapped away though.

"Those are all nice words, Arran, but you clearly have no concept of what this means nor the impact of it. You're a *child*," Hadden countered.

Arran's jaw tightened. "I'm the head of my kingdom."

"From what I've heard from your own refugees and allies, your kingdom is scattered," Veloth's king continued with a wave of his hand.

"We did what we had to for the safety of his people," Mihel broke in now, her voice hard.

She would've been a part of that decision, Adel realized. *Her judgement is being equally challenged.*

Hadden scoffed. "Children making adult decisions."

"All the more reason for us to stand together and guide them," Diah said calmly, but Adel could hear the dangerous edge in her tone. It practically raised the hair on the back of her neck.

Hadden met the queen's gaze, but she didn't back down, maintaining eye contact.

The king stood in a huff, quickly leaving the tent with his knight rushing after him. Jase groaned almost inaudibly and ran a hand through his dark hair.

"I'm sorry for my father. It was miracle enough we convinced him to leave the kingdom to fight Lavanai, and now you're asking him to do the exact opposite," the Veloth prince explained.

"And where does that leave you?" Arran asked, watching his fellow prince carefully.

He sighed but gave Arran a sympathetic look. "It's a complicated situation, Arran. It's not easy to let go of everything that's happened. I know you said we don't have to forget or erase it, but moving on will mean letting go. Maybe even forgiveness. That's a tall order for those of us who've have been hurt by the dahems, as you know. We're not all in the same situation as you, where it was literally a life or death decision to make."

"You could be though," Arran said.

"So they're going to threaten us into submission?" Jase raised a brow.

"That's not what I mean. Suppose Lavanai does sign a peace treaty with Nithle, Heta, and Piridet. If Veloth were to wage war, Lavanai would defend itself," Arran elaborated.

Jase took a breath. "And where would that leave Nithle, Heta, and Piridet? Would that mean you'd be our enemies? Would Lavanai call you to stand against us?"

The two princes stared at each other, but neither had the answer. Adel noticed neither her father nor Queen Diah seemed to be able to supply one either. *Or maybe the answer is clear and they simply don't want to say it.* A sinking feeling clutched at her chest. Something had to be said.

"It *is* a complicated situation," Adel echoed, drawing multiple sets of eyes her way. "I don't think anyone is trying to pretend it's not. But if we can all come to an agreement, at least we could work through it together."

She had the distinct sense that she hadn't contributed much

to change the way people were feeling, but at the very least it broke the pause. Jase shifted now and stood from the bench.

"I'm going to go talk to my father," he said without giving any sort of commitment to how he felt.

After he'd left the tent, Diah spoke again. "Let's retire for the evening. Hadden will need time to think, and I'm sure you'd like to rest after your travels."

"I think that's the best idea for the moment," Criph agreed, standing from the bench and stretching. "We'll meet again on the morrow."

Diah nodded in agreement, and she and her children departed, seeming to sense there was more to be said between Criph, Adel, and Arran. Adel could feel it, too, and chewed on the inside of her lip.

Yet, all Criph said was, "However this goes, Arran, your father would be proud of you." The king then left the tent with Britta following closely behind.

Adel's breath caught, and she turned to see Arran's reaction, but the young man simply stared after Criph. It was her turn to leave the bench now, and she rounded the table to sit beside him, back facing the table, and encircle him in her arms.

Her voice was quiet, just for them, as she spoke. "I can't tell you how relieved I am you're all right."

He returned her embrace. "Me, too. I was so worried about you."

When he pulled back, she could tell from the look in his eyes that he had a lot more he wanted to say, but here wasn't the place.

"Let's go," she offered, hoping maybe he would open up in a more private setting. She was puzzled that whatever he wanted to say, he wouldn't say with Ley standing in the corner and wondered if it somehow involved the knight.

Arran nodded in agreement, and she kissed him lightly before standing again and donning her cloak. He joined her a moment later, and they left the tent hand in hand.

O n the way to Arran's tent, Adel shared what had happened between the last time they'd seen each other and the moment they walked through the tent with Hadden and Jase in tow. The prince listened intently as she shared how King Hadden had proven to be the only obstacle.

"We may have gotten him out of the castle, but he's still very much the same man he was locked away in his kingdom's borders," Adel commented quietly, not wanting her dissidence to be overheard.

"We can't expect him to change his mind in such a short period of time. Convincing him to fight Lavanai still fits his narrative that dahems are the enemy, but what I've done... It's completely turned that on its head. Even if Lavanai doesn't agree to this treaty in the end, I'm not confident the ties between Nithle and Veloth will be the same," Arran brooded. They'd made it to the tent, and he held the flap open for Adel.

She ducked through, welcoming the break from the direct exposure to the cold air. She heard Arran bid Ley goodnight and felt bad she hadn't done the same, but it was too late to change that since Arran came through the flap a moment later and secured it closed.

Adel waited for him to turn to her, then reached her hands to him and said, "Whatever happens, I'm with you."

He took her hands and pulled her close, holding her against

his chest. When he leaned back to look at her, she saw a look in his expression she didn't quite understand.

She decided to ask. "What is it?"

"I'm not used to the armour on you," he replied with a small smile.

She bit her lip. "And what do you make of it?" Despite any progress they'd made, she worried recent events might undo all of it. Killer Ryla had died, after all, and if such a formidable person could die…

He pushed the shoulder of her cloak back to run his fingers along the mail near her collarbone. "I've never seen the likes of it. It seems you're well protected though, which I'm in favour of."

"I hadn't either." Adel swallowed. She could feel the light pressure from where he touched the mail, and it sent a thrill through her. "Nea said their mother designed it. Queen Lelleth wanted their people to be well protected, just in case."

Arran nodded but didn't say anything, his eyes fixated on the mail. This sobered the moment as she could see, despite their proximity and his touch, his mind had taken him elsewhere.

"Talk to me, Arran," she prompted, her voice quiet but as reassuring as she could muster.

His silence loomed on, but she didn't push him. She imagined he was gathering his thoughts, which was why she was surprised when his hand moved from the mail at her shoulder to the side of her neck, and his lips met hers. Warmth flooded her, and her eyes fluttered closed as she kissed him back, hanging onto the moment.

Arran was the one to pull back but rested his forehead against hers. "I love you."

"And I, you," Adel replied, meeting his blue gaze. This

close, his turmoil was even more evident. It permeated off him. "Whatever happens, I'm with you," she repeated.

He took a deep breath. "I'm out of my depth. I wasn't prepared for any of this. We met Jasim on the battlefield where Ryla died. We almost killed Mithos, then he and his group surrounded us. He held a blade to my throat."

She couldn't help but lean back as her eyes dropped to his neck; she saw only a hint of a mark there. She recaptured his gaze as he continued.

"Some probably think it's fear for my life that's prompted this, but I was prepared to die... The end of the war has always meant victory over Lavanai. I don't understand why my parents never told me what King Gerge did..."

"I can't answer that, either. I'm sure they loved you and were just trying to protect you somehow," Adel told him softly. "I think now it's a matter of trying to accept that they didn't and moving on. We have this information now, and it looks like we may be able to use it for good. Heta and Piridet are with Nithle."

"That's easy to say when thinking of ourselves. Our people though..." he trailed off.

"Our people will respond to strong leadership. No one is trying to pretend this is going to be easy, but people will respond to the possibility of peace. Not everyone, maybe, but that's the nature of running a kingdom, isn't it?"

He sighed, his shoulders going slack. "You're right. It's just completely different being the one making those decisions."

"You've been making decisions on your own for years," Adel offered gently, accompanying it with a small smile.

His brow furrowed with confusion.

"I'm sure you've made decisions for the knights and fielders that they didn't like, even without active fighting, but they still trusted your judgement. Even deciding to strike out after Lavanai. Leading a kingdom has a lot more at stake, but it's another form of strategizing, isn't it?" Adel explained. She watched for his reaction and did see recognition in his gaze, but there was still something else there, too. "It's okay to feel uncertain. You've been delivered this in the middle of a war. Nobody expects you to be perfect."

"It's still a lot of pressure," he countered, looking away.

"I know."

His doubts reigned on. "What if I can't save my people? I tried to save Ryla. She said her death was inevitable—a product of her being a Killer. I didn't want to accept that. The Union abandoned her just as they did us. They sent her to this battle to *die*, but even if they hadn't, she said they would have killed her because she wasn't what they had made her anymore. I wanted to give her a chance at life."

"Killer Ryla was never yours to save," Adel said, and Arran's eyes reconnected with hers. "If you think about it, even as our protectors, the Union was their own domain. We know so little about them, except they forge humans into weapons that protect us from dahems."

"All Killers were once our people. If they hadn't been taken as babies, they would have been our people. Villagers, knights, even royalty," Arran said.

"That's not the life they were given," Adel replied with a small shake of her head, wrapping her own mind around it even as she spoke. "Regardless, that doesn't mean we can save everyone. It's a noble idea, but you can't blame yourself for every single death under your rule. Knowing you, you did everything you could."

"I can't help but question if I did..."

"Of course you did. You said so yourself—when you

learned she'd disappeared, you went after her. You risked your life and your ruling to do so." Unbidden, the rumours flitted through her mind again, but she found she didn't feel jealous. If anything, they felt more absurd than ever. "If you have some notion you would've been able to physically detain her, then you need to rethink that. You also said that even tainted, or whatever label people want to give her, she was still a force. Some people simply cannot be contained." She finished with a small smile.

Arran didn't quite return the smile, but she could see some of the weight leave his shoulders, even with his heavy cloak draped over them.

"I knew you'd be the best person to confide in, even though I wasn't sure I was going to, given our current situation with the potential treaty," Arran admitted.

"Why would the treaty make a difference?" she asked.

"It's a lot to take in. Like Hadden, you arrived expecting a war but instead were met with a stay of battle," he said with a small shrug.

She considered it a moment. "Well, I'm glad you told me. The situation is what it is. You shouldn't have to deal with your troubles by yourself."

Now a small smile crept onto his face. "I was an idiot."

Adel had no idea where he was going with this, but it felt like he meant more than just his hesitation to talk to her about these recent events. She didn't say anything, letting her confused expression do the talking instead.

"I'm an idiot for ever trying to protect you by pushing you away. Without you, I wouldn't be where I am. You're the voice of reason against the chaos in my head. The one who calms my inner storms," he said, his gaze never leaving her.

While the words made her heart swell, Adel couldn't help

the teasing tone that slipped in as she said, "I never took you for a poet, Arran."

He actually laughed now, and she grinned in response. It was nice to hear him laugh again; it'd been so long.

She took his hands again, lacing her fingers through his between them. "We'll get through this," Adel said, feeling confident about it as she did. "Whatever shape this takes, we'll get through it."

CHAPTER

SIXTY-NINE

The guards around the human camp were tense, shoulders rigid and eyes locked on Jasim and his entourage as they approached. Lord Jasim's personal guard accompanied him, something he rarely made use of, but he knew it was safer than going into the camp alone. The choice rang as particularly sound when he saw the banners for Nithle, Piridet, and Heta among the tents before him; Heta had made it, so that meant the army would be larger.

He was impressed that Arran had managed to rein in his allies—none had sought out Lavanai's camp, and even now, despite their nervousness, the guard didn't raise their weapons.

The dahem lord was glad for the milder day to make the trek from one camp to the other since the distance between meant the better part of an hour on foot. They could have reduced the time by taking it at a run, a jog, or on horseback, but there was no point. There was no rush, even with him carrying the letter he'd received from King Ottel.

Jasim had wanted to send Mithos, but although a few weeks had passed, she still wasn't quite herself. For the first few days, he'd wondered if she'd even survive. The initial assessment on the field had seemed fine, but her wound had gotten infected, a fever taking her and leaving it touch and go for a period. Even as the fever subsided and the wound healed, she wasn't immediately well. She was awake now but not ready for much more than resting in the camp.

"Stay alert," Jasim instructed his following in their own language. "Don't attack, but if they make a move against us, you have my leave to defend us."

"Yes, My Lord," Commander Anxer, newly promoted, replied.

Jasim brought his group to a halt with enough space to keep everyone comfortable while still effectively communicating. The humans glanced at each other, but still made no move to attack. Jasim then heard boot steps across exposed rocks where some of the snow had melted, and a knight stepped out from between the guard, his eyes sharp as he surveyed the group. He had a lavender scar running along his left cheek.

"Lord Jasim of Lavanai, I am Knight Feon of Nithle. What might I do for you?" the man asked, his voice strong and even.

"I have word from my king and seek audience with Prince Arran," Jasim responded. He was sure the entire camp had been apprised to the situation but allowed the formalities. It was best to be cooperative.

"Very well." Knight Feon looked, dare he say, hopeful. The man took a moment to give some sort of quiet instruction to one of the perimeter guards, who scurried off almost immediately. "This way, if you will." He gestured the same direction the guard had gone.

Jasim hadn't bothered to eavesdrop on what they'd said, but imagined he'd sent the guard to collect Arran and whoever else might be joining them. He strode forward and heard his group fall into step behind him.

He let his eyes roam as they made their way through the camp. It didn't look much different from his own, with rows upon rows of tents, except it stretched out across an open field instead of being intermingled among the trees. There were some fires where people cooked or sat around to keep warm and socialize. Unsurprisingly, many outside stopped to watch the Lavanian group pass by, but still no one made a move against them, even those who looked like they might want to. Jasim was intrigued as to what had been said to stay everyone's hands.

The tension from those around them followed all the way to a large tent, outside which stood Arran. He was flanked by his knight—Ley, he had called him—and the princess of Heta, neither of whom came as a shock to the dahem lord. It would have been more surprising had they not been present.

"Lord Jasim, thank you for coming here yourself," Arran greeted. "I'd thought you might send a messenger."

He reached into his overcoat's inner breast pocket to retrieve the letter. "I figured it best to discuss these matters personally."

"That's sensible," Arran agreed, eyeing the parchment. "Please, join us." He gestured toward the tent before turning to enter with the princess and the knight.

"Anxer, with me. The rest, stay alert out here," Jasim instructed in the humans' language for their benefit. No sense needlessly setting them on edge.

Wordlessly, Anxer followed Jasim into the tent. The dahem lord ducked through the flap into the large structure, where a table had been set out in the middle for everyone to gather at. King Criph of Heta sat to the right of the head of the table where Arran and Adel now took up position. To their left, Queen Diah, Princess Mihel, and Prince Cavrin of Piridet. The kingdoms' royal knights lined the edges of the tent, watchful of his every move.

Intimidation was not something that even crossed his mind as his amber eyes flicked from person to person.

"Please, sit," Arran offered, this time gesturing to the stool at the opposite end of the table.

Jasim glanced over his shoulder at Anxer, who nodded and went to stand along the tent wall. The dahem lord approached the table, first laying the letter upon it and then taking the proffered seat.

"Welcome, Lord Jasim," Queen Diah spoke now.

The woman exuded steadiness, and he had no doubt her greeting was to show she wasn't afraid or hostile. Jasim offered her a nod.

"What news do you bring us?" King Criph asked next. His tone wasn't quite as even as the queen's, but Jasim didn't sense hostility either.

"I have word from King Ottel," Jasim confirmed but then ventured to ask, "Is anyone else joining us?"

Arran's sigh was subtle, but Jasim caught it in the way his shoulders lowered just a hair. It was a sigh of disappointment or frustration. "No. Although King Hadden did arrive at our camp, he left as soon as the current situation was made clear to him. Veloth wants no part of peace with Lavanai."

"I see." Jasim considered that and looked at the cream-coloured parchment before him. He'd read the letter already, of course, and this split in the kingdoms made things all the more interesting and potentially complicated. He took up the parchment, pulling back the seal once again and unfolding it. King Ottel was a concise man and had kept his missive to a single page. Jasim summarized, "My king has agreed to meet with you to discuss a peace treaty. However, he'd first like to ensure the Union is not simply hiding within their walls until things have calmed down. While we know a Killer's word can be taken as truth, I agree with him that it's wise to take this step."

Arran nodded pensively. Jasim noticed the others waited on the prince to speak, seeming to defer to his judgement.

"That's reasonable," Arran said. "Are we to travel to the Union grounds and then contact him again?"

Jasim felt a small grin tug at his lips. "King Ottel is already en route to the Union grounds. He has asked that those who want to be a part of this treaty meet him there." His amber eyes took in the furrowing brows while his ears took in their shifting all around him.

"Is it wise for him to go to the Union alone? What if Killer Ryla was wrong?" Arran asked, and there was genuine concern in his voice.

"King Ottel isn't without his protection. I have no doubt he has some plan in mind since he's likely to reach the grounds before we will," Jasim said. Moving with one set of forces rather than several sets like they'd have to would be quicker. Besides, the messenger who'd delivered the parchment said he'd travelled with their king until midway through the forest, where they'd parted ways. King Ottel and his contingent had continued north while the messenger headed west to convene with them.

"What happens if the Union *is* still there?" Princess Adel asked from where she sat beside Arran. "What will it mean for all this and what will you do?"

"The real question is what it will mean for *you*," Jasim countered. "Will you denounce the Union for this peace if you know your protectors haven't left you? It's one thing to declare peace when your protectors are gone and you're left alone. It's another to hold onto that declaration when those who would oppose it endure." He wondered if they'd even considered this as a potential. From the looks on many of their faces, it didn't appear so. At least not in any depth.

"I will stand by what I've said," Arran said firmly. "This war has consumed generations of my family. Begun on a lie. I can't in good conscience let it continue. I can't speak for all the United, but for Nithle, this is finished."

"We'll stand with Nithle," Criph spoke a moment later. "I've long carried this secret and watched my friends under siege because of it. My best friend has died because of it. If there's a real opportunity for peace, Heta will take it."

Jasim watched the two men carefully. Arran's sincerity was clear in his expression, and Jasim could see Criph's was as well. It was news to him that Heta had known of Nithle's secret, and he couldn't help but wonder for how long, but he also knew it didn't matter. There was no sense getting angry over it now. What was done was done.

"Piridet also stands with Nithle," Diah said, glancing at her children, and Princess Mihel nodded in agreement. Cavrin sat silently, watchful eyes locked on Jasim.

Queen Diah's statement was interesting to him, considering what he knew of Piridet's particular fealty to the Union, but he didn't pry. "So, Nithle, Heta, and Piridet will travel north with Lavanai to the Union?" the dahem lord asked pointedly.

The humans exchanged glances. Jasim presumed his wording made clear that Lavanai had already committed to this journey. When he'd delivered their king's message to his own camp, there had been stirring among the forces. The idea of setting aside their weapons was easier for some to accept than others, but Jasim had expected that. The idea of going to the Union was more readily accepted; that's where the army had been headed anyway before they were waylaid by Ryla.

Yes, Lavanai was ready to continue the journey north. Jasim felt eager enough for it himself, and if the trip could be sweetened by the promise of peace...

"We'll travel with you," Arran said finally, his voice strong and clear. "Nithle, Heta, and Piridet will travel to the Union with Lavanai."

"Then let us plan for travel," Jasim said, and as he looked at the grim but determined faces around the table, a sudden lightness pierced his heart.

Hope.

CHAPTER

SEVENTY

While the initial plan had been to tear down the following day and begin their venture north, a sudden snow storm delayed their departure. It beat against the camps for a day and a half before letting up, until finally they were able to dig out, salvage what they could, and tear down to depart.

Now, the bite of the winter air was sharp against any bit of exposed skin. Even with furs encasing most of his body, Arran felt the cold seeping through and knew everyone else felt it, too, as the horses, wagons, and humans all trudged through the snow.

He sat astride a horse, Adel on a horse alongside him, watching the three kingdoms' armies move out in unison. There had been reports of fielders and knights who'd slipped away over the days, probably secreting out in the middle of the storm when no one would judge, challenge, or harass them. He could only hope the storm hadn't claimed any of them.

Most of those who'd left were from Nithle. As much as it caused an ache in his chest, the prince understood their fear, or if it wasn't fear they felt, their apprehension. After all the war and death, it wasn't easy to accept Lavanai as a potential ally. Some part of him still questioned if he'd be able to fully accept it and if he was making the right decision. In those moments, he remembered Jasim's tone as he'd held the blade to his neck.

I assure you that our people are equally tired of this fighting.

He sighed, feeling the warmth and moisture collect in the material across his face.

"Our numbers are still strong," Adel commented beside him, her words muffled by her own face covering.

Arran glanced her way, connecting with her gaze just beneath the fur across her brow. "You're right. My hope now is that this cold lets up so we don't lose anyone to the elements. The Union is still a long ride away. We'll have to stop to rest."

"Everyone has prepared as much as they can," she replied. "It's unfortunate there aren't villages along the way to stop at. An inn would be nice."

"If there are any villages, they'll be the exiled or won't accept the dahems." He paused a moment as a thought struck him. "If this goes well…if we establish peace, we should reach out to the exiled communities."

"And do what?" Adel asked curiously.

"I'm not sure. Perhaps if the Union really has departed, we can let those communities know that their exile is lifted. If the Union hasn't…" he trailed off.

"If the Union isn't gone and Killer Ryla was wrong, then we'll be exiled as well." She shivered, and Arran wasn't sure if it was because of the realization or the cold. "What would happen? Only Veloth would be left under the Union's protection. If we ally with the dahems, would the Union come after *us*?"

"I imagine if we were to attack Veloth, they would." The weight planted itself on Arran's shoulders again. They were all taking a giant risk, and one way or another making new enemies out of old allies. "We've already sworn to Jasim that our goal is peace. Our only choice now is to deal with the consequences as they come."

"You're right." Adel's attention shifted back to the moving forces ahead of them. "We'd better get going to meet up with Lord Jasim."

Arran nodded in agreement, and they both encouraged their horses to move forward. The royal pair made their way alongside the moving bodies and vehicles to catch up with Criph, Diah, Mihel, and Cavrin, who were heading up the train. Their knights were already with them, and Arran imagined Ley might be getting anxious. Indeed, as they caught up to them, Ley parted from the group to ride beside Arran.

"Could I have a word?" the knight asked through his own bundle of cloth and fur.

"Of course," Arran replied and cast a glance at Adel. She gave a nod and guided her horse through the snow to ride alongside her father as Arran and Ley slowed their mounts just slightly. He watched her retreating form before giving Ley his attention.

The knight spoke before Arran could say anything. "I know you're set on doing this regardless of anything I say. Many have deserted, but I'm not going to be one of those people. I'm also not going to lie. The prospect of what we're about to do is…incredible. Terrifying, but incredible. If this works, we'll invariably still have an enemy though. Are you ready for that?"

"I'm not sure I'm ready for anything at this point. I think having Lavanai as an ally rather than an enemy would be best. As much as I don't want to be at odds with anyone, wouldn't it make sense to not be at war with those more powerful than us? As much as I feel treasonous saying it, even *with* the Union's aid, we barely survived. I'm grateful for Ryla and everything she did for us, but how much longer would we have lasted? This is our chance at survival. I feel it," he said as they rode.

Arran looked ahead, but he could tell from the silence between them that Ley was considering his words. For a while, the only sounds were the horse hooves, footsteps, rolling wagon wheels along the road, and idle conversation amongst the armies.

"You're right," Ley ceded. "There's no perfect solution here. The only certainty is peace with the dahems will end a century-old war between Nithle and Lavanai."

"Four kingdoms united is a strong force, especially with Lavanai as one of them," Arran said, then considered his own words. "But I suppose we shouldn't get ahead of ourselves. We still need to meet with Lavanai's king. That'll be the true indication of how we move forward."

CHAPTER

SEVENTY-ONE

The armies made their way north with less trouble than Arran thought there might be. Of course, it wasn't perfect harmony by any means; the human and dahem armies seemed to only want to be as close to each other as needed. Although they started and stopped each day at the same time, there was a physical gap between the forces, with Lavanai leading the way.

At least they weren't at each other's throats. Each camp had its guards, but still no one made a move against anyone else. While it wasn't full trust, Arran could tell the tension was easing between them at least a little.

In addition, no one else was lost to either desertion or the elements. Snow continued its descent on the band of travellers, but they were able to ward off the cold—a small victory Arran was willing to take.

Arran passed the time in idle conversation with Adel, Ley, or any of the others who might be riding near him. As much as everyone had the Union and what they might find there on their minds, no one truly broached the subject, instead talking about just about anything else. That was the case, at least, until a dahem on horseback rounded its company and approached the humans following not too far behind.

Commander Anxer, Arran thought, recognizing him by stature and the heavy cloak he wore with Lavanai's crest on it. His eyes traced the emblem's gold stitching. *I wonder what that creature is.* Instead of asking, he waited until the dahem was close and then addressed him. "Commander. Is something the matter?"

The dahem shook his head, then pulled down his face covering, which Arran guessed was to un-muffle his thick, accented words. "The Union stronghold is in sight. My Lord invites you to join us."

By then, the rest of the royals had joined him and heard what Commander Anxer had said. Arran glanced at them, and they each nodded, except Prince Cavrin, whom Arran still hadn't spoken to much despite the several day journey together.

Now, the young Piridetian prince spoke. "I'll stay here with our people." His voice was strong and sure.

The rest of the group followed Lavanai's commander around the dahem army, and while Arran tried not to outright stare, he couldn't help be glance their way as they rode. Many of the dahems walked, but there were some on horseback, and they also had horses pulling their carts and wagons along through the snowy plain. Much like the humans' own armies.

Finally, they rounded to the head of the company and, sure enough, there was a building looming in the distance with miles and miles of open territory around it. Arran took it all in, squinting against the brightness of the grey sky and the white-covered ground, but saw only that large, single-storey building and a smattering of tall, wooden watchtowers standing vigil closer to where they approached.

"I feel as though I'm looking at something I shouldn't be," Adel said quietly from Arran's right. She, too, swept her attention across the fields.

"I know what you mean," he agreed.

It invited an air of surreality, if not reverence. Here. Here was where babies were taken and forged into human weapons.

Here was where cloaked guides had stayed when they weren't speaking to kingdoms and doling out Killers. Here was where Ryla had lived.

And here is where she would have died. Arran forced the thought, sobering the moment and washing away the reverence.

The group was far enough away that the main building looked deceptively small. Yet, even from the watchtowers, there was no movement. No sound of alarm. Nothing but the sounds of nature around them.

"Is it what you imagined?" Jasim asked from where he'd stopped atop his own horse, turning his gaze from the building in the distance to the humans gathering around him.

Arran and the royals brought their mounts to a halt as well, each continuing to take in the scene before them.

When Arran spoke, his eyes still roamed. "It feels like a dream. It's exactly as maps said it would be, but to see it in person is something else."

Jasim nodded his understanding. "I've never seen it myself. No journey north has ever brought me this far."

"Nor I," Diah said. "The Union has never invited us to their lands. They've always come to us."

Criph nodded along as the queen spoke. "Even as far north as Heta is, it's still a great distance to travel."

"I'm going to take a group with me to the stronghold to assess the situation and determine if King Ottel has arrived," Jasim announced.

Arran jumped in, "I can gather a group, and we'll join you, as well." He glanced at Criph and Diah who both nodded their agreement.

"That won't be necessary," Jasim stated. "Let me take the lead on this, and I'll send for you when we're ready."

The prince's brow cocked in surprise, but he didn't vocalize it as he looked back to the dahem lord. Sitting astride the horse dressed in warm clothes similar to his own, his large form looked even larger than it had when Arran had faced him out in that field. His dark hair was swept back from his strong features, and while Arran had been avoiding his amber eyes, he made a concerted effort to connect with his gaze now.

Anxiety whirled in his chest and throat, but he focused on the details around him. The horse beneath him, the towers overlooking their group, Adel by his side. It stayed the memories, but did nothing for the anxiousness stirring within.

The silence stretched out for a moment as everyone waited for his decision on how to respond.

He took a breath to steady himself, hoping they didn't mistake it for doubt or suspicion. "All right. We'll keep order here until your return."

CHAPTER

SEVENTY-TWO

Hours later, Knights Ley, Kein, Britta, and Eridan, along with a smattering of royal guard from each kingdom, accompanied the royal families as they trekked through the snow toward the Union stronghold. Commander Kein, who'd come with news that Lord Jasim and King Ottel were ready, led the way across the open field.

Adel stuck close to Arran as they walked silently along, her arm linked through his. He felt her grip tighten as they walked between the watch towers and followed where the dahems had already forged a path.

Commander Anxer stood at the large doorway to the building with a few other dahem guards, their amber eyes keenly watching the approaching group. The commander seemed to recognize each of them, even dressed as they were, and turned to say something to the other guards who stepped back to make way.

The prince's eyes quickly wandered to the building. Up close, it was somehow just as imposing as it had been far away, even though it was only a single storey. It looked as designed for battle as the warriors it had housed.

"Somehow, I expected it to be more regal or elegant," Adel commented quietly beside him, voicing the thoughts that crossed his own mind.

It didn't have spires, grand windows, or even a stylish

doorway. The stone structure of the building was plain, with only a few windows along the perimeter, and the door was a dark, heavy wood of some sort that could have been on just about any building.

"King Ottel, Lord Jasim, and Commander Mithos are waiting for you inside," Anxer told them through his thick accent.

"Inside?" Arran asked almost stupidly. Somehow the thought of entering the building had never occurred to him.

Anxer replied nonjudgmentally. "Yes, they're just in the entryway."

Adel's grip tightened on Arran's arm, and he looked at her. He saw the hesitation in her features but also the curiosity and determination. She looked up at him and gave a firm nod. He found himself returning it.

Ley leaned in and spoke as quietly as he could to not betray his distrust of the dahems. "Would you like us to go first, Arran?"

"No." Arran shook his head and kept his tone just as low. "We should go in first as a gesture of good faith."

"He's right," Adel agreed.

Ley nodded but stepped forward all the same to push open the door. Rather than go through it first, however, he held it open for the royals to walk in.

As Arran moved forward, he got a distinct sense he was about to tread on hallowed ground. The feeling almost completely disappeared once he crossed the threshold. If they thought the outside was inelegant, the inside was even plainer. There were no tapestries, no décor of any sort. Even the wall sconces were for practical use only, not even the slightest carving or fanciful configuration in the metal frames.

The most ornate things in the room apart from the humans

were the dahems that stood waiting for them. Lord Jasim wore a more formal winter garb, gold stitching lining the cuffs and hems of his dark overcoat while dark trousers disappeared into tall, leather boots. Even these simple clothes and the way his short, dark hair was combed back seemed to elevate him, especially in comparison to the plainness of the building.

Beside him stood Mithos, who, despite looking worn down, held her head high. Her clothes were also stitched with gold but were a light charcoal colour with a few layers that appeared wrapped around her. Her dimmed and unfocused eyes stared straight ahead while she favoured the leg that had been struck by the arrow.

Has she gone blind? Arran wondered. *Her behaviour in that field would make sense if so.* A sourer thought struck him then. *Potentially blind and was still able to kill Ryla.* Melancholy was hot on sourness's heels. *Remember what you said: we've killed those we care about on both sides.*

To distract himself, he continued to push his attention along. By far the most ornate of the bunch was a figure that Arran assumed was King Ottel. There'd been much speculation about what Lavanai's king actually looked like, how he behaved, and who he was.

The human stories had painted him as the most ruthless of the dahems, with cold eyes and a hulking frame fortified by all the years of training he'd undergone to lead his people to victory. Some stories even depicted him as an ancient dahem, whose eyes were wildly gold with heavy magic use that unnaturally extended his life.

The dahem before him didn't match that description at all. He was younger than Arran had expected, with barely any lines on his face, and his amber eyes were a darker hue than he'd ever seen. The king's pale hair hung loosely around his broad shoulders and seemed to sharpen his facial features, but in a refined rather than harsh way. The expression he wore was inquisitive as he took in each of them, rather than cruel and dangerous.

"I am Lavanai King Ottel," he said, his voice the only thing that might not have been far removed from the tales. It had a rougher edge, emphasized by his heavy accent and stilted phrasing.

Arran took the lead, first pulling the coverings off his face. "I am Prince Arran of Nithle. These are Princess Adel and King Criph of Heta and Queen Diah and Princess Mihel of Piridet." Prince Cavrin had once again remained behind with the forces.

"A monumental day," Ottel continued, his eyes resting on Arran. "The royals of Lavanai and Nithle meeting at long last. You are not what I expect." He didn't give them any room to respond. "We found room where we can comfortably rest. Come."

"So the Union building is empty then?" Criph asked as they began to follow the king down a hallway. "The Keepers and the Killers are gone?"

Jasim was the one who responded. "Completely. Not a trace of any of them left. But for the building itself, you'd never know they were here."

"Incredible," Mihel commented, glancing around as if the walls might reveal something about the Union or would suddenly sprout the sort of décor she was used to seeing along her own hallways. "It does feel like no one has ever been here."

"I don't know about that," Adel replied. "It's not life as we know it, but there was life here. The walls feel like they're echoing with the souls of Killers…"

"I have agreement with Heta's princess," Ottel said. "The

Union has tried to erase itself...or maybe secrets only, but we are not ignorant completely."

The ease of conversation was eerie. If anyone would have said even weeks ago that their kingdoms would bond over talks about the Union, especially while *in* the Union stronghold, Arran wouldn't have believed it.

We aren't trying to kill each other, so that's a success in itself, he thought.

He was curious that the room they seemed to be going toward was deeper within the building, and he imagined Ley was probably still anxious that this might be a bad idea.

It would be a good move strategically; take the humans deep into the building that only Lavanai had explored, giving little chance for escape. There'd be the opportunity to kill a handful of royals at once, which would initiate a full-out war from all the kingdoms, but it'd first leave people in shock and leaderless—the perfect time to attack.

Still, Arran sensed that wasn't about to happen. He knew he was trusting his instincts on reading people pretty heavily, considering he'd only just met King Ottel. Yet, to this point, Jasim had proven to be trustworthy, if the short time they'd spent interacting with each other could demonstrate such a thing. He chose to believe it could.

He paused mid-step as they came to an open passageway that led downward, like a path to a dungeon. The Union wouldn't have dungeons, would it? What prisoners would they keep here? Was there anything so treasonous that it would result in imprisonment at the Union rather than exile?

"Arran?" Adel questioned, not leaving his side.

From the corner of his eye, he saw her peering down the passageway. The rest of the group had also paused, but no one moved any closer, except for Jasim. He'd been guiding

Mithos but left her where she was for a moment to stand beside the prince.

"What's down there?" Arran asked the dahem lord. "You scoured the entire building, right?"

"We did. There are many rooms that we can only guess the use of. Most are devoid of anything. Others have what could be training equipment. Some might be bedchambers. We can't be sure, of course. Mithos strongly suspects a number of the rooms involved the Union's magic, even that of Killers. She can sense magic that echoes Ryla's throughout this entire place," Jasim said, turning his gaze to the dahem, but she made no move to approach them.

Arran watched Mithos for a moment, wondering if her distance was because of the assault he'd launched on her. He wouldn't blame her if it were. The dynamics between their kingdoms were certainly not easy to manage; he'd tried to have her killed, she'd tried to kill him, she *had* killed Ryla, Jasim had been ordering Nithle besieged for his entire life…

As friendly or at least civil as they were all being right now, the aftershocks were still very real. The earlier sour melancholy returned.

"I'd like to go through this building," Arran commented to no one in particular.

Jasim spoke from beside him. "I'm sure everyone will want the opportunity to do so once this is done. The chance to learn the Union's secrets isn't an easy thing to pass up, even for the most loyal, I would imagine." He paused. "But it means something different for us, doesn't it?"

Arran met the dahem lord's gaze, blue eyes meeting amber. "Yes," he agreed with a nod. "It definitely does."

A hint of a grin tugged at Jasim's lips before he turned away. "Let's get going. There's a lot to talk about."

The prince watched the dahem's retreating form, then looked at Adel, who observed him patiently. He could see the curiosity in her gaze.

"I know, this is going to take some getting used to," he told her quietly.

She nodded. "You make me optimistic though. Despite all that's happened, you're able to work with them, and so far, they with us. Peace feels possible."

He placed a hand over hers and squeezed gently. "Let's hang on to that optimism."

SEVENTY-THREE

A rran could see why King Ottel had chosen the room. Its spaciousness, even with furniture, meant they could all comfortably occupy the space, including their guard. It was otherwise just as bare as the rest of the building. The stone walls had no adornments but for sconces where torches currently flickered light to chase the shadows away. There wasn't even a window to bring in natural light, which gave the room a strange sort of atmosphere. Arran was fairly certain they weren't near an outer wall.

The royals each took seats, forming a bit of an odd talking circle. Arran was used to having a table in front of him for formal meetings, where individuals might lay out documents or maps to talk over, but here, there were only chairs. His gaze fell on Criph and Diah to see what they made of the situation, but so far as he could tell, they seemed to be as out of their element as he was by the way they set and reset their hands on their laps or adjusted in their chairs.

Ottel spoke first, his stilted, accented words breaking the silence. "I have been long looking to the day we can end this war. That it is this way is a bit of surprise, but Lord Jasim tells me of your conviction and sincerity. That you are willing to risk conflict with your fellows, and that you were willing to risk ire from your protectors were they still here. This tells me much. Meeting on these grounds was not just for me to see confidently that the Union and its Killers are gone."

Arran's brows pinched together, but he didn't interject, only watching the king as he continued where he sat tall in his chair with his hands clasped on his lap.

"These grounds symbolized enemy, source of fear, for my people. For people of human kingdoms, they've been protection symbol and guidance or courage source. I wanted to meet here to show we can overcome fear and shed old allies. This is new foundation of faith in us each and shedding of past. We cannot easy paths promise for dahems or humans, but we can make effort. Let us start here. For my people, I say we will leave our fears, hatred, this war behind. Lavanai wishes to start anew." Ottel spoke in a way that addressed each of them, shifting his gaze around the room.

Even with his lack of full mastery of the humans' language, his declaration carried weight and rang as true in his tone as it did in his eyes.

Arran also cast his eyes around room. Jasim and Mithos stood quietly behind Ottel, their expressions neutral in deference to their king. Criph seemed to be lost in thought, considering the gravity of the situation now that he was actually in it. Diah and Mihel exchanged a brief look, but the women seemed settled.

"I speak for my people—for Piridet—when I say my kingdom will set aside the past to forge this new future," Queen Diah said, her posture similar to King Ottel's as she sat straight in her chair with her hands folded on her lap. Her daughter mirrored her poise beside her.

"And what of Piridet arms?" Ottel asked curiously. "I have watched long from afar your kingdom increase forces despite not having active role in war. Will your people so easily accept the peace?"

A small smile graced the queen's lips. "You're not wrong about my kingdom and how we've prepared our people for the possibility of going to war, but our citizens trust us. King Timith and I have ruled with honesty and transparency, preparing our people for battle without sacrificing the message that it might not be needed. They will trust us to lead them well."

Mihel picked up where her mother left off. "It is our duty to lead our people through fear to a better future. This situation may not look as we expected, but our role is no different."

Ottel nodded, the dark amber of his eyes now turning to Criph, who sat between Piridet's princess and his own daughter. The two leaders silently assessed each other, and Arran couldn't help but wonder what was going through each of their minds.

Lavanai's king spoke first. "As Nithle closest ally and friend to passed King Alden, I know this is difficult ask for you, King Criph. I expect you may wait to hear Nithle prince as you are tied both similarly. So, I say this to you both: although this began as orchestration by Nithle King Gerge, my people have not completely been innocent. The war began as retaliation of death of King Irkis and has continued for various reasons. Unrest on both sides, hatred and fear driving even our people to take matters themselves. There has been death and loss and tragedy for each."

"The fact that both sides have seen this loss doesn't erase it or the pain that's come of it," Criph spoke, his tone slightly dark.

"No, of course not," Ottel replied, the small shake of his head sending his hair swishing across his shoulders. "We live with realities we have created for ourselves. Not only live with them, but live through and beyond. That is what I am asking. Forgetting does memories a disservice. Ignoring our hurt does not benefit anyone."

"I can see why Lord Jasim thinks of you so highly," Arran said now, somewhat surprising himself alongside the rest with his interjection.

While everyone else's eyes fixed on him, his own fixed on Jasim. The dahem lord only inclined his head in acknowledgment, as if understanding the prince entirely. Arran returned his attention to Ottel, who was watching him curiously.

Arran took a breath and continued. "He never said the words, but I could tell you're a well-respected leader and your people trust you. Despite all the…propaganda I heard of you growing up, you're fair with your words and offer sagacity. You know what we're proposing isn't easy, but since it could mean the betterment of so many, you're willing to try. I maintain my position: Nithle will lay down its weapons and stop this war. I admit, it's a challenge to look those in the face who've taken almost everything from me."

A sick feeling in his stomach brought his words to a stop. He looked away, the silence of the room a hum around him. Warmth encased his hand as Adel took hold and gave it a squeeze. His eyes trailed from where their hands joined to her soft, encouraging expression. He could see the strain in her own features from what he'd said.

Ashla. How had it been so long without her already? He took another breath and brought his attention back to Ottel. "Being in this place, where my kingdom's protectors once dwelled, with those who I've only known as the enemy, calls for adjusting my mindset and perspective. This is a cycle I have the power to put an end to, and I'm going to do it," Arran said. His heart raced with each word.

There was a hum of energy about Arran that felt almost tangible beyond how it sung through his body. But for the fact that Ottel's gaze held him, he would have looked around to see if the others felt it, too.

For a moment, he worried about slipping away into the dredges of his memories. *I'm sitting in the Union stronghold, in a room with no adornments. The air smells stale. The chairs are worn and hard.* Whether it was due to reciting details of the space or something different about the dahem king's dark amber eyes, the memories remained silent.

Ottel's approving expression turned back to Criph, whom Arran saw nod out of the corner of his eye.

"Then it is settled," Ottel said, looking from person to person again. "Lavanai, Nithle, Heta, and Piridet enter era of peace. We can finalize with a peace treaty. This will outline and guide us and our peoples to move forward."

There was a relaxed tone to the king's voice now. Arran hadn't thought that his voice or demeanour was particularly tense before, and he wondered if maybe the accent had disguised it, but there was a difference, he could tell. Had the king been nervous that this wouldn't go the way it did?

In the past, this would've been a time to say the Alliance Pact, but he dashed the thought away. This was a new alliance, and if there were going to be any sort of phrase they would say to solidify that, it should be new. He'd have to retrain his instincts on a lot of things, but if he could look the dahem king in the eye without either of them trying to kill one another, then he could embrace other changes, too.

CHAPTER
SEVENTY-FOUR

"Another empty room," Arran muttered more to himself than anyone else, even though Ley trailed a few steps behind him.

As much as the prince couldn't fathom there being *no* evidence left behind by the Keepers, the stark, grey walls, room after room, elicited nothing. Not even a sign of life that anyone had lived in the building. Yet the Keepers and all their Killers must have lived in the Union stronghold—there were no other structures on the grounds. No villages or cities nearby.

Arran had spent hours searching these lower-level chambers in the days following their arrival to the stronghold. It in equal parts provided some reprieve from the ongoing treaty negotiations and also gave him a chance to sate his curiosity. Or at least try to.

Each booted step to cross the room echoed a reminder of just how empty the room was. The heavy thud of his footfalls sounded heavier than they ever had, accompanying him to the walls. Bare fingers traced over the stonework, hoping to find some sort of hidden compartment similar to that in the High Chambers in Nithle Castle. The rough surface scraped against his skin, but he felt no gaps in their binding or looseness in their structure.

He cast his gaze to the ceiling, which was just as blank as the rest of the room. *It could have been a weapon's room.*

Sleeping quarters. Anything, Arran mused silently. *What else would Keepers and Killers need? What else might they have hidden from us?*

He'd thought about asking Lord Jasim or Mithos what they might have discovered in their searches, but that connection still felt closed off to him. To be fair, it wasn't one-sided. Arran's unsettled feelings about the general and his commander were still a work in progress. He was well aware of what he'd said—about putting things aside for a better future—and he meant it. But putting it into practice was proving much more difficult than speaking the words.

Giving up his search for secrets in the stonework, Arran turned to find Ley waiting patiently in the doorway. The knight stood with his hands behind his back, feet shoulder width apart and attention fixed on Arran. The navy and silver brocade he wore glimmered just slightly in the torchlight surrounding them.

Arran's next words came to him unbidden. "Thank you for being here, Ley. I know you have reservations."

"Of course," Ley replied, a neutral expression along his scruffy face.

"Don't say it with that tone," Arran chided gently and closed the gap between them.

"What tone?" Ley countered.

"A tone that says you *have* to be here," Arran explained, trying to keep the hurt from his voice. "That it's your duty. You've been my personal guard for years. I'd like to think we're also friends."

Ley's expression softened. "I also see us as friends. You well know I haven't agreed with every aspect of this, but I support you. Your conviction eases my worries, but it's hard to shake everything we've been told. Still, I trust you."

"There are still moments where I question everything I'm doing, but we can't pass up this chance at peace, right?" Arran looked to him for reassurance. He'd already been over this dozens of times with Adel, but Ley's thoughts mattered to him, too.

Ley considered his words only a moment as they resumed their trek through the lower levels of the building. "This is the first real chance at peace we've had in our lifetime. Potentially in the entire war, if we can believe everything we've been told. A defeat of or surrender from the dahems would be easier for people to accept, but we have to work with the situation we have."

It didn't alleviate all weighing on Arran's soul, but it did help.

"You'll make a fine king, Arran, and your parents would be proud of how you've handled things so far. There was a time when I thought we might lose you, too, but you've pulled through. That's no small feat, and I'm glad you're still here."

Arran felt a hitch in his throat when he looked to where Ley walked beside him. The man looked back at him with a smile that he couldn't help but return.

"I've still got a lot of work to do, I know, but I appreciate your support," he told the knight.

The duo climbed the stairs to the main level. As much as Arran wanted to continue his exploration of the lower chambers, he knew the time was coming for the next stage of transforming the peace treaty from talk to reality.

Approaching the top of the stairs, Arran saw Adel waiting for them. The chandeliers in the hall cast light across her features in a way that highlighted the maturity which joined her beauty. Her features had sharpened without becoming hard. Her eyes piercing without becoming severe. Even the long navy dress and charcoal overcoat she wore seemed to speak of someone who'd aged much in only a few short months. Maybe even in only a few short weeks.

A knowing smile broke out across her face when she saw them. "I suspected you might be traipsing the lower chambers again."

Arran reached for her hands and pulled himself toward her to plant a kiss on her cheek before replying. "You suspected correctly."

"And how'd today's search go?" she asked.

"No different than any other time," Arran grumbled against his own disappointment.

Adel's smile turned sympathetic now, and she squeezed his hands. There was a pause before she spoke again. "Let's leave it be for now. We've got the address with King Ottel to get to."

Arran nodded, and he, Adel, and Ley made their way toward the entrance. The halls were quiet except for their footsteps, which led them to the large, plain doors. Royal Commander Kein stood waiting for them, a pair of charcoal cloaks in his arms. He extended them toward Arran and Ley as the group neared.

"Thank you, Commander," Arran said as he accepted the garment and wrapped it around his shoulders.

"My pleasure, Your Highness. Shall we?" Kein gestured toward the door. "Everyone else only stepped out a few moments ago, but I imagine they're eager to get started."

The prince let out a heavy sigh. "Yes, let's do this."

The brisk air bit against his sinuses, and Arran pulled his cloak tighter around him as he stepped through the crowd made up of the Heta and Piridet royals and their commanders, as well as Lavanai's general and commanders. The group pressed in behind him at the entrance of the Union stronghold, leaving only himself, Adel and King Ottel in front of their collective forces.

In the distance, he could see the sea of tents, another of Ottel's ideas. As the rulers had been tested on Union grounds, so too should their people, he'd said. It made sense, although Arran would have to say something if the kingdoms' entire populations were expected to make the journey to prove their allegiance.

He couldn't think about that now, though. Instead, he was fixated on the mass of faces staring back at him with everything from apprehension to open curiosity. Eyes the colour of clear blues to chilling ambers held him in place.

Arran took a deep breath and closed his own eyes to block it all out for a moment, but it only served to amplify the murmurs that rippled around him. A sudden tightness grasped his chest.

What have I gotten my kingdom into? Who am I to lead my people? Do I even have a kingdom to lead?

His thoughts swirled violently, going through every personal failure that had led to this moment. Every ineptitude. Every lesson he hadn't had the chance to learn. And he'd deigned to propose and push for a treaty with their longest enemies?

Even Ley is apprehensive. I saw the apprehension in these people. We only just barely agreed on the foundations of the treaty.

Arran, Ottel, Criph, and Diah had agreed they needed to start with the foundation before diving into the intricacies and individual impacts. Things like land, trade, and the change of alliances among the kingdoms were easy additions to the document. But then there was magic and ensuring that each kingdom had its interests and concerns addressed, which is where the tensions started to mount.

How will these people react to what we've agreed to?

Fingers threading through his own drew Arran's focus to Adel, who watched him patiently.

She whispered, "We'll take on this new era together."

It was as though she'd sensed his thoughts. His heart swelled, her words a balm against the rising panic in his chest. "What have I done to deserve you?" his reply also a whisper.

She smiled again before nodding to Arran's right. He turned and noticed Ottel watching them, a similar patience to Adel's meeting him.

Ottel wore a kind half smile. "You are ready?"

Arran tried to straighten his shoulders, although he wasn't sure how effective the attempt was. "Let's proceed."

Ottel made no comment and instead faced the crowd. Arran stepped beside him, where the mass of gazes threatened to overpower him again. Ryla's guidance came, almost second nature.

I am Prince Arran of Nithle. It's midday, and I stand on Union grounds in the cold. I am surrounded by those who support me. Ley stands with me. Queen Diah and King Criph stand with me. Adel stands with me.

His mind wandered as he endeavored to continue the exercise.

I have sworn a peace treaty with Lavanai, and the Union has vanished. Killer Ryla has been killed by those I've sworn peace with. My parents have been killed by those I've sworn peace with.

He took a shuddering breath to stop the course of his thoughts as Ottel opened his mouth to address this mixed group of people that had been, until recently, mortal enemies. Watching the dahem king stirred a sort of reverence in Arran.

What had been overwhelming a moment before suddenly felt tinged with a glimmer of hope.

We will rebuild. As long as I am here, I will try to build something better.

And I'm still here.

PRONUNCIATION GUIDE

NAMES

Adel — ah-DEL

Alden — ALL-den

Anxer — ank-SHER

Arran — ARR-an

Ashla — ASH-law

Britta — BRIT-aw

Calar — kaw-LAR

Cavrin — KAH-vrin

Criph — KRIFF

Dalam — daw-LAWM

Diah — DEYE-ah

Eridan — AIR-ih-dan

Feon — FAY-on

Fyrah — feye-RAW

Gath — GAHTH

Gerge — DZERDZE (soft Gs)

Hadden — HAH-den

Halfa — HALL-fah

Harben — HAR-ben

Irkis — ER-kiss

Isuh — EYE-suh

Jase — JAYCE

Jasim — JAH-sim

Jeet — JEET

Kein — KAY-in

Keretuw (Keret) — KARE-eh-two (KARE-eht)

Kurisha — ker-EE-shaw

Lamis — lah-MIS

Ley — LAY

Nea — NAY-aw

Ottel — AW-tul

Megnata — meg-NAH-taw

Mela — MELL-aw

Mihel — MEE-hell

Mithos — MEE-thohs

Naxala — NOX-aw-law

Raynold — RAY-nold

Rold — ROHLED

Ryla — REYE-lah

Rynn — RIN

Shron — SHRAWN

Timith — TIM-ith

Ufrala — oo-FRAH-law

Veena — VEE-naw

Woxla — WAHKS-law

PLACES

Bunthle — BOON-thlay

Jenthle — JEN-thlay

Harthlen — HAR-thlen

Heta — HEH-taw

Hetaen — heh-TAY-en

Lake Pol — lake POLE

Lavanai — LAH-van-eye

Lavanian — lah-VAN-ee-an

Nithle — NITH-lay

Nithlean — nith-LAY-an

Piridet — PEER-ih-det

Piridetian — PEER-ih-deh-SHE-an

Sirama — see-RAW-mah

Sothle — SAW-thlay

Thlake — THLAYKE

Thlent — THLEHNT

Veloth — VEL-awth

Velothian — vel-OH-thee-an

Wendur — WEN-der

Yandana Fort — yawn-DAW-nah fort

OTHER

Cevrla — SEH-vruh-law

Cizeth — see-ZETH

Dahem —dah-EM

Fanahray ehntehs oahcl — fah-NAW-ray EN-tess AW-cle

Inatin — ee-NAW-tin

Tora — tor-AW

Torshid — TOR-shid

Yastalai — YAW-staw-leye

ACKNOWLEDGEMENTS

Like every author who's never done one of these before, I have no idea where to begin. So, I'll just begin.

I'll start by thanking every alpha reader, beta reader, critique partner, and pre-publication reader I've ever had. Given that this book has taken me nearly 20 years from first draft (NaNoWriMo 2005) to final copy, the list is extensive. Most recently, thank you to Azulina and M.H. Woodscourt. Named and unnamed, you all are incredible, and I haven't forgotten the time you've given to my book. *Killing Secrets* wouldn't be what it is without your insights.

Speaking of people whose insights have helped shape *Killing Secrets*, my deepest gratitude to my editor, Rachel Weisbrot. Your guidance has truly taken this story from great to magnificent. You helped me see where I could push for greater impact. You've taken my words and made them shine. And to think, I used to be afraid of editors.

Next, I thank every teacher who ever cheered me on. When there were people in my life telling me I should pursue other more financially friendly paths, you heartened me by encouraging my passion. Thank you for putting up with my long-as-hell short story assignments.

I'd be remiss if I didn't thank the online writing and bookish communities. Our shared passion for stories and books is something I'd never trade. The sharing of resources and uplifting of each other to reach our goals makes this challenge of self-publication easier. Let's keep kicking ass, okay?

Thank you to my friends and acquaintances alike who've watched this journey and said they want copies of my book long before it was close to publication. (Don't worry, I won't hold you to it if you've changed your mind.) Your eagerness to see my world is heartwarming.

To you, the reader. You took a chance on my book, which means so much to me. It's said there are over 158 million books in the world, and you picked up mine. Thank you doesn't seem like a strong enough word. I'm forever grateful.

To my mom, who has always had my back: your support is unmatched. You've read my bad writing and my not-so-bad writing and never once made me feel like I shouldn't do this. You did everything you could to try to make my dream a reality. You encouraged my imagination and never made me feel wrong for it.

And finally, Brad. My heart. My non-book-loving cheerleader. I don't expect you'll ever read a word of this or any other book I write, but to know you're in my corner is everything. I'll never forget the year I participated in a Twitter agent pitch day, how I didn't get any interest, and how your response was, "F*ck 'em!" I'll never not smile over that.

ABOUT THE AUTHOR

LAURA A. BARTON has a knack for getting lost in worlds that don't exist. Whether of her creation or another's, she loves magic-stained realities and living, breathing characters. In the "real world," she lives in Ontario, Canada with her fiancé. You can connect with her on Instagram: @labartonwrites.